THE BONE PUZZLE

A NOVEL BY

CLAYTON E. SPRIGGS

This book is a work of fiction. Names, characters, places, events, and situations in this book are purely fictitious. Any similarity to actual persons, living or dead, is entirely coincidental.

Published by
Penn Mill Publishing.
Slidell, Louisiana
www.pennmillpub.com

ISBN: 978-1-945842-90-0

For Matthew

PROLOGUE

"Push it through the mouth like this and twist it a bit 'til it comes out his gut," Lucius explained as he demonstrated his well-practiced technique. "But not too much, or he'll split in half and fall right off."

The old man watched as his great-grandson attempted to bait the hook. He tried not to laugh as the slippery minnow fell apart in the boy's tiny fingers.

"That's okay. You'll have plenty of time to learn how. Here," he said, handing his cane pole to the child, "take mine. It's ready to go. I'll get yours fixed up in a jiffy."

The boy smiled and dropped the line into the murky water. He held onto his great-grandfather's heavy pole with both hands. Lucius baited the boy's hook in no time, and they exchanged fishing poles, much to the relief of the child. His pole was considerably smaller and easier to manage, plus it was painted sky blue. His great-grandfather's pole was scarred and worn, having seen years of service by the avid fisherman.

"Do you want to know Paw Paw's secret to catching the really big cats?" Lucius whispered to the boy. "You gotta find a quiet spot near the reeds and go deep. Them catfish can't resist a tasty morsel, and they'll practically jump right into the frying pan."

Lucius smiled and patted Clifton's head. He loved the boy and wished that he had more years in front of him to watch the youngster grow up. He'd fathered six children—all of them girls. Two had died as infants; another succumbed to scarlet fever when she was eight. Of the three who had survived, only one lived long enough to bear children. Ophelia had made up for the family's lack of offspring with a vengeance, producing eleven children and twenty-seven grandchildren.

By the time Clifton Brewer made it into the world, it seemed to Lucius Jones that half the county must be related to him in some manner or form. Well, half of the colored people in the county, anyway.

His light skinned neighbors didn't much care for his kind and let him know it at every opportunity. Lucius' parents had been born slaves, and they felt the same way about the white folk.

Lucius didn't pay it no mind; he didn't have a mean bone in his body. Preacher man told him that you had to 'forgive others lest you doom your own soul to the pit of fire,' and that's just what Lucius tried to do. Considering his good health at eighty-seven, he considered it to be good advice.

"I feel them nibbling," Clifton whispered with excitement.

"That's good! Keep still, and maybe you can bring supper home."

Moments passed, but there were no more signs of the hungry fish. After twenty minutes, Lucius dropped his line into a quiet area that he had a feeling about. Right away, his line got snagged on the bottom.

"You got one!" Clifton exclaimed.

"I don't know 'bout that. I think I just got it caught on a root or something. It's mighty heavy, whatever it be." Lucius pulled on the line from several angles, trying to free it without breaking his favorite fishing pole. Just when he thought he'd have to cut the line, he felt the object give way. Whatever he had hooked was heavy, but Lucius pulled it out of the muddy water and swing it onto dry land between himself and the boy.

"It's a shoe," remarked Clifton with amazement. "Look, Paw Paw, there's something in it."

Lucius squinted to examine his catch, and wished he hadn't. He dropped his pole and grabbed hold of Clifton, pulling the boy to his side and covering his eyes.

The boy was right. There was something in the shoe.

PART ONE:

HOCUS POCUS

What the eyes see and the ears hear,
the mind believes.

Harry Houdini

CHAPTER ONE

"Ladies and gentlemen, what you are about to see will amaze and confound you. Please, do not be alarmed. At no time will you be in danger."

Richard looked around the tent. Most of the chairs were empty as usual, but at least the people who were there made up for the lack of audience with a lack of interest. He thrust his arms into the air in a dramatic fashion and continued his spiel. "As you can see, there's nothing up my sleeves. At no time will my arms ever leave my side."

Someone coughed, and his lame joke fell flat, as it always did. Three teenage boys were wrestling with each other in the back row. A rotund man wearing suspenders was slumped over in the second row, snoring. A woman in the middle row on the right was simultaneously rocking an infant in her arms while tending to two toddlers who fidgeted at her side.

"As you can see, this is an ordinary deck of cards." Richard picked up the trick playing cards and fanned them out for their inspection. He pushed them back into a pile, shuffled the deck, and nodded to Ruth, who was waiting in the wings behind the curtain.

He waited. Ruth was too busy checking her mascara in a compact mirror to notice her cue. Richard cleared his throat, but to no avail. He repeated his line. "Yes, as you can see, this is an ordinary deck of cards."

Richard glared at his wife, who remained unaware that she'd been summoned. Leaving him little choice, he said the line again, "This is an ordinary deck of cards."

"We heard you the first time!" yelled one of the teenagers.

Ruth snapped her compact shut, slipped it into a hidden pocket in her skimpy outfit, and pranced out onto the stage. The three youths catcalled and hooted as she gave a bow and smiled.

"May I present my lovely assistant," Richard announced, "the incredible Miss Matilda the Mysterious!" The introduction called for another series of whistles and hoots as well as a polite round of applause from the small crowd. Ruth ate up the attention that was considerably more than the magician had garnered so far. "Matilda, if you please," he continued, "draw a card, any card, from the deck, but don't let me see it."

Richard turned his head to the side and closed his eyes tight to show the audience that he had no way of knowing which card his wife was selecting. He did his best to hide his annoyance when he felt her select a different card than the one she was supposed to pick. They'd practiced the routine for hours the previous day without a single mishap, but now, when it mattered most, Ruth spoiled the trick.

"While my eyes are closed, show the audience the card, then put it back into the deck," he continued as if nothing had gone awry.

Ruth waved the card for the crowd to see. When she attempted to slip the card into the middle of the pile, Richard pushed the deck slightly askew so that he would be able to find that particular card later. Unfortunately, Ruth bumped his arm, making him lose his place as well as his temper. Richard did the only thing he could do at that point. He dropped the deck, sending playing cards scattering across the stage.

"Gosh golly, Svengali!" Richard exclaimed. "It appears the lovely Matilda knocked the cards out of my hands."

"Looks more like the Remarkable Richard is a clumsy oaf!" a voice called out.

"Fifty-two pick up!" shouted another.

The sound of laughter drifted up from the audience. Richard ignored it and moved on. "What I'm about to show you now is nothing short of a miracle. Years ago, as I traveled through the Dark Continent, I came across a witch doctor who, after a great deal of convincing on my part, agreed to share with me the secrets of the netherworld. I will now give a demonstration of this great power as I perform the mystical art of resurrection."

The baby wailed, encouraging another round of abuse from the teenagers.

"I feel like crying, too!" shouted one.

"You suck!" yelled another.

Ruth brought out an object covered with a colorful silk cloth and placed it on the table. She moved her hands over it as if presenting the item for inspection, then backed away. Richard stood behind the item and waved his arms in the air, as if pushing away invisible cobwebs. Closing his eyes and lifting his face toward the ceiling, he chanted, his voice starting low, then increasing in intensity.

"Humma bumma hoodoo voodoo inna mona lisa. Abdu rabdu onu locust, dippy doodoo, hocus pocus!" He waved his arms and opened his eyes with a dramatic flair, only to realize when he looked down that he'd skipped the beginning of the trick. Quickly trying to recover as if nothing had happened, he lifted the silk cloth off of the object to disclose a wire cage sitting on the table. Inside it, a white dove lay on its side.

"I tawt I saw a puddy cat!" one of the teenagers yelled.

Everyone, except the magician, laughed—including Ruth. Richard ignored the heckling and continued. "This poor creature of the heavens has recently expired. But fear not, for I, the Remarkable Richard, will resurrect the bird's spirit, and again it shall take flight amongst the living! At no time will anyone here be in any danger, but I must warn you, do not try this at home. Only the greatest of mystics, wizards, or magicians can perform such miracles. Do not, I repeat, do not interrupt me as I summon the spirits. They will not take kindly to mockery."

"Just get on with it already!" one of the boys shouted.

Richard sighed and covered up the cage once again. As he fitted the cloth over the bottom edge of the cage, he pushed a hidden latch, but it refused to budge. He pushed harder, but it remained stuck. He looked up and smiled nervously. Pretending to smooth out the table cloth, Richard slipped his hand around the back of the cage and tried for a third time to release the latch. This time, he pushed it too hard, and the whole contraption went flying off the end of the table, crashing to the floor. As the dead bird spilled out of the cage, a live bird, caught in a fake compartment along the bottom, flapped its wings in a desperate attempt to break free of the trap.

The audience exploded with laughter. Richard looked away in embarrassment, only to see Ruth yukking it up with the crowd. His face grew red with anger and humiliation. He felt like crying, but he held it together and tried to steady himself until the room stopped laughing. He picked up the dead bird and tossed it into the cage. As he did, the spring popped, and the bottom flipped open. The live dove broke free, flying out and hitting Richard in the face, knocking his glittery turban to one side. The crowd responded with another round of laughter and jeers.

Once the audience quieted down, he began again. "You have angered the spirits, and they seek to send curses your way. Lucky for you, I am here to protect you from their wrath."

"Lucky us!" someone yelled. The crowd laughed again.

"I am the Remarkable Richard!" Richard's voice boomed with authority. "And I will now present to you the most fantastic and incredible act of magic you will ever see in your sad and pathetic little lives."

The insult was met with hisses and boos.

"In my journeys to the Orient, I met a Hindu mystic who imparted to me the gift of the Magi. This is a great power that was bestowed on me, and I will demonstrate the greatest of all illusions. I will saw Miss Matilda the Mysterious in half, right in front of your eyes, only to restore her to her lovely self with the powers vested in me by the holy Brahman of India. At no time will any of you be in danger. And please, I beg of you, do not try this at home."

A long table carrying a wooden casket rolled out from behind the curtain on the right. It made it out to about a third of the way before halting abruptly. Richard looked over and saw that Ruth was struggling to push the heavy object onto the stage. She tried again, but it refused to budge. Richard saw that the cover from the bird cage had gotten twisted up in one of the wheels, so he ran over to try to dislodge it. Ruth pushed the table backward and forward as Richard pulled at the cloth, which only knotted it further around the wheel.

Screech! A high pitched squeal erupted as the pair forced the table out onto the stage. By the time they made it to the center of the stage, the corners were starting to collapse a little, causing the whole contraption to sway. Richard glanced apprehensively at his wife, who stared at him doubtfully.

"If it pleases my lovely assistant," Richard announced to the audience, "I will help her into the box."

"It does not please me," Ruth snapped.

"Don't do it, lady!" someone yelled. "Remember the bird."

A howl of laughter erupted from the crowd once again.

"At no time will you be in any danger," Richard pleaded.

"At no time will I climb in that box," she answered, much to the approval of the crowd.

"But Miss Matilda——," Richard stammered.

"Ruth," she corrected him.

"But I am the Remarkable Richard! I command you!"

"Put a sock in it, Dick."

The crowd howled in delight. Pretty soon, everyone in the tent got in on the heckling. Shouts of "The Remarkable

Dick!" and "At no time will we see anything worth seeing!" were only interrupted by boos, hisses, and the occasional thrown food items. Richard stormed off the stage in disgust, finally earning a huge round of applause. Ruth stayed behind to take a few bows. The crowd loved her as much as they loathed her husband.

Richard threw off his turban and stewed in anger. He vowed that he was going to make his poor excuse of a wife pay for her actions, if it was the last thing he did.

CHAPTER TWO

Richard remained silent as Bossman Wallace chewed him out over his poor performance. He'd been summoned to the Wagon when word spread of the debacle, and he had to explain once again why he'd be short on the take. Wallace pretended not to want the meager funds offered to him. He threatened to kick the magician off of the bill and replace him with another human oddity. But the ruse was up when he pocketed the cash and nodded for Richard to leave. Wallace's inappropriate comment about sending for Ruth to make up for the lost wages didn't help. Richard was furious.

When he got back to the trailer, he let his wife know, in no uncertain terms, that her sabotaging of their act could not continue.

"What the hell is wrong with you, woman? Can't you see how much we need this?"

"We, Dick?" Ruth had had enough. "Don't you mean you? When are you going to face it? You're a horrible magician."

"I wouldn't be if I had an assistant who was worth a crap."

"Don't you lay this on me. I'm the only reason people clap at all. Even Bossman says—"

Richard's hand cut through the air like a bolt of lightning, catching Ruth across the cheek. Ruth held the side of her face, tears welling up in her eyes, her heavy mascara running in rivulets.

"Don't tell me about what Bossman says, slut. It doesn't matter what Bossman says. It matters what I say. I'm your husband, which means your ass belongs to me." He hated to be so hard on the woman, but she had it coming.

Ruth cast her sad eyes down and Richard knew the crying would come next. Normally, that would mean he would cave in and apologize, but her power over him was beginning to wane. He looked at her and tried not to laugh. Her makeup was a mess, and she looked like a raccoon. The red outline of his hand on her cheek didn't help her appearance any.

"You purposely screwed up our routine. You embarrassed me. We're barely getting by as it is, and you pull a stunt like this. What's the matter with you? Why would you do such a thing?"

"You know why, Dick," Ruth sobbed. "I'm not happy."

"You're never happy. No matter what you want, as soon as you get it, you want something else. We discussed this before we started, if you remember. You said you didn't want a humdrum life. You wanted to travel. You wanted the glamour of the big top. You wanted to be in show business. I gave you all those things, and this is how you repay me?"

"Take a look around us, Dick. Do you think this is glamorous?"

"We have to pay our dues, Ruth."

"We can't even pay our rent."

"Not yet, but one day, we will. You'll see. Remember what I told you. Stick with me and one day you'll be farting through silk."

"That's disgusting. Come on, Dick. You're a second rate magician at best. Even if you were the greatest magician in the world, we'd be struggling. You're not Blackstone or Houdini, and you never will be."

"I'm not trying to be."

"What are you trying to be? The Remarkable Richard? Where did you come up with that name? Your name is Dick Henderson, from Toledo, Ohio. We're just a couple of average yokels. We don't need fortune and fame. I don't even want that anymore."

"What do you want, Ruth?"

"I want a family." She finally said what had been on her mind for months. She'd gotten tired of the grind almost as soon as they'd set out. Everything he said was true. They had discussed it. She'd been all for it. He'd made it sound so exciting. It turned out to be just the opposite. They lived in a tiny, cramped trailer with a leaky roof and a window that didn't close all the way. They traveled from town to town with whatever sideshow they could manage to hook up with. Most of the time, they were searching for a new sponsor every couple of months. The act was terrible and showed no signs of getting better. It was time for a change.

"A family?" Richard laughed. "Kids? You know we can't have any, Ruth. Besides, we can barely afford to feed ourselves. How are we going to take care of a baby?"

"We could if you got a job."

"I have a job."

"A real job, Dick."

"So that's what this is all about? That's why you sabotaged the performance?"

"Now wait a minute, Mr. Remarkable. You can't put all the blame on me. You haven't exactly been holding up your end of the bargain. I've yet to see anything even remotely resembling remarkable."

"Watch that mouth, Ruth."

"Don't you mean Matilda?"

Richard raised his arm, but paused as he looked at his wife. She had that crooked smile that he found so endearing, and he felt his heart melt.

"The Mysterious," he said.

They laughed. Richard sat down and put his arm around Ruth. He apologized. They kissed. She cried in his arms. He comforted her. By morning, they came to an agreement. Three more performances for Bossman Wallace, and they'd part ways when the show moved on.

At the end of the week, they'd head to Memphis. Ruth had heard about a woman with the Tennessee Children's Home Society who could help them. They were going to be parents.

CHAPTER THREE

Things were looking up. Ruth's brother-in-law, Ray, agreed to hire Richard. She'd convinced Richard that he would need a steady job if they wanted to adopt a child, and he conceded, but not without a good deal of resentment. Ruth didn't care. She wanted a baby, and as far as she was concerned, the magician idea was childish and unrealistic. Much to her surprise, when she announced that the new job would require them to relocate to Chattanooga, Richard offered little resistance.

"How was work, darling?" Ruth said, pouring it on a few weeks after their arrival.

"I shovel shit all day, Ruth. How do you think work was?"

"It's a job, Dick."

"When I agreed to work for Ray, you didn't tell me he worked for the sewage department."

"He works in the office. How was I supposed to know where you'd be working?" She had known. She also knew that, if she had told him, he'd still be trying to saw her in two while a dozen bored half-wits heckled them.

"This wasn't part of the deal, Ruth," he said. He grabbed a towel and a change of clothes and stormed out, slamming the door behind him. They'd found a place to rent in a small hotel that offered little more than a room with a bed. There was a bathroom with a shower at the end of the hall that was shared by everyone on the floor and generally required a long wait in line to use it. Richard came home filthy, and he needed a shower before all else, right about the time every other person on their floor needed one, too. Ruth knew he'd be a while, and his temper was not likely to improve until he was clean and fed.

When he returned to the room, he found his wife dressed for dinner. Richard was suspicious.

"Where's my dinner?"

"I thought it would be a nice change if we went out tonight, honey."

"You did, did you? Who's going to pay for that?"

"I have wonderful news! Alice and Ray offered to help us pay the adoption fees. There's a little bit left over from what they gave me for the train to Memphis and a hotel. I figured we could also squeeze out a couple of bucks for dinner tonight to celebrate. You work so hard, you deserve it."

"I'm not taking charity from Alice and Ray. We can make due until we save enough on our own."

"It's not charity. They want us to have a family, and they see that you're trying so hard. They just want to help."

Richard was not convinced. He never liked Ray, and Alice was a stuck up bitch. They seldom gave anyone anything unless there was something for them attached to it.

"What are we going to tell the good people at the orphanage? We live in a flop house?"

"That's another thing I wanted to talk to you about, but I was going to wait for dinner."

"Oh no!" Richard interrupted. He didn't like the sound of this. "We're not moving in with your sister and Mr. Wonderful."

"Of course not! I would never suggest such a thing."

Richard looked at his wife and waited.

"If you're going to spoil the surprise, then I guess I'll tell you. Remember that room above Alice and Ray's garage—"

"No, no, no—"

"Please, I'm not finished. They are fixing it up into an apartment. It'll have a kitchen and a bathroom, a living room, and a bedroom. There's even space for a nursery! I'll have help with the baby, and—"

"No, Ruth, I said no," Richard was insistent. "I said I didn't want charity, and I meant it."

"It's not charity, Dick. Ray assured me that the rent would be reasonable."

"Rent? They're charging us to stay in their garage?"

"It's an apartment, not a garage. I thought you said you didn't want charity. If we pay rent, it's not charity."

Richard cursed under his breath but relented. It appeared his wife had planned everything out. He knew it was pointless to argue about it. She was going to get what she wanted no matter what.

Richard figured that what she wasn't saying was that she thought her husband was an idiot who was too stupid to see what was really going on. He suspected Ray had other ideas and that Ruth was a part of those ideas. He assumed that, slowly, but surely, good ol' Ray was setting him up, making him completely dependent on his goodwill so that he'd be able to get whatever he wanted from him, including his wife. Richard believed that he had no choice but to play along.

For now.

CHAPTER FOUR

The train ride to Memphis went without a hitch. Before long, they found their way to the Tennessee Children's Home Society. The excited couple waited in an open area for awhile before being escorted into the plush office of Georgia Tann, the highly regarded and well respected proprietor of the orphanage.

"Hmm." The dour woman grunted behind a frown as she rifled through the mountain of paperwork that the Hendersons had been required to fill out. After she'd flipped through the forms one last time, Miss Tann stacked them neatly in the center of her desk, folded her hands in front of her, and sat back. Her disapproving eyes examined the humble couple in front of her. Eventually, she leaned forward and addressed the pair.

"I'm sorry you two came all this way, but I don't think we'll be able to help you."

Well, that's that, thought Richard, shifting in his chair. At least they'd tried. He reached over to hold his wife's hand, and he felt the tension right away. Sneaking a glance at her, he saw that her head was bowed as she fought back tears. This would not do at all.

"I'm not sure I understand you, Mrs. Tann," said Richard.

"Miss," she responded. He wasn't the least surprised.

"Miss Tann," Richard corrected himself. "Surely, there's something we can do."

"Is there? I'm not so sure. After reading your application, I see that your work history is somewhat, how should I say it, brief? Neither one of you have any money to speak of nor a permanent residence of any note."

"Money isn't the only thing that makes a good parent," said Richard. Everything the woman had said was true, but he'd be dammed if this ugly, no good hose beast was going to disparage him and break his wife's heart without him putting up a fight.

"This is true, but money pays the rent. It buys the groceries. It buys clothes and diapers, doctor's bills, school supplies. You get my point."

"Absolutely, I would agree with you. It does all those things. Sometimes, it does more."

"I'm not sure I follow you."

"I think you do."

Ruth picked her head up and silently watched the standoff that had developed between her husband and the woman behind the desk. She'd never seen her husband like this before, and she liked it. Sure, he could be a bully when he tried to push her around, but this was something different. He was standing up for her, for their imminent family. Maybe she'd misjudged him after all.

Miss Tann considered the man before her. It was time to put the bite on the couple. "From what I see in these forms, I doubt we have much to discuss, Mr. Henderson."

"What makes you think I put everything on paper, Miss Tann? Do you?"

For the first time, the plump woman behind the desk smiled. It was almost as scary as her frown. "Our Society deals with discretion, Mr. Henderson. Our transactions are confidential, as is expected. Therefore, it is customary to periodically destroy our files. It is all on the up and up, I assure you."

"I'm sure it is, Miss Tann. Let's get to the bottom line. We are a loving couple who want to share our stable home with a needy child. That is all. We intend on doing just that. Somewhere in this building, there is such a child who needs us as much as we need him."

"Her," Ruth spoke for the first time.

Richard looked at his wife with surprise. They hadn't discussed whether or not they'd adopt a boy or a girl. It made no difference to him, but clearly, his wife had thought about it and made the decision for them, as usual.

"A girl!" Miss Tann said with delight. The price just went up.

"So I ask you, is there any way we can come to an agreement, or should we go elsewhere? It's up to you. I'm not here to tell you how to run your orphanage, but we are not going back to Chattanooga empty-handed. Maybe with an empty wallet," Richard added not very subtly, "but not empty-handed."

"There may be something we can do, but it's not as easy as you might think," Georgia responded. "There's a complication with availability at this time. Given enough time, I can get you whatever you want—for a price, of course. But if you're adamant about doing this now, we'll have to make do with what we have in stock, for lack of a better term."

Ruth was horrified by the woman's demeanor. If she could, she'd take every last child away from this monster.

"Go on," said Richard.

"Would you consider an older child? Perhaps even a toddler?"

Richard began to nod yes, but his wife interrupted, and he quickly changed the direction of his head movement.

"I want a baby. A beautiful baby girl," said Ruth.

"That's what I thought," replied Miss Tann. "Unfortunately, that might be a problem."

"Why is that?" asked Richard. "Do you mean to tell me you don't have at least one baby girl for us to choose from?"

"Not exactly."

"Not exactly?" Richard replied.

"Come," Miss Tann announced, abruptly standing up. "Follow me. I have something to show you."

CHAPTER FIVE

Georgia led the couple out of her plush office and down an ornate flight of stairs. They walked through a long corridor before the woman nodded for an attendee who waited by the exit to unlock a steel door with a square, wire-meshed window. After that, the Hendersons followed Miss Tann around a corner and through another set of locked doors. They entered a large room with dozens of cots lined up along one wall. A row of windows with iron bars allowed a fair amount of light into the room. No other decorations were present. Richard thought it looked more like a prison than an orphanage.

They followed Miss Tann until they came to three cribs tucked away in the corner of the great room. The first crib was empty. The second and third each held a sleeping baby wrapped in a pink blanket.

"I thought you said you didn't have one baby girl," said Richard.

"We don't," explained Miss Tann. "We have two."

"Very funny."

"It's no joke, Mr. Henderson. Take a closer look."

"They're twins!" Ruth exclaimed.

"Identical twins," Miss Tann corrected her. "Which is the problem."

"So?" Richard asked.

"So, we won't separate the pair. It would be cruel," explained Miss Tann. "Besides, we have a policy against such things."

Miss Tann was full of shit. There was no such policy. They split siblings apart all the time, but she knew a couple of marks when she saw them. Either they didn't have the funds to adopt a child, and this new development would drive them off, or they had enough, and she could squeeze them dry. Either way, she had nothing to lose.

"I, I don't know," Ruth said. "I mean, one baby is a handful, but two…"

Richard stared at the twins, deep in thought. Ruth didn't like the way he was looking at them one bit. It was the same look as when he proclaimed his interest in starting the magic act. She could practically see the wheels turning inside his head. He was hatching a scheme. Whatever he was planning was undoubtedly doomed to failure.

"Well, if you think they'll be too much for you—" Miss Tann said.

"No, that's not what we're saying," interjected Ruth. "Is it, Dick?"

Richard's gaze shifted from one of the girls to the other, and back again. It was as though he was hypnotized.

"Dick? Is it?"

"We'll take 'em!" he exclaimed, snapping out of his trance.

Miss Tann smiled. She could already count the dollars before she even deposited them in her substantial savings account. Ruth was happy, yet wary. Two babies would stretch their resources thin, and tax her abilities as an inexperienced mother. *What on Earth was Richard thinking?*

CHAPTER SIX

Not long after the couple returned to their garage apartment with the twins, the world erupted in flames. The Japanese bombed Pearl Harbor. Ray was able to secure a stateside position with the civil service, but Richard knew his chances of not being drafted to the front lines were slim to none. In the patriotic fervor that gripped the nation, Richard Henderson enlisted in the Navy.

Ruth was not happy about her new predicament. The girls were infants and required round-the-clock attention from her. Her fantasies about motherhood turned out to be just that—fantasies. The reality of caring for two children by herself was overwhelming. She let Richard in on her displeasure at every opportunity. Every letter, which she sent sporadically at best, was filled with complaints.

Richard had bigger concerns. Twice, the ships he was assigned to took on torpedo fire. He barely escaped with his life when a third ship went down in flames after a brutal kamikaze attack. His leg suffered shrapnel damage, and his forearm was severely burned during one of the battles, earning him a six week furlough in a Hawaiian hospital and a Purple Heart. Ruth expressed her concerns for his injuries by whining about her inability to buy pantyhose and having to help Alice with their victory garden.

While the other sailors received care packages and letters from their sweethearts professing their undying devotion, all

Richard heard from Ruth was how horrible it was to live in safety and comfort. She griped about the noise the girls made when they cried, but Richard was certain it was far better than the explosions and whimpering of wounded men. He found himself feeling jealous when one of his fellow seamen received a Dear John letter, and he secretly harbored a romantic crush on Tokyo Rose.

Eventually, the war ended and Richard returned home, but things were different. He was different. His wife was different. The world was different. He no longer had any interest in working for Ray. Instead, he took a gig as a stagehand at one of the rundown playhouses left over from the days of vaudeville. The hours were sporadic and the pay was meager, but Richard didn't care. He hadn't survived the war to go back into the sewers. Life was precious, and he'd made a promise to himself that if he made it home in one piece, he was going to do what he wanted to do. And he wanted to be a magician.

Ruth was disgusted. Opposite of most soldiers, Richard left as a man and came back as a child. She already had two children to look after; she didn't need a third. Even if it was true that Richard was able to supplement his income with his monthly disability payment from the Navy, which was hardly the point. He was around too much. She found out almost immediately that she didn't know how good she'd had it when he was gone.

Richard soon knew something was up with Ruth and her sister's husband. She'd moved out of the garage apartment only to rent a run-down double in a sketchy neighborhood, coincidentally owned by Ray. Alice gave Ruth an icy stare on the few occasions they'd come in contact with one another, and she refused to help out with the girls altogether. Ray, on the other hand, was more than helpful whenever the slightest repair was needed. Richard noted that the neighbor's rabid Doberman Pincher didn't bark when Ray came around, despite trying to attack any other soul who happened by. Things were definitely suspiciously askew.

The only thing that made Richard's homecoming worthwhile was Lacey and Laura. The girls were as cute as could be and loved the attention he poured on them. They were fascinated with the magic tricks he showed them. He used every opportunity to teach them and they took to it like pros. More importantly, it was impossible to tell them apart. It was a magician's dream.

Richard knew that in a few years they'd be old enough to become his assistants, which is why he'd insisted on adopting both of them in the first place. As long as he only brought one of them out with him at a time, no one would be the wiser. His head swam with the possibilities.

Richard studied his craft at every turn. He watched the performers at the playhouse and learned a great deal about showmanship. He peppered the most skilled entertainers with questions and rehearsed for hours on end. Richard converted the garage into a workspace and built a variety of contraptions for use when the time came.

Soon, all would be ready. The only thing he had left to do was to get rid of Ruth.

CHAPTER SEVEN

"You son of a bitch!" Ruth couldn't believe her ears. The loser she'd made the mistake of marrying was threatening her with a divorce. "I stood by you while you went gallivanting around the globe with your Navy buddies, and now this?"

"Gallivanting? It was war. Are you mad, woman?"

"You didn't have to go, Dick. You enlisted. You wanted to go."

"You're fucking nuts!" Richard exclaimed. "Go on; tell that shit to the judge. Not only will he grant me the divorce, he'll lock you up in the loony bin."

"This is going to cost you big time, Mr. Magic. Let's see you conjure up those alimony payments, not to mention child support."

"Alimony?" Richard laughed. "Child support? I think not."

"What do you mean, you think not? No judge in his right mind is going to let you run off scot free."

"Run off? I'm not running off. I'm going to Nashville. I already have a job lined up. The girls are going to love it."

"The girls! Now I know you've lost it. Did a torpedo hit you in the head? They're staying with me."

"Are you sure about that?"

"Oh, I'm sure. Just like I'm sure you'll be paying through the nose for alimony. I'll be taking those Navy payments, bucko."

"Will you?" Richard rubbed his chin as if in deep thought. "Since you put it that way, I guess I'll stay. I can't wait to tell Alice and Ray all about it. Should I spring it on them before or after?"

"Before or after what?" Ruth didn't like the sound of that. He was up to something.

"Before or after I show them the photographs?"

Ruth felt her stomach churn. She had told Ray they were going to have to be more careful. Still, whatever Richard thought he knew, it wasn't the half of it. "Oh, I see. You have photographs. So what? It's going to take more than that, Dick."

"Like medical records from a Dr. Bill Thornhill?"

"I, I don't know what you mean," stammered Ruth. *How the hell did he find out about that?*

"Adultery is frowned upon, Ruth. Abortion is illegal. You're fucking your sister's husband and cheating on a war hero."

"War hero? You really have a high opinion of yourself. May I remind you that you're practically unemployed? A magician! That's comical. What kind of idiot do you think that judge is going to be?"

"I wouldn't call Judge Faraway an idiot, Ruth. Far from it, if I remember correctly. Did I mention we served in the Navy together? I pulled him into a life raft when our ship went down. But I'm sure he won't be biased in any way. I doubt he even remembers that."

"You bastard!"

"Slut!"

Ruth stewed. How dare he do this to her—humiliate her like this. She wasn't going to stand for it.

"Don't get too upset, dear," Richard offered. "I'm not going to leave you in a lurch, even if you deserve it. I know you had it rough, in your own way, bringing up the girls. I'm just thinking of you."

"Thinking of me?" Ruth started to cry. This couldn't be happening. "How is this thinking of me?"

"You said it yourself. I hardly bring in any money, at least on paper. I'll make sure it stays that way if I have to. What do you think you'll get from me? Raising girls is expensive. Living as a single mother is expensive. I'm not sure Ray wants the girls around, anyhow."

"Ray? What's Ray have to do with this? He's married to Alice."

"For now."

Ruth stared at Richard. She knew that look. It was the same look he'd given Georgia Tann when the woman had sworn they'd never be able to adopt a child. Once again, Richard had thought ahead.

CHAPTER EIGHT

Things went exactly as Richard had planned. Ray left Alice and ran off with Ruth. Richard feigned surprise and indignation at the prospect of raising the girls on his own.

When they got to Nashville, Richard used his new name, A. M. Villanova. In no time he established his new persona as a renowned magician with one daughter, Natalia the Gypsy Princess. He'd grown a mustache and long, pointed goatee. He spoke with a vaguely Eastern European accent at all times. Richard instructed his daughters never to speak at all on stage, if possible. If they had to speak, to only whisper to him or mumble strange gibberish that he'd interpret.

He had learned a great deal about showmanship and used that information to transform himself and the girls into what he wanted the world to see. He was the Amazing and Magnificent Villanova—from parts unknown. His silent assistant was an orphaned gypsy who he'd rescued during one of his many travels. Her age was undetermined. As far as anyone knew, there was only one assistant.

The girls loved the new adventure their father had brought them on. Their mother had taken care of them without much enthusiasm. To her, they were a nuisance to be put up with, and they got in the way of her dalliance with her lover.

Their father was the opposite. He included them in his plans and ambitions. They learned the tricks and rehearsed with a passion that only amplified their father's resolve. He promised them that they'd become what they pretended to be as long as they maintained the illusion at all times and worked hard. They believed him, believed in him, and learned to believe in themselves. Once they received their first standing ovation, they were hooked forever.

What little funds Richard had left over after the move, he poured into the act. He used his connections from the playhouse and from his days traveling with the sideshows to find the right people to complement the act. He hired three freakishly tall black men to dress like African witch doctors and beat on conga drums, a skinny Indian to wear a loincloth and turban and act like a snake charmer swami, and an Asian woman who looked like she was pushing a hundred to wear silk robes and geisha makeup. He even found a Hungarian refugee who could play gypsy dance music on a violin.

Richard took out a full page ad in the local newspaper and tipped a half-dozen paperboys two dollars each to publicize his upcoming show on street corners. With his last few dollars, he and the girls made posters and went out in the middle of the night to tack them up on every telephone pole in the vicinity, so that the next morning they seemed to have appeared as if by magic.

Friday night was to be the first show at the Tennessee Luxor. If all went well, there would be many more to follow; success would finally be his. If it didn't, Richard and the girls would be ruined.

CHAPTER NINE

"**D**addy, you won't believe it!" Lacey exclaimed. They were backstage at the Luxor, where they'd been since early that morning. The rehearsals had gone well, but Richard wasn't taking any chances. Their future was on the line.

"What won't I believe, sweetie?"

"There must be a million, jillion people outside waiting to get in!" said Laura.

Richard smiled and hugged the girls. It was a rare occasion when they could be together in the same room without the risk of others seeing. He knew what sacrifices they were making by having to live a lie. It was particularly hard on the girls since they were not allowed to speak around others and were never to be in the same place at the same time. If the girls were right about the size of the audience and it went well that night, it would all be worth it.

Their intimate moment was cut short by a tapping on the door. Richard nodded and slipped on his wig and turban while Lacey hid in the box, one of the stage props they used for that very reason. It was literally a box with a hidden compartment big enough for one of the girls to hide in. It had a secret latch and air holes. Laura waited until they were ready, then opened the door.

"This is amazing!" The venue manager was elated that throngs of people waited outside even though they'd sold out of seats hours before.

"Amazing and magnificent!" agreed Richard in his thick, phony accent.

"Right, amazing and magnificent," the man corrected himself. "We've filled every seat, and there's at least a thousand more people waiting to get in. They're lined up around the block. It's too bad we're not having two shows tonight."

"Yes, yes, too bad," Richard agreed.

In order to book the venue, he normally would've been required to put a large deposit down and employ his own personnel. Since he didn't have the funds to do that, he and the owners had come to an agreement over the take. Half of the money from the ticket sales, along with all of the concession dollars, went toward the venue. An additional twenty percent went to the stage hands and other personnel. Richard had no idea how much the greedy bastard who managed the place was skimming, but he had hardly been in a position to quibble. Judging by the successful results of his marketing campaign, that position no longer applied.

"I'd really hate to turn those people away," stammered the man. "They've come all the way down here and—"

"And have all that cash to fork over?" finished Richard.

"Something like that."

The manager was actually rubbing his hands together, practically salivating at the prospect of selling out two shows in one night. When Richard said nothing more, the manager pushed the issue. "What would it take to make that happen?"

"Magic!" exclaimed Richard with a dramatic wave of his arms. The manager smiled nervously. "Just kidding," Richard continued, turning back to the mirror to touch up his makeup. "But, since I believe we've more than covered your overhead expenses, perhaps a more fair distribution of the profits is in order."

"Not exactly," the manager said. "I mean, I'll have to pay my employees overtime, and that won't come cheap. Besides—"

"Pity," Richard interrupted. "The second show is usually the best. The first one always has a few rough edges, but the next is spectacular. Once word gets out, you might have to make those overtime payments a regular thing. I'd be profoundly heartbroken to be the cause of so much trouble on your behalf. I'll make it a point to convey that to the owners of this fine establishment. I'm sure they'll be absolutely beside themselves with gratitude over your concern for your employees. But I doubt that'll be necessary. Word will get out that no second show was offered to the disappointed people who waited all that time to get in. It might prevent them from going to the trouble of coming all the way down here the next time. I'm sure there are other theaters that offer adequate entertainment for their enjoyment."

"No, no, I'll hear none of that," said the manager. "It's your special night. You've worked hard for this. I'd be happy to pay the workers out of my own pocket for their extra time as well as the considerable expense of keeping this place open for another couple of hours. Consider it a gift, Mr. Villanova. Fifty percent of the box office will cover us just fine."

"And the concessions?" added Richard.

"The concessions? I'm not sure. The owners are quite clear about how we—"

"A mere twenty percent is all I ask. For charity."

"Charity?"

"The gypsy orphan's fund," said Richard, nodding at Laura.

The girl ran to her father's side and said in a strange tongue. "Nanno cholati mallu rentisimo flora vespuci cammerarone."

"What's she saying?" asked the manager.

"She's expressing her gratitude over your generous offer. Her people have suffered so greatly. Very few have expressed a desire to help them. As one of the last members of her tribe, she's deeply touched by your gesture."

"Are her parent's deceased?" the man asked.

Richard nodded his head sadly. "Not only her parents, but all of her relatives. Burned in the ovens at the hands of the Nazis. I was able to help her escape by means of my unusual talents, and I've looked after her ever since."

"You are truly a remarkable man, Mr. Villanova. It's an honor to host your performance."

The men shook hands, and the manager left. The deal was made.

"A second show, Daddy!" said Lacey, climbing out of her hiding space. "Aren't you nervous?"

"Actually, my little gypsy princess, I'm relieved." With a second show, he'd have plenty of money to get by for awhile. If they tanked, there would be no shows the next night, or the one after that. With only one show, there'd be little left over after expenses. Two guaranteed them that they'd get by.

Richard said no more as they made the final preparations. They'd be on in less than fifteen minutes. The place was pulsating with the anticipation of three thousand fans waiting for their chance to witness something extraordinary. The Amazing and Magnificent Villanova was going to give it to them.

CHAPTER TEN

Under the instructions of the magician, the beginning of the presentation was delayed. The crowd grew restless. The theater manager paced nervously back and forth in the wings, wishing he hadn't agreed to the magician's demand that the show start fifteen minutes late without giving notice to the anxious crowd. The stage manager in charge of the performance ignored him and smiled; the magician knew what he was doing.

On cue and without warning, the lights dimmed, and the three black trumpeters blared out a sound reminiscent of a royal announcement. The trio set down their horns and beat an ancient rhythm on heavy bass drums. Minutes later, they were accompanied by the elderly Japanese woman plucking on a *koto*. The curtains moved unseen in the darkness. A strange purple-bluish glow radiated from an odd-shaped obelisk at center stage. As the light grew in intensity, so did the volume of the peculiar Hindu melody emanating from the *pungi*, an instrument used by snake charmers, now played by the elderly man from India.

The odd mixture of exotic instruments and compositions was both hypnotic and unsettling. When the Hungarian refugee played a gypsy melody on his violin, the effect was electric. After a crescendo, the musicians abruptly stopped, and the theater fell into darkness once more. After a long pause, the drums beat wildly, and cymbals crashed as pyrotechnics exploded in bright flashes on the stage, momentarily blinding all onlookers.

A backlit silhouette appeared in the fog as the sound rose again. The horns blew loudly once more, and the stage became bathed in light, revealing a lone figure where the obelisk had stood. From the loudspeakers erupted the voice of the house emcee: "The Luxor Theater is proud to present a once in a lifetime chance for you to witness a legend in the world of magic. Known for his incredible feats of miraculous illusions as the Wizard of Eurasia, Swami of the Far East, Mystic of the Orient, Magus of Persia, Sorcerer of the Dark Continent, and Conjurer of the Amazon, ladies and gentlemen of Nashville, in his first North American performance, it is my honor to introduce the Amazing and Magnificent Villanova!"

Richard raised his arms in a victorious pose, his glittery purple turban reflecting the bright spotlights in every direction. A red plastic ruby set in the center of the headpiece glowed, thanks to a battery powered light behind the stone. Richard's heavy eyeliner made his eyes appear almost too big for his face, an illusion which he heightened with a fiery stare at the darkened crowd beyond the lights. His cape flapped gently behind him in the light breeze from one of the fans set up to blow away the smoke and designed to make him look as if he were in motion amongst the clouds. Richard posed for a moment for effect, then lowered his arms.

"I am the Amazing and Magnificent Villanova!" he exclaimed in his fake European accent. To Richard, it sounded like a cross between the stereotypical Russian and Count Dracula, but it fit his phony persona. "It is true, I have traveled the world in search of the unexplainable and terrifying, and I bring to you some of the miraculous illusions that I have discovered. But I must confess something to you, something I've never told anyone before. I have seen the most amazing of sights, the most incredible natural beauties, the greatest treasures of mankind, and the richest of kings, emperors, and tyrants in all their splendid palaces and castles.

Until now, I have been unable to make this statement. You are truly a privileged people, for you live in a place like no other. Yes, the Amazing and Magnificent Villanova will state for all to hear. Now that I have seen the world with my own eyes, I can state without a shadow of a doubt that the United States of America is the greatest nation on earth!"

The crowd went wild with applause. Everyone jumped to their feet in delight. The magician bowed humbly in return and tried to hide his smile. The suckers were eating it up with a ladle.

"Let us begin!" Richard swung his cape around his body three times in an ever-widening arch before stretching out one arm from his side. He draped the cloth like a matador at a bullfight and stomped his feet. Spanish music drifted up from the orchestra pit as roses fell down on the stage from above.

"As I wandered the narrow alleys of Pamplona, a lovely señorita once said to me, 'Señor, you must be careful. The mighty Taurus will strike you down.' I smiled at the Spanish princess and told her, 'Not I. The wild beast holds no power over me. But beauty such as yours is truly dangerous.'"

The audience laughed. Richard smiled and winked. The cloth in his hands began to bulge, and he looked at it with confusion. He held the cape gingerly as the bulge took the shape of a bull's head, complete with horns. The cape seemed to come alive as if the garment itself had transformed into the beast.

"Toro, toro!" The magician called out. "Feo toro para chica boñita yo te mando! Hocus pocus." He turned and smiled at the crowd. "I'd better focus!"

More laughter drifted up from the audience. Richard turned back to the cape that now appeared beyond his control, and shouted, "Gypsy girl, arise!" He pulled the cape away to reveal his daughter, Laura, dressed lavishly in an exotic, brightly colored genie outfit. She held up both hands to her head, her thumbs and fingers in the shape of horns, and dragged her right foot along the floor as she walked toward him. She blew air out and snorted like a bull. The crowd erupted in applause and laughter. Laura bowed as her father introduced her. "Ladies and gentlemen, I present to you my lovely assistant, Natalia, the Gypsy Princess. Natalia, say hello to the wonderful citizens of Nashville."

Laura looked at the audience, then at the magician with a perplexed look on her face. She turned to the audience, and back to Richard once more, but remained silent.

"What's the matter?" Richard asked, "Cat got your tongue?"

"Neeeiiiigghh!"

The crowd laughed again at her antics.

"That's a horse," said Richard.

Laura opened her mouth, as if trying to force the words, but nothing came out. She tried again with more effort, rocking back and forth, but only garbled mumbles came forth. The girl looked at the magician in dismay. A determined expression appeared on her angelic face. She bent over and heaved as if she were going to vomit on the stage. Richard reached out and patted her back with one hand while putting his other hand in front of the girl's mouth to catch any foul contents that might spill out if she violently retched. As the cymbals crashed in the orchestra pit, Laura slowly stood up and extended one arm toward the magician, who now held a kitten in his previously empty hand.

"Meow," the feline cried. Richard handed it to Laura, who took the kitten and stroked it gently. She took several small bows, then headed off stage with the cat.

After a couple of steps, the magician called for her to stop. "Natalia," he said sternly, "is that all you have to say to the fine people of Nashville?"

She glanced at the magician, and back at the audience. She smiled broadly and shouted, "Yee haw!"

The patrons returned her cowboy yell and awarded her with another round of applause. She curtseyed slightly and hurriedly disappeared into the wings as Richard took a bow.

"Bulls and horses and kittens," he said, "are wonderful creatures that grace this world. But of the beasts that crawl and swim, run, gallop, hop, and, dare I say it, even walk upright on two legs," Richard said, then paused to glance around the room. He pretended to make eye contact with several audience members even though the spotlights made that impossible, and continued, "have nothing on the blessed creatures that the Lord has granted the gift of flight." Richard threw the cape he'd kept casually draped over his arm into the air. As it fell to the stage in front of him, a dozen white doves appeared from the magic garment and soared above the crowd. One by one, they flew into the shadows off stage, leaving the magician standing alone, his cape now lying flat on the floor at his feet.

"Cape's are overrated," he said as he held his hand above the cloth, palm down, and said the magic words. "Alacazam! Cain and Abel! Lose the cape, find a table!" The garment ascended from the floor as if pulled by an invisible force from the magician's outstretched hand. As it reached a level slightly above Richard's waist, it stopped. The cape had become a tablecloth draping an unseen table.

Gasps drifted up to Richard's ear from the packed theater. He'd made them laugh; he'd made them cheer; he'd entertained them with simple illusions and witty banter. Now he'd begun to amaze them. The magician's face held its stoic expression, with the exception of his eyes, which burned bright with a supernatural glow. Inwardly, he smiled because he knew. *They ain't seen nothin' yet.*

CHAPTER ELEVEN

Leaning forward, Richard examined the table-like object in front of him, exaggerating his moves. He ran his hands around the edges and tapped on the top with his knuckles. *Tap, tap, tap,* he knocked as if expecting a reply.

"Who's there?" a voice shouted from the audience.

Richard smiled and nodded. "We have that joke in the old country, too," he said. "Allah," he replied.

"Allah, who?" more voices shouted from the crowd.

"Alacazam!" Richard exclaimed and abruptly pulled the cape away. The space was empty. Oohs and aahs drifted up from the audience. "I'm afraid the joke's on me. I needed that table." The crowd laughed.

"I guess we'll have to do this the old fashioned way," the magician stated. "I don't know how things work in your country, but where I come from, if you want something done–"

"You have to do it yourself," someone shouted.

"Oh, yes, yes, I see." Richard laughed. "No, things are much different in the old country. We keep our tables in the kitchen and, in the kitchen, if you want something done right, you ask the woman of the house. But you'd better make sure you ask her kindly and with gratitude if you know what's good for you."

More laughter drifted up from the crowd. Richard was beginning to think he should ditch the magic tricks and focus on being a comedian.

"My dear, sweet Natalia, princess of the gypsies." Richard paused to smile and wink at the audience. "Would you be so kind as to bring me a table, at your leisure, of course?"

This time Lacey entered the stage, dressed identical to her sister. Richard knew that it was better to rotate the twins as much as possible. That way, what small differences they might exhibit would be harder to pick up on by others. She trotted up to Richard, handed him what appeared to be a business card, and tugged on his shoulder. Richard stooped over to let Lacey whisper in his ear. His expression went from confusion to surprise to understanding. He eventually nodded, patted his assistant on the back, and watched as she smiled at the audience and skipped off the stage. The magician read the card in his hand and turned it over a few times before addressing the crowd.

"It seems my table is on backorder," he explained. "The salesman at the furniture store was kind enough to give me his card and apologize for any inconvenience this might cause." He paused to give the audience time to laugh again. "He even wrote a personal note on the back," Richard continued, pretending to read what was written on the business card. "It says here that he personally expedited the order and that it should arrive at any minute now. Should we wait?"

He looked at the crowd. A unanimous 'No!' was the answer to his question.

"But he promised it would arrive momentarily," pleaded the magician.

More shouts of 'No!' came booming from the audience.

"Perhaps you are right," Richard agreed. "I'll just dispose of this card," he said. He began to tear the paper in half, but instead of it tearing, it unfolded, then, unfolded again. The magician looked stunned and gaped at the crowd as if to say 'Did you see that?' He unfolded the paper again and again. As it grew in size, he pretended to struggle with the complexity and resistance that the object presented. Laura, returning to her role as Natalia, ran onto the stage to lend a hand. The two unfolded and turned, turned and unfolded the paper, stopping at times to discuss their progress and give each other instructions. Minutes later, they grabbed opposite ends of the contraption, stepped back, and let go. A wooden table fell onto the stage between them, the sound of the hard wood reverberating throughout the theater. The crowd exploded in applause.

"It appears the salesman was right," said Richard. He took a bow, and nodded to his assistant to take a bow. When the applause dissipated, he reached for Laura's hand and continued, "Many of you don't know this, but my lovely assistant here is a renowned fortune teller. I can personally attest to her skill. But don't take my word for it. I will let her demonstrate her power for you so that you may see for yourselves. Ladies and gentlemen, I give you Natalia the Gypsy Princess!"

Richard took a step back, waving in Laura's direction as she curtsied. She took her place behind the table and looked around. Motioning for the magician to come closer, she whispered in his ear again.

"A chair?" Richard asked. He glanced around, but there was nothing on the stage. Addressing the audience, he said, "It seems we have forgotten to provide a chair, and it is standing room only tonight." Cheers from the packed theater. "If only we had a business card Natalia could sit on," he mused, more laughter followed. "I guess we'll just have to make do," Richard said. He unfurled his cape, held it at his side, shook it, then pulled it away in a grand gesture, leaving a chair on the stage where none had stood before.

Natalia smiled and sat down. Motioning once again for the magician's attention, she whispered in his ear.

"I see. Now, that is a quandary," Richard said and addressed the crowd. "Does anyone here have a crystal ball by chance?" He paused and asked again, "Anyone?"

When no one came forward with the prized item, the magician and the gypsy fell into a long discussion – not heard, of course, by the audience. Several of the musicians played intermission music in jest as the two appeared to argue. The girl pointed to the ruby on the magician's turban; he emphatically shook his head no. She insisted, and he refused again, turning his back on her and folding his arms. The girl feigned tears and wiped at her eyes despondently. Richard glanced back, saw his assistant in distress, and hung his head in defeat.

"Once again, I'm afraid I must confess our cultural differences," Richard said to the audience. "I'm sure, in America, where the men are strong and brave, once a man puts his foot down, there is no further discussion. Unfortunately, where I come from, that is not always the case. Oh, don't get me wrong. We try, but our women have a secret weapon that renders us helpless." The audience laughed. "The truth be told, they have more than one," he added and winked. The crowd howled in delight and applauded.

Richard looked over at the forlorn gypsy girl and relented. He unpinned the ruby from his turban and placed it on the table. Laura glanced at the jewel and back at the magician.

"What?" he asked. She stared at him without a word, raising one eyebrow.

"Apparently, it's not big enough," Richard said to the audience and shrugged his shoulders. "That's not the first time I've heard that." More cheers and laughter greeted him.

Richard turned to the audience and told another story. "When I traveled through the ancient and mysterious lands of the Orient, I came upon a most wondrous sight." A small spotlight lit up an object on the left at the back of the stage. Seated on a fanciful throne of pillows was an elderly Asian woman in full kabuki makeup. On both sides of her sat two statues of fearsome dragons, backlit with purple lighting, their eyes glowing with red lights, and smoke drifting out of their mouths. The woman plucked at the *koto* on her lap, its exotic melody echoing around the now silent theater.

"I was walking down a dirt road in the middle of a Japanese village when I saw a blind beggar in the distance, sitting beside a ditch," Richard continued. "I stopped and watched the man, and, more importantly, I observed the hundreds of people who passed by without seeing him. At that very moment, as if the man could read my mind, he shouted at me—in my native tongue, no less. I was astounded. How did this blind beggar even know I was there? I drew close to ask him. Yet again, he was ahead of me. 'I knew you were there because I felt your eyes upon me' he said. Before I could say anything in return, he added, 'I can feel the eyes of others'. I said one word— ironic. He did not find it amusing."

The theater was silent with the exception of the haunting melody. "He conceded that his eyes could not see as other's see, but he had a gift. I did not understand because I couldn't. The old man laughed and explained. He said that, although his eyes could not see, he could see with the eyes of others, while they were only able to look. He explained that it was looking that rendered the eyes useless, for it blinded the person from understanding the truth. What could I say? The old man was right."

Richard looked over the crowd with a mournful expression before finishing his story. "Not a day goes by that I do not think about the old man's warning. I'm not here to lecture you fine people. I'm sure your shortcomings are not as great as mine. But I do know a thing or two about illusions."

Richard pulled a handkerchief out of his jacket pocket and dropped it on the table, covering up the small ruby. He held the cloth down at the edges and said, "The size of a jewel does not define its worth. This is true of any object. An object of use should be valued above an object of vanity, but we deem it not so. What does that say about us? A shovel has more use than a diamond." Richard's hands trembled, shaking the table. "What we value defines us, not the object. The size of one's heart is where I place my treasure. If you care to see the future, ask the gypsy girl. But I warn you. You may not see what you want to see."

The handkerchief grew as if it were a balloon being inflated with helium. "Abracadabra! Is this what you're after?" he exclaimed, pulling the rag away to reveal a giant crystal ball sitting on a pedestal in the center of the table. The crowd cheered as Richard finished his warning. "Remember not only to look, but most importantly, to see."

The audience rose to its feet and applauded. Richard bowed and added, "I am the Amazing and Magnificent Villanova!"

He slowly backed away and exited the stage. The crowd settled down and took their seats. The houselights dimmed. Only a small spotlight remained on the gypsy girl in the center of the stage. It was Laura's turn to shine.

CHAPTER TWELVE

Natalia sat motionless as the theater grew silent. All eyes were on the gypsy girl sitting behind the crystal ball. Laura's eyes were closed. She swayed back and forth, almost imperceptibly. Her hands went into motion around the glass ball on the table, as if polishing an unseen barrier inches from the surface of the smooth object.

"Simi zooso ruishuisu laperedi moe," she chanted with a strange accent. "Moelentojia ramucassa cassenoveni zito bellarumeo." Laura hummed an odd tune, interrupted occasionally by more chants in the bizarre pretend language. A silhouette of a horse-drawn wagon appeared on the curtain in the background as if the sun were rising behind a gypsy encampment in Eastern Europe. The shadow of a Hungarian violinist materialized in the scene, accompanied by a poignant melody.

Tension grew as Laura's voice swelled, and her movements quickened. Unseen drummers beat on *doumbek* gypsy drums, and the tempo of the violin music increased.

"Ammano charo tini wesbroo cambraisi mahoo!" the girl sang, her hands flying into the air, her face pointing upward.

The lights flicked off as the music and chanting stopped. Slowly, a backlight appeared behind Laura, a pale, blue spotlight bringing her shadowy figure into view. Her eyes stared in wide open intensity at the orb in front of her. The glass itself swirled with a smoky radiance from within.

A familiar object became visible in the cloudy glass of the crystal ball. It was the face of Villanova.

"Sheebarisu nanna jarikito," mumbled Laura.

"The gypsy sees all," the magician's disembodied head announced from inside the orb. His voice seemed to come from every direction, echoing off the walls of the auditorium. Members of the audience, jarred by the extraordinary effect, gasped audibly.

Laura mumbled a few more lines of bogus dialogue, and once again, the face inside of the crystal ball interpreted for her. "Dark clouds are on the horizon."

The girl spoke again and again, pausing each time for the magician to interpret. "Winter comes, but not as before. The darkest days are behind us. The cold will not be as bitter. Spring comes again, and with it, life. With life, comes hope." The magician relayed the cryptic messages. "Avoid hastiness; relish the company of friends. Be wary of flattery; truth should guide you in your endeavors." Richard and the girls collected daily horoscopes, and they peppered the routine with some of the better ones whenever possible.

"No!" the magician's head shouted from inside the orb. "You must not!" His voice boomed throughout the theater.

The gypsy girl stopped speaking. She put her hands on the globe and shrieked. Thunder and lightning appeared in the crystal ball as the magician's head spun in circles. A tornado twisted inside of the glass. The sound of thunder erupted in the theater. Strobes of light erupted as smoke poured onto the stage. A cacophony of howling wind and rainfall crackled from hidden speakers that Richard had placed in the shadowy corners of the room.

The storm raged beyond control. A sudden burst of wind blew onto the audience, courtesy of several large fans hidden in the rafters. Cymbals crashed from the orchestra pit. A near panic swept through the crowd before everything halted in an instant.

"Stop!" the magician commanded. He now stood alone in the center of the stage. There was no sign of the crystal ball, the table, or the gypsy girl.

The audience warily settled back in their seats, apprehensive after the horrendous sights and sounds they had just witnessed.

"My apologies to all," said the magician. "That was unexpected. Please, allow me to explain. Natalia is a gypsy who strives to use her power for good. In her rituals, she is wont to contact the spirits of the netherworld. Usually, this poses no threat. But occasionally, bad spirits try to use her as a conduit to enter our realm. What we experienced was one such occurrence, but I am certain that I intervened in time to stop it."

Richard could sense that the crowd was less than convinced, just as he'd planned. They were anxious and nervous, many believing that otherworldly forces were now at play. He had them right where he wanted them. Now all he had to do was reel them in.

CHAPTER THIRTEEN

A shadow in the shape of the Taj Mahal surrounded by palm trees appeared on the curtain at the back of the stage. The Indian flute player, dressed in white robes and a turban, sat cross-legged on the floor. He blew into his *pungi*, the exotic notes floated in the air.

"In my youth, I traveled across the world in search of truth and the unknown, and I found both on the subcontinent of India," said the magician. "Many things of beauty were there for my eyes to behold. And some things of terror."

A creature emerged from the basket at the swami's feet. It swayed to the beat of the flute, its head following the end of the musical instrument as if hypnotized.

"At this time, I request the cooperation of the audience. Please, no sudden noises or movements. Unlike the beasts of the spirit realm that tried to crash our performance, this beast of the earth is already present. I must warn you. It is not only a creature to be feared, but the king of such creatures. Ladies and gentlemen, I give you the king cobra and the man who controls it, Swami Raj Taneesh, the Mongoose of Makrana."

The cobra rose from the basket, spreading the skin on its head as if poised to strike and inject its deadly poison at any moment. The charmer appeared unfazed by the threat within arm's reach, and he continued to play the hypnotic melody as the snake danced to the rhythm. Without warning, the charmer reached out and slapped the cobra's head. The crowd held its breath at the sheer lunacy of the action, but the snake did not respond and continued to dance. The charmer repeated the action twice more to prove his point. When he abruptly stopped playing, the snake fell back into the basket.

The audience cheered as the swami put a lid on the receptacle, took a bow, and exited the stage. Richard clapped with the crowd and saluted the man as he left.

Turning back to the audience, Richard said, "Amazing, isn't it? I wished to learn the great secrets that could tame the mighty cobra, but alas, I was halted by an unforeseen impediment." He nodded to the wings and Lacey appeared as Natalia, took a bow, and ran to Richard's side to hand him a *pungi* of his own. She took a step to the side and covered her ears with her hands as the magician blew into the flute. A horrible screech emanated from the instrument.

"A lack of musical talent," he finished. The crowd roared with laughter. "Fortunately, I was able to overcome my deficiency of this highly prized ability with my knowledge and skills of illusion."

Lacey ran off to the wings and returned with a basket identical to the one that held the cobra. She handed the basket to the magician and took the *pungi,* taking care to hold it away from her at a distance as if it were infected with a deadly communicable disease. Richard frowned at his assistant's antics and chided her. "It's not the flute's fault, my dearest Natalia, for only a poor musician blames his instrument." The gypsy girl rolled her eyes and shook her head, eliciting a few chuckles from the audience.

Richard gingerly slipped the lid off the basket and carefully peered inside. Once he was certain that it posed no danger, he gave an exaggerated sigh of relief and held the basket on its side in the direction of the crowd so that they could see that it was empty.

"Luckily, there are no king cobras inside of this basket."

"How come?" someone in the audience shouted.

"I'm a magician, not an idiot," replied Richard.

"You're just chicken," the heckler returned the taunt.

"I am the Amazing and Magnificent Villanova, not the stupid and dead ex-magician," Richard said. "But, if you insist—" he stammered as he reached his hand into the empty basket without looking while glaring in the direction of the unwelcome heckler. "Does this make you happy?" he asked, pulling out his hand, this time clutching a handful of wiggling serpents.

The crowd gasped with horror. Richard pasted a confused expression on his face and looked over at what he was holding. He swayed as if he were going to pass out from fright, only to take a deep breath and compose himself.

"Whew! I almost scared myself to death," he explained. "Don't worry, these aren't cobras. They're merely rope snakes." Richard stuffed the irate reptiles back into the basket and added, "See for yourselves!" Without warning, he flung the container in the direction of the audience, and long, serpentine objects flew into the first few rows of the audience. Shrieks erupted from the people near the front as they jumped out of their seats in a panic. Laughter and applause soon replaced the screams when those individuals held up strands of rope.

"I am the Amazing and Magnificent Villanova!" exclaimed Richard, taking a bow. The ovation was deafening. Things could not be going any better for the magician. His hard work had paid off. He could smell money in the air. Now, for the finale.

CHAPTER FOURTEEN

The lights dimmed, and moments passed while the audience settled down. The rhythmic beating of conga drums resonated in the air.

A warm green glow emerged from the back of the stage, illuminating two incredibly tall African drummers, one in each corner. The two men were dressed in full witch doctor regalia, complete with makeup and bones protruding from their noses. The sounds of unseen jungle creatures echoed from the rafters, adding to the exotic atmosphere.

A spotlight lit up the center of the stage to unexpectedly reveal the magician, as if he'd materialized out of thin air. His voice boomed above the din of the drums.

"I once traveled through the forbidden realms of the Dark Continent. Such wonders I saw! Those miraculous sights were only surpassed by the dangers that stalked my entourage. Of the twenty-three souls who set out from Cairo, I was the only one to return. But I did not return the same, and I did not return alone."

"Yeaaaaah!!! Molo holo buli muli!" shouted a third African, jumping onto the stage. He was wearing a loin cloth made of zebra skin, and he carried a long spear. Around his neck hung a necklace made of crocodile teeth. On his head, he wore a wooden mask of grotesque proportions.

The man danced to the primitive beating of the drums, occasionally blurting out Swahili-like mumbo-jumbo as if he were performing some ancient and forbidden tribal ritual.

"Deep in the jungles of the Congo lives a tribe of people with notoriously horrifying disposition. To travel to such a place is not only difficult, it is dangerous. Our expedition made that mistake, with disastrous results."

"Yeaaaahh! Molukoluki mayo! Sensa pari mo!" the witch doctor shouted as he danced around the stage.

"They came out of the shadows of the dense rainforest, surrounding us like spirits from the netherworld. But they were not spirits; they were very real. And as we soon found out, very hungry."

"Buta buta goola hayo! Yah!"

"We offered them what little rations we had left, but they preferred a different sort of nourishment. Our guides would not translate their requests, but it didn't take long for us to realize that we were on the menu."

"Juju carasi hazo mutibi!" the witch doctor held his spear in a menacing fashion, circling the magician in an aggressive, but cautious, manner.

"One by one, they took us to their fire pit, until only I was left. I remember it well. It haunts me still."

The beating tempo of the drums increased, accompanied by the calls of exotic birds and the growls of an unknown predator. Tension rose in the theater.

"At last, they came for me. The tribe looked at me, a white man, with disgust, with hatred. Worse yet, they looked at me like I was dessert. I knew I had to think fast, so I gathered what was left of my courage and dug deep into my knowledge of magic. It was then that I conjured up my greatest illusion as if my life depended on it, because it did."

Silently, the gypsy girl wheeled a table with a rectangular box on it out onto the stage. Richard paid no attention but continued his story.

"I knew that I had to do something to distract them in order to escape. I also knew that this would not be enough. I'd never survive in the jungle on my own. It was an untenable position to be in, and I knew I had but one shot of making it out alive."

Lacey locked the wheels of the table in place and stood next to the box, the stage lights revealing the colorful contraption. The Africans stopped and stared at the mysterious object and at one another in confusion.

Richard went to the box, flipped up the top, and knocked opened the side facing the audience to show that nothing was in it but empty space. He and his assistant closed the side, but left the top open. The magician looked at the girl and nodded. Lacey bowed her head and took his hand.

Richard continued with his story. "I was in a perilous state, but my resolve was unshakable. The only other time in my life I felt so afraid was when I was courting my dearly departed wife."

Richard bowed to the gypsy girl as if they were in a fanciful ballroom. Lacey twirled and the two waltzed to the strains of an unseen violin coming from offstage. When he started to dip the girl, Richard froze, raised his face to the audience and continued. "We had a much better selection from the caterer at my wedding, I assure you."

With that, the girl collapsed. Richard scooped her up and placed her limp body in the box, leaving only her feet and her head sticking out of the holes at each end. When the waltz began again, the magician unlocked the table and spun around the stage, rolling the table and box in a circle as if it were his dancing partner. When the music stopped, Richard was standing behind the box, the side facing the crowd.

"Unfortunately, the tribe of cannibals wasn't as civilized as we are, but some things they did do the same as us. For instance, we generally don't throw the whole cow on the pit, and neither do they. The butcher cuts it up into smaller pieces first."

Richard pulled out a large, gleaming metal saw with a serrated edge. He tapped on the terrifying looking device, and the shrill clang of steel echoed throughout the room. An audible exclamation arose from the crowd.

Setting the sharp saw edge against the box, he paused and said, "It was also unfortunate that there were dozens of them and only one of me. It seemed that slicing me in half would be required. The irony struck me as sharp as this blade. For you see, I always wanted to be taller."

Richard pushed down and sawed into the wooden box. His violent movements tore through the lumber, and, presumably, through the gypsy girl's flesh and bones, with a horrendous sound. He exaggerated the motion of the saw, knowing from the chatter coming from the crowd that they were feeling every thrust of the blade as if it were cutting into their own bodies.

"Whew! Pardon me. This is hard work," said the magician, pausing momentarily while a stage hand brought him a glass of water. He took a few gulps, handed the glass back to the man, withdrew a handkerchief from his shirt pocket, and pretended to wipe sweat from his brow.

"It's okay," he assured the audience. "I'll be alright."

Richard grabbed the handle of the saw and shoved it even more violently into the box while the gypsy girl's head contorted from side to side and her feet kicked about wildly. After a half dozen more thrusts of the saw, he was through the box. Leaving the thick blade sticking in the box, Richard stepped back to catch his breath.

"I'm glad that's over," he joked, leaning against the table and causing the two sides to push apart. Richard was now standing between the two halves. He bowed as the crowd exploded in applause.

When the clapping faded, he continued his tale. "So there I was, half the man I used to be." The audience laughed. "But I was not dead. In fact, I began to sing."

Lacey hummed a pleasant tune as if she were skipping through a field of dandelions without a care in the world.

"The only song that came to me at that time was as inappropriately pleasant as that one coming from my assistant."

The unmistakable melody of *Dixie* could be heard coming from the loudspeakers, sending the crowd to their feet in appreciation. "This confused the natives to no end, I must tell you. Flabbergasted is the word, I believe."

The three faux African Bushmen stood on the stage in a state of utter confusion. The subtle nodding of their heads and tapping of their feet in time to the Southern anthem provided comic relief, just as they'd rehearsed.

"I took advantage of their confusion and chastised them in what little I knew of their native tongue, insisting that they reattach my top half to my bottom half so that I could kick their collective asse—. I mean, derrieres. Pardon my French, or Swahili, or whatever." There was more laughter from the crowd. "So, reattach me they did. After that, none dared to defy me. So, here I stand."

Richard pushed the two halves of the box together and removed the saw in one quick movement. He lifted the top and the side fell open to reveal his assistant, back in one piece. The magician approached the box and helped the girl roll out. She smiled and curtsied as Richard held her hand and presented her for the crowd's approval. She then skipped off the stage to join the three pretend cannibals waiting in the wings.

"Wait!" Richard called out to the girl, but she was already off stage. He turned to the audience and said, "My lovely assistant forgot to remove this horrible contraption." Richard eyed the box with feigned disgust before turning back to the crowd. "No matter. A gypsy girl is always underfoot," he exclaimed. He unfurled his cape to reveal Laura, standing at his side. Another round of applause greeted the pair.

"Ladies and gentlemen, Natalia the Gypsy Princess!" The girl smiled and bowed before pushing the wheeled table off the stage.

The crowd cheered. Richard stood alone at center stage until the noise of the audience died down. He waited a moment longer, then still another moment. At last, he waved his arms in the air and pronounced in a booming voice before taking a bow, "I am the Amazing and Magnificent Villanova!"

The curtain dropped, and the house lights came up. Richard, exhausted but exhilarated, walked back to his dressing room. The entire building shook from the cacophony of three thousand people stomping their feet, clapping their hands, and shouting their love and admiration for the greatest performance they had ever witnessed.

CHAPTER FIFTEEN

The next show went on without a hitch, and the next. The crowds lined up and down the block for every event. It wasn't long before the owners of the Luxor attempted to get Richard to sign an exclusive contract, but he had bigger plans. They renegotiated his deal to give him a larger cut of the take. They invested their own funds for advertising. They even presented him with a new automobile to show their appreciation. Still, he refused to budge. Offers were coming in from out of town. He was on the verge of stardom.

When they ran out of incentives, management shifted gears.

"What's this all about?" Richard angrily shouted. "This is an outrage!"

"I'm sorry, sir, but we're just doing our jobs," the bookish man with the thick glasses and bowtie replied.

Richard stared at him, pretending the two goons on either side of the man weren't present. He knew this was a shakedown. He'd expected it. Knowing it didn't help. He figured it was only a matter of time before management played hardball. Still, he hadn't expected that they'd go after the girls.

"I assure you, all of our paperwork is in order. We are in this country legally, and I am the legal custodian of Natalia. So, if you'll excuse me, I'll have to ask you to leave at once!"

The men stood their ground.

"We know you are here legally, Mr. Henderson. As for the girls," the man continued, stressing the plural tense of the word, "it's not their immigration status that concerns us. Of course, I'm not sure of the status of the rest of your menagerie, the guru, geisha, and the rest of them, but that's not why we're here." He paused before adding, "Yet."

Richard wanted to argue with them, but he knew that his ruse was up. The bastards had done their homework. He remained silent.

"How old are the girls again, Mr. Henderson?"

"Sixteen," he lied.

"Not old enough for the stage, I'm afraid. I guess you'll have to wait a few years before you take your show on the road. I know for a fact that the boys in New York are pretty strict about such things. Actually, it wouldn't go over well here if word got out. The theater is taking a risk by allowing it, I'd say. It could prove to be quite a liability if it got out."

"Why would it?" asked Richard.

"Why, indeed," the man replied. "As it is, management has stuck its neck out looking the other way. Our legal representation thinks it would be best if we weren't involved in any sordid cover-up and we disclosed everything we know to the proper authorities. It would limit our legal liability. They've drafted a press release to that effect. I tried to convince them that it would dampen the appeal of your show and spoil it for the audience. I mean, once people know that there are two girls, it'll ruin the illusion, not to mention the very idea that the Amazing and Magnificent Villanova from parts unknown is actually Dick Henderson from Toledo."

"I don't see how that helps you, either," Richard remarked.

"It doesn't. It isn't good for anyone. I tried to explain it to management, but I'm afraid it's one of those 'if I can't have him, no one can' kind of things. Those things never end well, do they, Dick?"

Richard looked at the trio. There was no expression on the small man's face, but the two large Italian-looking goons who flanked him glared at him. One even cracked his knuckles. The scene reminded Richard of some film noir Bogart movie, but it was all too real. He was screwed, and he knew it.

"No, they don't," he agreed. "However…"

"However?"

"What do you know about show business, Mister—?"

"Blank," the man replied. "You can call me Mr. Blank."

"How original. Mr. Blank, tell me, what do you know about show business?"

"What are you getting at, Mr. Henderson?"

"See, that's what I'm getting at. Mr. Henderson—Dick the Great. That wouldn't sell many tickets, now, would it?"

"Obviously not, which is why you created your little persona. We get that. In fact, we are most impressed by your commitment. It's one of the reasons we felt so comfortable showering you with gifts and offering you such a generous contract. It's you who forgot the rule of reciprocation."

"I didn't forget, Mr. Blank. It's part of the illusion. Let's get to the point. I can't keep doing the same act in the same town, night after night. I'm constantly tweaking and changing things, but I can only do so much. Eventually, the crowds will stop coming. The act will play out. Worse yet, my secrets will be exposed, as you are threatening to do now. Magic is a hit and run act, Mr. Blank. It's all about misdirection. Given enough time, even the simpletons will figure it out. Like it or not, we'll need to cut back on the performances. Not when the crowds start to thin, but when the demand is the greatest. Then, we can swoop in unexpectedly from time to time, take the money, and run. That will ensure that they keep coming. They won't want to miss out. Otherwise, they can always wait until next time. We have to make them believe there may not be a next time."

"I'm listening."

"If we can't go to New York, or Los Angeles, or any of the big show business Meccas, and we can't stay here, what can we do?"

"Tell me."

"No, you tell me, Mr. Blank. Does management have any other venues that need to fill seats? Do any of their constituents have such a venue? Even further, dare I say it, would not our success in the Big Apple or City of the Angels raise our value on our triumphant return to the mighty Luxor, the home away from home of the Amazing and Magnificent Villanova?"

"Perhaps."

"Notwithstanding our current dilemma, of course," Richard reminded them of the threat. "It's unfortunate that this has come to light now. Our mutual business interests might have proven most lucrative."

"I see no dilemma, Mr. Villanova," the man said as he placed his briefcase on the desk and removed a manila folder. "Our contract can and will be amended to include those things. I'm sure our arrangement will be more than satisfactory to you and yours."

"Then, I see no reason not to sign it," stated Richard.

The man flipped open the folder and turned the forms of the contract to the last page. He pushed it in front of the magician and offered him a pen. Richard held his palm up, paused, and made a fist, a pen appearing in his grasp from out of thin air.

"Bravo!" The man smiled.

Richard paused again and looked at the man.

"What?" asked the man.

"The girl," Richard said, exaggerating the singular, "will be of legal age soon. At that time, there will be a need to revisit our arrangement."

Silence fell over the room for a moment. No one blinked. Eventually, the man with the bowtie nodded. "As you wish, Mr. Villanova."

Richard signed the contract with the name of a man who didn't exist. *A. M. Villanova.*

CHAPTER SIXTEEN

The new contract was just what Richard needed. They were able to take the show on the road to a few select theaters in the region, which allowed them to improve and refine the act. Even better, they were getting paid handsomely to do it.

Richard wasn't greedy, and he was smart enough to realize that his success depended on everyone who contributed. He gave his employees a raise and made it a point to comp meals and give bonuses to the musicians and assorted performers with whom he shared the stage. The magician routinely handed out gifts and handfuls of cash to the various stagehands and theater personnel who he came into contact with, which made him popular at every stop along the way. It was more than an act of altruism on his part. It was a calculated maneuver that ensured his act's success and reinforced the nondisclosure agreement every employee was required to sign. He was more than happy to play the role of grand benefactor. His future success was all but guaranteed. The act was spectacular.

After months on the road, they were slated to return to the Luxor the following weekend. The theater had been sold out in advance in anticipation of their return. Richard was happy. His girls were happy. It was going to be their homecoming, and they planned on giving the people of Nashville their best efforts. Just one more show in Memphis, and they'd be on their way.

The presentation the previous night had gone well, but Richard was unhappy with the venue's security. He saw a few unsavory looking characters hanging around backstage. They appeared to serve no purpose that he could ascertain, which made him suspicious. As an extra precaution, he'd had the stagehands load up his props in the truck out back, where they would remain, locked up, until show time. The last thing he needed was to have someone poking around, discovering his secrets. He also took special care with the girls. He didn't want them to be seen together by anyone not under contract and whose palms he hadn't greased.

Their grand finale had almost been a disaster during the last performance. It needed some tweaking, so he had the table, box, and saw brought out of the truck and placed backstage. The three burly men with the thick Southern drawls who helped unload the truck acted as disinterested as could be. Something about it wasn't right. Richard made a mental note to take it up with the management when they came in later.

"Yes, yes, place it over there," he instructed. "And be careful. It's a valuable commodity. You can't just mosey on down to the corner store and pick one up."

He hated to be so sarcastic to the rednecks, but their IQs didn't seem to be much higher than the amount of teeth defiantly clinging to their rotting gums. Richard didn't know or care what backwoods swamp these hillbillies came from, but he knew he'd better lay on a bit of charm for the sake of good community relations. So he struck a more cordial tone and attempted to engage them in a bit of small talk to ease the tension before he dropped the boom on them later and had them fired.

"I really must thank you gentlemen for all of the help. Tell me, do you hail from this vicinity?"

"Do we what?" one of the men asked.

"Are you from around here?" Richard clarified.

"Alabama," one of the others replied. His two companions glared at him as if he'd spoken a curse word. He offered no further explanation.

"A beautiful state, I hear," Richard continued. "I hope to go there soon. Maybe we'll be fortunate to work together in the future."

The men nodded but said nothing. Richard felt uneasy, and he wished they'd go away. He tried to ignore them by fiddling with the box and pretending he was doing something important. Unfortunately, the men didn't take the hint.

"That'll be all for now," said Richard at last.

The men stood their ground.

"Where's the girl?" a voice from the corridor disrupted the silence. An elderly man with a long, grey beard entered the room, carrying a crooked wooden stick he used as a cane, and flanked by two younger men.

"I beg your pardon," replied Richard.

"The gypsy girl," the old man said. "Where is she?"

"I don't see where that is any of your business," stated Richard. There was something wrong about this. Who would want the girl?

For a brief moment, he wondered if his ex-wife had learned of his financial success and planned on fighting for custody to try to squeeze money out of him, but he quickly dismissed the idea. They would've asked for the girls, not the girl. Richard had a feeling that this was going to be much worse than anything Ruth could do.

"I'm makin' it my business, heathen!" the old man bellowed.

The gang of unkempt hillbillies circled him. Richard swallowed hard as his mind raced.

"Now, gentlemen," he stammered, "whatever it is that you want, I'm sure we can come to a mutual understanding." Richard wondered if his reputation for generosity had attracted the wrong sort. Maybe they had the impression that he carried around a wad of cash, and they were there to liberate it from him. He wished he had some. They weren't going to like it when they found out he didn't have much pocket change on him at the moment.

"That gypsy girl," repeated the old man, "The one you're turnin' against the Lord. We come for her. She must be saved from your wickedness, demon. Tell me where she is, or else."

"Or else what?" Richard said with defiance. He'd never considered himself a brave man, but he'd be damned if he was going to let these thugs get a hold of his little girl.

The old man laughed. He nodded to the others. The two biggest men each grabbed Richard by the arms. The others closed in.

"Ain't nothin' goin' to save you now, Devil man," said one of the men standing next to the old geezer. His outburst resulted in a tap on his shin from the old man's cane. He winced in pain and hopped on one foot. The younger man on the other side chuckled, which earned him the same fate as his companion. The old geezer shot him a dirty look before turning back to the magician.

"I ask the questions here, sinner. But for the cowardly and unbelievin' and abominable and murderers and immoral persons and sorcerers and idolaters, and all liars, their part will be in the lake that burns with fire and brimstone! Hand over the gypsy so that I may save her from the terrible fate that awaits you. Heed my words, sorcerer!"

"Go to hell," spat Richard.

"Daddy, I think Lacey has the ruby," said Laura, rounding the corner and skipping into the room.

Richard's heart dropped. The man with the limp grabbed the girl and held his hand over her mouth. The old man nodded his approval, turned back toward Richard, and smiled.

"Rescue the weak and needy. Deliver them out of the hands of the wicked." He turned to the man holding the girl, "Take her. Put her in the truck. Jeremiah, you go with him."

"But, Paw," the man holding Laura said, "you promised I'd get to—"

"Do not merely listen to thy words and so deceive yourselves. Do what I say. Now go, boy, before I spare not my staff again on your worthless ass."

Laura tried to break free, but the man's grip proved too strong. His companion, chuckling again at his brother's berating, helped subdue the struggling child. Together, they disappeared down the corridor, leaving the magician alone with his tormentors.

"I seen your magic show, sorcerer," the old man said. "It was mighty impressive, I must say. 'Course, I know it to be a false illusion. Only the Lord Jehovah holds such power, and you are not a true believer. Any fool can see that. You follow the path of the Morning Star, Lucifer! What sayeth you now, vile one? What demons can you conjure up on your behalf, sinner?"

"Leave the girl alone, bumpkin. Don't you have a sister you can fuck?"

The blow from the cane came with full force, striking Richard on the left side of his face. He felt his mouth fill with blood. He fought against swallowing a tooth that had been dislodged, and he shook his head to clear his thoughts. Once Richard regained his composure, he lifted his head and stared at the old man.

"I particularly liked the tale of you with the cannibals. You talk a good show, a real silver tongued heathen. We both know you are full of lies, viper. You ain't never been to no Africa. You ain't never been held by no tribe of niggers. You lie! But I wonder—"

Richard remained silent. He didn't like where this was going.

"They cut you in half, and you was whistling *Dixie*? That's what you said. What you gonna sing when we saw you in half, Devil? It better be a hymn. I'm partial to *Shall We Gather at the River*. Do you think you can sing that one for us, or do you need your legs to help you?"

The men holding his arms pulled at him. Richard struggled, but he could not break free. Another man grabbed his feet. He fought them off with everything he had, but he was unable to keep them from putting him in the box. They closed the lid, one of the men holding his feet in place, the other holding his neck. He was trapped.

"If your right eye makes you blind, tear it out and throw it from you!" the old man began his sermon. As if on cue, one of the men retrieved the saw and cut into the box.

"For it is better that you lose one part of your body than for your whole body to be thrown into hell."

The saw blade cut further into the box.

"Please, don't do this!" Richard pleaded.

"If your right foot makes you stumble, cut it off and throw it from you. For it is better for you to lose one part of your body, than for your whole body to go to hell."

The saw cut deeper still, the leading edge catching Richard's shirt.

"Please! I beg you! I have money! Lots of it! It's yours! Take it! Just stop!" the magician screamed.

"Better the little that the righteous have than the wealth of many wicked. We ain't here for your ill-gotten gains, trickster. But except ye repent, ye shall perish."

The blade slid down a little further, this time cutting into the magician's flesh.

"Aaaaaaggghhh! What, what do you want? Shall, shall we gather at the river, the beautiful, the beautiful river," Richard sang frantically. "Aaaauggh!"

"That's it, heathen. Sing them words like you mean 'em. It won't matter none, now. It's too late for that."

"Please! Stop! Please!" Richard cried.

"Stop?" asked the preacher. "Stop!" he held his hand up, and the big man halted the saw. "Do you consent for us to take the girl and set her on the path to righteousness? She's quite a looker, that one. I'd hate to see what sinful future she'd have if she stayed in this house of iniquity. Fornication no doubt awaits her. What she needs is a godly man to tend to her needs, a humble servant of the Lord, such as myself. Do you consent?"

Richard's face contorted as his mouth tried to force a reply. The preacher grew impatient.

"Spit it out, man!" he commanded.

Richard did as he was told, his tooth striking the old man square in the eye. The preacher howled and put his hand to his face.

"As you wish, foul demon. So it will be at the end of the age. The angels will come forth and take out the wicked from amongst the righteous."

The big man cut deeper with the saw. Richard screamed in agony until the preacher gagged his mouth with one of the colorful bandanas the magician frequently used in his act. This only slightly muffled the magician's cries, so the old man nodded to the others, who picked up where Richard had stopped singing.

"Gather by the saints at the river that flows by the throne of God."

"Humuna mahoo bibibi sharantui," the preacher mumbled incoherently.

By the time the saw made it all the way through the box, the magician had stopped moving; the singers had stopped singing; the preacher had stopped his maniacal chanting; and the congregation had fled the scene, leaving a bloody mess in their wake. The Amazing and Magnificent Villanova had performed his last disappearing act.

THE BONE PUZZLE

PART TWO:

HALLELUJAH

Those who can make you believe in absurdities can make you commit atrocities.

Voltaire

CHAPTER SEVENTEEN

The men drove south, passing through Mississippi before entering Alabama in the early evening. They'd agreed to meet up a few miles away from Cooter Yates' place outside of Vienna. The remoteness of the location all but guaranteed their privacy.

"What we gonna do 'bout that truck, Paw?" Jeremiah asked.

"Don't you worry 'bout that none, JT," Brother Eustice replied. "That's why we come all the way out here in the first place. It is the glory of God to conceal things. Where's the girl?"

Brother Eustice had ridden in the back of Joe Bob's sedan when they left Tennessee. His boys, Junior and Jeremiah Thomas or JT, took the magician's truck, and the others rode in Charles Ray's pickup.

They'd been careful not to attract attention. They knew that soon after they left the theater, someone would stumble upon the horrible scene. It wouldn't take long for them to discover that the girl was missing, along with the magician's truck. The vehicle was the only lead, and every law enforcement official in the region would be out looking for it.

"Junior's got her in the back. We didn't want anyone to see us."

"Get her out here. I want to have a look-see at what we got."

Earl Barber popped open the latch and let the back door retract upward. The truck was full of the magician's stage props, leaving only a small area in the back where the girl was gagged and tied. Junior Winchester hurriedly hopped down from the truck bed and headed for the nearest tree. "It's 'bout time. I gotta pee like a racehorse."

The elder Winchester paid him no heed, instead focusing his lustful attentions on the girl. After his initial inspection, he frowned.

"Why is her skirt hiked up like that?" he spat in disgust.

Junior returned, averted his eyes from his old man's fiery glare, and meekly mumbled his excuses. "We got jostled about somethin' awful during the trip, Paw. JT can't drive for shit. Not to mention, I had to keep all that satanic crap from fallin' over and crushin' us to death. You should be thankin' me for—"

Whack! Brother Winchester swung his cane, landing a fierce blow on his eldest son's shin. Junior yelped and hopped around. Jeremiah snorted in laughter at his brother's reprimand, then feigned a cough before the old man could turn his attention his way. He needn't have bothered. The old man's beady gaze never left the helpless girl tied up in the back of the truck.

"If I find out you tarnished her chastity in any way, you'll pay for it severely. Flee from youthful lusts and pursue righteousness. It's up to us to show this girl the light. She's seen enough of the ways of the unclean."

"I ain't done nothin'," Junior tried to explain. "Besides, she's just a child. She ain't old enough—"

"Old enough for what, you vile pervert? She ain't yours. We didn't go all the way to Memphis to find you someone to court. You got a wife, adulterer. Your younger brother got hisself a wife. Hell, all you men got someone. It would be sinful for any of you to even look upon her with foul intent. 'For whoever looks on a woman with lust has already committed adultery with her in his heart', sayeth the Lord. You fellers forget we doin' God's work here?"

The old man nodded to Buck to help him up into the truck. He made his way into the back and squatted down next to the girl.

"It's gonna be alright, my little angel," he assured the frightened child, brushing his fingers across her forehead and pushing her bangs out of her eyes. Laura looked at him and trembled with fear.

"Brother Eustice is gonna take good care of you. You'll be happy here, you'll see. Give it some time. I'm gonna make sure you'll never have to take part in those Devil shows again. No one's gonna hurt you. You'll learn to be a good woman— my woman."

Laura struggled violently against the ropes, trying in vain to escape her terrible fate. Brother Eustice ignored her, stood up, and addressed the men.

"Cooter, you and Earl take the boys down the road a bit. Make sure ain't no one followed us. Charles Ray, you and Joe Bob scamper 'round through them woods. We don't want no wayward hunters or fisherman happenin' upon us. Buck, stay close by in case anyone gets an idea 'bout disturbin' me. But not too close. This ain't no performance. I'm gonna baptize this young'un in the faith. Start teachin' her our ways."

Brother Eustice reached up and pulled on a strap. The overhead door fell closed behind him, leaving only a small crack along the bottom edge through which a sliver of light entered the cramped quarters. He looked at Laura and smiled, revealing the few yellow teeth that defiantly clung to his rotting gums.

"As an ordained minister of the Lord Jehovah, it is within my power to officiate our betrothal," the preacher said in a soothing tone. "Soon, I will baptize you in the waters of Jordan, and you will enter into the congregation of the spirit. The others will accept you, even though you're an outsider and have danced in the ways of Beelzebub. They'll accept you because you'll be a Winchester and the wife of the great prophet. Submit yourself to your husband as you do unto the Lord, for the husband is the head of the wife as Christ is the head of the church, his body, of which he is the Savior." He reached down and placed his hand on the girl's leg. "As the church submits to Christ, so also wives should submit to their husbands in everything," he continued, his hand slowly sliding up her thigh.

Without warning, Laura snapped her head forward, catching the unsuspecting preacher square in the forehead. Eustice lost his balance and fell backward with a thud, dazed by the blow. The girl fought with everything she had to break free. Her hands started to slip from the ropes that ensnared her wrists. Before she could get loose, Winchester had regained his composure and hopped up, kicking Laura in the face. He bent down and grabbed her hair, violently twisting her neck so she would face him.

"A wife of noble character is her husband's crown, but a disgraceful wife is like decay in his bones. Don't do that again, little angel. I can make this hurt." He slammed her head against the metal wall of the truck. Laura's head swam from the blow, but she clung to consciousness. She soon wished she hadn't.

CHAPTER EIGHTEEN

"**A**in't no one followed us out here," griped Junior. "The old man just wanted to get rid of us."

Cooter and Earl remained silent. Things had gotten dangerously out of control. Neither of them had known what the prophet's true intentions were when they set out on their mission. Now they were accomplices. All they had left was their faith. It would have to be enough.

"Do you think Daddy is gonna rape that girl?" asked Jeremiah.

"Shut your mouth, JT!" Earl interrupted. "You don't question the prophet, even if he is your paw."

"Earl's right," Cooter agreed. "He's never led us astray before. If it weren't for Brother Eustice, my soul would be damned to the fiery pit for all eternity. 'Sides, we've gone too far to back out now."

Earl nodded. It was definitely too late for second guessing. They had to stick together no matter what.

"It ain't right," Junior continued his rant. "He shouldn't talk to me like that. I'm his successor. You fellers would do right to remember that."

"She's just a girl," lamented Jeremiah. "He can't be thinking she's gonna be his."

"She's gonna be your new mama," Cooter joked. Earl laughed.

"Shut up, you two," said Junior. "Don't ever talk 'bout my maw again, or I'll whip the snot out of ya."

"Easy there, Junior," said Earl. "We wasn't talking 'bout your real maw, God rest her soul. We talkin' 'bout that gypsy girl. If'n the prophet marries her, she'll technically be your new step-ma."

"He ain't gonna marry her," said Jeremiah, his doubtful tone in contrast to his authoritarian pronouncement. "Is he, Eustice Adam?"

"Of course he's gonna marry her, you nitwit," interjected Cooter, "or he'd be committin' a sin. We all know the prophet can't commit mortal sins like we do. Nope, he'll make her his partner in the spirit, then she'll submit. It'll all be on the up and up."

"Cooter's right," agreed Earl. "Who are we to question him? He's the shepherd."

"She's closer to my age than his," said Junior. "I coulda had her if I wanted to. He's gotta have everything for hisself."

Cooter and Earl looked at each other and smirked. Junior was on one of his 'pitiful me' rants again. Experience had taught them that there was only one way to stop his whining.

"Maybe you should take it up with him yourself when we get back," offered Cooter.

"I'm sure Buck will be interested in what you have to say 'bout the matter," added Earl.

Buck McEwen was a giant. Deeply devoted to Brother Eustice Winchester, he was head Head Deacon of the Antioch Pentecostal Church and unofficial enforcer of security. The only thing bigger than his muscles was his ignorance. No one wanted to mess with Buck, not even Cooter and Earl. They'd seen what he'd done to the magician at the prophet's bidding.

"Ain't no need to talk about this to Buck," Junior replied. "I'm just lettin' off a little steam. It was a long trip in the back of that Devil truck, cramped up with all those sorcerer's tools. It was a might creepy, too. I swear I heard breathin' in there, like there was someone with us. Probably some demon or evil spirit."

"What we gonna do with all that stuff?" Jeremiah asked. "It'll incriminate us if anyone finds it."

"How they gonna find it out here, dummy?" asked Junior. "You think the magician is gonna drive down here looking for it?"

"I don't know," Jeremiah replied. "Maybe. What'd ya'll do with him, anyway?"

Cooter and Earl glanced at one another before looking away. Their lack of eye contact said it all.

"Well?" insisted Jeremiah.

"Let's just say he ain't gonna come lookin' for us and leave it at that," Earl said at last.

"We still can't just leave this stuff out here," said Jeremiah. "Someone will come across it sooner or later. It don't exactly fit in with the surroundings."

"He's right," said Cooter. "This is my land, and I don't want that stuff on it. I'll be the one goin' down. It ain't fair."

"Don't you fret about it, Cooter," Earl assured him. "I can help keep the authorities at bay for a spell. I'm sure Brother Eustice has a plan."

"He may have a plan, but it would be nice if, for once, he'd let us in on it," said Junior. "Did he tell any of y'all 'bout his plan to take that girl for hisself?"

"Give it a rest, Junior," said Cooter. "What's done is done. There ain't no fightin' City Hall."

"I thought ya'll said no one would come looking for us out here," Jeremiah said, nervously pointing in front of him. "Then what's that?"

The four men looked at the cloud of dust coming their way. A police car drove toward them down the remote dirt road.

CHAPTER NINETEEN

Charles Ray Wilson and Joe Bob Duncan did as they were instructed—at first. The two walked close to fifty yards into the woods before splitting up. Charles Ray went right; Joe Bob left. They hiked in a semi-circle until meeting up on the opposite side.

"Did you see anybody?" asked Charles Ray.

"Nope and ain't goin' to," replied Joe Bob. "You know that. Brother Prophet just wanted to get rid of us so he could defile that child."

"You shouldn't talk like that. You know it ain't like that."

"Isn't it? I didn't sign up for this shit, Charles Ray. Neither did you."

"Yeah, I reckon. Ain't much we can do about it now."

"It stinks to high heaven. Hell, I gotta girl at home older than her. This ain't right. Not to mention what Buck did to that magician back there."

Charles Ray nodded in agreement. He didn't want to think about that. He wished it had all been a bad dream and that he'd wake up. But it was no dream. It was a nightmare, and it was very real.

"What are we gonna do now?" asked Charles Ray. "We're in it up to our necks. If I'd a known that the preacher was after the girl—"

"You'd a done what? Same as we done. He's got us by the balls. We don't jump without word from the prophet. He says shit, we squat and strain. It's worse than bein' in the Marines."

Unlike his fellow parishioners, Joe Bob Duncan had served his country with honor. When the Japanese bombed Pearl Harbor, he'd been first in line at the county courthouse to enlist. As a Marine, he'd seen the worst of it at Guadalcanal. Only upon his return had he discovered that his fellow members of the flock had avoided serving altogether at the command of the prophet. Brother Winchester had proclaimed that the war was an earthly doing and not one worthy of spiritual beings.

Instead of honor and respect, Joe Bob had received scorn and ridicule for his service. In the end, he'd almost been forced to gather up his wife and children and relocate, but for the intervention of Brother Eustice. Once he'd stood up in front of the congregation, denounced his wicked participation in the war, and begged for forgiveness, Joe Bob had been allowed back into the fold.

Joe Bob never forgave himself for his cowardly actions. He'd faced the ferocious Japanese without hesitation, but relented to the iron will of the prophet. He'd disgraced himself in front of his wife and children, all in the name of social acceptance. As a reward, he'd been tricked into becoming an accomplice in a homicide and a child abduction and molestation. Where would it all end?

"It don't sit well with me," Charles Ray agreed. "It was bad enough before, with Buck always hangin' over the prophet's shoulder. But he owns us now. Poor ol' Cooter. He drove that girl and the magician's truck here. He'll be the one to take the fall if anythin' goes wrong."

"You don't think Brother Eustice will turn on us, do you?"

"Nothin' would surprise me now. My guess is that if any of us gets nabbed, we won't live long enough to implicate the others. The prophet's influence runs deep in these parts. Who knows how many of the flock are sittin' in high places? It seems like he's got somethin' on everyone 'round here, or they're mesmerized by his sermons."

"Just like us," noted Joe Bob.

"Yep, just like us," Charles Ray agreed.

CHAPTER TWENTY

Cautiously, Buck stood vigil near the truck—not too close, not too far. He followed the commands of the prophet without question. It was not for him to wrestle with uncertainty and moral dilemmas. Those things were for lesser men to quibble over; or greater men, such as Eustice Elijah Winchester, to set the record straight.

Bang! Buck heard something slam against the side of the truck. Whatever was going on inside, it wasn't any of his business. Unless the prophet called for his help, he'd remain right where he was.

The last few days had been exhausting. He'd been summoned by Brother Eustice to embark on their holy endeavor only hours before their departure. It was the way the prophet worked with him. The less he knew, the less chance of dissent. Not that Buck was ever going to dissent. He vowed to follow the prophet into the pits of hell, if need be. It was his only path to salvation.

Buck McEwen never forgot what Brother Winchester had done for him. He had been lost, on the road to eternal damnation, when the prophet found him. People despised him for the sins of his past. Atonement and forgiveness eluded him. That is, until Winchester stood up for him and offered him salvation. Now he had a family. He belonged. He mattered.

Buck was disgusted at the way some members of the congregation showed disloyalty to the prophet from time to time. Surely, they'd forgotten what the holy man had done for them. Occasionally, he'd be required to remind them, bring them back into the fold. It was his duty, and he performed it with zeal. It was important. Buck was convinced that, without it, the poor souls would stray so far off the path that they'd be doomed to the lake of fire. Not on his watch.

He glanced over at the truck. A rhythmic thudding could be heard, keeping time with the slight back and forth motion of the vehicle. Buck thought it was as if the vehicle itself were caught up in the spirit, like those whom the Lord saw fit to speak in tongues at the Sunday services. Buck had never felt the spirit grace him with the voice of the angels, and he hadn't spoken in tongues, or shook with the seizures that often accompanied those blessed events. He sometimes wished that he'd be granted such a sacred gift, but he understood that, if he bided his time and heeded the words and commands of the prophet, the blessing would come.

Buck felt bad about the way things had gone down. He knew that some of the others were grumbling right now about the unexpected turn of events. He would have plenty to do in the coming days. It was tough business doing the Lord's work. Not for the faint of heart, that's for sure.

He'd been delighted when the prophet chose him over the others to accompany him on the previous night to watch the performance of the sorcerer. He saw the disappointed way the others looked at him. Even the sons of the prophet were excluded from such a privilege. Junior had been particularly put out as always. Buck didn't care.

He knew why the prophet had chosen him. The others wouldn't have seen the show for what it was. They'd have been swayed by the extravagance of the performance and not repulsed by its wickedness as he'd been. When the time came to rid the Earth of the demon, he'd be the one to do what the others didn't have the faith to do.

Buck felt his stomach turn and took a pinch of tobacco out of the pouch in his pocket. He placed it between his cheek and gums and let the flavor fill his mouth. He fought against the image of the dead man's face and the blood that soaked the floor of the dressing room. He could still hear the man's screams, and he hummed to himself.

His baritone voice singing *Shall We Gather at the River* drifted out into the warm, evening air. By the second stanza, the revelation that it was that very hymn that had been sung while he cut into the dead man's torso made him swallow hard. A wad of tobacco caught in his throat and caused him to choke. Buck doubled over and spit the foul contents onto the soft mud, gasping for air.

Regaining his composure, Buck pushed the horrifying memory of his misdeed out of his mind. The last thing he needed was for the prophet to see him like this and question his resolve. The second to last thing he needed was for any of the others to see him. To them, he must remain a rock, as Peter was the rock for Jesus. It was his duty and his burden.

Buck glanced over at the truck. The movement had stopped. He thought he heard a strange wailing coming from inside, but he held fast. He could hear the prophet speaking in tongues. If and when the prophet needed him, he'd heed the call. Until then, he would resist temptation. One never knew when the Devil would tempt one's soul, and a person must remain ever vigilant to remain pure. Buck wasn't pure, but he would one day become pure again. It had been prophesized.

Woop! Wee ahh! An unexpected and unwelcome chirp made him jump. He turned toward the road, and through the fading light of the early evening, he saw the flashing blue and red lights of a police car. It was time to retrieve his bolt action Browning from the trunk of his sedan.

CHAPTER TWENTY-ONE

Unhappy about the situation the men found themselves in but unable to do anything about it, the foursome watched the approaching vehicle with trepidation. The last thing they needed was for the cops to spot the truck.

"Y'all let me do the talkin'," said Earl, "and act casual, for Christ's sake."

He looked in Jeremiah's direction to let his words sink in before turning back to the police car. He waved. The car stopped and the driver rolled down the window.

"Evening, Earl, Cooter," said the officer. The men nodded. The policeman eyed the other two men for a moment. "Ain't you the Winchester boys?"

"Yes, sir," Junior answered. Jeremiah kept his eyes averted and nodded.

The deputy in the passenger seat hit a button, and the siren chirped a couple of staccato wails as the flashing red and blue strobe lights lit up the area with an eerie glow.

Cooter jumped and nearly fell over. "Jesus, Clyde," said Cooter. "You scared me half to death."

The officers laughed.

"What y'all doing out here?" asked the officer in the driver's seat.

"We just robbed a bank," said Cooter. "Got the hostages tied up over yonder.

Either one of you know how to crack a safe?"

"Don't be an ass, Cooter!" the officer in the passenger seat yelled.

"We're on my property, Clyde," Cooter replied. "I need a reason to be on it?"

"You should tell your friend to be more polite," said the driver.

"You know how he gets, Ricky," said Earl. "What brings you boys out here?"

"Sheriff Fuller is looking for you."

"And how did you know I was out here?"

"We're detectives, Earl," said Clyde. "We figured it out."

"You're what?" asked Earl. "Detectives? Ya'll been promoted?"

"We called your home but no one answered, so the Sheriff sent us out to see if there was a problem and to fetch you." explained Ricky. "Peggy Lou said you took off with Cooter and Charles Ray a couple of days ago. We narrowed it down from there."

"What's the sheriff want with me now?"

"What's he always want? He needs you at the station pronto."

Earl sighed. Before he could answer, Joe Bob and Charles Ray wandered out of the woods on the opposite side of the police car.

"Is there a problem, officers?" asked Charles Ray.

"Evening, Charles Ray, Joe Bob," Clyde said. "There's rumors 'bout some nigger boy whistling at a white girl over by Reform. Sheriff thinks there might be trouble, so we're putting extra patrols on the streets."

Joe Bob whistled. "That has to be some crazy coon. There a meetin' 'bout it?"

"We ain't talkin' 'bout that here, Joe Bob. Not that it's any of your business," Clyde said. He looked over to where the Winchester boys were standing to make his point.

"We know you fellers from the Antioch church don't like to help in your civic duties," Ricky said. "But someone's gotta mind the store. You know the drill, Earl."

"Ya'll 'spectin' trouble?" Earl asked.

"Sheriff is adamant about stopping it. He thinks it'll bring the Troopers down, and we don't need no outsiders poking their heads in our business. Cyclops agrees and instructed the boys to go easy. But you know how quickly things can get out of hand."

Earl nodded.

Charles Ray spoke up, "Do we even know this happened? I find it hard to believe them colored boys in Reform don't know better."

"You know how them jungle bunnies are," said Clyde. "They see a white woman and can't control themselves."

"I have a hard time with that myself," joked Joe Bob.

The policemen laughed.

"Anyway, you'll be needed to cover the desk, Deputy," Ricky told Earl.

Earl relented. "I suppose so." He pretended to be disappointed, but he was inwardly relieved. So far, it appeared that nobody knew about the gang's involvement in the magician's homicide or the abduction of the girl. Working the night shift alone would give him access to the interstate reports. He'd quickly learn what the local authorities knew and what they didn't. "If it's alright with you, I'll need you to give me a lift. I'll have to swing by my house to pick up my uniform. It shouldn't take long."

"We'll drop you off."

"I'll need a ride to the station, too. Peggy Lou needs the car in the mornin' to go by her folks'. Her mama done got sick. I'll have to take one of the patrol cars when I get off tomorrow until she gets back."

Earl looked at Cooter and winked. Cooter nodded.

"Hop in the back. We gotta get going soon, or the Sheriff will be on our ass. If there's a lynching tonight, there'll be hell to pay tomorrow."

Deputy Earl Barber climbed into the back of the patrol car. They turned around and headed down the road. The remaining men stood and watched as they disappeared out of sight.

"Do you think they suspect anything?" asked Jeremiah.

"Nope," Cooter answered. "And let's keep it that way."

CHAPTER TWENTY-TWO

Buck watched the police car through the trees, his hunting rifle ready. Once he saw Earl get into the police car and the vehicle turn around, he relaxed and returned to his vigil by the truck. As he approached, he saw Brother Eustice standing near the rear, looking pale and sickly.

"Is everythin' alright, Brother?" asked Buck.

"Why you carryin' that gun?" Brother Eustice asked, eyeing the big man with caution.

"A couple of Fuller's deputies showed up."

"Did they now? Where are they?"

"They left. Took Earl with 'em."

Eustice nodded, leaned against the truck, and lit a cigarette. Buck waited uneasily, not sure what he was supposed to do next. He drifted closer to the truck and glanced inside. The girl lay motionless in a heap on the metal floor.

"The Devil took her," Brother Eustice explained. "Blessed are the dead who die in the Lord. I am widowed again, Brother Buck. Turn to me, oh Lord, and be gracious to me, for I am lonely and afflicted."

Buck wanted to comfort the old man, but he found himself unable to take his eyes off the dead girl. Her eyes stared unseeing into the abyss, her skin already fading to a ghostly white. The child's clothes lay in tatters around her; the ropes still bound her wrists. The only color left in her smooth skin was the bruising that bordered the ligature around her neck.

"Cursed Satan!" the old man shouted. "The thief comes only to steal and kill and destroy!"

Brother Eustice looked pensively at Buck. The way he was staring at the girl and clutching the rifle made the preacher uncomfortable. Behind him, the others approached.

"What's goin' on over there?" Charles Ray asked as they drew near.

"Brother Eustice—" Buck said before the preacher interrupted him.

"Your adversary, the Devil, prowls around like a roarin' lion, seekin' someone to devour. He has taken my lovely bride. It is the work of the magician. It was good that we rid the world of his wickedness. We must do the same with the tools of his trade."

"You killed her?" asked Junior in dismay. "You punished me for touchin' her and then you murdered—"

Whack! The old man's cane struck Junior on the side of the head and knocked him to the ground.

"How dare you question the prophet, boy! If Elijah Andrew were here, he'd smite you mightily. Your older brother looks down on you from his place in paradise with shame. I hope he shields your saintly mother's eyes from your lack of faith. It is as I say. The one who doubts is like a wave of the sea, blown and tossed by the wind."

The men stood by, visibly distraught by the sight of the murdered child. Yet no one spoke their misgivings. The prophet's hold was strong. Brother Eustice stared at his congregation, waiting for anyone to challenge his authority. None dared.

Joe Bob, Cooter, and Charles Ray looked away. Eustice could see they were conflicted inside. Junior staggered back up to his feet, clutching the side of his head. His face was flushed with anger. Tears fell down Jeremiah Thomas' cheeks. Buck continued to gawk at the dead girl, as if hypnotized by the repugnant image. His hands tightened around his hunting rifle. Eustice took control.

"We gotta rid Cooter's land of this evil," he stated. At the sound of his name, Cooter looked up. He couldn't have agreed more with the preacher.

"You got a saw somewhere 'round here?" Eustice asked. Cooter couldn't believe his ears. Things were going from bad to worse. The others looked appalled at the suggestion.

"The work of the demon is afoot. Mark my words. The beast will conspire against us if we ain't careful. Behold, I have given you authority to tread upon serpents and scorpions and over all the power of the enemy, and nothin' shall hurt you. There is but one path to salvation. Let me show you the way."

"Brother Eustice," Charles Ray said, "you can't mean—"

"If Satan has risen up against himself and is divided, he cannot stand. We must divide his vessel. The evil one seeks to deceive us. We will deceive him."

"I'm not—" said Junior.

"Enough! Buck," Brother Eustice said, addressing the big man. He saw immediately that Buck wasn't going to be pressed into chopping another body into pieces, so Eustice changed his plan. "Buck, go with Cooter. Bring back a saw and some shovels, and a tarp."

Buck nodded, and the two turned to leave.

"Come back quickly," Brother Eustice instructed. "We're losing light. When you come back, we ain't going to argue 'bout this none. Buck took his turn with the sorcerer. It's on the rest of us now. Remember them cops coming out here? There'll be others, sooner or later, if we don't do this right. We all gonna take a turn at her. Each one of us is gonna take a part. Each one of us is gonna get rid of it. There ain't gonna be no one inclined to speak 'bout it to the authorities without implicatin' himself. Is that clear?"

A few mumbles and grumbles could be heard, but nobody challenged the prophet.

"What we gonna do with 'em?" asked Joe Bob. "We can't bury 'em 'round here. It wouldn't be fair to Cooter."

"We ain't," replied Brother Eustice. "Don't you worry none. I know just the place."

CHAPTER TWENTY-THREE

Once Cooter and Buck returned with the hacksaw, Brother Eustice chose the order. Jeremiah went first. Brother Eustice knew his youngest son was weak. The longer he'd have to think about it, watching the others hack away at the corpse, the more cowardly he'd become. Eustice was firm in his command, but gentle enough so that the boy wouldn't break down and embarrass the family name in front of the others.

Jeremiah Thomas' job was to hack off the feet. The boy turned green and threw up when the blade hit the bone the first time, but eventually he finished the grisly task and gladly handed the saw to his brother.

"Not yet," said Brother Eustice. "Joe Bob, you're up. Take an arm."

Joe Bob looked disgusted, but did as he was told, hacking off the girl's left arm with little hesitation. He looked at the prophet, who nodded to Charles Ray.

"Take the other arm."

Charles Ray grabbed the right arm, pushed his boot against the girl's torso, and sawed the appendage off at the shoulder. He threw the saw on the ground and wandered away from the group to cry.

"I'll take a leg," said Junior, reaching for the saw.

Whack! The old man's cane struck him on his ass. He spun around, his fists balled up, and his face flushed with anger.

"It ain't your turn, pervert," his father announced. "Cooter, you're up. And show some respect."

Cooter wanted to punch the old man, but he restrained himself. Buck was still keeping watch, clutching his rifle with a white-knuckled grip. Cooter just wanted to get it over with. He regretted allowing them to use his property for their heinous deeds, and he felt vulnerable. He pushed what was left of the child's skirt over her privates and bent down. Once he cut through both of the femurs, he looked at the preacher with disgust. The old man nodded; his cue to hand the blade to Junior.

"Remove the head," instructed the old man.

"What're you gonna saw off?" Junior asked, careful to keep out of range of the old man's walking stick.

"Just do as I say, boy."

"You said we were all gonna take a turn."

"What'd I say? Take the head, dummy."

"He don't need to do nothin' to share in the guilt. He's the one that dragged us into this," said Joe Bob.

Brother Eustice nodded to Buck, but the big man ignored him. Eustice glared at Joe Bob. "Why do you look at the speck of sawdust in your brother's eye and pay no attention to the plank in your own eye? You were well acquainted with murder long before this. Weren't you?"

"I've repented the sins of my past. It's you that brought this upon us," replied Joe Bob.

"I'll not argue with a heathen and a killer like you. How many Japs did you kill, Marine?"

Joe Bob held his tongue. The old man was right. They were all guilty.

Junior placed his handkerchief over the girl's face and sawed through the cervical spine. He picked up the head, dropped the saw, and walked away.

"It'll be dark soon," said Brother Eustice. "We'd better get going. Each of you take a piece of that tarp over there and wrap up your portion. Buck, you take the torso. We'll load 'em up and dump 'em while we can still see where we're goin'."

"Where are we goin'?" asked Cooter. He didn't care where they were headed as long as it was off his property.

"Dead River Swamp."

CHAPTER TWENTY-FOUR

Inside the small confines of the magic box, Lacey watched through the tiny air holes, terrified of the prospect of being found. She was already in the back of the truck, searching for her father's fake ruby amulet, when the men came. Quickly, she'd hidden herself and waited.

When the truck had unexpectedly started to move, Lacey almost jumped out of her hiding place. She saw her sister tied up next to the ugly man in the rear of the storage space. Lacey did her best to keep her breathing quiet, not wanting to be found by the foul-smelling deviant next to Laura. She watched the man make his way over to where Laura lay motionless. Although she couldn't see in the dark, she knew what he was doing to her sister. Lacey sobbed silently into her hands. *Where was her father?*

The truck rambled on for hours before stopping. Before long, the compartment filled with light as the back door ascended to reveal a gang of hillbillies. Lacey wanted to scream, but she had no choice but to remain quietly in hiding. She could do nothing to help her sister, even when the old man with the beard climbed in and shut the door behind him.

Lacey watched with horror as the old man beat and raped her sister. When it was over, he choked her until she no longer moved.

"Aaagh!" Lacey sobbed before she could stop herself. The old man froze. He'd heard her cries.

She held her breath and tried to remain as motionless as possible. The bearded man turned his head and stared right at the box in which she was hiding. Lacey was certain that he could see her, but she was unable to move.

"Oooooohhh!" A strange, high pitched wail came from the old man. He howled eerily and mumbled incoherently as if speaking an unknown language. Rocking back and forth on his haunches, he looked as if he'd come across the dead girl by accident instead of murdering her with his own hands. After calming down, he opened the door of the truck and climbed out. Lacey waited in silence.

When the others returned, they saw what the old man had done, but no one did anything about it, not even the big man holding the gun. Lacey knew she'd get no help from those men, so she stayed where she was.

The men took her sister's body out of the truck and walked away. Awful, sickening sounds drifted in to where Lacey sat in the box. She waited. After a while, the light dimmed, and she heard car motors start and drive away. She waited a bit and listened. All was silent.

Slowly, she climbed out of the box and stretched her aching muscles. She'd been contorted in the box for hours. She could barely move, but she had no choice now. To stay there was to die. Lacey quietly slipped out of the truck and looked around. She was alone.

She crept around the area, keeping a sharp eye out in case any of the men had stayed around to keep watch. *Scrunch. Scrunch.* Her footsteps echoed through the dead leaves as she tiptoed through the woody area. *Slurp. Slurp.* She looked at the wetness at her feet, expecting to find mud.

"Aaaaauuugghh!" she gasped and felt her stomach churn. She was standing in a huge pool of blood in the dirt. Now she understood what those terrible sounds she'd heard meant. Horrified, she ran into the surrounding wilderness, her hand still clutching the plastic ruby from her father's turban.

CHAPTER TWENTY-FIVE

Darkness had descended by the time the group returned to the clearing on Cooter's land. With the exception of Earl, who was pulling duty at the sheriff's office, none of the men were allowed to return to their homes at the command of the prophet. Brother Eustice was adamant that they dispose of the truck and its foul contents at first light and solidify their alibis. He wasn't about to risk anyone babbling to their spouse about the horrific events and incriminating them all.

Cooter and Charles Ray built a fire, and the rest gathered around. The crickets chirped in the distance. The fire crackled. The men sat morosely, lost in thought. Brother Eustice eyed them all, one at a time, sizing up their commitment and looking for the weak links. At last, he offered a prayer to put the day to rest.

"As it says in Isaiah, 'You are wearied with your many councils; let them stand forth and save you, those who divide the heavens, who gaze at the stars, who at the new moons make known what shall come upon you.' This is the word of the Lord."

"Amen," the men replied.

"It has been a tryin' day, my brothers," Brother Eustice continued, "and it has come to its end. Our faith has been tested as never before, and your prophet is pleased. The Lord came to me, speakin' to me as is His desire. He, too, is pleased. I am humbled before the Lord and humbled by your devotion."

Brother Eustice smiled as his eyes wandered around the circle of men. No one looked back, so he laid it on thicker and heavier as he went on.

"Proverbs instructs us, 'In all your ways, acknowledge Him, and He will make straight your paths.' We must acknowledge the Lord in our works, my brothers. I tell you, it is His will, we are only the vessels that carry it out. Remember, 'All the paths of the Lord are steadfast love and faithfulness, for those who keep his covenant and his testimonies.' Do you hear and understand, oh brothers?"

"Amen," the reply came without enthusiasm.

"Keep his covenant and his testimonies," repeated Brother Eustice. "There are many who would question our actions and our resolve to keep on the path of righteousness. This has been true for the faithful from the beginnin'. Peter once said, 'Dear friends, do not be surprised at the fiery ordeal that has come on you to test you, as though somethin' strange were happenin' to you.' It's as though he was speakin' directly to us, because he is. 'He will not let you be tempted beyond what you can bear. But when you are tempted, He will also provide a way out so that you can endure it.'"

Brother Eustice paused and lowered his voice. He talked to the others, not as their preacher, but as one of them. "I must confess, I am but a frail man, many times not worthy of my burden. But the Lord commands me, and I must obey. It is only by the strength of you, my brethren, my friends, that I find the energy to go on. Forgive me my trespasses, and don't think poorly of me. I can bear many things and will stand up for the Lord as long as I have a breath in my tired body, but losin' the respect and friendship of the likes of you men I could not endure. You've shown me what faith truly means and exposed my weaknesses. I thank you as much as I ask for your forgiveness."

Silence greeted him. None dared look him in the eye. Not to be dissuaded, Brother Eustice stood up, stared into the heavens, raised his arms, and spoke with authority.

"Dear Lord, look down upon your unworthy servants and bless us with courage in the comin' days. The Devil will come upon each and every one of us, seekin' revenge for castin' out his demon and the demon's spawn. We will remain steadfast in our resolve—to a man."

"Amen," mumbled Buck.

"We will withstand the onslaught of the evil one and not be trapped by his devious schemes."

"Amen," said Buck and Cooter.

"We will return evil with righteousness, resist temptation with resolve, and answer cleverness and trickery with silence."

"Amen," the group replied.

"Your word has given us the way, oh Lord. 'Even fools are thought wise if they keep silent, and discernin' if they hold their tongues.' There's 'a time to be silent and a time to speak.' This is the time to be silent."

"Amen!" The chorus grew louder.

Brother Eustice smiled and sat down. He bowed his head, and the others followed suit.

"We end this day givin' thanks to you, oh Lord. Tomorrow, we rid the world of the tools of the sorcerer. What we hide will remain hidden, for we know that you will protect your holy servants. It will be as you have whispered to your humble prophet, so that his chosen disciples will find comfort in their shepherd. Praise be!"

"Praise be!" echoed the men.

"Let us get some rest," concluded Brother Eustice. "When the morrow comes, we'll put the matter behind us and never speak of it again. Let Satan search all he wants, the swamp will hold our secrets."

CHAPTER TWENTY-SIX

Lacey ran through the forest in a panic. It was past midnight before she stopped next to a small creek and rested, trying to catch her breath. Her eyes wide with fright, she looked around the thick woods, paranoid that the men were following her.

The girl was lost. She didn't know where she was or where she was going. Her surroundings all looked the same to her. For all she knew, she'd been running in a circle. But that didn't stop her from moving on. Lacey saw what had happened to her sister, and she could only imagine what might have been her father's fate. She was terrified of being caught, so she pushed on through the night.

By the time dawn came, the girl was covered from head to toe in mud, dirt, and dried blood. She'd sustained multiple scratches on her arms and her legs from the thick underbrush as well as a few bruises from the dozens of times she'd stumbled over unseen branches and downed trees. She didn't dwell on her condition. She only wanted to get away from the monsters pursuing her.

In the rising morning light, Lacey spotted a gravel road and followed it, wary of any other travelers that she might come upon. It was still early, and none could be seen or heard. All the same, she proceeded with caution. Just in case.

An hour after dawn, she heard the tell-tale sound of tires on the gravel road. Lacey ran into the nearby woods and lay on the ground behind a mulberry bush to keep out of sight until the vehicle passed by. Minutes later, a white dented-up pickup truck pulling a small boat on a trailer drifted by. Lacey stayed well hidden for a good five minutes until she was certain that the truck was long gone, and then she continued on her journey.

She desperately needed to get away from the men who had murdered her sister. She wasn't sure that she'd be able to recognize the men, so she was scared to approach anyone who might be connected to the others. Her plan was to remain hidden and keep moving until she came upon a town or someone whom she felt could be trusted, someone who could save her.

It seemed like hours before she heard another vehicle approaching. Once again, Lacey ran and hid in the safety of the trees and watched pensively. Moments later, another vehicle drove by.

When she spotted the six pointed gold star on the car, Lacey ran into the road, waving her arms in a desperate attempt to catch the attention of the vehicle that had just passed.

"Help!" the girl cried, her voice breaking. "Help!"

Much to her dismay, the car kept going, its occupant seemingly oblivious to the distraught child in the middle of the road.

"Please, help me!" she cried as she stumbled and fell onto the hard dirt.

The unmistakable sound of screeching brakes broke through the quiet Alabama air. Lacey looked up. When she saw the brake lights come on and the roof of the car suddenly illuminated with flashing, twirling blue and red lights, she knew that she'd been spotted. At last, her ordeal was over. She'd been saved.

When the door of the sedan swung open, she knew that, from then on, everything was going to be alright. No longer able to hold her emotions in check, she laughed and cried all at the same time and waited for her savior to end her nightmare.

The deputy had been driving through the quiet area, lost in reflection, when he thought he heard someone scream. He slowed down and glanced at his radio, thinking that a sudden call from dispatch was forthcoming, but all was silent. Shaking the cobwebs from his brain, he drove on, wondering if he'd nodded off in his exhausted state. The last thing he needed was to drift off the road and into a ditch. He'd never be able to explain that to his superiors without being mocked about it for years to come.

The officer slapped his cheek and shifted in his seat, determined to rouse himself. He glanced up into the rearview mirror and slammed on the brakes. *What the hell?*

The deputy threw the gearshift into park, flipped on the flashing lights, and stepped out of his police cruiser. He looked over at the pitiful child lying in the middle of the road. His ruddy complexion paled as if he'd seen a ghost.

CHAPTER TWENTY-SEVEN

Lacey lay curled up on the back seat of the police cruiser, the deputy's jacket covering her torn dress and bruised and battered body. The car lumbered on down the dirt road, lulling her to sleep. The serenity of the rural area was a stark contrast to the terror that had constituted her last twenty-four hours. The horror was now over. Lacey could finally rest.

Charles Ray's head popped up at the unexpected sound. He sat under a shade tree, trying to stay out of the bright, morning sun. The relative comfort of his position made it difficult to stay awake, and he knew that he must've dozed off. It was his turn to watch the road. If Brother Eustice got wind of his failure, Charles Ray knew the prophet would send Buck to have a private word with him. He shuddered at the thought and stood up to confront the approaching vehicle, his hunting rifle ready.

Minutes later, a dust cloud appeared through the trees to reveal a black and white police car coming down the lane. Charles Ray took his position in the center of the road and waited.

"Who's that comin'?" Charles Ray heard a familiar voice behind him.

"Not sure," answered Charles Ray, "but I'm hopin' it's Earl."

Cooter stood at his friend's side as they watched and waited. Before long, the car pulled up. Deputy Earl Barber nodded, and the two men stood aside to let the vehicle pass. Someone was in the back seat. Charles Ray and Cooter eyed each other with suspicion and followed the car to the clearing.

Earl drove the car into the center. He exited the vehicle, taking care to close the door behind him, and walked over to where the others waited. The deputy felt sick, but he pushed his ill feelings inside and addressed the group in a calculated, measured tone.

"I came out here as soon as I was able to get away," he said. He spat a glob of tobacco-laced saliva on the ground. "It's a good thing, too. You boy's missin' somethin'?"

The others looked at each other with confusion. Earl had left before their unfortunate situation with the girl. Nobody wanted to be the first to tell him of the previous night's activities.

"The only thing we was missin' was you," Brother Eustice replied. "You put on that uniform and badge, and you think you're somebody all of a sudden. Don't be comin' 'round here and pretendin' you wasn't a part of our mission."

Earl paused. He wasn't expecting to be on the receiving end of hostility for doing his duty. The deputy nodded, spit again, and said, "I beg to differ, oh holy one." The sarcasm cut into the morning air like a knife. Buck instinctively pushed out his chest and tightened his grip on his firearm. Earl rested his hand on the revolver in his holster without batting an eye. "I say you're missin' something. You want to argue with me 'bout it?"

"Boys," interjected Joe Bob, "let's not lose our heads. Ain't none of us got any sleep, and we're all a bit testy. Earl, stop playin' Gary Cooper and get to the point. We ain't in the mood for your bullshit right now."

A whistle echoed from the direction of the police car. The group turned and looked. Cooter and Charles Ray were backing away from whatever they'd seen hiding in the back seat, both looking as if they would faint at any moment.

"My bullshit?" Earl asked. "It ain't my bullshit that need concern you boys. It's the bullshit that I seen on my way over here that you should be worried about."

Earl walked to the car and opened the door. The girl was asleep on the seat. He gently picked her up and carried her out. She began to wake as he placed her on her feet. He pulled his jacket from around her shoulders, took a step back, and motioned toward his find.

"It can't be!" shouted Jeremiah.

The men gasped in horror as they stared at the very girl that they'd dismembered and tossed into the swamp the night before. Buck fell to his knees and prayed, finally speaking in the tongues he so desperately sought after. Joe Bob ran to the edge of the trees and hurled the few contents that remained in his stomach. Jeremiah cried. Charles Ray and Cooter backed away, their faces pale as they looked at the ghostly apparition in disbelief. Eustice Junior showed no emotion at all, his mind unable to grasp what he saw.

Brother Winchester shouted to the heavens, "My God, my God, why have you forsaken me? The serpent who deceives the whole world was thrown down to the earth, and his angels were thrown down with him!" The prophet threw himself on the ground and punched the dirt with his fists.

Earl watched the display before him in a state of bewilderment. When he'd spotted the girl trying to escape, he figured she had snuck out in the dark while the others were asleep, and she'd ended up on the road in the morning. He retrieved her without difficulty, being that she had no clue who he was and where he was taking her, and he brought her back into the fold. Earl had been lucky. He used that now to display his usefulness to the group, and he added a measure of swagger to remind everyone that he was an officer of the law. He figured he'd get a round of back slapping and a show of appreciation on his return. Instead, it was as if he'd brought on the rapture.

All of a sudden, he noticed that the girl was gone.

"Shit!" he screamed. "Where she'd go?"

The men turned and looked at the spot where the girl had stood moments before. It was empty.

CHAPTER TWENTY-EIGHT

Lacey had drifted off to sleep in the back of the police car, secure in the knowledge that her nightmare was over. Exhausted from the previous night's events, she'd closed her eyes for what seemed to be only a moment before feeling the deputy's arms gently pull her from the car and stand her up. She felt the stagnant heat of the morning sun on her exposed arms when the deputy removed his heavy jacket, and she fought against her lethargy to gain her balance and open her swollen eyes. She heard voices around her. Squinting from the bright sunlight, she stretched and attempted to push the cobwebs from her sleepy mind. As her blurry vision slowly cleared, she froze in horror.

Lacey found herself right back in her nightmare. She panicked and ran into the woods. Through the underbrush and around the pine trees, she flew with the grace of a deer, disappearing without a sound under the green canopy.

Unlike the girl, the men ran with all the subtly of a herd of spooked bison. She could hear them behind her, gaining ground. To the girl, it sounded like a gang of giants were on her heels, tearing through the forest in a vengeful wrath.

Lacey sprinted over fallen trees and hurdled over a small creek, determined to escape; but no matter how fast she ran, the others still came. She was out of breath, and she knew she'd never outrun the beasts, so she found a hiding spot at the bottom of a burned out tree and slipped into the shadows. Lacey desperately tried to slow her breathing, frightened that any noise would give her away. Minutes later, she heard the men approach.

"Where'd she go?" asked one.

"I don't know, but she couldn't have gotten far," another replied.

"She's 'round here somewhere."

The disembodied voices surrounded her, each sounding more menacing than the next. Lacey tried to hold her breath as tears ran silently down her flushed cheeks.

"We gotta get her 'fore she escapes."

"No shit, dumbass!"

"How the hell did y'all let her get loose in the first place? She was tied up in the back of the truck when I left."

"Shut the fuck up, Earl. You don't know shit."

"You shut the fuck up, Junior. I don't care who your paw is, I'll whip your hide if you talk to me like that, you little piece of shit."

"I'd like to see you try."

"Shut up, you two! Shut the fuck up!"

"Calm down, JT. Everythin's going to be alright. Soon as the prophet catches up, he'll know what to do."

"Yeah, like he did last time."

"Don't be sassing the word of the prophet, Charles Ray. Do you want Buck to set you straight? Ain't that right, Buck? Buck?"

"Even he ain't having this shit, Cooter. I mean, what the fuck?"

"It's the Devil's work, I tell you. More reason we listen to the prophet."

"It was him that brought this down on us."

"Maybe so, but he's the only one who can deliver us now."

"What the hell are y'all going on about?"

"The girl, Deputy. We're talking about the girl."

"What about her?"

"Winchester killed her yesterday, Earl."

"What? What do you mean?"

"He raped and strangled her in the back of the truck."

"Don't you be castin' your aspersions on the prophet like that."

"It was the Devil that did her in. My daddy didn't rape no one. She was his bride."

"Don't be an imbecile, Junior."

"Buck, are you gonna let him talk about the prophet like that? You were there. Tell them."

Silence greeted the request. Lacey choked back her tears and balled up in the shadows. Her heart beat so loudly that she was certain the men would hear it. She trembled in terror, praying that they'd leave.

"Buck? You were there. Tell them."

"I ain't had nothin' to do with it."

"Ain't had nothin' to do with what?" Lacey recognized the old man's voice and whimpered.

"Nothin', Brother Eustice. We was just talkin'."

"Talkin'? Why were y'all just talkin' and not chasin' after the gypsy girl?"

"We lost her."

"Then find her. She'll be the undoin' of us all if you let her get away. She is the Devil's plaything. He will not escape from darkness; the flame will wither his shoots."

"We don't know where she is."

"What's this I hear about you rapin' and killin' her?"

"The hell you say, Brother Earl. A false witness will not go unpunished, and he who breathes out lies will perish."

"How did she come back, Brother Eustice? We cut her up. I threw her arm in the swamp myself."

"Stand firm in the faith, be courageous; be strong. This is one of Satan's tricks. We must continue to fight. We shall prevail."

"You cut her up?"

"Shut up, Earl. You weren't there."

"Yeah, Earl, you weren't here. Don't be castin' your judgment on us. We did as the prophet commanded."

"For Christ's sake, Cooter; listen to yourself."

"How dare you use the Lord's name in vain, heathen!"

"Y'all are nuts. I picked the girl up on the road this morning. She ain't dead. I don't know what you think you saw—"

"Fuck you, Deputy. I cut her head off myself!"

Lacey couldn't keep from recoiling in horror, her foot slipping in the moist dirt. A loose pebble rolled down the embankment, making a slight sound.

"Shhhh! Did y'all hear that?"

"Hear what?"

"I didn't hear shit."

"Shut the fuck up, Junior."

"You shut up, JT."

"Both of y'all shut up!"

Whack!

"Ouch! What did you do that for?"

"Ha ha."

"Shut up, JT!"

Whack!

"Owww! Cut that out!"

"Shut the fuck up! I hear somethin'."

Silence. The only sound Lacey could hear was the beating of her heart and the breathing she tried so desperately to quiet.

"Well, well, look at what we have here."

CHAPTER TWENTY-NINE

The group of angry men stood in a circle around her, discussing her fate as if she were an inanimate object. Lacey lay on the hard dirt, a rag stuffed into her mouth, her arms and legs bound with rope. Tears ran down her pale cheeks, her cries muffled by the gag.

"How can this be, Brother Eustice?" asked Charles Ray.

"It's the trick of the Devil," replied the prophet. "The serpent is craftier than any of the wild animals the Lord God has made. We must not give him a foothold."

"What can we do? Beelzebub will come for us!" cried Jeremiah.

"Submit yourselves to God. Resist the Devil, and he will flee from you. JT, my son, we will defeat the dark one. Of this, I swear."

"What are we gonna do with her?" asked Cooter, nodding to the girl.

"Same as we done with her before."

"What do you mean we?" asked Junior.

Whack! Brother Eustice's cane struck Junior in the shin. Jeremiah laughed despite himself.

"He makes a valid point," said Joe Bob.

"I ain't cuttin' no one up again!" exclaimed Charles Ray.

"Neither am I," Cooter agreed.

"I say whoever missed their turn last time does it this time," Joe Bob offered.

"This ain't up to a vote," said Brother Eustice. "Jesus himself spoke: 'You are my friends if you do what I command.'"

"You ain't Jesus," said Joe Bob.

"Buck," replied Brother Eustice, letting the unfinished threat hang in the air.

Buck paid no heed. Instead, he watched the helpless girl in silence.

"Speaking of Buck, he gets a turn this time, too," stated Junior.

Buck woke from his daydream and glared at the son of the prophet. "I did my part back in Memphis." He held a wave of nausea that rose in his gut and turned his eyes towards the girl. Nobody dared to argue with him about it further.

"Yes, you did," said Brother Eustice. "We all done our part. All except Earl, that is."

"Me? I'm the one that found her and brought her back here," Earl reminded them. "If it weren't for me, we'd be in a world of shit trying to explain this to Sheriff Fuller."

"No, we wouldn't," explained Brother Eustice. "If it weren't for you, she'd still be buried in the swamp. She come back because of what we missed. For once, Junior is right. Until we all do our part, she'll keep coming back. Buck, my dearest friend, I'm sorry, but it's the only way. We all gotta take our turn. This means you, too, Earl."

"And you, Brother Eustice," said Joe Bob.

"I did my part."

Cries of protest erupted from the group before the prophet quieted them down. "But I'll get my hands dirty if it sets y'all's minds at ease."

The group fell silent and looked at the girl. "'Course, we can't do this while she's looking at us like that," Brother Eustice noted.

Lacey squirmed in vain against the tight ropes. It was hopeless. Her fate was sealed.

"You had your turn with that," Junior offered. "Maybe I can take her as my bride before we—"

Whack! Another round of howls from Junior and laughs from Jeremiah ensued. No one else found it funny.

"We ain't doing that," said Buck, tightening his grip on his rifle. He sighed, held his breath, and pointed the muzzle before clenching his eyes shut and pulling the trigger. A lone shot rang out in the quiet Alabama morning. A flock of doves escaped from their nests nearby, leaving the scene as if they were next on the menu.

Lacey's body lay still, blood dripping slowly from the hole in the center of her forehead, her unseeing eyes staring into infinity. Tears ran down Buck's face as he turned and walked away without another word.

Brother Eustice hobbled out of sight, then returned with the bloodied hacksaw. He offered it to Earl. "You're up, lawman."

Joe Bob intercepted the exchange and pushed the prophet's hand away. "No. It's you who goes first."

Brother Eustice stared at the man with fire in his eyes, though it did little good. He saw the others gather behind the challenger. He knew better than to push it, so he let it go. Despite their current insubordination, he knew had them all right where he wanted them. They were in too deep to back out now.

"Take care, brothers, lest there be in any of you an evil, unbelievin' heart, leadin' you to fall away from the livin' God," Brother Eustice sermonized as he waved the saw around. "You seek to pull me down, to humble me, your great prophet, to your level of debasement. You lead me into temptation and rejoice at my failures."

Brother Eustice looked at the girl. His knees buckled. He steadied himself and tried again. This time, the hand that held the saw shook as if he were having a seizure. He dropped the foul instrument and threw himself to the ground. "She is my bride! I cannot do this vile deed. You serpents, you brood of vipers, how are you to escape bein' sentenced to hell?"

Brother Eustice wailed and spoke in tongues. A strange, high-pitched wail emanated from his throat, and he gasped for air. The others looked at him with a mixture of pity and disgust.

Charles Ray spat on the ground and shook his head. Cooter reached down and picked up the saw, handing it to the deputy. "I guess you're up, Earl."

Earl wanted to puke, but he held himself in check. He reluctantly grabbed the saw from Cooter, knelt beside the girl's corpse, and hacked her left leg off at the knee.

"Save a leg for me," said Junior.

Jeremiah ran deeper into the underbrush to throw up. Cooter, Charles Ray, and Joe Bob waited their turn in silence. Buck stood at a distance, refusing to even look at the others. Junior eyed the dead girl as if she were a rack of ribs at a Sunday picnic. Brother Eustice wept his alligator tears, all the while sneaking glances at the dismemberment of the gypsy girl.

When they were done, they returned to the swamp and disposed of the girl's parts as they had before—hopefully for the last time. They made it back to Cooter's camp by late afternoon and dismantled the magician's truck. The men stacked the stage props and whatever else they could remove from the vehicle in a pile and lit it on fire. In the early morning, before dawn, they'd take what was left to an auto salvage yard owned by one of the faithful, where they'd have the truck and its scorched contents crushed into a cube.

In the meantime, they sat silently around the campfire and examined what was left of their souls. Brother Eustice offered no sermons. Whatever salvation had been promised them had been squandered. There could be no redemption for their sins. They had fought the Devil, and the Devil had won.

CHAPTER THIRTY

The next morning, the men prepared to separate and return to their families. No one spoke. All they wanted was to go home and forget about the horrendous deeds they had performed. Brother Eustice knew he couldn't allow the men to leave without a stern warning.

"A prudent person keeps silent in such a time, for it is an evil time," he said. "I know many of you have doubts, as your faith has been tested. Much of that is because of me. I have failed you as a pastor and as a holy man. I am unworthy, but unable to escape. What y'all don't know is that I didn't choose any of this. I didn't want to be a prophet or a preacher. I just wanted to live my life quietly and look after my own. It was the Lord that commanded otherwise. Who was I to question the will of God?"

Brother Eustice stood up. He looked at the others, one by one, as a parent would look at a child. "I know now that you know how I felt. You know the doubt. You know the struggle. Yet it is in these times that one's faith must not falter. For all have sinned and fallen short of the glory of God, even you—even me. But we should not fear if we hold fast to our faith and remain strong. As the Lord said in Revelations, 'Do not fear what you are about to suffer. Behold, the Devil is about to throw some of you into prison, that you may be tested, and, for ten days, you will have tribulation. Be faithful unto death, and I will give you the crown of life.' I say, we need not fear even that. If we stick together, if we all tell the same account, we will remain free from this testin' and tribulation. Brother Earl, tell us what you tell people when you arrest them."

"What do you mean?"

"Suppose you arrest someone. You ask them questions. What if they don't want to answer those questions? What if they ask for a lawyer? What do you do?"

"We don't do nothin'. We give them a lawyer. It's the law," answered Earl.

"You can't make them talk?"

"No. How can we? I mean, we try sometimes, but if they don't—"

"You can't make them," Brother Eustice finished the deputy's sentence. "What if they do talk?"

"We use it in court."

"You use it to set them free?"

"We use it to convict them," Earl corrected him.

"Exactly. You use it against them. What does their lawyer tell them to do when he shows up?"

"He tells them to shut up."

"But what if they start asking us questions?" asked Cooter. "Won't all of us refusin' to talk make us look suspicious?"

"Yes, it will," Earl conceded. "It'll make us all look like we're hidin' something."

"So we talk, but tell the same story," Brother Eustice explained. "What'll happen then, Earl?"

"Sheriff Fuller and the boys won't take it any further, I'll see to that."

"But what if it ain't Dale we're talking to?" asked Joe Bob. "We killed that magician in Tennessee and took the girl. That's kidnappin' across state lines. What if the state police or the FBI come around hasslin' us? They're a might more clever than the sheriff."

"That they are, Joe Bob. That they are," replied Brother Eustice. "But we've got the Lord on our side, and let's not forget it. We'll be just fine if that time ever comes. As long as we stick to our story."

"What story?" asked Jeremiah.

"The one we're all going to tell. We've been on a religious retreat, brothers, to bring our spirits closer to God. We don't know nothin' about nothin' past that. Y'all got that straight?"

Everyone present nodded.

"Besides, I wouldn't fret it none. The magician died miles and miles away. Nobody saw us comin' or goin' from there. The truck's gone. There's nothin' left of that hunk of junk. Ain't no one gonna find that girl where we put her. The swamp will hold our secrets."

"You said that before," Joe Bob reminded him.

"Just stick to the story, Marine. Stick to the story."

THE BONE PUZZLE

PART THREE:

THE HOLY RELIC

Foot bone connected to the heel bone,
Heel bone connected to the ankle bone,
Ankle bone connected to the shin bone...
Dem bones, dem bones gonna rise again.

James Weldon Johnson

CHAPTER THIRTY-ONE

Months passed without any inquiries about the dead magician or the missing girl. Earl kept a close eye on the interstate reports, but no one suspected the involvement of anyone in Alabama. It was a Tennessee problem, and it looked to remain so. Eventually, tensions eased up among the church group, though Brother Eustice never quite regained the respect from the men that he'd lost.

The story they'd rehearsed eliminated any suspicions by their spouses or the local authorities. By all accounts, they'd gone on a spiritual retreat into the woods where they fished, hunted, and camped out while drawing closer to God. It sounded stupid to Joe Bob and Charles Ray, but much to their amazement, everyone bought it without further inquiry.

When the call came in, Earl almost panicked. Sheriff Fuller drove out to the location with Deputy Halpin and Deputy Smith. Earl wanted to go but wasn't invited. He'd been ordered to attend to a domestic disturbance call near Aliceville. It turned out to be just another redneck who'd had too much to drink and took umbrage with his wife's nagging. The woman looked like she had the beginnings of a black eye, but she denied any abuse, so Earl let it be. By the time the officers arrived at the station, it was all Earl could do to act calm.

"How goes it?" he casually asked as the sheriff and deputies strolled in.

"It's a gruesome mess," replied Clyde.

"What did y'all find?"

"A shoe with a foot in it," said Ricky.

"What?"

"You heard me right—a shoe with a foot in it. It was mostly bones by the time we found it. Must've been out there awhile."

"Who found it?" inquired Earl.

"Lucius Jones," Sheriff Fuller replied. "He was out fishing with his great-grandson when he snagged it with his cane pole."

"Do you think he had anything to do with it?"

"Old man Lucius? Hell, no. The geezer is practically a saint. Besides, he's a might old to be carrying on with such evil deeds."

"Whose foot do you think it is?" Earl couldn't let it go.

"Hell if I know," the sheriff replied. "Looks to be a child's shoe—a girl. We'll have to dig through our missing person's files, along with those statewide and in Mississippi, being that we're so close to the border. That ain't the worst of it. We're gonna have to comb those woods to see if we can find the rest of the body. It's damn hot out there, and the going is tough. This ain't going to be good. We'll get some publicity and some heat. We're going to have to dot our *i*'s and cross our *t*'s. We don't want a whole lotta scrutiny about the goings on in these parts, if you know what I mean."

"It was probably one of those coloreds over in Reform. If not, maybe a transient passin' through," Earl offered. "We got good Christian folks in these parts. I don't see any of our own doin' something like that."

"God, I hope it ain't someone from around here" Sheriff Fuller said. "Ricky, get on the phone to Jarvis. We're going to need his bloodhounds on this. Clyde, call over to Greene, Sumter, Lamar, Tuscaloosa, and Fayette Counties. We're gonna need some help. See if any of them can spare a few men and ask them about anyone missing. Earl, you're still part of Eustice Winchester's church group, aren't you?"

"Well, yeah," Earl stammered. "Why do you ask? I'm sure none of them know anything about this."

"I didn't think they did, Earl. I was hoping you could put a word in. We could use a few volunteers, people with boats."

"I suppose I can do that."

"Good, because we're going back out there first light. Gentlemen, let's make this happen."

The officers got to work. The logistics of the search would be a nightmare. The swamp was a difficult place to investigate. It wasn't going to be easy, and it wasn't going to be fun. Sheriff Fuller was doubtful that they'd recover any more of the body parts. Earl wasn't as certain.

That evening, an emergency meeting was held between Brother Eustice and his select group of deacons. They used the request of the sheriff as an excuse.

"I told you someone would find her," said Jeremiah.

"They found a foot," said Junior. "You had the feet. It's all your fault, dumbass."

"Brothers, let's get a hold of ourselves," interrupted Brother Eustice. "So they found a foot? So what? That's all they're gonna find. Besides, we'll volunteer. We'll comb the areas where we know there's parts and come up with nothin'. It's perfect. Deputy, do they know about the girl?"

"No, and I doubt if they'll figure it out. The dragnet for the missing child didn't come down this far. There's nobody that suspects any involvement by us. The evidence is gone."

"Except the foot," said Joe Bob.

"Right. Except the foot," Earl agreed.

"All of y'all remember our story?" asked Brother Eustice.

"Word for word," said Cooter.

"Good. Let's keep it that way. Brothers in Christ, let's bow our heads in prayer," Brother Eustice said. "Only conduct yourselves in a manner worthy of the gospel of Christ, so that whether I come and see you or remain absent, I will hear that you are standin' firm in one spirit, with one mind, strivin' together for the faith of the gospel. Amen."

"Amen," the men replied.

They would assist in the search, as agreed. No one was going to find anything.

CHAPTER THIRTY-TWO

By the time the sun rose above the horizon, three dozen men stood ready to scour the swamp. Many of the search party had boats; the others were on foot. Jarvis Brown and his cousins, Vernon and Travis Davis, held the bloodhounds. Deputies from around the region were gathered, looking at maps and deciding on which areas they would be responsible for.

"We can look at these spots," Earl offered, pointing to a section of wetlands on the map.

The sheriff eyed his deputy for a moment before grunting his approval. Earl glanced at his accomplices and nodded. Brother Eustice felt emboldened enough by the fortunate turn of events that he offered up a prayer to begin their search.

"Lord, we beseech thee, guide us in our righteous endeavor," he said. The men bowed their heads. "What man of you, havin' a hundred sheep, if he lose one of them, doth not leave the ninety and nine in the wilderness, and go after that which is lost, until he find it? We, your humble servants, are on such a quest. With your blessings, will we be successful, for thy have declared 'Seek and ye shall find'. We seek, not only for the answers to your worldly riddles, but for your grace and forgiveness. Praise be, amen!"

"Amen," the men replied.

The search party split up into groups and headed out to their agreed upon areas. Sheriff Fuller and Deputy Halpin retrieved a package wrapped in plastic from an ice chest. They carefully untied the wrapping and offered a whiff to the canines, who barked loudly. Earl and the boys from the Antioch Pentecostal Church looked away. They knew what was in the bag. They didn't want any reminders.

"You think they got it?" the sheriff asked Jarvis.

"They'll find the rest," Jarvis assured him. He instructed his cousins, "Vernon, Travis, you boys let Pup and Tick loose first."

The cousins undid the leashes on two of the dogs, and they ran into the brush, chasing unseen quarry. The other dogs barked and pulled against their restraints, eager to join their companions.

"Hold onto Yonder and Ambrose, but follow the leaders," continued Jarvis. "I'm gonna give Mojo here a few moments, then I'll come up fast behind y'all. We'll find what's left of that girl. My hounds ain't failed me yet."

The men faded out of sight, but the yelping of the dogs echoed through the trees. Earl looked at his friends and shook his head. None of the boys in the Fellowship liked the fact that Jarvis had brought his bloodhounds, but there was little they could do about it. They set out to search the area where they knew they'd disposed of the body parts and prayed for the best.

Hours passed without anyone finding even the tiniest of clues, much to the relief of Brother Eustice and his followers. The morning turned into afternoon, and soon evening was upon them. When the light faded, they gathered their things and went back to where their search had begun.

"Barroooo!" the canine's howl unexpectedly made the group jump.

"What the hell, Jarvis?" Earl shouted. "You scared the hell out of us!"

Jarvis paid them no mind. His attention was drawn to the dog pulling ferociously against the leash in his hands.

"We already looked there!" Junior shouted. "You're wastin' your time."

"Yeah, get that mutt out of here 'fore he cuts loose and we have to shoot him," said Buck, cradling his shotgun.

"You ain't touchin' my dog," Jarvis said with a coldness in his voice that left no room for argument. "Mojo, what you got there?"

"We told you we looked there," Earl insisted.

"Well, you ain't looked hard enough, Deputy," replied Jarvis. "Mojo smells somethin' under that bush."

"It's probably a rabbit or some dead coon, you dumbass redneck!" shouted Cooter.

The men pushed as close to the barking dog as they dared. Before long, the cousins came up with the rest of the hounds in tow. Five dogs yelped and howled as they fought against their leashes, each desperately trying to get at the unseen object hidden in the muck. Brother Eustice and his followers tried to protest further, but the ruckus made their attempts futile. Buck thought about accidentally firing his weapon at one of the dogs to distract any further investigation, but the sheriff and three deputies had arrived at the scene.

"What you got there?" asked Sheriff Fuller.

"Mojo got somethin' under that bush," Jarvis replied.

The sheriff nodded, and one of the deputies from Tuscaloosa County approached the site as Jarvis and his cousins pulled the dogs away. The officer bent over and poked and prodded through the mud, eventually retrieving a small piece of tarp. He opened the tarp and pulled away quickly, trying not to throw up. The smell hit the others, and they, in turn, did their best to retain the contents of their stomachs.

"What is it?" asked the sheriff, coming closer, a rag held over his nose and mouth.

"A foot," answered the deputy.

"I guess we found the other one then," noted the sheriff.

"I don't think so, Sheriff," said the deputy.

"Why not?"

"Remind me, what was the other foot we found?"

"It was a child's foot, most likely a girl's."

"So is this one. But I meant, what foot was it, the left or right?"

The sheriff, temporarily thrown off by the confusing question, looked at the man and answered, "The right one, I think."

"The right one, you think?"

"The right one," replied the sheriff with more confidence.

"Holy shit!" the deputy spat and looked at the sheriff in dismay.

"What?" asked Sheriff Fuller.

"So is this one."

CHAPTER THIRTY-THREE

"Take a seat, Robert," said the captain, pointing to the empty chair on the other side of his neatly organized desk. "I think I've found just the assignment for you."

Detective Stallworth nodded and sat down. He glanced at Captain Warner and Lieutenant Reid, but their expressions didn't betray their feelings. Robert had only recently been promoted, and he knew that he'd be given an impossible case to investigate as his initiation into his new position. It was standard operating procedure at the state police. His superiors and peers wanted to know what he was made of. Robert had no intention of disappointing them.

"A dismembered body part was found in the swamp over in Pickens County," said Warner. "Actually, two parts have been discovered so far. Obviously, there are more. The local authorities have bumbled around clueless for two weeks since the discovery without anything to show for their efforts, despite having employed local volunteers and officers from neighboring counties in the search. With your reputation—"

Robert nodded. His talent for finding hidden dead things had followed him into the force from his previous stint of duty in Army Intelligence. His duties during the war had been highly classified and remained so, yet enough information had leaked out to the top brass of the Alabama State Police. Together with his father's reputable career and ultimate demise in the ranks, Robert was sure it helped him climb the ladder into his fledgling position as homicide detective.

"You were personally recommended to us by one of the deputies at the scene," said the lieutenant.

"Is that so?" Robert had met countless members of law enforcement throughout the state, but he couldn't recollect knowing anyone working in Pickens County.

"Deputy Brian Gibbs," said the captain.

"Gibbs? The only Gibbs I know works in Tuscaloosa."

"He was one of the ones helping in the search," said Warner. "According to him, unofficially of course, it's a real cluster-fuck over there. His exact words were, 'They ain't going to find shit with those bumpkins leading the investigation'. We agree. What's more surprising is that he mentioned that there was, quote, 'a guy I knew in the war that could smell a rotting corpse under ten feet of concrete', unquote. That would be you."

"I wouldn't go that far," Robert said. He preferred not to think about the things he had witnessed in his previous occupation. They had haunted his dreams ever since. "With all due respect, it isn't that unusual to find an occasional body dumped into a swamp. I'll be more than happy to investigate, but what I find curious is that two of you called me in here and spoon fed me this with such fanfare. There has to be more to it. Spill it."

Lieutenant Reid glanced at Warner. The captain's eyebrow rose slightly, and Robert saw the subtle smile that formed at the corners of his mouth.

"Two body parts have been found," said Captain Warner, "both of them feet. From what we've learned from forensics, they were both deposited in the area no more than four or five months ago and no less than two. They weren't found near each other. The first was retrieved on a fishing line approximately half a mile from where the other was found by bloodhounds—by the aforementioned Gibbs. Both appear to be that of a girl. Based upon the type and size of the shoes, most likely pre-adolescent. So far, no one has been able to ascertain who the victims are."

"Victims?" asked Stallworth.

"Both were right feet," said Reid.

"So, you see why we're sending you," said Warner. "The local sheriff, one Dale Fuller, is not equipped, or manned, to handle this investigation. That is clear."

"Has he sought our help?" questioned Robert.

"Do they ever?" Reid replied.

Robert knew the locals would never admit that they were in over their heads. They would resent his being sent there and would react accordingly, making his life miserable and hamstringing the investigation as much as possible. Once again, Robert understood that was standard operating procedure.

"Where in Pickens County?" he asked.

"Dead River Swamp," said the Captain.

"That sounds about right." Robert shrugged and stood up.

"This is the first big case you're investigating on your own, Detective," said the captain. "Don't come back empty handed."

"I'll find something. But don't say later that I didn't warn you."

"Warn us?" asked Reid.

Robert put a hand over his mouth and suppressed a belch. "I haven't even stepped foot in Pickens County yet, and my stomach is already churning. I'm going to find something, alright. My hunch is that it's going to be one of those things we're going to try to forget later."

"Careful down there, Robert," said Warner. "We've heard rumors about Fuller and his men and their nocturnal activities."

He nodded. The captain's warning was unnecessary. It was Alabama, after all. He hadn't been afraid of the SS or the Red Army, and he wasn't afraid of the Klan. It was going to take a lot more than a few slack-jawed yokels wearing dirty laundry to intimidate him.

Robert left Warner's office and headed out the door. After a quick stop at the house to pick up a few supplies, he was going to head over to the location and start cracking skulls. He wasn't going to Pickens County to make friends. He didn't give a damn whose toes he stepped on. Sheriff Fuller and his men were going to hate him. He was going to make sure of it.

CHAPTER THIRTY-FOUR

"It's a real mess they got going on down there," said Deputy Gibbs.

Robert had stopped by the police station in Tuscaloosa to go over a few details before heading into the lion's den over in Pickens County. Although he hadn't seen his old army buddy in awhile, he knew the man was a straight shooter and wouldn't hold any punches in his assessment of the matter.

"I wouldn't be going otherwise," said Robert.

"No, I guess you wouldn't. I hope you're not mad at me for dropping your name. It kind of just slipped out. I had no idea that you'd get the short straw on this one."

"Don't worry about it. I was recently promoted, and they've been waiting to throw me to the wolves on one of these disasters. They want to see if I can handle it. Little do they know, I've seen worse."

"That we have." The deputy cleared his throat and paused, doing his best to push unpleasant memories away. "Do you ever think about what we saw over there?"

"I try not to," said Robert.

"So do I."

Robert detected a hitch in his friend's voice and quickly changed the subject. "I understand you were the one who found the second appendage."

"The dogs found it. I'm just the one who dug it up."

"Who else was there?" asked Robert, pulling out a small pad to take notes.

"Everyone. Well, most of us. The Pickens County Sheriff and a few of his boys were there, along with me and a couple of deputies from the assorted regional counties who were sent over to help out. Some skinny redneck and his cousins were tending to the bloodhounds, and there was a group of local volunteers as well. A secure crime scene it was not—not that it mattered. It's a swamp. From what I hear, the feet had been there awhile. I doubt there's much evidence left at this point as to who put them there."

"I'm going to need names."

"It's all in my report. I'll fish you out a copy before you leave. Don't worry, it's detailed, unlike the ones you'll get from anyone else around here," said Gibbs, shaking his head.

"Good," said Robert. "Tell me, what were the reactions?"

"Nausea and disgust, as you'd expect. What did you think they'd be?"

Robert ignored the question and continued, "Tell me about the volunteers. Did they get there before or after the rest of y'all?"

"I know what you're thinking, but it wasn't like that. One of them was a cop."

"Is that so?"

"Yeah, they were part of some church group that one of the deputies belonged to. He gathered them up at the request of Sheriff Fuller, if I remember correctly. They looked as sick as the rest of us when I fished the bones out of the muck."

"A church group?" asked Robert. "How do you know that?"

"The leader of the group offered up a prayer to start the search. 'Seek and ye shall find' and all that. You know the drill."

"It seems like an odd group to involve in the search for dismembered body parts."

"I never thought about it that way," conceded Gibbs. "But I guess beggars can't be choosers. It's hot and humid out there. Not exactly the kind of place you'd want to be if you could avoid it."

"Yet there they were."

"There they were. I think one or more of them might've lived nearby, and they knew the area. They seemed to know where they were going."

Robert nodded but said nothing for a moment. He flipped the page on his pad and continued after a brief pause. "Tell me about the dogs."

"The dogs? They were dogs."

"How many were there?"

"How many? Hell if I know. Is that really important? I might've left that out of my report."

They laughed.

"I suppose not," said Robert.

"It's funny you said that, though," continued the deputy. "The owner of the dogs was having a spat with the church group. Some big guy was threatening to shoot one of the dogs when we showed up. I think the barking was getting to him." Gibbs laughed.

Again, Robert said nothing, but he jotted a few lines in his pad before flipping it shut. He tucked it into his pocket, grabbed his hat, and started to leave before turning around to ask one more question. "Off the record, what do you think I'm going to find?"

"Nothing good."

Robert nodded. "I'm going to need that report before I leave."

"I'll have Sarah fetch it for you. I have to say, it's good to see you again, Robert. It's been a long time. I get notices occasionally about reunions with the old gang, but I must confess, I just can't seem to motivate myself to go. I hope none of the boys think I'm being unsociable."

"I wouldn't know," said Robert. He received the same invitations from time to time and threw them in the trash on sight. He'd put that part of his life behind him, or at least he'd tried to. It had proven much more difficult than he'd imagined it would be. The last thing he wanted was reminders.

"I wouldn't worry about it. There's not many of us left anyway. The ones who are still around probably feel the same as we do. What would we talk about? It's all classified. You know as well as I do that nobody is ever going to release those files. No one wants to read about those things. No one wants to see those pictures. The whole lot was likely destroyed years ago, seeing as what's in them."

"Do you think so?" asked Gibbs. "I mean, I'd feel much better if I knew for sure."

"We aren't ever going to know that. It's how they keep us in line. Heads would roll if anyone ever..." Robert stopped himself from finishing the sentence. The past was the past and he wanted it to stay that way. "Anyway, don't worry about it. If anyone up top thought it would come out, the likes of you and I would end up like those body parts. Every day is a blessing. Just remember that."

A middle aged woman with graying hair and thick framed glasses handed Robert a folder, and the deputy escorted him out of the station.

"Good luck with your search," Gibbs offered as they shook hands.

"Thanks, I'm going to need it."

"Don't go too hard on 'em. They're ignorant as fuck, but most of them are good people."

"Would I do that?" asked Robert.

They laughed.

"Watch your back. They ain't going to like you poking around over there."

"I'm not there to bust up any stills or Klan rallies. If they aren't involved in what I'm investigating, they have nothing to worry about."

"And if they are?"

"They'll be more files to burn."

The deputy shuddered. That's what he was worried about.

CHAPTER THIRTY-FIVE

Robert reversed course and headed back to his office in Birmingham with Gibbs's file in his briefcase. It would be too late to start the search that day, and he didn't want to swoop in on the local authorities until he was properly prepared.

Back in his office, he opened the file and made notes. Once he'd read through the report a dozen times, he formulated a plan. The first order of business was to assemble a team. Since he was a fledgling detective and had no subordinates in an official capacity to assist him, he had to improvise. Robert made a list of what positions he needed filled, and he started making calls.

The first position was forensics. Robert had a gut feeling that the investigation was going to be a difficult one, but it also offered an opportunity for someone looking for a challenge. The leading state coroner was Dr. Russell Barrett, but he was pushing seventy, and Robert knew from experience that the man looked for quick solutions so that he could spend as much time out of the office as possible. What professional curiosity the man had once possessed had long since been replaced with laziness and the longing to retire. He wouldn't do, so Robert found the next name in the directory and smiled. Dr. Jack Hall. *Perfect!*

Robert had once had the pleasure of working with Dr. Hall in the investigation of a particularly grisly case of lynching. The body had been found hanging from an oak tree, still smoldering from the torches that had burned it beyond recognition. No one wanted to touch the case, or the repulsive corpse. No one, that is, except Dr. Hall. The man had proven to be resourceful, and Robert had taken notice. He knew that once prodded with the possibilities, the good doctor would be chomping at the bit to be involved in his current investigation. Robert only had to sell it properly.

The detective sat back and pondered. He needed to come up with a catchy name, something worthy of a Sherlock Holmes novel. The location of the body parts suggested the first option for a working title: *The Dead River Mystery.* Robert laughed at the choice. It sounded more like the Hardy Boys than Sherlock Holmes, but he was at a loss for a better idea, so he put the task on the back burner for the time being.

Robert knew that he'd need someone to look for similar crimes throughout the region and inform him of any possible connections or leads. He'd be too busy digging up body parts and dealing with the locals to dedicate any reasonable effort to the thankless, but vital, task. He had only one person in mind—Billy Watts.

Billy had been his father's old partner and had retired a decorated hero from the department. By the time he'd left, he'd cemented his reputation as a homicide detective of the highest order. Watts maintained endless contacts in the department as well as throughout the region, which gave him almost unlimited access to information. His decades of experience had taught him how to sort through mountains of random data and hone in on what might be valuable. Robert was sure Billy would be an enthusiastic and effective collaborator, as long as Robert presented the challenge appropriately.

"Two Feet in the Swamp," he muttered. It was worse than the previous title. Robert shrugged and moved on.

He knew that he would be an unwelcome intrusion to almost everyone in Pickens County. He figured his best course of action would be to use that to his advantage. If he was going to be the bad cop, someone would have to be the good cop. Robert smiled.

Officer John Turner of the Alabama Highway Patrol was the perfect candidate. His grandfather and father had both served as sheriff of their county, as had John for a number of years before he'd moved on to the state level. A nasty run in with an escaped convict had left Turner with a hero's reputation, a bad limp, a desk job, and a huge gut. His jolly disposition and white beard reminded most people of Santa Claus. He was beloved wherever he went. He owed Robert a favor, and he'd jump at the chance to get away from his desk.

"*Backwoods Country Conundrum*," said Robert. It sounded particularly dumb when stated out loud.

That left only one position to fill. He needed a private investigator who would work for practically nothing, incognito, with great discretion, and with an almost supernatural ability to get people to talk. He knew of only one person on the planet who could do the job, but he hesitated. His head told him that he had no choice but to make the call. His heart whispered not to.

Claire Montgomery was a knockout. She was a genius. She was brave and resourceful. She didn't need the money, but Robert knew she'd be intrigued by the investigation. He also knew she'd do anything he asked, just because he asked. She was also the only woman he'd ever loved.

When he had come home from the service, she was waiting for him. He did his best to put on a brave face, but she knew better. He couldn't tell her what he'd been through, what he'd seen, and he didn't have to. Yet it tortured him. He didn't deserve her, and he'd pushed her away. She reluctantly let him. There was nothing left to be said between them, and they'd both moved on. Now, here he was, ready to call her back at the first opportunity. He didn't know if he truly needed her help, or if somewhere deep down, he just needed her. Robert tried to convince himself he could do it without her.

It was futile. There was no way he'd get anywhere without her involvement. He couldn't allow his feelings to get in the way. At least two children had been murdered and dumped in the swamp, and no one else was going to do anything about it. Robert knew he'd make the call. He'd never forgive himself if he didn't. Still, he'd need a selling point.

"*Pickens County Body Parts,*" he said. Robert dismissed it. It sounded even more stupid than the last one.

He was at a loss, so he rifled through the file one more time. The detective let the pages direct his vision. His eyes landed on the black and white photographs, each one of a set of foot bones, partially covered with rotting flesh. He knew that it was going to be a huge undertaking digging up the rest of the skeletons and assembling them into something useful they could work with. Despite the repulsive images in front of him, Robert caught himself smiling as the words left his lips.

"*The Bone Puzzle.*"

CHAPTER THIRTY-SIX

"**S**heriff!" Deputy Smith yelled to the back of the station house. "There's someone here to see you."

The deputy eyed the unexpected visitor with disgust. Robert saw the same expression on the other curious onlookers who glanced up from their desks. He ignored them and waited. *If they think they hate me now,* he thought, *wait till they get to know me.*

Minutes later, the sheriff appeared out of a back office and warily approached the front desk. He eyed the detective for a moment before offering his hand.

"I'm Sheriff Dale Fuller. And you are?"

"Detective Robert Stallworth of the Alabama State Police," said Robert, reaching over and shaking the other man's hand.

"The state police, you say? And to what do we owe this pleasure?"

"I've been sent here about the body parts found in the Dead River Swamp."

"Have you now? I don't remember asking for help from the state authorities."

"That's irrelevant, Sheriff. Here I am."

By the furrowed brow on the sheriff's face, Robert could tell his answer had not gone over well. The rest of the room was silent. The detective doubted that anyone had dared question the sheriff's authority before, and they waited for his response.

"It might be irrelevant to you, Detective, but we have jurisdiction in this county."

"My jurisdiction covers the state of Alabama. The last time I checked, Pickens County was in Alabama. Are we going to do this here, or would you prefer we go into your office?"

"I haven't invited you into my office," replied the sheriff.

"Then we'll do it here. I'm officially taking over the investigation. You and your men will assist me in any and every way I require regarding this case."

"Will we now?"

"Yes, you will," replied Robert decisively.

"I don't know who you think you are, Detective, but I don't work for you."

"You do now, Fuller. If you have a problem with that, I'll just have to work around you. Seeing that you've gotten absolutely nowhere, I don't see a downside to that."

"Wow, you really are a son-of-a-bitch, aren't you?"

"You have no idea. I'm not here to make friends, Sheriff. I'm here to get results, and I expect to do just that. What we have is two murdered and dismembered children and we don't know who they are or how they got that way. More importantly, we have zero suspects. I'm not sure why you became a policeman, Fuller, and I certainly can't speak for the rest of your men, but I find that unacceptable. Are you telling me you feel otherwise?"

Whatever smart ass defensive statement was about to escape Sheriff Fuller's lips died in his throat. The detective had a point. He may have made it with all the diplomacy of a raving lunatic, but the point was well taken.

"No. We feel the same as you do about it. Forgive me, Detective. We didn't expect your arrival. It would've been nice to get a courtesy call about your coming. Please, let me show you to my office. Ricky!" he shouted to one of the deputies sitting nearby, pretending not to pay attention. "Grab the files of the Dead River case and join us."

Sheriff Fuller escorted Robert to the office in the back and offered him a chair. The sheriff sat behind the desk and waited. Minutes later, Deputy Halpin joined them, carrying a large brown envelope and holding a rolled-up map under one arm. He handed the envelope to the sheriff and unrolled the map out on the desk.

"Excuse my attitude at your arrival, Detective. We're happy to have you onboard with the investigation. I'll debrief you on what steps we've taken in the matter, and we can figure out how best to use you at this point. But I doubt we'll get very far. You'll soon learn that we've pretty much done everything we can do, with little to show for it."

"I understand your feelings at my intrusion here this morning, Sheriff. But I don't think you fully understand. I'm not here to assist you. You are here to assist me. Now, before you get all worked up over the situation, let's be clear about this. You have a county to run. This investigation is but a small part of what you have to deal with, and I appreciate that. That is why I've been sent here. This isn't a reprimand over your lack of progress. It's in recognition that you've spent countless man hours and resources on it and will be unable to continue to do so. I, on the other hand, have only one thing I'm responsible for, and that is bringing this investigation to a close. You are correct. I have barged in here and I haven't a diplomatic bone in my body, and that's for a reason. These people in your county aren't going to like me poking around. They're going to despise me from the get-go, regardless of my personality. Since I'm not going to win them over with flattery and small talk, I'm not going to try. What I am going to do is make them uncomfortable. People don't like being uncomfortable. They will resist talking to me, but I am persistent. Every man here, including you, will want to get rid of me as soon as possible. So be it. There's only one way that's going to happen. Once everyone figures that out, you'll be surprised at the level of cooperation that'll come my way."

"I wouldn't be so sure about that," said the sheriff. "People here have their own secrets, and they ain't about to share them with an outsider, particularly one with a badge and an attitude. You may get more than you bargained for."

"If you're referring to the history of lynching and white power terrorism activities in this region, I'm well versed and not at all intimidated. We know more about your involvement than you think we do, Sheriff. Notice I used the term *your*. Now, you go to whatever meeting you're going to have to arrange and discuss your misgivings about my coming here with your Grand Wizard, or Cyclops, or Rooks, or Grand Poobahs, or Mighty Wazoos, or whatever. Devise your schemes, hatch your plans, and do whatever you think you have to do. Frankly, I don't give a shit. At this point, I have no reason to suspect your little boy's club has any involvement in this matter, and until I start getting threatened or harassed, it'll stay that way. If I'm correct and this crime had nothing to do with your clandestine organization, I have little interest in peripheral investigations. However, if things go south, we'll know how wrong that assumption was, and this will go all the way up to the federal level. You may want to convey that to the boys at the next cross burning. Get me what I want, and you'll get rid of me. Do otherwise at your own peril because, I swear on my last breath, I'm going to do what I came here to do if I have to burn the whole county down and everyone in it."

The sheriff and deputy held their tongues. This was an unexpected revelation, and it gave them much to think about. Robert saw their unease and used it to drive his message home.

"Now that we've gotten that out of the way, gentlemen, may I offer a point you may have overlooked? Whoever did this may have done more and is likely to continue. Whoever it is walks among you. It could be your neighbor, your friend, or one of your co-workers. This is a small county. My guess is that one or both of you know the perp or perps on a first name basis. Let that sink in for a moment."

"Actually, we've thought about that very thing, but the feeling around here is that it was done by someone passing through and probably not a local," offered Deputy Halpin.

"I doubt that," said Robert.

"Why do you say that?" asked Fuller. "And what do you mean perps? Do you think there was more than one?"

"I don't know how many there were and neither do you. In fact, I don't know who he, she, or they are; yet."

"But you said you doubted that they were from somewhere else," chimed in Halpin.

"Look at this map," replied Robert, pointing to the section marked with arrows. "The place is remote. It's not easy to get into, not easy to get out of. So far, only two body parts from two victims were found. Whoever did this took the time to dismember the body and spread the parts around. That's a lot of effort. Why bother if you were just passing through? It also would take a considerable amount of time. Well, it would if it was one person. So that begs the question, could there be more than one culprit? Sure, there could. Would someone unfamiliar to the terrain dispose of the evidence there? Possibly, but unlikely. Who lives nearby? Who knows the area? Have you followed these leads in your investigation?"

"No, now that you mention it, we haven't," said the sheriff. "But you raise valid points to consider. We've spent most of the time scouring the area for the rest of the remains and checking on similar crimes or reports of missing persons from the region. No hits that have panned out yet, but we've put a lot of time into it."

"Good solid police work, Sheriff. I'll need to see everything you have on it so far. I'm bringing in a man of my own to help out with neighboring communities and possible suspects. This should ease the burden on your department. I'll personally take over the area search, but unfortunately, I will need at least one officer from your department to assist."

"We expected that, but I doubt you'll have much luck. We've gone over it with a fine toothed comb. Even the hounds have been unable to find anything else. Unless you have a special way of uncovering dead bodies, I don't know what you'll accomplish."

"Don't worry about that, Sheriff. I've got that covered."

"If you say so," said the sheriff. "But, other than giving you our somewhat scarce files and accompanying you on your futile search, I really don't know what else we can do on our end."

"I do. If I need to spell it out, I'll do so. There will be reports I'll expect to receive—at least one a week, more if the situation warrants it."

"Reports? What kind of reports?"

"Detailed."

And so it begins, all three men thought simultaneously.

CHAPTER THIRTY-SEVEN

Robert drove straight out to the area where the feet had been discovered. Deputy Ricky Halpin showed him the sites, which were marked with wooden stakes with pieces of police tape attached.

"Is this where the first or second one was found?" asked Robert.

"The second one," Ricky replied. "One of Jarvis's dogs found it."

"Which one?"

"Pardon?"

"You said one of his dogs found it. Which dog?"

"I'm, I'm not sure. Does it matter?"

"Probably not, but we don't always know what's important. Which is why we get all the details."

Ricky grunted but said nothing. As much as he resented the detective showing up, he suspected that he might be able to learn a great deal by observing the man in action. "I can find out if you want."

Robert looked over and smiled. "That won't be necessary, Ricky. May I call you Ricky?"

"Yes, sir, Detective."

"Call me Robert. Ricky, how long have you been a cop?"

"Five years now, I reckon."

"Drop the 'I reckon'."

"Five years, sir."

"Very good. Don't take this the wrong way, but it's hard to get ahead in your situation. You learn from your boss. It's no knock on the good sheriff, but you're not going to pick up good habits for advanced investigation techniques out here in the sticks."

"We mostly deal with traffic violations, public drunkenness, small time thefts, and domestic disputes out here."

"And terrorizing the colored folk with the occasional lynching. Which is promptly ignored."

Ricky kept silent.

"Don't worry about it, Ricky. I'm not here for that, unless this has something to do with it. Does it?"

"No, sir."

"Good answer. It better be the truth. If I find out someone in the department is making me chase my tail, it's not going to end well. I have contacts in the state penal system, and imprisoned ex-policemen don't generally fare well—unless special considerations are followed. I assure you, they won't be if someone pisses me off. Am I making myself clear?"

"You are, but I swear I haven't heard of any involvement of you know who in this."

"I hope you're right. I also hope that we don't get pushed to a false suspect of a darker skin tone just because of said pigment. I won't stand for it. For one thing, it's disgusting, and I'll make sure that hell will descend on Pickens County. For another, we don't want whoever did this to get away with it. Do you have any kids, Ricky?"

"I have a son and two daughters."

"Someone's two daughters were chopped up and thrown out here. Never forget that."

"No, sir."

Robert wandered around the area, seemingly following an invisible path. Ricky followed, curious as to what the detective was up to but not brave enough to ask. Twenty minutes and a hundred yards later, Robert stopped in front of a shallow pond and stared at the center.

"Ricky, have you ever thought about becoming a detective?"

"Well, not really."

"You mean, 'yes I have, but I didn't want to say'."

"Why do you say that?"

"Because you said 'well' before you answered. You qualified your statement before you made it. It's okay. This conversation is between us. If you like, I'll give you a few pointers, but only if you want. I'm not one to give unsolicited advice."

"That would be great. That is, if you don't mind."

"I don't mind. One caveat though."

"What's a caveat?"

Robert laughed. "Good question. I like that. Ask whatever questions you have. There's no such thing as a stupid question. Caveat means 'stipulation'. Our conversations stay between us. You'll soon learn that I am considered the enemy by your friends and fellow officers. I don't want your career to go down in flames because of me. Keep cool about what you learn and what I tell you. Eyes open, mouth shut. Think you can do that?"

"Yes, sir."

"I thought as much. Another question: Do you think there's a gator in that pond?" Robert pointed to the water in front of him.

"I doubt it."

"Why don't you go in and see?"

"Me? I'm not dressed for that. Why don't you go?"

Robert laughed. "Looks like I'll have to. But next time, it's your turn."

Robert waded out into the shallow water, his way impeded by the thick mud that pulled his feet lower with each step. Ricky looked on in amusement. When Robert got to the middle of the water, thigh deep in the muck, he reached down, soaking what was left of his uniform with slimy mud. He felt around, coming up every few minutes with a branch or rock and discarding it before going back for more. After several minutes, he froze, then stood up and examined the item in his grasp.

"Well, well, what do we have here?" he asked rhetorically and looked at the deputy.

"What is it?" Ricky asked.

Robert waded to the shore and placed the item on the ground.

"It's wrapped up in a tarp, but I can tell you right now what it is," said Robert. "It's a femur. Go call it in and get something to mark the area. We'll need forensics on this. Nobody touches this until I say so, is that clear? I'm calling my own man on this."

"Your own man?"

"Forensics, Ricky. It'll make or break you, don't forget it. Don't trust whatever dipshit gets elected or appointed, but find reliable people you trust. Make them part of your own personal team. It'll pay off. Trust me on this."

"But how did you know you'd find it there?"

"Watch and learn. Let me give you another piece of advice, Ricky. When you discuss this later with Fuller, pretend that you don't want to follow me around anymore. Insist on it."

"But I thought—"

"Do it. He'll override your request and assign you to me with explicit instructions to relay everything we talk about. Are you going to do that?"

"Not a chance."

"That's what I thought."

"But how do you know he'll do that?"

"Same as I knew where that leg was."

"How did you know?"

Robert smiled. "Before this is over, Ricky, you're going to help me find the rest of the parts. You'll see. Now, go on. This thing is only going to smell worse the longer we stand here. I've smelled enough death already."

The deputy nodded and made his way to his police car as instructed. Robert waited till he left, took a few steps back, and leaned against a tree. He'd been out there for a less than an hour and he knew that more of these horrible discoveries awaited him.

He regretted having involved the deputy in the search, knowing what a toll it would take on the young man in the years to follow. Ricky would be excited when he found his first bone, like catching his first fish. He'd be proud of his professional accomplishment. He'd get a pat on the back and a toast in his honor. Then, he'd go to sleep, only to find the nightmares begin. Robert knew that they would never stop.

CHAPTER THIRTY-EIGHT

By the afternoon, a team of officials had marked off the site, taken photographs, and gathered around, pretending to be busy. Robert took Dr. Hall aside to discuss his findings.

"What do you think?"

"It's probably connected to one of the feet that were found earlier. The size matches, and the tarp looks to be the same," answered the coroner.

"Yeah, that's what I figured, too. There's not much flesh still attached that I can see though."

"The tarp wasn't secured too well, and the critters got to it. Off the cuff, I'd say, three months, maybe more."

"Same as the others."

"Yep," agreed the pathologist, "same as the others. Find me more parts, and hopefully, we can piece this together—no pun intended."

"*The Bone Puzzle*," Robert smiled.

"That was a clever one."

"It got you down here."

The men paused and scanned the area. The heat and humidity were oppressive; the swamp was overgrown with dense vegetation and filled with swarms of insects. Dr. Hall took a handkerchief out of his pocket and wiped the sweat from his face and neck.

"I don't envy you having to search out here. Do you think you'll find something else?"

Robert nodded. "We'll dig up what we need." He glanced over at the group of useless law enforcement officers gathered around the pond and frowned. Dr. Hall noted the detective's disapproval.

"I see you're not exactly surrounded by the best and brightest this time."

"Am I ever?" Robert agreed. "Still, that's not what troubles me."

"Is that so?"

Robert ignored the question and returned to where the others were standing, with Dr. Hall following. He motioned for the men to circle around.

He addressed the group. "We have three separate parts now. There's plenty more out here, and we're going to find every last one." Grunts of disapproval could be heard from the group.

"That's the spirit!" he replied. "I knew I'd find some enthusiasm. Now gentlemen, I realize that, for some of you, catching a child killer might not be as rewarding as breaking up a bar fight or directing traffic, but it's what we're going to be doing."

"We've searched out here for weeks already," Deputy Smith complained.

"I was only here twenty minutes before I found the femur," Robert said. "Care to go on?"

His question was met with silence.

"But since you've made your feelings known, Deputy Smith, we'll exempt you from further involvement. You may go."

The deputy stood awkwardly by, not sure what had just happened. He looked around for support from his fellow officers but found none of them willing to make eye contact with him. At last, he looked to Sheriff Fuller.

"Go on," the sheriff instructed.

"I'll volunteer," Deputy Earl Barber offered. "I can muster up a group of locals that know the area pretty well, too. They'll be willin' to help, I'm sure."

"Is that so?" asked Robert. "Get in the car with Deputy Smith."

"What?"

"You heard me. Get in the car with Deputy Smith and high-tail it out of here."

"I, I don't understand."

"You will."

"Detective Stallworth," Sheriff Fuller asked, "is there any of my men that you'll need to assist you?"

"I'll need one. Is there one worth a fuck that you can spare?"

"I'd offer Deputy Halpin, but—"

"But?"

"I just had a talk with him and, to be perfectly frank with you, he ain't too keen on working with you."

"Is that so? And why is that, Deputy Halpin?"

Ricky hemmed and hawed, unsure how he was supposed to play the charade. "No offense, Detective, but you ain't the easiest person to work with. This swamp is ripe with vermin, and it's hot out here. I was out here with you this morning and I hated every second of it."

"Go on."

"With all due respect, Detective, you're a bit of an ass. You talk down to us and treat us like dog meat. I might not be as college smart as you are, but I'm not a moron, and I don't appreciate you treating me like one."

"He'll do just fine," Robert said to the sheriff.

"Dale!" pleaded Ricky.

"Dale what? You're now assigned to the detective," said Sheriff Fuller. "Is that clear?"

"Yes, sir."

"And as such you can now take over writing the weekly reports that he requires," added the sheriff.

"I don't think so," said Robert. "He'll be glued to my side. I'll already know what he thinks, or doesn't think, as the case may be. I'll need the reports to come straight from your desk, with your signature on them."

"What's the point of that? What am I supposed to be doing that you're not?"

"You're the sheriff, aren't you? Figure it out," Robert said. "But don't sweat it too much. I'll point you in the right direction with my red pen. Just get it done."

"Detective, I don't know what—"

"Yes, you do, Sheriff." Robert glared at the sheriff. The look in his eyes said the words that would remain unspoken between them: *I know what you've been up to.*

"Now, before you start complaining, remember, your deputy and I will be wading through the swamp looking for the rotting body parts of murdered children."

Dr. Hall looked on in amusement. Same ol' Robert, he thought. He could feel the hatred in the air. They all despised the detective. Well, maybe not all of them. To the doctor, the deputy assigned to assist the detective seemed to be acting. Hall figured the detective had worked his charms on the young man and had previously set the whole thing up. The doctor smiled. He'd been played the same way. It's why he was there.

Dr. Hall glanced at the others. Yep, they all hated the man, with one exception. The deputy who had volunteered to help and been rejected didn't look as angry as he appeared scared. The doctor wondered if the detective had noticed.

Robert had.

CHAPTER THIRTY-NINE

Earl was nervous. Just as he was preparing to leave for the day, the detective requested his presence in the interrogation room. The deputy shrugged and casually did as he was told, as if it were an afterthought. Deep inside, he suspected the worst. How could the detective know? There was no way he could, but Earl felt uneasy all the same.

"Good evening, Deputy," Robert greeted him as he joined the officer in the cramped room. The detective took a seat and opened a file. He shifted through a few papers, then pulled a notepad out of his pocket and clicked his pen. He was ready to take notes. "I'm glad you could join me. Please, don't be nervous." Robert eyed the man across the desk and paused.

Everything the detective did made Earl nervous. Telling him not to be nervous and then preparing to take a statement while giving him the evil eye made it virtually impossible to be calm. All the same, Earl did his best to pretend it was just another day at the office.

"Why would I be nervous?" he asked, his voice cracking.

"Right. Why would you be?" Robert asked rhetorically. He waited another moment for effect, and then shifted gears. "I hope you weren't insulted by the way I called you out earlier. It's not what you think. I appreciate the fact that you've been so willing to help out when others haven't been. There are reasons for the decisions I make. And some of those reasons will become clear, in due time, to those who pay attention."

Robert glanced at the man and asked, "Are you paying attention?"

Earl nodded, but he had no idea what the detective was talking about.

"I see that, early in the investigation, you not only went out of your way to search the area in question, but you also rounded up a group of locals to help you. That's very impressive, Deputy. That's the kind of initiative that we need."

Robert smiled, forcing Earl to respond in kind. Things were getting more confusing by the minute for the deputy.

"Your friends have provided an invaluable service, one that we will need in the future. They must be an extraordinary group of individuals to volunteer their time like that. Tell me, Earl—May I call you Earl?"

"Yes, sir."

"Call me Robert. Anyway, Earl, tell me, how did you manage to find men so willing to help out like that? You must really have a way with the powers of persuasion."

"No, sir, I mean Robert, it weren't me at all. That's just the kind of men they are."

"You know them personally?"

"Yes, sir, I'm proud to say. We're all members of the same church."

"Well, that explains it," said Robert. He nodded his head and smiled. "Good Christian men. We men of faith understand what's really important, isn't that so?"

"You, you're a believer?"

Robert laughed. "Don't be so shocked. Am I that much of an asshole that you find that hard to believe?"

"I didn't mean—"

"Yes, you did." Robert laughed again. "It's okay, Earl. It's all part of the act."

"The act?"

"Surely you've heard of the good cop/bad cop routine? I'm the bad cop."

Earl laughed. "Funny, I didn't realize—"

"That's the whole point. We used to play that in the army, too. Only then, the bad soldier was able to do much more than pretend."

Robert looked Earl in the eye. The detective's face was without expression, which made the implication all the more disturbing.

"But that was a long time ago. It's hard to stay the course in our profession, walk the narrow path, as it were, and remain part of the flock. One gets tested at every turn. A small gesture here, an exemption there, and, pretty soon, one is on his way to the fiery pit. I must confess, I have failed on more than one occasion. I suppose it's what makes the Lord's gift of redemption so important. Wouldn't you agree?"

"Yes, sir. It's like my pastor says, 'The Lord sacrificed himself on the cross so that we all can be forgiven.'"

"Amen. Your pastor sounds like a wise man."

Earl remained silent. He once believed the words that the detective spoke, but he'd been having doubts since the incident and its aftermath.

Robert gave no indication that he'd noticed. He'd make his notes on the matter later. He shifted through some papers in front of him and retrieved a form. He scanned the page for a brief moment before setting it down and addressing the deputy.

"I have a partial list of your friends who helped in the search. I'm hoping you can add anyone that I missed and fill me in on some details regarding these righteous men. Don't fret about it, Earl. There are reasons for what I'm asking. May I speak to you in confidence?"

Earl nodded.

"We've known for quite some time about the nocturnal activities of this county. By we, I mean, the state police. We also know that there are many, if not most, of the county officials involved in this, including in this department. Do you see where I'm going with this?"

Earl nodded again, and then shook his head. "No, not really."

"I'm talking about the Klan, Earl. This county has the third highest number of lynchings in the state. Not one conviction. That's nothing to be proud of."

"I'm not proud of it."

"I noticed. I also noticed that you're not exactly one of the gang with your fellow officers. It doesn't take a genius to put two and two together."

"I don't believe in what they believe in."

"Neither do I, and that's because we believe in justice. I'm guessing the members of your flock don't participate in those activities, either."

"No, we don't."

"And y'all were the ones out there searching. I didn't see mention of any other group of hunters or fishermen helping out."

"That's because there were none."

"Precisely."

Earl nodded. *This was perfect.* If the detective suspected the Klan, he'd get nowhere, and they'd all be off the hook. Earl relaxed a little. Stallworth wasn't as smart as Earl had originally thought he was.

"So you can see why I need your help."

"But you said earlier—"

"That I didn't want your help? Now, why would I say that?"

"Because you don't want them to know I'm helpin' you," Earl replied.

Robert winked. Earl smiled. Robert took his pen and motioned to the list.

"I'll need more than your help, Deputy. Do you think the members of your flock might be willing to see that justice is done?"

"Yes, I do. I'll have to speak with them first, of course. They'll be hesitant to talk to you, being that you're a detective and from out of town and all."

"I figured as much, which makes you even more valuable to me. I'll leave them to you, for now. We can go through this list, and you can help me with the details. We'll update it accordingly. I know this will make you uncomfortable. You'll feel like your ratting on your friends. But that's not the case. I consider you and them allies of mine. The problem is, if we don't do this correctly, we'll have problems later when we go to trial. It's complicated, I know, but you'll have to trust me. Once the lawyers get a hold of this, even the slightest irregularity will set the perpetrators free. We can't have that. When this gets to court, our cover will be blown. If we get anything less than a conviction, there'll be hell to pay. Of course, if we never get to court, none of this will matter. It'll stay hidden in a file until it gets trashed. Do you understand what I'm saying?"

"Yes, sir, I get it, and you'll get full cooperation from me. I'm glad you came to me with this. I might be the only one that's willin' to help you."

"That's what I was hoping for," Robert said. "Keep in mind that I'll keep this all confidential. No one will know you and your friends are helping me—maybe not even them. We don't want to spook anyone or make them unwelcome with their not as enlightened neighbors. We'll have to be discreet with this. Do you think your friends can keep a secret?"

Earl smiled. "You have nothin' to worry about."

Robert nodded. *I know I don't, but you do.*

CHAPTER FORTY

Three weeks passed, and the body parts started to accumulate. Each one was photographed on location, and a stake was placed at the site. A colored pin with a number attached was placed on the giant map at the sheriff's office in the conference room that doubled as Stallworth's command center. Each part was numbered, tagged, bagged, and brought to Dr. Hall's morgue to process. Once he was finished with his examination, the bone, or bones, was laid out on a giant tarp on the floor in the middle of an empty room at the morgue, as per Robert's request. Dr. Hall thought it was curious but did as instructed.

"Don't you think you're taking this bone puzzle thing a little too seriously, Detective?" he asked one day as they gazed over the exhibit taking shape on the floor.

Robert laughed. "Maybe, but I'm a visual learner, Jack. I'm wondering how you know which bones to put where."

"An extensive knowledge of anatomy is required for a man in my field."

"Yeah, I know that, but that's not what I mean. I see three femurs and four humerus bones. How do you know which goes with which skeleton?"

"I don't, but it doesn't matter. They're identical."

"So we have twins?" The detective's question proved to be more of a statement.

"It would appear so. But we haven't found all of the bones yet, so there's that."

The men looked at the partial skeletons lying side by side and paused. There was something odd about it, but Robert couldn't quite figure out what it was.

"Do you think they were attached?"

"You mean as in conjoined twins?" the doctor asked, surprised by the question. "I doubt it. There's nothing so far to indicate that. But until we get the rest of the bones, we can't be certain. Why do you ask that?"

"I'm just ruling things out."

"They were identical though," the doctor added.

"And you know this because the bones of the two are so close to being the same?"

"That and because we've compared partial toe prints and hair samples from the little bit of flesh still attached."

"Do we have enough to identify the victims?"

"Probably not," the doctor conceded. "But how many missing identical twins could there be?"

Robert was way ahead of him. Billy Watts was looking into the matter at that very moment. So far, no reports of missing identical twins had been discovered.

Robert sighed and stared at the macabre display. Dr. Hall watched the detective and waited. When he remained silent, the doctor pressed the issue.

"What's troubling you, Robert?"

"What's missing?"

"There are a lot of parts missing."

"Right, but most are missing from one or the other, and I know we have partials of some of the ribs and vertebrae. What I mean is what major parts are missing from both?"

"The skulls."

"Right."

"Do you think the killer kept the heads as a memento?" the doctor asked with disgust. "That's pretty sick."

"And this isn't?" Robert said, indicating the assortment of bones.

Dr. Hall whistled and shook his head before adding, "I don't know how you do what you do."

"I could say the same for you."

They wanted to laugh, but the gravity of the situation prevented it. Tears were more appropriate. Those would only come later when each man lay awake in the darkness alone, trying desperately to confront their inner demons.

CHAPTER FORTY-ONE

"That's the dumbest thing I've ever heard. You told him what?" yelled Charles Ray.

"I thought we agreed that we'd keep our mouths shut," added Cooter.

"Loose lips sink ships," said Joe Bob.

"It's not like that," Earl tried to explain. "I had to tell him somethin'. He had me cornered."

"The prophet ain't going to like this one bit," Buck said, spitting a mouthful of tobacco laden saliva on the ground at the deputy's feet.

"You dumbass," Charles Ray went on. "He get you to confess yet?"

"Fuck you, Charles Ray," Earl countered. "I keep tellin' you, it ain't like that; not that he didn't have me worried at first. Hell, he done dragged me into the interrogation room and scared the crap out of me. He looked at me as if he could see right through me. He's a crafty one, that sumbitch. But not as smart as he thinks he is. He's convinced it was the Klan that done it."

"What makes you say that?" asked Cooter.

"'Cause he done told me so himself. That's why he wants our help. He said he could tell I wasn't part of that and, by association, y'all ain't either. Said that he knew 'cause he's a man of the Lord himself, and only a true believer can spot another one."

"You really are a dense motherfucker, you know that?" Joe Bob said. "A man of the Lord. Give me a break."

"Why, because he's a cop? I'm a cop. Are you sayin' I ain't a true believer?"

"Dumbass," insisted Joe Bob.

Earl lunged at his friend, but Buck intervened between the pair. "Easy now, brothers. I'm sure Brother Eustice will have something to say about the matter. He'll be here any minute. I think you'd better get your ducks in a row, Deputy, because I reckon his holiness ain't gonna take kindly to your yappin'."

"I ain't told him nothin' he don't already know."

"You better be right about that," said Cooter.

"Dumbass," Joe Bob repeated.

The rusty Buick arrived, kicking a cloud of dust into the hot morning air. Brother Eustice and the boys exited and joined the others, clearly displeased at being called out to the remote location unexpectedly.

"What's this all about?" Eustice asked, daring anyone to answer.

"Earl's been runnin' his mouth," said Buck.

"That true, Earl? You been runnin' your mouth?"

"It ain't like that, Brother Eustice. I keep tellin' y'all, but ain't no one listenin'."

"The prophet done told your sorry ass not to say shit," Junior said. "What the hell is the—"

Whack! Brother Eustice's cane smacked his shin.

"Oooww! What you done that for?"

"Shut up, Junior," Brother Eustice replied. "Now, Earl, go on now. You tell us who you been talkin' to and what you been sayin'."

"It was that smarty pants detective from Birmingham," Charles Ray said.

"What do you know about it?" Brother Eustice turned to Charles Ray.

"I know what everyone knows. People talk. They all hate him. Say he's a real thorn in their side. Bossin' everybody around, treatin' people like they was dirt. Brother Earl here thinks he's a member of the flock, though. Ain't that right, stupid? Ain't that what you been tellin' us?"

Brother Eustice looked at Earl, one eyebrow cocked.

"That ain't what I said."

"Yes, it is, dumbass," Joe Bob insisted.

"Yeah, dumbass," Junior echoed.

Whack!

"Ouch! Stop doin' that!"

Jeremiah chuckled until his father's glare ended the frivolity.

"Tell me 'bout this here detective," said Brother Eustice. "What did he want to know?"

"Mostly about us," Earl replied.

"Us?" Cooter exclaimed.

"What do you mean, us?" Eustice asked.

"About us, the flock," Earl explained. "He wanted to know about us."

"How'd he even know 'bout us in the first place?" asked Cooter.

"I don't know, but he knew," said Earl. "He had a list. All of our names were on it."

"But I don't see how—" Cooter started before Eustice motioned for him to be silent.

"It's from that damned search," said the prophet. "I was afraid that might happen. One of them out of town officers must've gotten our names from the sheriff and put it in his report. What did he ask about us?"

"Not much," said Earl. "He wanted to know if everyone that helped on the search was on the list and if anyone was missin'."

"And?"

"We was all on it already."

"And?"

"And what? He wanted to know general things, like where everybody lived and who was who in the church."

"Did you tell him?" asked Cooter.

"Sure I did."

"What? You dumbass!" Joe Bob shouted.

"Why you done that for?" Brother Eustice calmly asked.

"'Cause I could see his list, and everyone's addresses was already on it. I didn't want to look like I was hidin' anything, so I played along. I gave him general descriptions of what we looked liked and offered whatever information that I knew he'd already know or could easily find out, like I was tellin' him our deepest, darkest secrets. He ate it up with a spoon."

Brother Eustice nodded his head and ran his fingers through his scraggly beard. "Clever."

"Who's the dumbass now?" Earl said to Joe Bob. "Dumbass!"

"Enough of that, brothers," said the prophet. "You done right, Earl. Quick thinkin'. But don't get too cocky. This detective feller is likely a might smarter than you think he is."

"He ain't. He thinks the sheriff and the Klan is—"

"That's what he says he thinks," Brother Eustice interrupted. "He wants you to think that's what he thinks. That's what we know. What we don't know is what he actually thinks. I can tell you one thing I know 'bout this feller before I even meet him though, and I want everyone here to listen up when I say this. I don't know what he thinks, but rest assured, he thinks. He didn't get to be a detective with the state police because one of his cousins knew somebody."

"So, what should we do when he comes nosing 'round?" asked Jeremiah.

"That's the real question, ain't it?" replied Brother Eustice. "'No advantage would be taken of us by Satan, for we are not ignorant of his schemes.' We're gonna play along with his game—to a point. But we're not gonna deviate from our story. Remember, he's going to ask us the same questions in different ways, over and over again, lookin' for a crack. Don't let him find one. As long as we remain steadfast, we will be invincible. He'll move on to greener pastures. 'For lack of wood, the fire goes out, and where there is no whisperer, quarrelin' ceases.'"

"Are you sure that's gonna work?" asked Junior. "You said yourself this guy is—"

Whack!

CHAPTER FORTY-TWO

Identical houses lined the dirt road outside of Dancy. Chickens ran freely through the street, ignored by the half-dozen children who played in the open space. Two goats were tied up next to a feeding trough, oblivious to the poverty that surrounded them.

The majority of the dwellings appeared abandoned. The few remaining in use were decorated by the elderly inhabitants who sat idling their few remaining days away on their front porches. As if on cue, every citizen of the small enclave stopped in their tracks to watch with trepidation as the unexpected vehicle approached. Only the chickens and goats remained blissfully unaware of the intrusion.

The sedan stopped in front of one of the dwellings. Two men exited the vehicle and approached the elderly couple sitting on the front porch.

"Pardon me!" Robert called out. "Is this the home of Lucius Jones?"

"Yes, sir," the old man answered.

A large, middle aged black woman appeared in the doorway. "Don't answer him, fool," she protested. "You don't know who he is."

"My apologies, ma'am," Robert said as he and his companion approached. Robert removed his hat and offered his hand to the gentleman seated in the rocking chair. "My name is Robert Stallworth. I'm a detective with the Alabama

State Police. This is a friend of mine, Mister Billy Watts." Robert motioned to the man on his left.

The old man shook hands with both men; the men nodded to the woman.

"You a cop, too?" Lucius asked Billy.

"Not any more. I'm retired. I'm more of a fisherman now."

Lucius smiled. "Well then, you're in good company. I've caught my fair share of cats 'round here, goin' on three quarters of a century now. Although I've slowed down a might over the past few months since—"

Lucius felt no need to continue the sentence. He figured if the police were coming around to question him again, they surely knew about the incident.

"Yeah, I suppose not," said Billy. "That'd keep me away for a spell. If you don't mind me asking, how's the boy taking it?"

"He don't seem too troubled 'bout it no more. He done had a bad dream or two right after, but he seemed to get over those. The boy'll be just fine. I doubt he'll ever forget, but 'fore long, he'll grow up and find worse things to occupy his nightmares."

"Yep, that he will," agreed Billy.

"I hope you don't mind us coming out here like this," said Robert. "We promise not to keep you too long."

"That's alright, Detective. You're just doin' your job. I'm not sure I'll be able to help you much. I done told the sheriff and his men everything I know, not that there was much to tell."

"That's what we figured, but I'll have to say that I talked to you in my report."

Lucius laughed. "Yeah, I ain't thought 'bout it like that, but you got a point. I ain't never had no job that made me fill out forms and such, and can't say as I wish I had."

"You have no idea," Billy agreed.

He'd done his due diligence in his background check of the elderly black man. No arrests, no convictions, not so much as a traffic violation was in the man's file. Until he'd fished the girl's foot out of the swamp, there was only one mention of the man in any police investigation—the death of his daughter and her unborn child.

The incident had happened decades in the past. The files were purposely vague. No arrests or actual police work had been done about it. By all accounts, the girl was a victim of violence stemming from a person or persons unknown, following a racially charged riot in Pickensville. Due to the lack of interest in the case by the local authorities, it was assumed that the local Klan had been involved. Rumors swirled that the same men who wore police uniforms during the day were the ones wearing the white sheets and burning crosses at night, including several on Lucius' front lawn following the murders.

At the time, Lucius had a house full of children to protect. Although the horror of the crime and the terrorist intimidation that followed weighed heavily on his mind, he turned to the church to find comfort. When the church was burned to the ground, presumably by the same group that killed his daughter and unborn grandbaby, Lucius found another.

Many of the culprits, and even his neighbors, initially looked down upon Lucius because of his lack of response. He was called a coward and worse. But over time, his example turned the hate into admiration. Eventually, even his greatest detractors came to respect him as a righteous man. Unknown to Lucius, his example caused many a man to cry for mercy and beg forgiveness for their despicable acts on their death beds, not that it would've mattered. Lucius hadn't chosen his actions to provide comfort for those who took so much from him, but rather to help his family and himself to find meaning and purpose in a cruel world.

"Ain't you fellers done enough?" the heavy set woman interjected. "You need to leave Paw Paw alone. We ain't got nothin' to say to you."

"Now, now, Anna May, I taught you better than that," Lucius chastised her. "Pardon my niece, officers. She just doin' her best to look after me. She don't mean no harm."

"It's okay, Mr. Jones," said Robert. "I don't blame her one bit. Do you mind if I level with you? I'm not here to talk about what you found."

"You're not?"

"No, sir. We can see you didn't have anything to do with the crime, but I'm curious about a few things."

"Shoot."

"The sheriff ever ask you if you saw anyone else out there?"

"Sure, he done asked, but I ain't seen nothin' or nobody."

"I figured as much," continued Robert.

"Then why you asked?" Anna May asked. "You see he's old. His heart can't take all this nonsense."

"It's one of those things I'll have to put in my report."

"Your report? That why you came out here—to hassle us so you can fill out some dumb papers?"

"Anna May," said Lucius, "you hush now. They'z gonna get to the point. Ain't that right, Detective? You ain't asked what you wantin' to ask me yet. Go on, I knows what's on your mind."

"Why hasn't anyone come around here accusing you or one of your relatives?"

"'Cause they knows I ain't had nothin' to do with it. That thing had been there a good spell 'fore I came along."

"That hasn't stopped them before," Billy pointed out.

"Now why you goin' to bring up that? That was a long time ago. I let it go and ain't had a lick of trouble since."

"That was mighty big of you, Mr. Jones," said Billy. "I'm not sure many people could've done that."

"We mourned our losses and put our trust in the Lord. Do you know I made eighty-eight last month? I ain't gotta lot of regrets. My days ain't long in front of me, and I'm good with that. I done what the Lord asked of me, and I can meet him on the other side with a clear conscience. Can you say the same?"

Billy couldn't answer, so he remained quiet.

"I know I can't," Robert said at last. "For one thing, I'm kept up at night thinking about those girls who ended up chopped into pieces and thrown into the swamp."

"Good Lord!" Anna May protested. "I done told you, Paw Paw ain't got a good heart. Don't be comin' 'round here sayin' stuff like that."

"It's okay, baby girl," said Lucius. "The man's just doin' his job. Detective, what you want to know is how two white girls done got murdered in Pickens County, and ain't nobody been lynched for it. What you wonderin' is why ain't no one burned no cross in front of my house. Isn't that right?"

"That about sums it up, Mr. Jones."

"I don't think you'd understand, but you're the cop. You tell me. You think they involved, but now that you're here, they tryin' to sweep it under the rug?"

"Is that what you think?" Robert asked.

Lucius rocked in his chair for a bit and pondered the question. Robert and Billy waited. At last, he answered, "I think they ain't had nothin' to do with it. They would of gone out of their way to blame someone else and put a noose 'round their neck. Lord knows, ain't nothin' would of come from it. Case closed, and you wouldn't be here."

"You are a wise man, Mr. Jones," Robert replied, "and a better man than I. I don't know that I could've endured what you did and remained untroubled and able to not seek revenge."

"Don't think I'm untroubled. As far as revenge, I'd of settled for justice. Denied."

"Yeah, well, at least you sleep at night," offered Robert.

"That's 'cause men like you don't," Lucius replied. "It was good to meet you. You too, Mister Billy. You want to come fishin' sometime, you're welcome. I promise I'll show you where the big cats are bitin'." Lucius shook their hands, and the men began to leave when he added. "And I'll do my best not to pull something vile out the water next time."

"You do that," Billy replied. "And I might just take you up on that offer when this is all over with."

"And Detective," said Lucius, "I heard it was two girls they found out there. You do me a favor and find their parents. You tell them I'z prayin' for them. And then find the demon that done this. Bring them to justice this time. Do it for my little angel."

"Rest assured, I won't stop until I do."

"I know you won't."

The men returned to the car and left. Just as Robert navigated the narrow dirt road, Billy looked at the three figures, watching them from the front porch. For all the disapproval Anna May had voiced, Billy noted that she nodded at them as they drove off.

She might've been unsophisticated and seen little of the outside world, but Billy could see that Anna May had an astute sense of character. She knew that Robert meant what he had said, as assuredly as Billy knew it. Whoever did this was going to pay. This time, justice would not be denied.

CHAPTER FORTY-THREE

Billy waited until they well on their way before probing Robert's mind. "So, what do you think?" Robert was driving purposely slow on their trek back to the hotel where Billy was staying at in Aliceville. It would give them time to talk.

"The old man?" Robert replied. "I doubt if he knows any more than what he told us."

"Agreed, but not that. I meant, what do you think overall? Do you have any suspects in mind?"

"Everyone in the county, except for Lucius Jones."

They laughed.

"I know you better than that, Robert. I heard you were questioning one of the sheriff's men the other day. What was that all about?"

"Probably nothing."

"Probably?"

"He was an outlier from the start, from what I could ascertain from Gibbs's report. Deputy Earl Barber."

"I ran the name. He's clean as far as I can tell."

"He's a cop, so I figured that."

"So, what about him brought him to your attention?" asked Billy. He knew that Stallworth did very little without a plan of action in mind.

"First of all, he was jumping over himself to help me when everybody else was avoiding any involvement in the investigation like it was a venereal disease."

"You have such a way with words. Yes, that is rather suspicious, but I suspect you had him in your crosshairs before that."

"He's not one of the gang, which means, it's unlikely he's one of the Klansmen. And if they aren't involved, where does that leave him?"

"So you think they aren't involved?"

"They could be, but I'm thinking less and less," Robert conceded.

"And what else about the deputy bothers you?"

"His band of merry men."

Billy laughed. "You mean like Robin Hood?"

"More like some weirdo cult. Did you run the list I sent you?"

"I'm working on it."

"And?"

"They are a colorful group of possible deviants, but it'll be tough to get past the church doors and single them out. They'll close ranks once you start applying pressure, whether they're guilty or not. These cult types live off the premise of being persecuted. They're paranoid by nature, and you're the Devil incarnate."

Robert glanced at his friend, one eyebrow cocked. "Am I?"

"To them, you will be. Isn't that part of your plan?"

Robert laughed. "You know it."

"What about this other deputy? The one helping you look for bones?"

"Ricky Halpin," Robert answered. "He's okay, just a tad wet behind the ears. He wanted to learn a thing or two about investigating, so I gave him a few pointers on how to find dead things."

"I'm surprised and impressed. I'd of thought it was a trade secret with you. After all, you're famous for that talent."

"Don't remind me."

"So, how is the young deputy coming along with his training?"

Robert sighed. "Better than expected, I'm afraid."

"Is that a bad thing?"

"He looks ten years older already. I don't think he's getting much sleep at night."

"Join the club."

Robert nodded. Switching gears, he asked, "Any headway on identifying the victims?"

Billy frowned. He'd spent the greater part of his time following up on one dead end after another, without making progress. It was frustrating and depressing. How could two girls of such a young age, twins no less, go missing without a national manhunt instigated? "Not yet. None of the girls near that age who have been reported missing have been sisters or twins. As far as I've determined so far, none of them even knew each other."

"It's a sad state of affairs when there are enough missing children that you had to use the term 'none of the missing girls'," noted Robert.

"That it is, Bob. That it is." Billy waited, but he could sense Stallworth wasn't going to bring it up, so Billy breached the subject at long last. "I'll look into that church group, and I'll follow up on known criminals and similar crimes committed throughout the Southeastern United States. But we both know, we're going to need someone else to find out who the victims were. I've tried and failed. Doctor Jack hasn't gotten anywhere. When are you going to call her?"

Robert felt a pain in his chest, but did his best to hide it. "I already did."

"And?"

"She'll be here the day after tomorrow."

Billy nodded. He knew it was going to be tough for Robert to see Claire again. It wasn't going to be easy for her, either. Nevertheless, Billy let out a sigh of relief. If anyone could find out who the girls were and where they came from, it would be Claire Montgomery.

CHAPTER FORTY-FOUR

"It looks like you've found another one, Ricky," Robert said as he watched the deputy pull what looked like a rib bone out of a dank pool of slush. "By my count, there'll be seven more and some loose vertebrae."

Ricky wanted to puke. He'd been standing in the knee deep muck for over half an hour, fishing the assorted bones from the mud, one at a time. This particular assortment was devoid of the tarp that had been wrapped around the majority of the parts they'd discovered, which the deputy was grateful for. The material usually prevented total decay, leaving bits of flesh teaming with parasites and smelling like the bowels of Satan himself. The detective preferred the parts come up that way because he said it preserved valuable evidence, but as far as Ricky could determine, nothing useful ever came from that evidence.

The loose bones were good enough for Ricky. He'd been having nightmares ever since he'd found his first package. He'd thought the bundle was little more than a discarded wrapper left in the brush by a fisherman or hunter until Robert insisted they open it. The hand had been close to being perfectly preserved. Ricky found it impossible to rid his mind of the memory. He suspected that he'd live with it for the rest of his life. The detective seemed unmoved, which left nobody he could complain to about his predicament. If only he'd known what he was getting himself into when he'd insisted Stallworth teach him the ropes.

"Are you okay?" Robert asked. His assistant looked a little woozy.

"I'm fine," Ricky answered. "It's just—"

"Speak."

"This will be the majority of the two corpses. I'm sure there are a few bones we've missed, but this makes almost the complete torso. Yet the heads—"

"Right, the heads." Robert nodded. "He, she, or they kept the heads."

"He, she, or they? You think a woman did this?"

"I highly doubt it, but it's been known to happen. We can't rule it out, so we won't."

"They?"

"I'm not sure we're looking at just one sick individual here."

"Why do you say that?"

"You tell me, Deputy."

Robert could state several reasons for his suspicions, but that wasn't going to teach Ricky to think for himself. The young officer had been coming along in strides. He was twice the policeman that he was less than a month prior, when they'd started working together. He'd be three times that once Robert left.

"This took a lot of time and effort. Staying out here that long would've increased the risk of being seen. Just dismembering the girls alone would've taken a great deal of work. But if there were more than one—"

"Go on."

"I'm not sure I'm buying it. More than one would also increase the chances that someone would talk."

"They may still. Once we hone in on them, they'll start to turn on each other to cut a deal for themselves no matter how much they swear allegiance now. They always do—like rats on a sinking ship."

"But we have to catch them first, and we don't have any idea who they are or if they're even from around here."

"Don't we?"

Ricky was stunned. How could Stallworth possibly know who the perpetrators were, and, if he did, why didn't he make an arrest? Why were they wasting valuable time digging around in the swamp for the rest of the bones if they had the crime solved already?

As if he could read the deputy's thoughts, Robert asked, "How likely is it that whoever dumped the bodies here didn't know the area?"

"Not likely," Ricky replied. "They'd get lost out here in a heartbeat."

"That's what I'm thinking. How many locals know this area well enough?"

"A few. That old coon that found the foot for one."

"Lucius Jones? Do you think he did this?"

"No," said Ricky. "I suppose not. A few others that live nearby maybe."

"Not many of them. Suppose it was more than one though. How many people who live or have property nearby are members of, for lack of a better word, a gang of miscreants who might do something as vile as this?"

"I know what you're thinking, but I'd of heard if the Klan was involved in this."

"Why would you have heard, Ricky?"

Robert looked at the man with an accusing stare. Ricky hesitated, hung his head in shame and mumbled, "No reason, but I'd of heard."

"I'm sure you would've. Maybe I've misjudged you, Deputy. Perhaps I should relieve you of your duty in this investigation."

"Detective Stallworth, please," pleaded Ricky. "Robert, I, I, I swear I'll—"

"Yeah, yeah, I'm sure you will. A word of advice—don't ever use the word coon to describe another human being in front of me again."

"I didn't mean anything by it. It's just how we talk 'round here. I didn't know you were so sensitive to things like that."

The young man had no idea, thought Robert. He knew he wasn't going to change the man's thinking overnight, but he wasn't going to lose the opportunity to teach him a valuable lesson. As reluctant as he was to dredge up old memories, Robert felt compelled to relay a horrible experience for the sake of the young man.

"Have you ever heard of a place called Majdanek?"

"Majda what?"

"Majdanek. It's in Poland."

"I ain't never been to Poland."

"But have you heard of it?" asked Robert.

"No, sir." Ricky had no idea what the detective was talking about, or how a town in Poland had anything to do with Alabama, but he listened for the sole reason of wanting to keep his assignment. He'd learned a great deal from the detective and, although he wouldn't ever admit it to anyone in the department, he wanted to be just like him. The man was clearly a master at his craft.

"Have you been having trouble sleeping at night?"

"Uh, well, yeah I guess."

"Then be glad you've never been to Poland. Did you serve in the war?"

"I was in the Merchant Marines. We took on some torpedo fire once, but that was about it. I was a cook."

"I can't tell you what I did, and you don't want to know, but I found some things in Poland that no one was supposed to find. How do you like coming across a few bones once in awhile? Is it everything you thought it would be?"

"No, sir. I don't really care for it."

"Try digging up a trench with thousands."

"I don't see what this has to do with—"

"Do you like Jews, Deputy?"

"I, I, can't say as I know any."

"The Germans didn't care for them, even the Jews who were German. They liked Polish Jews even less. They had names for them, too, so casually cast about like you did with Mr. Jones."

"I said I ain't meant nothin' by it," Ricky protested.

"I've met Mr. Jones, Ricky, and I've worked with you for a bit. Don't take this the wrong way, but you ain't half the man Mr. Jones is."

Ricky fumed inside. He didn't understand where he had gone wrong. The old man was just a nigger. Why was Stallworth getting all worked up over it?

"Thousands, Ricky, thousands of bodies. There were other places, too. Some had emaciated bodies stacked up so high you couldn't see over them. Women, children, you name it. Millions. All because some people thought they were better than other people."

Robert looked at the man before him and wanted to shake him. He wanted to make him see what he'd seen. Anything to get through to him, but he knew it was futile.

"But, this ain't Poland," Robert continued. "Is it, Ricky?"

"No, sir. Good thing, too."

"Agreed. We don't do things like that here, do we?"

"No, sir."

"Yeah, I used to think that, too, until I found a burnt sixteen year old boy hanging from a tree one day. The boys at the local sheriff's office said, and I quote, 'He had it comin'.' I found out later he was accused of talking to a white girl. You think he had it coming, Ricky?"

"I suppose not."

"You suppose not, but we ain't Poland. You're standing in the mud digging out rib bones. We have a collection lying on a tarp at Dr. Hall's. But we ain't Poland."

"I get your point. I'm sorry. It won't happen again."

"See that it doesn't." Robert said all he was going to say on the matter. He'd meant every word. One more racial epitaph and Ricky was on the shit list permanently. "So, let's suppose there was more than one person involved in this, maybe even a group, but they aren't the Klan. One or more resides nearby and is familiar with the area. That narrows it down quite a bit, doesn't it? Considering that nobody has come forward yet, they must be pretty close to stick together. Just imagine how gruesome this task was. We're not left with much, which is good."

"I'm not following."

"You will." Robert changed course and inquired, "Have you heard the phrase, 'habeas corpus' before?"

"It's a legal term pertaining to having enough evidence to hold someone and charge them with a crime," Ricky proudly proclaimed. He had learned about it when he was training to be a policeman, and he'd always liked the exotic sound of the words.

"It's Latin for 'you shall have the body'. It's fitting, don't you think?"

"We have them," said Ricky. "Well, except for the heads."

"Who are they?" asked Robert.

Ricky had no answers.

"Which brings us back to square one," said Robert. "We'll find suspects soon enough, and once we isolate him, her, or they, I'll squeeze them so tight they'll sing. We might even find the mementos that were so lovingly kept."

"The heads?"

Robert nodded. Someone had them. If it were more than one person who had done this, Robert wagered that only one kept them and hadn't told the others. If they found them, it was all over but the crying.

"But first things first," Robert continued. "Two girls are dead. They came from somewhere. Someone is missing them. We solve this puzzle first. Then, we bring down the hammer."

"How come no one's reported them missing?"

"You tell me."

"I, I don't know. Maybe they were the ones that did it."

"Yep, that thought has occurred to me. Or?"

CLAYTON E. SPRIGGS

"Or?" Ricky asked. He drew a blank.

Robert's eyes drew away, scanning the surroundings. He was not seeing what was in front of him as much as he was looking within that dark place that he fought to keep hidden. It was that same dark place that kept him up at night and helped him understand the evil that others do. He used it to hunt them down, knowing full well that the same inner thoughts resided in him. It's why he was so good at his job. It's why he could find the buried secrets of others. It's why he knew what the other option was and had little doubt that it would be the answer to the riddle.

Robert sighed and turned to the deputy, asking again, "Or?"

"Or they're dead, too," said Ricky.

CHAPTER FORTY-FIVE

A buzz hung in the air when Robert stopped by the sheriff's office the next morning. He went to the station in spurts, careful to make his visits as hard to predict as his motivations. The detective's presence kept the officers on edge. He wanted to keep it that way.

"Okay, I'll go ahead and ask," Robert announced as he passed the front desk. "What's all the commotion about?"

"Commotion?" asked Deputy Smith, the unattractive smile he fought so hard to hide in sharp contrast to his question.

"Don't play coy, Deputy. It doesn't suit you. I can feel it in the air. What am I going to find back there?"

Clyde surrendered to his excitement and gushed, "She's a real looker, I'll say that much."

Robert looked at the blushing oaf behind the tall desk and allowed himself to smile in return. He was much better at hiding his inner feelings than the deputy, but he was just as delighted with the turn of events. Claire Montgomery had arrived.

The detective made his way through the maze of desks, noting how the men present were doing their best to suck in their guts and exhibit whatever version of masculinity they imagined appropriate. Robert observed that even the petty criminals in various stages of being questioned or detained mimicked the officers.

The policemen smiled and nodded towards the detective as he passed. That was definitely a new development. Up to that moment, he'd been greeted with scorn and disdain. *Leave it up to a woman to change the dynamics in any room*, thought Robert. And Claire was not just any woman.

He walked straight to Sheriff Fuller's office, briefly tapped on the closed door that was usually open, and went right on in without being invited.

The sheriff jumped at the intrusion. His face morphed into a grimace before he caught himself. He grinned like a politician as he stood up, greeting the detective warmly as if they were long lost brothers. He offered his hand and squeezed Robert's upper arm, then motioned for him to pull up a chair and join in the discussion of the investigation.

Claire was standing at the sheriff's side, examining the map sprawled out on the cluttered desk. She pretended to be unaware that, while she'd spent the last fifteen minutes pouring over the details of the swamp's terrain and assorted colored pins marking the spots where they'd recovered the body parts, Sheriff Fuller had been pouring over the woman's ample cleavage and firm derriere outlined through her thin, crimson summer dress.

Same ol' Claire, Robert thought. He suppressed the urge to throw a faux tantrum at the sheriff's lack of good sense and protocol at giving an unknown civilian unlimited access of evidence in an ongoing criminal investigation involving the double homicide of two children. He knew it would've been wasted effort. Nobody could resist Claire. She was as talented at getting information out of people as she was beautiful. Robert recognized that the two were hardly contradictory attributes.

"I believe you know Miss Montgomery," said the sheriff as if he were doing Robert a favor by introducing her to him.

"Oh, don't be so formal, darlin'. You can call me Claire." She laughed and patted his back. Robert noted that the physical contact made the sheriff adjust himself in his seat.

"Miss Montgomery." Robert nodded, reaching over and gently shaking her hand. "It is still Miss, isn't it?"

Robert stared intently into her dazzling green eyes and tried to hide the sudden rush of excitement he felt in her presence. She met his gaze without wavering and replied coolly, "Why yes, yes it is."

"Well, well, that does surprise me," Fuller interrupted, growing jealous of Stallworth's intrusion. *Who invited this asshole in here anyway?* "A pretty girl like you should have no trouble finding a good man."

"Oh, I've found them, darlin'," said Claire. "It's keeping them that's been the hard part."

Robert tried not to laugh as he watched the sheriff blush when Claire subtly emphasized the words *hard part*, even as the deeper meaning of her comment hadn't gone unnoticed by him. He ignored it and moved on. It was part of the game.

"I see the good sheriff has been going over the investigation with you," said Robert. "Do you have any thoughts on the matter?"

"More questions than thoughts for the moment," she replied. "I feel stupid for asking this, but don't y'all have any idea who these girls were? I know if they were my little ones, I'd be beside myself with worry. Surely, someone has reported them missing."

"Not a clue, Miss Mont—, I mean, Claire." Fuller smiled despite himself at the use of the attractive female's first name. "You'd think missing twins would be easy to track down."

"How do you know they're twins?" she asked.

"We're pretty sure. Their remains match identically, according to the medical examiner. I'm sure the detective can tell you better than I can about that."

Robert stayed silent. He knew Claire was working the sheriff, and he was curious as to where she was going.

"How many twins live in the area?" she asked.

"Not many," the sheriff responded. The truth was, he didn't know. They hadn't bothered to check on anyone not reported missing.

"Four sets," Robert was compelled to answer. Billy had researched the lead at Robert's request on the first day. "One of the sets is no longer a set and another is middle aged or older; the others are accounted for."

"No longer a set?" Claire asked.

"One of the gentlemen passed away years ago. The other pair is in their fifties."

"What do you mean accounted for?"

"By the size of the bones, Miss, I mean, Claire," the sheriff offered. "We're looking for girls in early adolescence or younger."

"They could be midgets," she said.

"They're accounted for," Robert replied. Leave it to Claire to consider all the possibilities. There's an old saying amongst investigators, 'When you hear hoof beats, think of horses, not zebras'. In the majority of cases, the most obvious answer turns out to be the correct one. Many a detective fell into the trap of over-thinking only to find out the man standing over the body holding a bloody knife was the culprit all along. Claire thought of horses, and zebras, and antelopes, and bison, and the occasional horse dressed up as a unicorn. If it turned out to be a goat, she'd be the one to have mentioned that it could've been a goat.

"Maybe they're just similar and not twins," she said.

"Maybe," said Fuller, "but the detective thinks otherwise." The sheriff hadn't put much thought into the matter. It had been the detective who had pushed the idea of twins. His theory was seconded by the medical examiner, and Fuller went along. In truth, he was intimidated by their discussions of anatomy, and he didn't want to expose his ignorance and ask questions.

Claire skipped past the remark. She'd get an update from Robert later. This was all about the sheriff. "And there are no reports of missing twins or girls of that age in neighboring counties or states?"

"We haven't found any," said Fuller.

Claire looked at Robert.

"Watts looked into it and came up blank," he said.

Claire nodded. If Billy hadn't found anything, her job was going to be tough. "I see by the pins in the map that the parts were found to be haphazardly strewn about the area, both corpses intermixed with each other, but put there at roughly the same time. About four to five months ago. Is that correct?"

"Yes, ma'am, it is." There was something in the way Claire asked the question that made the sheriff think they'd missed something vital.

"Are y'all sure they were put there at the same time?"

"We're sure," Fuller said.

"Approximately," corrected Robert.

"Approximately?" Claire asked.

"The same relative time," Robert explained. "By the pattern of where we found them, Hall thinks they were cut up, packaged, and mixed up at another location and disposed of on one visit."

"But you don't?"

"I don't know, but my gut says that they were murdered elsewhere at separate times, cut up, and deposited on separate visits within days, if not hours, of each other. I'm going with days," added Robert, "consecutive days."

Sheriff Fuller was getting annoyed at being left out of the discussion, but he had no clue why any of this mattered, or how on earth the detective and medical examiner could possibly know such a thing.

"Consecutive days?" asked Claire.

"The first on day one; the next, the following day."

"I hate to leave you out of this, darlin'." Claire smiled at the sheriff and patted his back again. "But I really must hear this."

Fuller smiled at the slightly mocking tone that Claire had used. *She's not buying this know-it-all's bullshit, either,* he thought. Quite the contrary to her act, Claire knew better, and she was dying to know what was going on in Robert's head. She'd loved his dry wit and warped sense of humor, and she'd been attracted to his bookish, but strangely rugged, good looks since the first time they'd met. But it was his keen intellect that drew her in. His sense of justice and empathy was what ultimately made her fall in love with him. Thanks to the war, those were the same traits that had shattered her hopes of a happy future with him.

"Going out there at night is out of the question. It would take time, and a strong stomach, to murder and dismember even one person. I'm thinking one at a time would be the limit for anyone to handle. Once you finished the task, you'd need a break, so it's likely, the next day it was the second girl's turn."

"Maybe it was more than one person," said Claire.

"Most likely," Robert agreed, "but still, two bodies, two days. It's a lot of mayhem for one day."

"Why the next day?"

"Too many trips, the more likely you'd be seen. More time in between, the more likely the parts would be spread out or a different location used. No, they wanted to get it over with and forget about it. Well, all but one. One of them wanted to remember."

"The heads?" asked Claire.

Robert nodded, "The heads. Not that it'll matter soon enough. I'm quite certain that none of them have been able to forget what they've done."

Yep, that's the Robert I remember, thought Claire. "I'm quite certain you won't let them, darlin'."

"That's why you're here," said Robert.

Claire nodded, stood up, and patted Sheriff Fuller on the back one more time before announcing, "Then let's get to work."

CHAPTER FORTY-SIX

Much to Sheriff Fuller's delight, the two didn't leave together. Claire hung around briefly, going over copies of the reports that Stallworth had insisted the sheriff write. Robert excused himself to run some unnamed errand.

When Claire left, she headed straight to meet with Billy. He'd have a summary of every avenue related to his search for the girls' identities that she'd need to get started. After that, she agreed to meet with Robert at the medical examiner's office.

Claire was both excited and wary of the meeting later. She'd heard about the macabre display Robert had constructed in the empty room at the morgue. It was classic Stallworth. As much as she yearned to hear his theories on the girls and their untimely demise, seeing their remains scattered about the floor would bring the horror of the situation from the theoretical to the very real. Claire knew she'd have the stomach for it. It wasn't her first go round with murder victims, but she lacked the depth of detachment to such repulsive visions that Robert had earned. She was grateful. She remembered what a changed man he was when he had returned from Europe, and she wanted no part of it.

Billy opened the door to his hotel room before Claire had the chance to knock. He gave her a fatherly hug, kissed her on the cheek, invited her in, and closed the door.

The place was a mess. Papers and reports were stacked up in various piles throughout the cramped quarters. The walls were covered in maps, documents, and, most disturbing of all, photographs. The pictures ranged from mug shots of sexual offenders, ghastly photos of the recovered body parts, to rows upon rows of missing children posters.

Sadness crept into Claire's heart. How so many children could have been abducted from their homes, yet nobody but the loved ones seemed to know about it? It was a well known fact in her line of work that, no matter how horrendous and terrifying an incident was, it was soon forgotten by the general public within weeks of occurring, being systematically replaced by other shocking events. Claire knew firsthand that the families of those missing children would never forget, and neither would she.

"I see you've done your homework as usual, Captain Watts."

"Awe shucks, ma'am," Billy kidded as he pretended to be embarrassed by the compliment. He put his hands in his pockets and looked away while swinging his feet awkwardly to enhance his impersonation of a bashful kid.

Claire laughed. Billy smiled in return. He'd noticed the depressed look in her eyes when she'd seen the posters, cognizant of the tragedies in her own family's past. So he took it upon himself to lighten the mood.

"I've about exhausted every lead I found when it came to identifying the girls," said Billy. "It's going to be up to you now. I hope you're ready for a challenge."

"That's why I'm here."

"Is it?" asked Billy, his knowing gaze shooting through Claire's hardened shell.

"Yes," she answered, not wholly convinced of her resolve in the matter.

"Well, we're happy to have you aboard."

"I'm not so sure everybody is happy," protested Claire.

Billy knew where she was going. "He is. It's just hard for him to see you again after all this time."

"And it's easy for me?"

"I suppose not." Billy felt like he was intruding on the pair's unspoken agreement, but he had no choice but to continue. "We really need your help on this one. Robert has made unbelievable progress so far, but it's not going to be enough. To tell you the truth, I don't know how he does it. His father was my partner, you know."

"I know," said Claire. She knew little about Robert's father because he'd refused to discuss it in all the time she'd known him.

She knew that he was a veteran from the First World War, along with Watts, and they became partners in the state police after their time in the service. She also knew that the senior Stallworth had remained bitter about his stint in the army, and he'd felt burned over the Bonus Army fiasco that occurred when it came time to get what they'd been promised.

By all accounts, Robert's father had been detached and unloving with his family and had ignored his son altogether. His wife, Robert's mother, exhibited signs of depression and paranoia, probably the result of an undiagnosed mental illness, which left Robert to raise himself. Robert, inquisitive even at an early age, had thought of himself as an unwanted addition to the family, a disappointment in the eyes of his parents.

In reality, his father bent his partner's ear relentlessly about the boy's intellectual gifts, confiding to Billy that even he felt intimidated at times by his boy's capacity to find the truth. This unspoken phenomenon created more distance between the two as time went on, or they might've otherwise bonded. The elder Stallworth was afraid of what his son would think about him if he knew about his violent actions and cowardice in the trenches when the flamethrowers made their unwelcome appearance. He was ashamed of his mistreatment of Robert's mother and his ever-escalating drinking problem.

Watts had listened to his partner's lamentations and encouraged him to bide his time. He recognized that Robert already knew how poorly his mother had been treated and might not harbor as much resentment as his father imagined. The boy understood his mother's illness in ways the older man never could. As horrified by the outbreak of the Second World War as Billy had been, he knew the younger Stallworth would see his share of atrocities and have a greater understanding of the torments his father suffered.

He'd prayed that, one day, the two would come to terms with their estrangement, but it was not to be. A routine traffic stop ended the elder Stallworth's life on the side of a little used, rural highway. He bled out on the lonely stretch of Alabama highway, taking his last breath at the hands of a lone gunman. The result was that father and son lost the chance to really know each other. The unknown gunman was never apprehended.

"Even the old man would've been impressed by Robert's abilities. He had his own methods of getting to the truth. Let me tell you, they were very effective."

"I've heard stories."

"Nobody but me will ever know the real stories, and I'll never tell," Billy said. "In any case, with the Stallworth brain or not, we're dead in the water without the Montgomery charm."

Claire laughed, ceremoniously fanning herself and replying in her best Scarlett O'Hara impression, "I do declare!" Taking a more serious tone, she said, "Now that we got the schmoozing out of the way, where should I start?"

"Dr. Jack's office," said Billy. "Is Robert going to meet you there later?"

"You know it. I can't say as I'm looking forward to it."

Billy cocked an eyebrow, so Claire elaborated, "About what Robert has waiting for me over at the medical examiner's. Not about meeting up with him. I saw the good detective earlier."

"Did you now? And?"

"Same ol' Robert," said Claire. "He's mighty popular at Dale's place."

"Dale?"

"Sheriff Fuller," Claire explained.

They laughed.

"Same ol' Claire," said Billy. Claire smiled but said nothing. Her eyes scanned the posters on the wall again. Looking for a place to rest, they found a picture of the dismembered foot with the fishing line attached that had started the investigation. The corners of her mouth turned down; the skin on her forehead furrowed.

"No doubt, you've heard about Robert's little display at the doctor's," said Billy.

Claire remained silent. She'd heard. It was what brought her there. Robert's eccentric methods notwithstanding, she was going to find out who the girls were and take them home.

CHAPTER FORTY-SEVEN

"How come we always have to meet over at my place?" asked Cooter.

There was a time when he loved coming out to the secluded stretch of land he'd inherited. He used to find solace in taking long walks, surrounded by the wonders of nature. Cooter ingratiated himself with his friends in the church by offering his place for gatherings of the other deacons. Even Brother Eustice and his sons looked forward to the invitations, and, over time, the place became a retreat for the disciples of the great prophet. Cooter had been pleased. It made him feel like a big shot.

"We always meet here," Charles Ray replied. "What's the big deal?"

"You know what the big deal is," protested Cooter. "Don't play dumb."

Since the incident, he no longer wanted to set foot on the property. He was even more hesitant to have the deacons there, especially with that pesky detective from the state police nosing around. The man made Cooter nervous by sheer reputation. He hadn't actually talked to him, and he wanted to keep it that way.

"It's the only place where prying eyes won't see us all together and ask questions," Joe Bob explained.

"We're usually together," said Cooter. "We've known each other our whole lives. It's not seein' us together that'll make people wonder."

Over the past few months, their devotion to the cause had waned. Few members showed up together or acknowledged each other at services, with the exception of polite nods and brief small talk. Someone always had an excuse why they were unable to attend some function or another.

"My wife has already asked me about it," said Charles Ray.

"Mine, too," Earl agreed.

"You ain't said nothin' to her, I hope," Cooter said.

"Of course not," said Charles Ray. "What am I gonna say? 'Sorry, honey, we're takin' a break from each other since we murdered that girl.'"

"Twice," added Joe Bob.

Their attention was drawn to the sedan. The Winchesters had arrived.

"I'm glad to see we've all managed to gather at the same time for a change," Brother Eustice said accusingly. "We've become an assembly of backsliders. We must be careful, brothers, lest we let the Devil see our weakened resolve and seek to divide us."

"I was just sayin' that," said Cooter.

"You were also whinin' about us meetin' here," Charles Ray added.

"Were you now?" Brother Eustice said. "And why is that?"

"Because you know why," answered Cooter. "That nosey detective is bound to come around sooner or later."

Brother Eustice nodded. He looked to Earl for an explanation. "He's right. Do you have any idea why he ain't asked us any questions yet? He has a list of all of our names. Seemed mighty interested in us when he first come down here. Since then, zilch."

"How am I supposed to know?" said Earl. "It ain't like I can rightly ask him that."

"No, I suppose not," said Brother Eustice. "Still, it seems odd. What's he up to?"

"I've heard things," said Earl. "Weird things that don't make no sense."

"Such as?" asked Junior. Unlike the others, he wasn't afraid of the detective. Let the man come and ask him whatever he wanted to. He'd learn soon enough who the smart one was.

"For one thing, some dame he knows came in askin' questions. Dale pretty much let her have full access to whatever they had. He won't even share that with me, and I'm an officer of the law."

"Why the hell did he do that?" asked Junior.

Whack! Brother Eustice's walking stick found its favorite target.

"Ouch!" screamed Junior, clutching his shin. "What did you do that for?"

"Don't use them vile words," said Brother Eustice. "'For his mouth speaks from what which fills his heart.' Tell us, Deputy, why did the good sheriff give that woman free reign?"

"If you'd seen her, you wouldn't be askin' that," Earl replied. "Not that it matters. He did."

"What else troubles you about the detective?"

"There's a rumor he has a display at the medical examiner's office."

"A display?"

"They say he has the bones laid out like a giant puzzle. They're puttin' the parts together to figure out where they came from."

They? Buck thought. Something deep inside of him stirred.

"And what do they know?" Brother Eustice asked.

"Not much, from what I gather, or they wouldn't still be lookin'."

Brother Eustice nodded. The deputy wasn't as dumb as he looked.

"Have they found all the parts yet?" asked Jeremiah.

"Save for a few small pieces," Earl said. "But that's another weird thing. I've heard through the grapevine that the heads are missing."

"Heads?" asked Buck. "As in more than one?"

"Yeah," said Earl. "They think the girls were twins."

"Are you shittin' me!" shouted Buck. "Twins? Goddamn it, Eustice. What have you gotten us into?"

All eyes turned to the preacher. He wanted to respond with force and indignation at his accuser, but it was Buck McEwen. Buck was big, and Buck was now furious. He was also Brother Eustice's most faithful servant. If he turned on the preacher, the others would soon follow.

"This is exactly what I warned you about," said the prophet. "'Put on the full armor of God, so that you will be able to stand firm against the schemes of the Devil.' The detective is trying to trick us. We've turned from the Lord, and now we're turnin' on each other. It is not I that led you astray, brothers. It is the unholy one who seeks revenge for our pious acts."

No one replied to his sermon, but the preacher could see the doubt behind their angry glares. He needed a distraction.

"How and why?" Brother Eustice asked the deputy.

"How and why what?"

"How did he find all them parts? We were the ones that put them there. It would've been impossible to find them all, but he did. It's unnatural, I tell you."

"I, I don't know," said Earl. "Ricky was helpin' him, but he doesn't like to talk about it. He's been actin' strange lately, like he thinks he's better than us. That detective has him under some kind of spell."

"That's what I'm sayin', you fools," said Brother Eustice. "He was sent from the pit of hell itself. Satan works in him. There's no other explanation."

"You asked why," noted Earl. "Why what?"

"Why ain't they found the head if they found everythin' else?"

"You mean head*sssss*," said Buck, the anger in his eyes unabated by the preacher's feeble explanation.

Brother Eustice ignored the taunt. "We didn't do anythin' different with it than we did with the other parts. Why ain't they found it, too?"

"I don't know," said Earl, "but from what I hear, it means somethin' to them."

"Who had the heads?" asked Cooter.

"It weren't me," said Charles Ray.

"Me, neither," said Joe Bob.

Buck shook his head.

"Don't look at me," said Earl. "I wasn't even here for one of them."

The men looked at the sons of the prophet.

"It wasn't me, Daddy," Jeremiah said. "I had the feet. Remember?"

Junior took a few steps back, ensuring he was out of range of his father's staff.

"What did you do?" asked the prophet, turning on his son.

Junior was at a loss for words. His mind raced with possible excuses, but he couldn't come up with a single one.

The sound of a car approaching interrupted the interrogation. The men turned to see who dared to ignore the half-dozen PRIVATE PROPERTY: TRESPASSERS WILL BE SHOT signs prominently posted on the secluded dirt road.

"I guess if you have any more questions about the detective," Earl said to Brother Eustice, "you can ask him yourself."

CHAPTER FORTY-EIGHT

The group huddled together as they watched the detective's unmarked police cruiser approach.

"Y'all let me handle this," said Earl. "And try to act natural."

"Don't fuck this up," said Charles Ray.

"Shut up," Earl replied, "and that means all of you."

The car stopped, and the detective climbed out. He walked over to where the men waited.

"Howdy," he announced and tipped his hat. "I'm Detective Stallworth of the Alabama State Police. Y'all can call me Robert."

Silence greeted him. Robert smiled as if they were old friends.

"Deputy Barber, it's a pleasure to see you again."

Earl nodded. "Detective. What are you doin' out here?" Earl's voice cracked slightly. He hoped the detective hadn't noticed. Robert had.

"You got a warrant?" Cooter blurted out.

Earl felt his heart drop. *What part of 'shut up' didn't Cooter understand?*

Robert paused, as if surprised by the response. "A warrant? Now why would I need a warrant?"

"This here is private property. You got no right to come out here to harass us or search," Cooter protested.

"Search? Why would I search?" Robert asked as if it were a rhetorical question. He furrowed his brow and scratched his chin, letting everyone know that the man's objection had presented a new lead.

"Don't mind him," Earl interjected. "He acts that way when anyone comes out here. He even does it to me, and we've known each other since the third grade. Is there anything we can do for you, Detective?"

"Right, right," said Stallworth, playing along. "I've been meaning to get together with you and your friends. It's just that we've been so busy. We've found most of the bones that we know of so far, so I hadn't actually required your offer to help with the search. I know you boys have already given a great deal of your time and effort, and I didn't want to impose on y'all any further. I did want to add how much I appreciate what y'all did. I don't know if the sheriff ever thanked y'all for helping out, but it didn't go unnoticed by me."

Robert paused to let that last line sink in.

"We appreciate that," said Brother Eustice.

"And you must be Brother Eustice Winchester," Robert announced. "I've heard a lot about you, and I must say, I've been dying to meet you."

Brother Eustice nodded but held his tongue. As pleasant as the words sounded coming out of the detective's mouth, the preacher knew it was a veiled threat.

"Excuse my lack of manners," said Earl. "Let me introduce everyone."

"No need, Deputy," said Robert. "Let's see if I can guess. The man to your left is Joe Bob Duncan; next to him is Charles Ray Wilson. The big guy, who looks sick to his stomach, is Buck McEwen. The guy who's afraid I'll have a look around is Cooter Yates. The scared looking young man over there in the overalls is Jeremiah Thomas Winchester, also known as JT. The other fellow with the smug expression and missing teeth is Eustice Adam Winchester, also known as Junior. Of course the ring leader, I mean, the pastor of the

Antioch Pentecostal Church is none other than Eustice Elijah Winchester, self proclaimed prophet."

"How'd you know all that?" asked Joe Bob.

"I'm a detective, Mr. Duncan. It's my job to know things. I have files on each and every one of you. I know where you live," he said as he glanced at Cooter. "I know your wives and children's names. I know your criminal history." He glanced at Buck. "I probably know what you had for breakfast in the third week in May when you were six." Robert laughed. "But don't feel special. I know that about half the people in the county."

The men were beginning to believe the preacher may have been right about the detective. Only supernatural forces could explain how the man could know so much about things he had no way of knowing.

"What do you want from us?" Brother Eustice asked coldly.

"I want your help," Robert replied. It wasn't the answer they expected.

"How can we help you? You already seem to know everything."

"Not everything or I wouldn't be out here. First, I need to know if you men can keep what I'm going to tell you in strictest confidence. Can I trust you men? Do you know how to keep a secret?"

"Yes, we do," Junior blurted out and flinched, expecting a sharp blow to the shin that never came.

"I thought as much," Robert replied.

Earl didn't like this one bit. It was as if every comment the detective made had some hidden meaning. It was as if he were telling them all, *I know what you did, and I'm going to hang you for it.* Earl swallowed hard and fought against his instincts. He told himself it was his suppressed guilt getting to him.

"You boys popped up on my radar from the very beginning," Robert continued. "I mean, it just didn't fit. Y'all didn't fit. Everyone involved in the investigation from day one had some obvious and explainable reason for being where they were, and they acted accordingly. Nothing was out of place, except you boys. That's why I know so much about y'all. I made it my business to know."

"If you're suggestin' we had anything—" Cooter said.

"What Cooter means is that it sounds like you are makin' accusations," Earl interrupted before Cooter could finish. *Shut the hell up already, for God's sake.*

"Accusations?" Robert replied as if it he'd never thought of that. "No, no, absolutely not! Is that what y'all think? Oh, my goodness, no wonder y'all are looking at me like that. Please, forgive me. I completely mucked this up. Accusations? Y'all are men of God. A church group would be the last people I'd suspect of doing something so horrible. I can't share with you what I know of the case, but let me tell you, it's bad. Whoever did this was a sick, depraved pervert. Nobody with a shred of decency could've committed such a heinous act on another human being, much less a child. If they could, I don't see how they could live with themselves. I'm sure men of such high moral standards as yourselves would agree. Sick, sick, sick."

"Then why are you—" Cooter asked again.

"Like I said, y'all stuck out, but not in the way you're thinking I mean it. Let me tell you boys a story. Again, it's not something I want repeated."

"You have our word," said Brother Eustice.

"Despite my college background, I came from a small town just like this. I was raised to be a devout follower of the local Southern Baptist congregation. I truly believed in our Lord and Savior, Jesus Christ, and I still do. However, something happened when I was fifteen that shattered my illusions about my fellow men. A child had been raped, strangled, and dumped into a nearby river. The town elders, including the pastor of my church, who also happened to be the sheriff, quickly nabbed a suspect. He was a colored fellow from the wrong side of the tracks, some ex-convict with a rap sheet a mile long. We didn't waste time on a trial or jury, not that it would've mattered; we hanged him that night for all to see. I witnessed the hate and violence of the very people I'd sat next to in church my whole life and I slept soundly that night. It's something that I've thought about ever since. Anyway, seven months later, it happened again. Even then, it didn't occur to me that we'd murdered an innocent man. No, this time, we had a lead. A group of fishermen saw the car that dumped the body and wrote down the license plate."

"Who was it?" asked Earl.

"The sheriff," said Robert. "The very man who led our Sunday sermons and taught us the value of leading a moral life. Can you believe it?"

They could.

"So that's why I'm here."

"I'm, I'm not gettin' what you're sayin'," said Cooter.

"Don't you get it? It was a conspiracy. Others knew what the sick bastard had done but helped cover it up. They sat idly by while we murdered an innocent man. Notice I said we. I'll have to pay for that come Judgment Day, along with a long list of other things. I'm not going to let that happen again. I can't trust a soul in this county, up to and including anyone at the sheriff's office. Well, maybe one. Like I said, you boys don't fit. That's a good thing, but it might be bad for y'all, too."

"What do you mean?" asked Earl.

"Whoever did this is going to need someone to pin it on. They'll need that colored fellow to hang for it. Unfortunately for them and you, it was old man Lucius who found that foot. No one is going to stand for blaming him, not even the Grand Wizard of the Ku Klux Klan. Once I start the endgame, the pressure will be on to find someone else to take the blame. Who do you think that'll be?"

"But they can't do that," said Jeremiah. "That's not right."

"If you'd only seen what the sick bastard did to that girl," Robert replied.

"I heard there was more than one," said Buck.

"You're going to hear a lot of things, Mr. McEwen," Robert said and winked.

"Why, you clever son of a bitch," said Joe Bob.

Robert smiled. "Just don't say I didn't warn y'all."

"But I still don't know what we can do to help you," said Brother Eustice.

"Play along," said Robert. "At some point, I'm going to lure those responsible into thinking they're going to get away with it. I'll set the trap, and they'll walk right into it, practically handing the evidence to me on a silver platter. Now, think about it. How do you think I'm going to do that?"

"By blamin' us," said Earl.

"The bullshit interrogations are going to be brutal, guys. I'm letting you know now. I'm going to stay in character, and I'm expecting you to do the same. The walls have ears over there. One by one, I'll eventually drag y'all in and go through the motions. Don't be alarmed, but I'm good at what I do. It's going to seem very real, and it'll be very scary. I know you boys think you're brave and will skate right through it, especially since you know it's a con. But trust me, I can get you to confess to the Lincoln assassination, if I want to, so don't get cocky. We'll get through this, and everything will be fine. You'll all get a medal when it's over, and you'll deserve it. But first things first, we may never get to that stage unless I connect a few dots. Let's pray that I do."

With that, Robert bid his adieu and parted. The group pledged their support and thanked him for the warning. They promised that they'd do whatever was required to find and convict the guilty parties. They watched him leave with relief.

"I told you he wasn't as smart as he pretends to be," said Earl.

"Don't be naïve, Deputy," said Brother Eustice. "He knows it was us."

"He knows it was you," Buck corrected him.

"No, he knows it was us, just like he knows what you done. How do you think that's going to look, pervert?"

Brother Eustice was losing control of his flock at the worse time, but he'd be damned if he was going to go down alone.

"How could he know?" asked Charles Ray.

"I told you how," Brother Eustice replied. "Because he was sent by Lucifer."

Robert guided his car down the lonely dirt road, lost in his thoughts. The meeting with Deputy Barber and the church group had gone exactly as he'd planned. He'd waited patiently until he could catch them all together, and they didn't disappoint. They'd even led him to the likely scene of the crime. Unfortunately, it appeared that they'd done a rather thorough job of cleaning it up. It would be extremely beneficial if he could find some physical evidence to link the girls to Cooter Yates' property. Robert wondered if the heads were buried there.

As Stallworth pondered his predicament, a strange glint coming from an unknown object off to the side of the road caught his eye. It was as if a divine answer to his prayers had suddenly appeared. He stopped the car and walked over to the nearby ditch. He shifted through the dirt until he found the item. Robert stood up and examined the unusual object before slipping it into his pocket and resuming his journey. It was time to meet Claire at Dr. Hall's office. He couldn't wait to show her his latest work of art.

CHAPTER FORTY-NINE

Robert arrived at the medical examiner's office to find Claire and Dr. Hall already in the adjoining room admiring his handiwork.

"Well, darlin', it looks like you've really outdone yourself this time," said Claire. "*The Bone Puzzle.*"

Robert nodded in appreciation, and the three returned their collective gaze to the pile of bones on the floor. Robert and Dr. Hall had painstakingly positioned the skeletal remains, side by side, as they'd collected them. By the time Claire had arrived, they were nearly complete. The result was two identical sets of miniature skeletons without the skulls. As detached as they tried to be, the three struggled to hold their feelings of sadness and disgust in check as they looked down.

"It makes me want to cry," noted Claire.

"It should," said Dr. Hall.

"And you haven't been able to identify them?" she asked.

"No, not that we haven't tried," said the doctor. "We know they're twins, or we are pretty sure, anyway. We know they were girls. We know they were anywhere from eleven or twelve years old to maybe sixteen tops. We know they were murdered and dismembered separately anywhere from four to six months ago—we're going with late April, early May, for now—by person or persons unknown and unfamiliar with anatomy. We know that no one has reported them missing as far as we can determine. We know they weren't from around here because of the previous fact, but that the killer or killers were familiar with the area in which they were dumped. So he, she, or they either reside here at the present time, or has resided here in the past. We don't know how they died, or who killed them."

"Do we?" Claire asked Robert.

"Do we what?"

"Do we know who killed them?" she asked again. He'd been up to something in the weeks before she'd arrived, other than to construct the macabre exhibit on the floor, and she was curious as to what that was.

"Possibly," he replied.

"Is that so?" asked Dr. Hall, clearly surprised by the revelation. "Do tell."

"I'm keeping that to myself for the moment," said Robert. "It's only a theory at this juncture. I don't want us to do this backwards. Let's let the evidence, or lack thereof, guide our hands for now. If we're unable to find success once Miss Montgomery does her thing, then I'll proceed with plan B."

"Plan B?" asked Dr. Hall.

"Pressure," replied Robert.

"What kind of pressure?"

"The kind that makes diamonds from lumps of coal, darlin'," Claire said. She'd tangled enough with Robert over trivial matters, like whose turn it was to walk the dog or who left the top off the toothpaste tube, to question his skills at interrogation. If they couldn't find out what they wanted to know one way, she had little doubt he'd get it another way.

Robert knew it, too, but he preferred it didn't come to that. If pushed hard enough, some people confessed to things they had no part in. They could be convicted and executed for crimes they hadn't committed, leaving the guilty party free to kill again. If exonerated, it left enough reasonable doubt to allow the correct suspect to walk.

"I see," said Dr. Hall.

No one said anything for a moment, but Claire could sense that there was something on Robert's mind. She watched him out of the corner of her eye until she noticed him subconsciously fiddle with an unseen object in his jacket pocket.

"What do you have there, darlin'?"

"What? Oh, nothing," he responded.

"It's not nothing. It's something, so what is it?"

"Just something I found in the dirt," Robert replied, pulling the object out of his pocket and holding it in the palm of his hand for Claire to see.

"That is unusual," said Claire as she examined the item.

"Where did you find that?" asked Dr. Hall.

"On the side of the road," said Robert, preferring to keep its exact location to himself for the moment.

"It doesn't look like it's from around here," noted Dr. Hall. "At lease, I've never seen anything like it around these parts."

"My thinking precisely," Robert agreed.

"It looks familiar," said Claire.

"Does it?" asked Robert.

Claire racked her brain. She couldn't remember where she'd seen it before, but was sure that she had. It was frustrating, and she let it go for the moment. "Yeah, but I'm drawing a blank."

"It's obviously fake," said the doctor.

"Yet unusual, all the same," Robert added. "I know one thing. It didn't belong where I found it."

"Do you think it has anything to do with the murdered girls?" asked Claire.

"It's hard to say, but I have a hunch." Robert was almost certain that it did, but he had no idea how, or in what manner.

"It looks like a ruby," said Claire. "Costume jewelry, for certain. Given its size and uncommon shape, I can't think of a piece of jewelry that it would adorn. What are you calling it?"

"Calling it?" asked Robert.

"Yeah, what are you calling it?" she answered. Claire glanced at the pile of bones meticulously placed on the tarp in the middle of the floor. "We have *The Bone Puzzle* here. What creative moniker are you going to subscribe to your phony ruby?"

Robert smiled. Claire knew him too well. He had a habit of giving things names, some sarcastic, some exaggerated, some comical, and, most of them, inappropriate. He already had one picked out for this one, but had yet to admit it.

"I call it *The Holy Relic*."

"*The Holy Relic?*" asked Dr. Hall. "Why *The Holy Relic?*"

"It's a sign from God."

PART FOUR:

REVELATION

But the beast was captured, and with him, the false prophet who had performed the signs on his behalf.

Revelation 19:20

CHAPTER FIFTY

Claire got right to work. She pored over the files that Watts had summarized as well as the reports that she'd gotten through her own channels, and soon determined that nothing was going to come easy. Cases of missing twins should've been an easy thing to track down, but since it hadn't turned out that way, something told Claire that there would be an unexpected reason that wasn't going to be pleasant. All the same, she needed an angle to pursue, and she found it.

As a private investigator, Claire had a collection of favors people owed her, and she wasted no time in cashing them in. Before long, her desk was covered in birth announcements. She was going to trace every report of multiple births in the Southeastern United States within the proposed age range of the missing girls and go through them one by one, paying particular attention to any that might've involved orphanages, adoptions, or foster homes. On the third day, she found something that had red flags waving all over it.

The Tennessee Children's Home Society was still occasionally in the news, even though the place had been shut down for years. She remembered hearing the sad and startling reports when the woman who had run the place had been arrested. Claire remembered thinking at the time how difficult it would be to clean that mess up. Since then, her misgivings had been proven correct. Inaccurate records, when there were records, had created a situation that resulted in hundreds, if not thousands, of children disappearing into the homes of strangers without a trace. Miss Georgia Tann, the proprietor of the disgraced Society, passed away in custody. Her name was forever tainted. She was the face of human trafficking.

The details of the crimes were horrendous. Children were taken from parents by a variety of means, only to be sold to anyone who had the cash. Minimal background checks were done on the new parents, false histories made for the children, and no little to no records kept after the adoptions. Even after the scam was exposed and shut down, no investigation was held to determine the fate of the children, and consequently, none were ever returned to their rightful parents.

Something told Claire that her answers would be found at the Home, and she quickly packed for the trip to Memphis. With or without the despicable Miss Tann, someone knew something they hadn't shared with investigators, and Claire was determined to find out what that something was.

The next morning, Claire talked her way into the abandoned orphanage. Rows upon rows of cots still lined the walls of several wards, a silent testament to the unlimited cruelty that evil people could inflict on the innocent while preying on the desperate. Each empty bed held a story of a lonely child, now, no doubt, grown into a damaged adult. Some told stories of mothers who had their babies snatched from their arms, never to be seen again. Others told of children who would know only victimization and exploitation in an uncaring world. Claire held back tears as she wandered through the maze of sadness, consoling herself with the realization that some must've found homes in the arms of loving parents.

"I know what you're thinking, ma'am," said Birdie, "and, believe me, it'll break your heart if you let it."

Birdie Andrews had worked in the orphanage for a brief spell over a decade before its closing. She'd left in disgust when her husband had a stroke and her two sons died in the war—long before anyone suspected the terrible abuses that had transpired there. In her grief, Birdie had tried to put the unpleasant memories behind her, but often found herself unable to forget about the children that she'd seen traded off as if they were nothing but commodities.

"How could it have gone on for so long?" asked Claire.

"I don't know, ma'am, but it did."

"And nobody ever asked you about it, even after the true nature of this place was discovered?"

"You're the first. Why would anyone want to talk with an old black woman like me? I was just a cleaning lady. They didn't pay me no mind when I worked here, and they ain't paid me no mind since. I ain't never forgot, though— 'specially them babies."

Birdie led Claire to a section at the end of one of the wards where a few empty bassinets stood, frozen in time.

"This is where they kept the little ones 'till they found them homes. Or at least, that's how they said it. In truth, they sold them." Birdie shook her head with dismay.

"Only three? I was expecting more," said Claire in surprise.

"The babies rarely stayed long. Most people want to adopt them when they small. Heck, most of the babies had homes before the Miss acquired them. It's a damn shame how she did that. Even I was shocked when I heard them stories. I knew that woman wasn't right in the head, but I'd of never thought she could of done what she done."

"I know what you mean, but she wasn't alone," Claire remarked. "What scares me is how many others were involved, and nobody said a thing."

"Now, I don't want you thinking I had anything to do with this," Birdie explained.

"No, of course not. I was referring to the doctors and prospective parents, and everybody else along the line."

"Yeah, I know what you mean. Those poor, poor children."

Claire couldn't agree more. "Miss Birdie, do you ever remember there being twin girls around the time you worked here?"

Birdie paused, as if she'd been slapped in the face. She looked at the empty bassinets and slowly nodded before replying, a tear in her eye, "I remember something."

CHAPTER FIFTY-ONE

After her preemptive investigation in Memphis, Claire drove around the suburbs of Chattanooga until she found the small cottage she was looking for. The neighborhood was middle class at best, but Claire could see that it was on the verge of decline. The only people living there now who would still be living there a decade later would be those unable to afford to move.

Claire adjusted her ill-fitting jacket and donned a pair of fake eyeglasses before marching up and knocking on the front door in her best 'serious business' imitation. After a couple of minutes, she saw someone peer through the curtains in the window to her right. Claire gripped the briefcase in her left hand and knocked again.

The door opened only a few inches and a disembodied voice asked, "Can, can I help you?"

"I'm looking for Mr. or Mrs. Ray Valence," replied Claire curtly.

"Who's asking?" the wary voice returned.

"Mrs. Ruth Valence, otherwise known as Ruth Henderson? Is that you?"

A pause told Claire that she was at the right address.

"Who are you, and what do you want?"

Claire sidestepped the introduction and said in an authoritative voice, "I'm here about the improprieties at the Tennessee Children's Home Society. I'm sure you're familiar with it, so let's not play games, Mrs. Valence. Are you going to let me in, or do we have to do this in a more public and humiliating way?"

Another pause, and the door swung open. A haggard, disheveled woman smoking a filter-less cigarette waved Claire in and closed the door behind her. Claire followed the woman to a small kitchen in the back and sat down at a worn dinette table. Ruth smashed her Lucky Strike out in an ashtray overflowing with the remains of at least half a carton of spent cigarette butts and lit another one. She offered Claire a drink, which Claire turned down. She stood up, retrieved a glass of what looked like water, but which Claire knew was vodka, then sat back down.

"I ain't got nothin' to say about what went on there," Ruth said. "I ain't seen my girls, Lacey and Laura, in years. If you want to know anything, you'd have to ask my good for nothing ex-husband, Dick. He took the kids from me and never looked back. The bastard."

"And where can I find your ex-husband?"

"Look under a rock or follow a swarm of flies. He's a real piece of shit."

Ruth took a swig of her elixir and another puff of her cigarette, clearly disgusted by how her life had turned out.

"I appreciate the sentiment, but that's not very helpful," said Claire.

"He's a bum," Ruth said, her voice sharp with bitterness. "Always was a bum; always will be a bum. Ray, my husband now, got Dick a job once, even helped us adopt two beautiful baby girls, and my ex shows his appreciation by quitting the job and running off to be in show business. Dick always had his head in the clouds. What a pathetic loser."

"Once again, not very helpful," countered Claire. "I've looked up Richard Henderson and came up blank. We have no current address. We looked up Lacey and Laura Henderson and got the same results. No school records. No records of any kind. Surely you know something that can help us."

Ruth laughed. *Cackled* was a more appropriate term for the offending sound, thought Claire.

"You ain't going to find out nothing that way," said Ruth. "He changed his name. He's in show business." Another burst of sarcastic laughing erupted. Ruth took another swig of her vodka and added, "The loser was going to use the girls in his act. Probably changed their names, too."

"I see," said Claire. She was getting nowhere. Her hopes were being diminished by the minute, but she had no choice except to pursue her line of questioning. The more she heard, the more her intuition told her that the Henderson girls were the ones she'd been searching for. "Tell me, Mrs. Valence, are the girls twins?"

"Identical. Ain't no way to tell them apart. Shit, even I couldn't tell. That's why Dick was so interested in them in the first place."

"I don't understand."

"For his stupid act," Ruth replied, as if that explained it all.

"His act?"

"He's a magician. Can you believe that? A grown man trying to make a living doing card tricks and such. I told you he's a loser."

The hair on the back of Claire's neck stood up. She thanked the bitter, drunken woman and quickly left.

When Claire had heard about the Children's Society, she remembered the news reports and connected the dots. It hadn't been too hard. The crime was well publicized; the reports went nationwide. When she heard the word 'magician', it was déjà vu. She recalled the grisly reports of the magic show gone awry in Memphis. The irony of a magician cut in half and the sick jokes it had spurred. She remembered it vividly because she remembered the magician.

Claire had been single for a number of years after she and Robert had broken things off. Although she'd never let go of her feelings for him, she occasionally accepted the offer of a night on the town from an available suitor. One such man, Frederick Mansfield, a successful business man who owned a string of feed stores, had taken her out for a night she couldn't forget. They'd eaten at a wonderful, out-of-the-way restaurant on the outskirts of Nashville, then he'd surprised her with tickets to the hottest show in town, the spectacular performance of The Amazing and Magnificent Villanova. It had been one of the greatest shows she had ever witnessed.

Memories flashed through her mind as Claire revved the car engine and hit the accelerator. She recalled the stage alive with snake charmers, Eastern mystics, and, most compelling of all, a small gypsy girl who seemed to appear and disappear at the magician's request, as if by magic. *Or,* Claire thought, *as if there were two of them.*

She also recollected the giant poster that graced the lobby. The fierce eyes and hypnotic pose of the great magician made you believe in his powers. His twisted mustache and long, pointed beard created an exotic, unearthly aura about him. Most of all, she remembered the strange turban on his head, with the odd shaped jewel at its center, the one Robert now had in his pocket—*The Holy Relic.*

CHAPTER FIFTY-TWO

"Looks like that didn't take long." Billy Watts couldn't believe his ears. Claire had been gone less than a week and seemed to have cracked the case wide open. Although she'd shared little in the way of details, she'd been adamant of the need for him to join her in Memphis immediately.

He left at the crack of dawn and arrived at the Memphis Police Station a little after noon. Claire had already been there for the greater part of the morning by the time Billy was escorted to the back.

"What did you find?" Billy asked. He could sense that a heated discussion had been ongoing prior to his arrival. Claire was in the company of two disgusted looking detectives. The men were clearly unhappy about Miss Montgomery's presence. Claire, on the other hand, was not the least put out by the men's stubbornness.

"She didn't find anything," one of the men said. "She's just some dame that came in to stir up trouble with a crazy story."

"I didn't get your name," said Billy.

"I didn't get yours either, Pops," the man replied.

"I'm Lieutenant William Watts, retired Chief Homicide Detective from the Alabama State Police."

"Retired, huh?" the man continued. "Shouldn't you be fishing?"

"Is that Billy Watts?" a booming voice called out from across the room.

The group turned to see a burly man with gray hair, wearing an impeccable police uniform, stroll up, his humongous hand outstretched to greet the unexpected guest.

"Charlie, it's good to see you again," Billy said as the two men shook hands.

"And who is this pretty lady?" asked Chief Charlie Higgins.

"Miss Claire Montgomery, a protégé of mine."

"So, you're Claire? I've heard about you."

"Have you now, darlin'?" said Claire, donning the crooked smile that had repeatedly gained her access to the most top secret files in law enforcement.

"I hope my men have been treating y'all right."

"Chief, we've already told her we've apprehended the killer. He's been tried and convicted," said one of the detectives.

"Is that so? What's this all about, Billy?" asked the chief.

Billy nodded towards Claire.

"It's about Lacey and Laura Henderson," she said.

"I've never heard of them."

"The twin daughters of Richard Henderson."

"It's not ringing a bell."

She looked around. "Anyone?"

Nobody said a word. Billy hid a smile. He didn't know either, but he was sure that whatever point Claire was trying to make, she'd already made it.

Claire pulled a faded poster from under a stack of files on a nearby desk and presented it like it was Exhibit A at the Supreme Court. "Otherwise known as The Amazing and Magnificent Villanova."

"You remember, Chief. The dead magician. We already know that Gibson did that, and the jury agreed."

"Yet you didn't even know his real name," noted Claire. "What else didn't you know, Detective?"

"I don't have to listen to this shit," the officer spat.

"Yes, you do, Jimmy," Chief Higgins corrected him. "Go on, Miss Montgomery, I'm sure there's more."

"The girls." Claire watched their reaction.

"See, that's what we mean, Chief," the other detective chimed in. "She keeps saying girls. Villanova only had the one assistant. We asked the stage hands and everyone else involved with the show. There was only the one, and we don't know what happened to her, but we can guess. No doubt Gibson raped and killed her. He's not talking and won't, not that it matters. We nailed him on the Villanova homicide and that's that."

Chief Higgins didn't look convinced. "What about you, Jimmy? Do you concur with your partner?"

"Of course," replied Jimmy. "There was only the one girl."

"And who was she?" the chief asked.

"You mean her name? It was Natalia—Natalia the Gypsy. It's right there on the poster," the detective pointed to the bottom of the advertisement in Claire's hand.

"I mean, what was her real name?" the chief insisted.

The detective shrugged.

"Dan?" the chief asked the other officer.

"We, we don't know," stammered Dan.

"Lacey and Laura Henderson," Claire interrupted. "They were identical twins. Richard Henderson adopted, or rather bought, them from Georgia Tann and the Tennessee Children's Home Society when they were infants. Does that name ring a bell, gentlemen?" Claire paused for effect, knowing full well no one at the Memphis Police Department would care to discuss that travesty.

"I see," said the chief, clearing his throat. "And with all due respect, how do you know this?"

"I asked his wife," said Claire. "Make that his ex-wife. Curiously, she has no idea that her ex-husband and her girls are dead. It seems nobody has bothered to talk to her."

"You're a real peach, lady," said Dan.

"Detective," chastised the chief, "we'll not have that here. Miss Montgomery, I see your reputation is well warranted, and I commend you. Unfortunately, we have somewhat of a sticky situation on our hands."

"Not to mention an innocent man on death row," added Claire.

"Charlie," said Billy, "I can appreciate your predicament, but Claire is right. Not only is the wrong man in jail, but the actual killer is still on the loose."

"Do you mind if I ask you two something?" asked the chief.

They both nodded.

"You're a private investigator," he said to Claire, "and you're retired," he added, glancing at Billy. "So, who sent y'all over here in the first place?"

"Bob," Billy answered. "He's heading the investigation."

Chief Charles J. Higgins sighed and dropped his head. This was getting better by the minute. "Little Bobby is all grown up, it seems. I've heard things. Is he like the old man?"

"In some ways, yes," said Billy. "In some ways, no."

"In what ways?"

"He's just as good at getting answers, but not as direct as his father in doing so."

'Direct' was a term that didn't have to be explained.

"And how is he different?" asked the chief, dreading the answer that he knew was coming because of what he'd heard through his contacts.

"He's smarter," said Billy, "and, if it were possible, more relentless."

"Who's Bob?" asked Jimmy, wondering what all the fuss was about.

"Your worst nightmare, darlin'," Claire answered.

CHAPTER FIFTY-THREE

Claire and Billy agreed to meet Robert at Dr. Hall's. When they'd told him about their findings in Memphis, Robert had surprised them by requesting total discretion. He didn't want any publicity about the magician or his assistants to find its way back to Alabama. Billy convinced him that once the situation leaked to the media, there would be no way to prevent nationwide exposure. Robert countered that, since the Memphis PD and the District Attorney weren't in a hurry to embarrass themselves, he could delay the inevitable for long enough to spring his trap.

"You do know Kevin Gibson is sitting on death row right now," said Billy. He realized that Robert knew but thought he'd remind him of it all the same.

"I'm aware of that, and we'll do everything we can to speed this up so he can go free."

"What's the plan?" asked Claire.

Robert turned his eyes to the poster of the magician that Claire had brought with her. The fake jewel on the showman's turban was an exact match to the item he'd found alongside the dirt road leading up to Cooter Yates' property.

"We'll have to reel in the suspects one by one and turn them against each other before they lawyer up and close ranks. I've already expanded on the files Billy gave me, and once I put in what y'all have brought me from Memphis, that should do the trick. Should, anyway, but we'll need some bait, a little time, and a great deal of luck. It's the luck part that troubles me."

"What luck do you need?" asked Billy.

"Two heads would do just fine," Robert replied.

"You may never find those," Dr. Hall pointed out.

"We probably won't, which is why I put it in the luck category."

"And the bait?" asked Claire. She was used to being a lure for unsuspecting males, but she knew Robert had other things in mind.

"A reason to suspect the sheriff and his men," said Robert.

"What!" Billy exclaimed. "How are you going to do that?"

"It's already done. With Dr. Hall's help of course."

"Jack?" Billy turned to the medical examiner.

"I'm not very proud of that. I want it known that I relented to the pressure under protest," said Dr. Hall.

"Duly noted," Robert said.

"Did what under protest?" asked Billy.

Dr. Hall remained silent. Billy turned to Robert, who winked, but gave no further explanation.

"I can't wait to see this, darlin'." Claire laughed.

"We're going to start the ball rolling tonight, around midnight. By morning, we'll be in full swing. Hopefully, our friend, Mr. Gibson, will be breathing free air again soon. Others might not be so lucky."

"Care to elaborate?" Billy said.

"And ruin the surprise?"

"I'm sure whatever Robert has in mind is going to be a real humdinger," said Claire, "but I do have one question."

Robert waited.

"You keep saying we. Who else is going to be involved in your elaborate scheme of deception?"

"Turner," said Robert.

"John Turner?" said Billy. "He's a desk jockey. What are you going to use him for?"

"I need a cop, but not just any cop," answered Robert. "He's the best person I could think of for the kind of cop I need."

"And what kind of cop is that, darlin'?" asked Claire.

"The good cop."

Claire and Billy laughed. Dr. Hall didn't understand and couldn't resist the temptation to ask, "A good cop?"

"Not *a* good cop," Robert explained. "*The* good cop."

CHAPTER FIFTY-FOUR

"Abomination! These niggras are running rampant, I tell you!" the man in the gold robe yelled from under his mask. "Why, just the other day, I hear tell one of them bucks was eyeing up the white girls at the church social, and not one of the congregation done nothing to stop him. I say, hang him high!"

"Hang him!" shouted the crowd.

"In my pappy's day, they knew their place," the man continued, "and when they stepped out of it, we reminded them of who runs things."

"Here, here." Mumbles of agreement drifted up from under the hoods of the thirty or so men present.

"We took care of them two girls back yonder, and we need to do the same to the rest," the man continued.

A hush grew over the crowd. Confusion ran through the ranks. The man in gold waited. Before long, a voice rang out, "What are you talkin' 'bout, Dale?"

"Exalted Cyclops, you fool!" one of the men in black shouted.

"You know damn well what I'm talking about," the leader said. He waved his torch around in a dramatic display as he stood in front of the burning cross. A sturdy breeze pushed the flame around the stationary wooden frame, giving the speaker the appearance of a demon resurrected from hell itself. "We did what we had to do."

"Did what?" another voice shouted out.

The dozen men in black aggressively stepped forward and spread out to encircle their leader.

"Who dares question the Exalted Cyclops?" one of them shouted.

"The Twelve Terrors know what needs to be done. Has not the Kleagle instructed you in the ways?"

Indiscernible protests could be heard from several of the men. The man in the golden robe continued.

"They ain't the only ones, my fellow Klansmen. Did you think we just come out here for a picnic? This is a war! We are his mighty soldiers! Our beloved Lord was a white man, and he spits upon the niggras and Jews of the world. His hand guides us to slay the dragons, pinkos, Catholics, Commies, and all the other mongrel races. Are you with me, brothers?"

Members near the back drifted away, hoping to be lost in the shadows before being seen. The dozen men in black made as if they were going to stop them, but it was all for show. Others followed the first few, and soon only a half dozen men were left standing around.

"Tell us, Exalted One, what other acts of bravery have you done in our honorable name?"

The voice from under the hood sounded strangely familiar, but the Cyclops couldn't put a face to it.

"Another lost soul we tried and convicted of racial impurities. She's buried behind the courthouse, where no one will ever look. White power!"

"White power!" the Twelve Terrors answered.

The few men left in the crowd looked at each other as if waiting for a cue. The man who had shouted the previous question took off his mask and said, "Under the authority vested in me by the great state of Alabama, I arrest you on the charge of homicide."

"Stallworth!" shouted the man under the gold hood. The men in black scurried away in every direction. The others in the crowd removed their robes and pulled out firearms. All of them were wearing the unmistakable uniform of the state police.

One of the men in black pulled out a shotgun and pointed it at Stallworth.

"I wouldn't do that if I were you," Robert said calmly, hoping the man didn't panic and squeeze the trigger in all the excitement. It would be a hell of a thing to be cut down at this stage of the investigation.

"Clyde, put the gun down," instructed the Exalted Cyclops. He removed his hood, revealing his true identity at last.

"Good evening, Sheriff Fuller," said Robert. "Deputy," he said, nodding to the man with the shotgun. Deputy Smith set his gun down and removed his hood, as did all the others except one. Robert recognized many of the pillars of the local community, and he shook his head in disgust.

The last hooded member squirmed as the handcuffs were shackled around his wrists. Robert walked over to him, reached up, and pulled the man's hood off. Stallworth felt sick when he saw the man in tears under the mask.

"Ricky."

CHAPTER FIFTY-FIVE

"Never, ever, are you going to believe this!" Jeremiah told his wife. "The sheriff's been arrested."

"Arrested? For what?"

"Murder! They say he killed them two girls, maybe even others."

Jeremiah could barely hold in his excitement. Ever since the incident, he was sure that sooner or later someone would figure things out and put them in jail. When the detective from the state police showed up, he was certain of it.

"Really? That's a little hard to believe." Brandine was doubtful. "Are they sure they got the right guy?"

"Of course they got the right guy. Why would you even say such a thing? Besides, it weren't just him. They arrested Ricky and Clyde, too."

"What they arrested them for?"

"'Cause they was in on it. Jeez, honey, why do I got to explain everything to you?"

"You mean to tell me the whole police department was in on killin' two girls?"

"And others," he explained.

"I ain't buyin' it. That don't make a lick of sense."

"Don't be so naïve, Brandine. They done it. That detective said they did."

"Ain't he the one you said was an idiot?"

Jeremiah huffed. Brandine Stonecypher wasn't the sharpest tool in the shed, but if even she doubted that the sheriff and his men were responsible, Jeremiah wondered if they really were in the clear. Just then, the dog howled. Jeremiah made his way outside in time to see his elder brother's truck pull up to the trailer.

"I guess you heard the news," Jeremiah said as Junior got out and walked over.

"Everybody heard. It came as quite a shock. I told you that detective was a fool."

"Yep, I guess you were right," Jeremiah agreed. His confidence had been shaken by his wife's nagging, so he welcomed his brother's assurance.

"We're goin' to be just fine, JT. You'll see."

"So, did you get rid of them yet?"

"Get rid of what?"

"You know. Them heads." Jeremiah couldn't see how Junior could've possibly forgotten. He'd have been unable to sleep knowing the things were lying around, but then again, his brother was an asshole.

"For Pete's sake, you gonna ride me 'bout those, too?"

"I ain't ridin' you, but you said—"

"Don't you worry 'bout them things. They as good as gone. 'Sides, the stupid cops think the Klan done did this. We're off the hook."

Jeremiah couldn't shake his doubt. He wanted to put it all behind him, but he felt unable. "You remember what that detective said. He said they'd try to pin it on us, and we're gonna be on the hot seat again."

"So what?" Junior hated his younger brother's meek ways. "Ain't none of us gonna say squat. What you so worried for?"

"He said it was gonna be rough, him questionin' us."

"Don't be a pussy, JT. I ain't afraid of that moron."

"But what if one of the others says somethin'?"

"Says what? They ain't, and you'd better not." Junior headed back to his truck. He'd hoped visiting his brother would give him the chance to gloat over the bumbling of the police. Instead, JT's outward cowardice made him uneasy.

The dang fool was bound to say something stupid sooner or later if given the opportunity. Junior knew it would be up to him to silence him if necessary. He didn't want to think about that at the moment. It was a day for celebrating. "Just keep your mouth shut. You hear me?"

Jeremiah nodded and watched as his brother turned his truck around on the front lawn and sped away, kicking a cloud of red dirt into the dry, morning air. He hadn't heard his wife open the door, and he jumped when her voice cracked the silence from behind the rusty screen door.

"Keep your mouth shut about what, JT? What's he talkin' about?"

"Nothing, Brandine. He wasn't talkin' about nothin'."

"He was talkin' about somethin'. I want to know what it was."

"It was nothin'. I already told you."

"Don't you lie to me."

"Damn it, woman, I ain't gonna tell you again. It was nothin'!"

Brandine felt her heart drop, but she remained silent and returned to the relative comfort of her kitchen. She scrubbed the counters as if she could wash away what she knew would forever taint them all. She held back tears as long as she could until they broke free and ran down her ruddy cheeks. Yet she continued to scrub the clean surface with all her might.

Brandine couldn't believe what she knew in heart to be true. Despite her husband's denial, the nothing that the men had been talking about could've only been one thing.

CHAPTER FIFTY-SIX

Earl was shocked when he received the call. Almost everyone in the department had been detailed out, leaving him the senior officer. Just as the first rays of the sun rose above the horizon he entered the station house with apprehension.

"Deputy Barber, it's good to see you again." Robert greeted him as if they only knew each other in passing. Several unknown officers from the neighboring counties and the state police mulled about, so Earl played along.

"Uh, Detective Stallworth, right?"

"Yes, sir, that is correct. Please join us in the back. There's much to discuss."

Earl followed Robert to a desk near the corner of the great room and sat down. The detective motioned for the others to gather around for the debriefing.

"As everybody here knows, last night we arrested Sheriff Dale Fuller, Deputy Clyde Smith, and, unfortunately, Deputy Ricky Halpin. What y'all don't know is that I just received word from over in Carrollton. Judge Early released all three of them only minutes ago on insufficient evidence."

An uproar erupted throughout the room. Robert gave them a moment before waving for silence so that he could continue.

"But they confessed," one of the unidentified officers complained.

"Well, that ain't what they're saying now," Robert replied.

"What about the others we arrested?" asked another.

"All charges have been dropped," said Robert.

The group couldn't believe their ears.

"Please, please," Robert continued, "bear with me. This was to be expected. We knew what we were up against. I assure you, this isn't over."

"What can we do now?" someone asked.

"I already have a plan. First, let me introduce Deputy Earl Barber, the only honest man in the sheriff's department." Robert motioned to Earl, who nodded sheepishly. "Despite our act, he and I are already acquainted with one another. Deputy Barber here provided a great deal of insight regarding the men he's been forced to serve with—indispensable insight. I went to him with my concerns weeks ago, and he more or less told me that this would happen. He said that they would find someone else to pin it on. They always do. I have to admit, he was right. I've already heard through the grapevine that this is what helped them convince the good judge to release them. That and, sadly, Judge Early's own possible involvement with the organization in question. Regardless, this is the hand we've been dealt, and we have to play our cards with all the skill we can muster."

"What does that mean?" one of the officers asked.

"It means we are going to play along," answered Robert. "Deputy Barber and I have already set our trap. Isn't that right, Earl?"

"You got that right," Earl replied in an overt show of false bravado. The group of unknown officials smiled and patted him on the back. Earl ate it up. He felt important. He felt smart. He glanced at the detective, who slyly winked at him. Earl winked in response. To hell with these idiots, he thought. In the end, it was going to be Deputy Earl Barber who outplayed the smarty pants detective at his own game.

CHAPTER FIFTY-SEVEN

Unable to contain her curiosity any longer, Claire finally breached the subject. "What are you up to, my clever darlin'?"

Robert smiled but remained silent. Claire laughed. She had missed him so much over the past few years. Not a day had gone by when she hadn't thought about him, hadn't wondered what he was up to. She'd heard things through the grapevine. They were generally about his string of successes and his meteoric rise to homicide detective. She wondered if he had thought about her as much as she had about him.

Claire stared at Robert until he returned her gaze. She felt herself begin to blush and looked away.

"Claire—" he said.

"You don't have to," she interrupted. They'd said what they'd needed to say years ago. There was nothing either of them could do now that would change things.

"Yes, I do," he continued. "I want you to know it was hard to make that call and get you involved in this, but not as hard as it should've been."

Claire wondered what he meant by that, and she turned to look him in the eye again.

"It's true. We needed you, and you came through for us. You are the most brilliant investigator I've ever known. I swear I don't know how you do it."

Claire nodded in recognition of his compliment, his kind words stinging in the absence of what she longed to hear.

"You know it's more than that. I, I..." Robert paused to arrange his words. "I find myself feeling like a shy schoolboy." He laughed. Claire bit her lip and waited for him to continue.

"I still love you, Claire."

Her heart stopped for a moment, and she held her breath. The man was always so full of surprises.

"I've tried to put it behind me, but just like everything else in my life, I haven't been able to. I know what you're going to say. I know we agreed that we can't make it work, and I know it's because of me and my stubborn ways. None of that's changed. . I can only promise you that in a few years when we both tire of all this, we'll make another go of it. Maybe then I'll be able to sleep at night. Maybe then I can be the man you need me to be. I know it's unfair, and I'm truly sorry. But I can't lie to you. I never could."

"I never asked you to," said Claire.

"But I needed to," Robert replied.

"I know."

She reached out to him, and he took her in his arms. Years of denial and regret fell away, and they unleashed the passion that each of them had fought so hard to forget. The evening passed into early morning, and the darkness outside waned as the dawn of a new day came to pass. Robert held Claire in his arms, watching the morning light begin to creep through the cracks in the blinds.

"What devious plans do you have in store for your unfortunate suspects today?"

Robert laughed. "I'm going to baffle them with bullshit."

"I'm sure you will," said Claire. "That was one hell of a performance—arresting the sheriff and his men. I don't know how you got so many people to go along with it."

"I dazzled them with diligence."

"You're full of clichés today, aren't you, darlin'?"

"Sleep deprivation."

"Cute. I didn't hear you complaining last night," said Claire.

"I wouldn't call it complaining."

Robert pulled her over and kissed her. God, she was beautiful. He must've been crazy to ever let her go.

"So, what's on your schedule today, my dear? Are you off to discover Eldorado, or find the Holy Grail?" he asked.

"Closer to the latter."

Robert cocked an eyebrow.

"I have to follow up on something regarding *The Holy Relic*, as you call it," she answered. "I'm heading up to Memphis."

Robert felt a pang of sorrow. After all this time, he finally had her back in his arms and he didn't want her to go, but he knew better than to try and stop her. He didn't have to ask her what she was going to do in Memphis. When he found out that Claire had gone to the Tennessee Children's Home Society orphanage, he knew she'd never be able to let it rest.

"Will you be back?" he asked hopefully.

"Eventually," she said. "As much as I wish I could watch you in action, there are things that require my particular expertise."

"I figured as much," he said. "Well, if not for the fun part, how about the trial?"

Claire smiled. "Aren't you the confident one? Trial? And pray tell, how long before that begins, being that you haven't even made an arrest yet. Correction, you haven't made a real arrest, yet."

"It won't be long," Robert stated. "I know what I'm doing."

Claire laughed. "Oh, don't I know that, darlin'. Don't I know that."

CHAPTER FIFTY-EIGHT

Shaking his head in an apologetic manner, Robert confided to the deputy, "I'm really sorry about this, but we have to follow up on every lead."

"I understand. I'm here to help in any way I can," said Deputy Barber.

"These are serious allegations, so I don't want you to answer anything that you don't want to. You can ask for an attorney at any time."

"Attorney?" asked Earl. "Why would I need a lawyer? Am I under arrest?"

"Of course not. I just didn't want there to be any misunderstandings. Do you waive your right to have an attorney present?"

"I don't need a lawyer. I ain't done nothin' wrong."

"I didn't say that you did," said Robert.

"Someone did, or I wouldn't be here."

Robert's eyes flicked to the one way mirror on the wall and returned to the papers in his hands. Earl gave a slight nod to let the detective know he understood. They were being watched by others who didn't know this was all an act.

"Deputy Barber, I see that you aren't exactly one of the gang here at the sheriff's department. Why is that?"

"You know why."

"Yes, I know, but can you tell us."

"Us?"

Robert smiled. "Me."

"Because I don't belong to their little social club."

"Social club?"

"I can't answer for what the others do. If you want to know about that, ask them. If you want me to rat out my fellow officers, you came to the wrong guy, Detective. Now, if you have anything to ask me about me, I'll be happy to answer, but other than that, I don't know what to tell you."

"Fair enough, Earl, fair enough. I can call you Earl, can't I?"

"You just did."

"Earl, I was reading that you helped to find some locals to search the swamp for the missing girls. How do you know these men?"

"We belong to the same church."

"Right, the Antioch Pentecostal Church, to be precise. Is that correct?"

"That's the one."

"And your pastor is Eustice Elijah Winchester. Is that correct?"

"He is."

"Some would say he is a prophet. Do you believe he's a prophet?"

Earl shifted in his seat. There was a time he would've shouted his affirmation from the rooftop to anyone who'd listen. Now he wasn't so sure, but he felt uncomfortable voicing his doubts. There seemed to be no right answer to the question.

"He could be."

"Anyone could be, but is he?"

"That's not for me to say."

"Then who is to say?"

"What does this have to do with anything? Is someone sayin' Brother Winchester had somethin' to do with the murders?"

"Did he?"

"No way in hell."

"Did you?"

"Of course not! I wasn't even there."

Fuck! What did I say that for? Earl couldn't believe he had been so stupid. He hoped the detective hadn't noticed his slip up, and he tried to quickly change the subject. "We're good Christian men, Robert. I can call you Robert, can't I?"

"You just did." Robert smiled. "You know that social group you aren't a part of burns crosses while they terrorize people. They're Christians, too. So am I. So were those Nazi scumbags I fought in the war. You'll have to do better than that to convince me you're not involved."

"I don't have to convince you I'm not guilty. You have to convince a jury that I am. Can you do that? Do you have any evidence?"

Earl smugly stared at the detective. The idiot detective had completely missed the stupid thing he'd blurted out. This was going to be too easy. He didn't know why he'd been so nervous in the first place.

"Yes," Robert answered coolly. "Why, yes, we do."

Earl pretended that he was unconcerned. "What evidence?"

"Tell me about Cooter Yates. Does your church group meet up over there a lot?"

"Cooter is Cooter. There's not much to tell. And no, we don't meet up at his place often. You just caught us over there by chance."

"Caught you?"

"You know what I mean."

"I know exactly what you mean, Earl. I did catch you, come to think about it."

"What's that s'posed to mean?"

"Joe Bob Duncan."

"What about him?"

"I'll see him next. I'll be talking to you again soon, Deputy Barber."

"Call me Earl." The deputy wasn't going to let Stallworth push him around. *He didn't have any evidence, did he? That stupid Junior and those damn heads. Why the hell did he keep them?*

"Okay, Earl. Mr. Duncan is on his way here at this very moment. After that, we'll move on down the list. Then I'll get back to you. In the meantime, do I need to say it? Don't leave town."

"Where am I goin' to go?"

"Who knows? Perhaps Memphis again?"

Earl almost choked.

"Oh, and when you meet up with the other members of the flock, don't worry if you forget to tell them that you clarified that you weren't with them when they murdered the girl. I'll make sure to mention it to each of them when the time comes."

"I don't know what you're talkin' about."

"Yes, you do. Do remember to pass one thing along though, just in case they need to be reminded of what's in store for them."

"What's that?"

"John Wilkes Booth." Robert winked.

Earl forced a phony smile and left the room. He didn't know what kind of game the detective was playing anymore. Earl just wanted to pick up his ball and go home, but it was too late for that. Whatever Stallworth had in store for them, there was only one thing Earl knew for certain—they were in big, big trouble.

CHAPTER FIFTY-NINE

Joe Bob sat nervously in the interrogation room, waiting for the detective to start. So far, all the man did was give him a cigarette and fetch him a cup of coffee. They'd made small talk for about half an hour, mostly about the weather and the best fishing holes in the region.

"Oh, I forgot to tell you, thank you for your service, Marine," Robert said. "Semper Fi!"

"Uh, thanks. I didn't know you were an ex-Marine."

"There's no such thing as an ex-Marine; there's only Marines. No, I'm not a Marine. I was in the army, served in Europe. It was cold as fuck, but I don't know if that's worse or better than the tropics."

"I don't like to talk about it," said Joe Bob. He meant it.

"I don't either. Besides, I'm not allowed."

"Not allowed?"

"Army Intelligence," Robert explained. "But that's all behind us now, isn't it? It must be tough for you belonging to that weird cult you belong to."

"We're not a cult. Why do you say that?"

"Because I checked, and you're the only notable member who served. That's odd, considering."

"Considering what?"

"Considering that most eligible men of age served. Not so for the men of the Antioch Pentecostal Church, though. Everyone there managed to find a way to weasel out of their duty; everyone except you."

"I wouldn't call it weaseling."

"I would, and I just did."

"They were practicin' their religious beliefs."

Robert laughed. "Okay, if you say so. I bet they even tried to sell you on the idea that you were the coward for fighting for your country and not the other way around. I'm sure you set them straight. Right?"

"What's your point?"

"Joe Bob? Man, I don't know what to say. Ooh rah? I guess I was wrong."

"Wrong about what?"

"There are ex-Marines."

"Look, Detective, I don't know what I'm doin' here. Are we goin' to start this or not?"

"Oh, we started long before you got here. You just didn't know it."

Joe Bob kept silent as his mind ran through everything they'd talked about. He was sure he hadn't said anything that would come back to haunt him. Well, he was almost sure.

"But if you'd prefer, I can make this more direct," Robert said, standing up. He grabbed the overhead light that hung from the ceiling on a chain and pointed it at Joe Bob's face. "Where were you on the night of the twenty-third?" He laughed.

"Very funny."

Robert let the light go and sat down. "No, I was being serious. Where were you?"

"On the twenty-third? I don't remember."

"The twenty-third of April. Where were you?"

Joe Bob felt his heart rate double, but did his best to play it cool. "I said I don't remember."

"You don't? Your wife remembers. Your kids remember. Your boss remembers."

"What do you mean my wife remembers?"

"According to everyone we asked, you were out of town. How was the show, anyway? Or did the Great Prophet forbid you to see The Amazing and Magnificent Villanova? You know, so you wouldn't be cursed by the Devil or anything." Robert laughed.

Joe Bob glared at him, but he felt scared. Stallworth wasn't as dumb as they thought.

"Imagine that, a grown man, an ex-Marine," Robert said, stressing the *ex*, "having to ask permission from a slack-jawed hillbilly for permission to see a show. Did he think you'd be mesmerized by a card trick? Tell me, do you give him a percentage of your wages?"

"It's called tithin'."

"It's called something alright. You'd think that, with all that mean, green Brother Preacher was pulling in, he could afford to get those teeth fixed. I guess they call him the prophet for a reason, spelled P-R-O-F-I-T. He's really raking in turkeys over at the Antioch church, I tell you."

"Fuck you." Joe Bob had had enough.

"Fuck me? That's not very Christian of you. How long before he turns on you, Joe?"

"He ain't goin' to turn on any of us."

"No? That's what they always say. You know, I've been doing this for awhile. Let me give you some advice, because you're going to need it. From one soldier to another—watch your back. When push comes to shove, and I'm telling you now, push is going to come to shove because I'm the one doing the pushing, when the time comes, everyone is going to run for cover. The first ones get the deal. The rest get the shaft."

"I ain't got nothin' to say to you."

"No, not yet, you don't. But you will. Who do you think you're talking to? I know what it means to follow orders, even bad ones. I also know there are some orders you don't follow. But that's easy to say after the fact. I was at Nuremberg. In fact, much of my work was a key factor at Nuremburg. Since I can't talk about it, I won't, but you being a fellow soldier and all, I'll say one thing you'll understand. Not everybody I had files on made it to Nuremburg. Poof!

Gone. The smart ones spilled the beans early on and walked clean. Be one of the smart ones, Joe. Earl is."

"What does that mean?"

"He already told us what he was doing the night after the twenty-third. And lucky for him, he has an iron clad alibi. He made a point to let us know. Wait, I wrote it down, word for word." Robert shuffled through some loose papers in front of him for dramatic effect. "Here it is: 'I wasn't even there when they did that.' I don't have to tell you that was good to hear, him being an officer of the law." Robert amended the incriminating statement. It was part of his baffle with bullshit approach.

"Are we done here?"

"For now," said Robert, standing up and signaling the end of the interrogation. "But I'll be seeing you again shortly. I mean, considering the shape the corpses were in, you are of particular interest to us as compared to your buddies."

"And why is that?" Joe Bob didn't like the way that sounded.

"Because you're the only one we know for certain who has killed before, Marine."

"Fuck you."

"Oh, come on, Joe. Don't be so sensitive. So have I."

Stallworth's revelation did little to soothe Joe Bob's nerves.

"Say hello to Winchester on your way out. He's next."

"The Prophet ain't goin' to tell you nothin'," Joe Bob defiantly proclaimed.

"Sure he will, but not yet. It's Jeremiah Thomas Winchester who's up next. A clever and confident man like him will toe the line. I wouldn't let it concern you none. He'll have plenty of time to stick to his story. I think I'll keep him awhile. See how he holds up. I've seen people go twelve, fourteen hours sometimes before they crack. I'd ask you if you want to get in on the office pool, but I'm sure your preacher daddy wouldn't approve of you gambling. Take care, Joe Bob. I'll be praying for you."

Joe Bob gave the detective the finger and left without another word. *The preacher's plan is not going to work*, he thought. Something had to be done, and it needed to be done quickly.

CHAPTER SIXTY

Jeremiah sat upright in the wooden chair, his foot tapping nervously on the tile floor.

"You can relax, son," Robert said. "This won't take long." He lied.

"Good, I got to get back to Brandine. She'll be expectin' me shortly."

"Brandine is your wife?" Robert played dumb.

"Yes, sir. We've been married goin' on two years now."

"That's good. It's good to have someone who'll look after you as only family can."

"Yes, sir."

"Children in the future, too?"

"What? Um, yeah. We'll be havin' our first pretty soon. How did you know that?" The expectant couple hadn't announced the news to anyone yet.

Robert ignored the question. He hadn't known. The couple was young and had only been married two years, so he made a calculated guess and hit pay dirt. It was time to mine that little tidbit for all it was worth.

"Good, good. Well, it's usually good, anyway. Does Brandine have any family around here? I mean, other than you."

"She's got kin up near Tuscaloosa."

"Good, good," said Robert. "I've seen what growing up in foster care can do. It's hard on a girl when she has to raise little ones on her own. It would be a damn shame to see your wife struggle, after all the faith she's put in you."

"What do you mean by that? I ain't goin' nowhere."

"Jeremiah, please. We both know how this is going to end. You can't be much of a husband and father behind bars. Your wife is a pretty young thing. As much as I'm sure she loves you, it's unrealistic to think she's going to wait for you. You can't blame her. Why would she? You'll be lucky to avoid death row, much less see the light of day again. No, no, I'm sure she'll find someone else; hopefully, someone who will be a good father to your child. Lord knows, you're not going to do it. You'll come around to the idea of her with someone else. You'll have plenty of time to get used to it."

"She ain't findin' no one else! Why would I go to prison? I ain't done nothin'."

"We have two dead girls, Jeremiah. Somebody killed them."

"It weren't me! I thought y'all busted the sheriff and his men for doin' that?"

"They said it was you."

"Me! Why would I do it? I didn't even know that girl."

"Girls."

"Girls, then. I didn't know them girls."

Robert shrugged his shoulders and paused to rifle through some papers on the table before continuing. "You were there when they started fishing the parts out of the swamp, right?"

"Yeah, we was helpin' them. I didn't think they'd use that as an excuse to pin it on us."

"I can see your point." Robert sighed and sat back. "This is a real mess, Jeremiah. You're saying it's them. They're saying it's you. Some of the men in the congregation are blaming other men in the congregation. And I'm the one who has to sort it all out. I'm sure you can see my problem here. Sure, the Klan boys have a motive to shift the blame to your church group, but why would some of your group implicate others, unless y'all were involved? It doesn't make sense. So that only leaves me one course of action. I have to figure out exactly who in your group did what."

"Ain't none of us done nothin'."

"That isn't what the others are saying, Jeremiah."

Damn it! Who the hell was talking? They'd all sworn they'd keep their mouths shut no matter what. Daddy wasn't goin' to like this one bit.

"I have to level with you, kid. I just don't see it in you."

JT felt better about that. Maybe the detective wasn't so bad after all.

"Unfortunately, we're going to be here for awhile. Let's take a break. I'll run over to the diner and pick us up a bite to eat. Want one of the specials? It's on me."

Jeremiah nodded in agreement, and Robert left the room. Billy was waiting in the hall.

"What the hell are you up to?" asked Billy, clearly upset.

"I have to run an errand. We should talk in the car. Sheriff!" he yelled on his way out of the station, "give it about an hour, then send someone over to the diner. Have them pick up a lunch plate for Winchester, but hold off on giving it to him. Let him sit in there and stew awhile. I'll be back shortly."

Sheriff Fuller nodded and returned to his paperwork. Robert knew he'd do exactly as instructed. He'd gotten him to wear the imperial robes of the Exalted Cyclops and dress his deputies up as the Twelve Terrors. He'd gotten him to stand in court in front of the real Exalted Cyclops after their mock arrest. Having him fetch a lunch plate for a half-wit paled by comparison.

Once they were in Robert's car and out of earshot, Billy laid into him.

"What did you promise that asshole?"

"What do you mean?"

"Don't play games, Bob. I was doing this before you were born. You must've made a peach of a deal to get that level of cooperation. What did you promise them?"

"See, Billy, that's the beauty of it. I didn't have to promise them a damn thing."

"Then it's implied. You can't make a deal with these people. You know what they are."

"Do you really think I'd make a deal with the Klan? Come now, you know me better than that."

"I thought I did. You better be careful. These ain't the kind of men you take lightly."

Robert turned south and headed down the highway.

"What did you promise them, Bob? What do they want?"

"What do they always want? They want me gone. There's only one way that's going to happen."

Billy sighed. *You can't tell this younger generation anything,* he thought. The boy was determined to learn everything the hard way.

"I hate to break it to you," Billy said, changing the subject, "but I passed by Claire's, and she's gone."

"I know," said Robert.

"You know? How do you know?"

"I saw her this morning before she left."

"I went over there at the crack of dawn. How did you see her before she left?"

Robert ignored the question. Billy took the hint.

"You are a careless man."

"Bold and daring," Robert responded. "She's off to Tennessee. It seems the lack of inquiry at the Tennessee Children's Home Society struck a nerve with her."

"As it should. I hope you know what you're doing."

"I don't," said Robert, "but since when has that ever stopped me?"

Billy braced himself as Robert turned the car onto a worn out dirt path that snaked through the pine trees. He pulled up in front of a trailer and parked.

"Where are we?" asked Billy.

"Brandine's."

CHAPTER SIXTY-ONE

Robert offered no other explanation, and Billy didn't ask. Instead, he accompanied the detective to the front door and stood by, looking official.

"Excuse me, ma'am, I'm looking for a Jeremiah Winchester," said Robert, pretending to read the name off of a blank page in his notebook.

"He ain't here," replied the wary girl from behind the rusty screen door. "What do you want with him anyway?"

"We're here to help him. Can you tell us where he is?"

"He ain't here. State your business, or leave. I have things to do." Brandine didn't like the looks of the two men. They spelled trouble.

"I'm sorry, I didn't introduce myself. I'm Detective Robert Stallworth from the Alabama State Police." He briefly flashed his badge before adding, "And this is my partner. We have urgent business with your husband. He is your husband, isn't he?"

"He is, and what urgent business might that be?"

Robert glanced at Billy. They made faces at each other as if deciding whether or not to divulge some top secret information to a civilian. After a moment, Billy shrugged his shoulders and looked away, absolving himself of responsibility. Robert gulped, and his eyes darted around to make sure nobody was watching. He said in a whisper, "We're here about the girls."

Brandine's face went pale, but she hid her fears. "Like I said, he ain't here. You boys should check with the sheriff's office. JT went down there hours ago. He said he was goin' to talk to you."

Robert feigned surprise and looked at Billy, who raised his eyebrows but remained silent.

"Did he now? That's rather curious."

"Curious?" asked Brandine.

"We just came from there," Billy interjected. "He wasn't there."

"What? That's where he said he was—"

"Now, now, let's not jump to conclusions," said Robert. "I'm sure there could be plenty of explanations of why he'd lie, I mean, why he might've not told you the whole story."

Brandine wasn't buying it. *That low down, dirty lyin', bastard!*

"I only hope he didn't—" said Robert.

"I'm sure he wouldn't go there," said Billy without a clue to where his friend was going with his bullshit story.

"No, I'm sure. Well, let's hope not."

"Go where?" asked Brandine.

"Nothing, ma'am," said Billy. "I'm sure there's nothing to worry about." He looked at Robert with concern.

Robert quickly flipped through his notebook in an overt attempt to change the subject. "Uh, Mrs. Winchester, I mean Brandine, can you verify an address for us? It's for a Eustice Adam Winchester, otherwise known as Junior. He's your husband's brother, I believe."

"Come on, Robert, I'm sure he wouldn't—" said Billy.

"Ma'am?" Robert interrupted his partner.

"...after we warned him," Billy slipped in as if by accident.

"Watts!" Robert chastised the man.

"Warned him about what?" asked Brandine, her voice trembling.

"It's probably nothing, ma'am. Precautions, that's all," said Robert.

"Now you listen here, mister, if my JT is in any danger, I have a right to know about it. I'm expectin'."

"Congratulations!" exclaimed Billy.

"Yes, ma'am, we already know about that, and congratulations," added Robert.

"How the hell did you know about that?"

Robert's lips clamped shut, and he looked away. Brandine glared irately at Billy, who sheepishly added, "I knew, too. Was it a secret?"

"Holy crap! That son of a—" Brandine said.

"Ma'am, please. We really want to help him, especially with y'all expecting and all," Robert implored. "If we can prevent another tragedy—"

"What do you mean another one?"

"Wasn't there an older brother?" asked Robert. Billy tried hard not to smile. Now he knew where Robert was heading. *That clever son-of-a-bitch.*

"Elijah Andrew," said Brandine cautiously, "but I don't see how—"

"It's probably nothing," said Robert.

"A hunting accident, wasn't it?" asked Billy. Robert shot him a dirty look, warning him to shut up.

"That was a long time ago," said Brandine.

"Wasn't it Junior who shot—" Billy blurted out again.

"Watts! I'm sorry, ma'am," Robert turned to the visibly shaken girl. "We've already said too much. I'm sure we're being overly cautious. It's just that, when Jeremiah called us up saying he had something about his brother he needed to tell us, well, you can see why we're concerned. But I'm sure it's nothing, or you would've heard. We only came out here because he didn't show up, and knowing how questionable the murder, I mean the accident, with his eldest brother was—"

"You don't think Junior did that on purpose, do you? It was an accident," Brandine protested, trying desperately to convince herself most of all.

"I've heard that one before," said Billy, a comment that got him an elbow in the ribs from Robert.

"Like I said," Robert continued, "I'm sure he'd of told you if his brother got him involved in something, and for all we know, he's over at Mary J—, I mean, somewhere else."

"Mary who? What are you talkin' about?"

"Nothing, ma'am," Robert assured her. "We're just hoping that she's, I mean, he's not with Junior, all things considered. That is our focus now, because of the danger. I'm sure if Jeremiah's brother got him involved in something serious, he would've told you about it."

"Well, there is one thing," said Brandine. She swore to herself and JT that she'd keep her mouth shut, but this was serious. For all she knew, Junior had lured her poor, innocent husband out into the woods with the intent of shooting him, as he'd done with Elijah all those years ago. If she didn't tell these detectives, who would stop it? Why should they cover for the horrible things that Junior did? JT wouldn't harm a fly. They'd see how he is and forget about him, and go after the real murderers, Junior and the Prophet.

"Go on," said Robert.

Brandine unlatched the hook on the screen door and invited the men in. There was something that had been weighing heavy on her mind, and it was time to let it out.

CHAPTER SIXTY-TWO

By the time Robert made it back to the sheriff's office, it was getting dark outside. He grabbed the bag with the daily lunch special and headed to the interrogation room.

When he opened the door, he could see Jeremiah was angry. "Where the hell have you been?" he asked.

Robert ignored his complaint and opened the bag, setting the container of cold meatloaf and soggy mashed potatoes in front of the young man as if it were the finest delicacy served to the King of Siam. Before Jeremiah knew what happened, he felt a cold wet mist hit him in the face.

"What the hell was that?" he asked, wiping the sticky wetness from his cheek.

"It's called *Lavender Blossom*. I commented on how much I liked it to the waitress, and she sold me a bottle. It turns out, she has a side business hocking this crap. I didn't have the heart to tell her I was just being nice. It smells like something that would gag a maggot. Now I know why they call it toilet water."

"Why the hell did you spray it in my face?"

Robert laughed. "Because you stink." He sat down and fumbled with a few papers. JT glared at him for a moment before picking at the food in front of him.

"It's cold! I can't eat this shit!"

"Boy, you really are hard to please," said Robert. "Still, it's a might better than you'll be getting at the state pen."

"Enough of that bull. I'm not goin' to jail. You don't scare me."

"You should be scared, but not of me. You have bigger problems on your hands."

"What do you mean?"

"Junior," said Robert. "You know how he gets."

"He's my kin. I don't need to worry about him none."

"That's what Elijah Andrew thought." In truth, Robert had no idea if the boy had been shot by accident or on purpose. Jeremiah had been left home that day, and the only ones present were the eldest two brothers and their father. The initial report was a bit sketchy, but it was later accepted that a misfire had occurred, which resulted in the death of the eldest Winchester boy. The middle boy took the blame, and no one pressed the matter. But people talk.

"That was an accident," Jeremiah protested.

"So they say. Accidents happen all the time. Make sure you aren't in one."

"You're tryin' to bluff me. I ain't worried."

"Brandine is," countered Robert. "She's wringing her hands as we speak, wondering where you done run off to."

Jeremiah laughed.

"Did I say something that amuses you?" Robert asked.

"She knows I'm here talkin' to you."

"That's not what we told her."

"What? What did you tell her? When did you talk to her?"

"We just had a long chat. She had some interesting things to say."

What the hell? That stupid girl! I told her to keep her mouth shut. "She don't know nothin'. What could she tell you?"

"Enough," said Robert, "but I'll let you two lovebirds sort it out after you tell her what else you've been up to, when you eventually go strolling through that door at an ungodly hour, smelling like a French whore."

"Why, you son-of-a-bitch!" Jeremiah cried. He paused and tried to force a smile before continuing, "She ain't gonna question me no how. She knows me," proclaimed Jeremiah, the timbre of his voice giving doubt to his resolve.

"She thought she did, but that's before our little chat. Now she's not so sure."

"You bastard!"

"Careful, JT. Don't let your anger cloud your judgment. Don't make hasty decisions or hold on to long-standing assumptions. Besides, you don't want to burn your bridges with me, kid."

"Why not?"

"Because, before long, you're going to realize that I'm the only friend you've got."

CHAPTER SIXTY-THREE

The sun was beginning to rise when Jeremiah finally exited the sheriff's office. He was exhausted and just wanted to go home and lie down, but he knew Brandine was going to give him hell as soon as he walked in the door. That asshole detective really did a number on him. Stallworth had warned them that it wasn't going to be a picnic. Truer words had never been spoken. Jeremiah didn't want to think about what the others had been telling the pesky detective.

He started up his truck and pulled out of the parking lot as Charles Ray was entering. Jeremiah waved to the man, but Charles Ray didn't see him. It seemed odd to Jeremiah, and he paused at the stop sign to watch his friend enter the police station in a hurry. A car came up behind him and honked, so he drove off, but not before he saw his brother sitting across the street in a strange vehicle. Jeremiah fought the urge to turn around and find out what was going on. He was in enough trouble already.

"Detective," the deputy announced. Robert was sitting in the interrogation room reading through his notes. "Mr. Charles Ray Wilson is here to see you."

Robert nodded, and Charles Ray hesitantly entered the room. Robert let him stand by awkwardly for a moment without acknowledging his presence.

"Should I sit or—?" Charles Ray asked.

"What?" Robert said without looking up.

"Should I sit down, or should I—?"

"No," Robert said and continued to read. He flipped through a few more pages and waited. Charles Ray balanced on one leg then another, not sure what he was supposed to do. Eventually, he cleared his throat to get the detective's attention. Robert responded by closing the file and jogging it neatly together before placing it to his left. He exhaled, picked up another folder, and flipped it open.

"Did you want to—?" Charles Ray asked again.

"What?" Robert's head popped up. He looked the man over, then went back to his previous activities.

"Did you want me—?"

"Did I want you to what, Mr. Wilson?" Robert asked.

"I thought you wanted to ask—?"

"You thought?" Robert laughed and shook his head. "Right, that's what you did."

"Pardon?"

"Why are you here?" Robert looked up again, this time his intense stare burned into Charles Ray's eyes.

"You said you wanted to—"

"Ask you bullshit questions so you can feed me bullshit answers?" Robert finished for him. "Really, what's the point? I already know what went down over at Cooter Yates's place back in April."

"I, uh, I mean, you—"

"How articulate," Robert observed. "You're not the first one from the Antioch church who I've talked to. Deputy Barber spent most of his time assuring me that he wasn't with you guys when you murdered and dismembered the girls."

"That's a damn lie!" Charles Ray protested.

"Which part—the murdering or the dismembering?"

"No, I mean, that's not what I was—"

"Or that he was only there for one and not the other?" *Now we're getting somewhere,* thought Robert. He tucked that tidbit of information away and continued, "I know what you mean, Mr. Wilson. Joe Bob clarified it already. I will say, he was a bit reluctant to do so. Give him a little credit, an ex-

Marine is hard to crack. He did his best, but the truth eventually comes out. Jeremiah Winchester couldn't stop spilling the beans. It was all we could do to tell him to shut up. He's going to be great on the witness stand. He even had us run over and talk to his wife. He's a little worried about his brother and his father, and I can't say as I blame him. Still, we eventually had to get him out of here. He begged us to stay, but he dug his own hole. Who'd a thought he'd be the smart one of the bunch?"

"I ain't got nothin' to say to you."

"Who asked you? You can get on now. You have nothing to offer me that I don't already know. There'll be no deals with you." Robert went back to his forms, but the other man remained standing. Robert looked up. "Go on, I said. Git!"

"But—"

"Deputy!" shouted Robert. Seconds later, the door opened, and Deputy Halpin poked his head in. "Ricky, get this piece of shit out of my sight."

Charles Ray didn't know what to do, but he had no choice. The deputy grabbed his upper arm and escorted him to the front door without so much as a word. Charles Ray hesitated in the foyer, but Ricky motioned for him to leave, like he was an unwelcome stray animal.

Charles Ray felt humiliated. He wanted to run back in and give the detective a piece of his mind, but then what? What could he do? He'd sworn to the others that he'd keep his mouth shut. What were they telling the cops? It was all so confusing. He exited the building and slinked over to his car, his eyes scanning the horizon. Charles Ray fired up the engine of his sedan and sped out of the parking lot in a hurry, almost slamming into oncoming traffic.

"How'd it go?" asked Robert, walking up behind Ricky and Dale, who were watching Charles Ray's hasty exit through the blinds of the front window.

"Like he was fleeing the scene of the crime," said the sheriff.

"He is," said Robert. "And Junior Prophet?"

"He's still watching from Jack Drury's Buick," Ricky answered.

"That's some stake out," said the sheriff. "Maybe we should send over some coffee and donuts."

They laughed.

"I gotta say, Stallworth," the sheriff mused, "you are one devious son-of-a-bitch. First, the cheap perfume, and now this. You keep Junior here all night and dismiss Wilson within minutes. The fake Klan rally, the pretty lady, the macabre bone display over at the medical examiner's. Them boys from the Antioch Pentecostal Church don't know which end is up."

"They don't need to know," said Robert, "yet."

Ricky smiled and winked at the sheriff. He'd tried to tell Dale how smart Stallworth was, but sometimes you have to see to believe.

"When do you think they'll figure out you're just messing with their heads?" asked the sheriff.

"When the iron barred doors slam behind them."

Junior watched the comings and goings at the sheriff's office. Something didn't add up. There was little doubt that the detective had questioned Earl, being that he was a deputy. Junior also knew that Joe bob had spent two hours in the hot seat. Then, his imbecile brother ended up spending the entire night. The detective left with another cop and returned hours later. And still, JT had remained. Junior knew he must've told them something. He'd had to. Now, Charles Ray runs in and out like he was hiding from the Devil himself.

Eustice Winchester, Jr. smelled a rat.

CHAPTER SIXTY-FOUR

"Is this here a starin' contest, or ain't you got nothin' to say?" Buck wasn't in the mood to play games. If the detective thought he'd be easy to push around, he had another thing coming.

"I'm just trying to figure you out, Mr. McEwen," said Robert.

"There ain't nothin' to figure out."

"Maybe from where you're sitting there isn't, but from over here, there is. We've been talking about you a great deal around here. I'd say y'all, but I mean you in particular, being you're a pervert and all."

"I ain't no pervert. You don't know what you're talkin' 'bout," Buck protested. He knew this was going to come up eventually. It always did.

"You like diddling little kids. That makes you a pervert, pervert."

"It wasn't like that. Besides, that was a long time ago, and I ain't like that no more."

"Once a pervert, always a pervert. Pervert," Robert needled the big man.

"I put that behind me, and I ain't like that no more. I've been saved."

"Saved? Is that what the great prophet of Alabama told you? Man, he really played you for a fool."

"You wouldn't understand," Buck insisted.

"Finally, something we agree on. You're right, I wouldn't understand, but then, I'm not the pervert. You are."

"I ain't no pervert. I've been saved. I told you that."

"Yeah, right. You've been saved from the fiery pit by none other than Brother Eustice Winchester, a pervert as well."

"What do you mean?"

"Come on, Buck. You know what I mean. Damn, it ain't exactly a secret he married his first wife when she was fifteen. It was a shotgun wedding at that."

"She was young, but so was he. So what?"

"He was twenty seven, Buck."

Buck attempted to reply, but the words were trapped in his throat. *Why that no good bastard! All this time, him tellin' me I was a pervert, and him doin' the same thing!*

"It's common knowledge he knew her, as it were, in the biblical sense for a spell before the nuptials. Made her about twelve or thirteen, I'd say. What's the word for that?" Robert shuffled through some forms on the desk as if he were looking it up in Webster's New Unabridged Dictionary. "I believe it's 'pervert.'"

"What's this got to do with me?" Buck asked. He was sick of this shit. No matter what he did, or how many years had passed, no one ever let him forget the sins of the past. That damn Winchester preyed on his weakness, and now, here he was, back in police custody having to listen to this.

"Did he share?" asked Robert and watched Buck cringe. "Now don't act all surprised at the question. There were two under-aged girls and two known pedophiles out there. It stands to reason," Robert explained. "But I can see that, maybe not. Did he let you watch? Is that it?"

"I ain't got nothin' to say."

"Of course, you don't. No, I'm guessing you wouldn't piss without permission from Brother Charlatan. I bet you kept guard so that the others wouldn't intervene."

Robert was fishing, but he detected a nibble and ran with it. "That's it, isn't it? No one there was a pervert like you, and they wouldn't stand for the old geezer pawing and defiling a little girl like that. But you would, because that's the kind of guy you are, Buck. A pervert."

Buck shook his head in denial. His reddening face told Robert he was spot on, so he continued, using the word 'pervert' at every opportunity.

"Yeah, that's it. You kept guard, probably getting all hot and bothered while you listened in. Did you sneak a peek?"

Buck clenched his jaw but said nothing.

"You did! A peeping Tom! I bet you tossed one off right there, pervert. You're getting aroused right now thinking about it. Aren't you, pervert?"

"Fuck you! I ain't like that!"

"Of course not, pervert. You're saved, pervert. Isn't that right, pervert? Thanks to Brother Eustice Pervert Winchester. He saved you so you could help him out. I bet you didn't know why, but you do now. Eustice used you because he knows you're just like him—a pervert. He used you to do his dirty work because he knew you would. Because you're a pervert, pervert."

"Stop saying that! I'm not no pervert!"

"No? What would you call it?"

"I don't know, but I ain't a pervert. You weren't there. I tried to—"

"Tried to what?"

Buck stopped. The tricky fucker almost had him.

"I want a lawyer."

Robert figured as much. It was right on schedule. He only wondered what had taken the guy so long.

"And you shall have one, Mr. McEwen," said Robert. "Should I get you a phone book, or do you have one you keep on retainer, just in case?"

"Public defender."

"But you're not under arrest. You are free to go at any time."

"But, but, I thought—"

"No, you didn't think, Buck. I bet you're thinking now. You'd better see about that lawyer, and I'd go for better than a public defender. This isn't going to be your first time. Repeat offenders of your variety go away for a long, long time. I'd shop around for the best. You're going to need it."

Buck got up to go, but before he made it to the door, Robert asked him, "Did you ever wonder how I fingered you for this, Buck? Let me give you a hint. The good prophet sent me your way. He informed me all about your indiscretions. He set you up, Mr. McEwen. You're what we call a patsy. A patsy and a pervert. That's a hell of a spot you put yourself in. Tell me one thing, though." Robert paused. Buck waited, so Robert finished, "How hard was it to cut all the way through a grown man with a hand saw?"

Buck's knees buckled and his face went pale. For a moment, Robert thought the man was going to pass out, but he steadied himself and left without another word.

Bingo!

CHAPTER SIXTY-FIVE

"My God, Bob," said Billy, "what the hell?"

"How did you know it was them?" asked the sheriff.

Billy, Dale, and Ricky had been watching from behind the one-way mirror. They were amazed at how the detective had masterfully handled the interrogations, and they used the brief interlude before the next suspect to pepper him with questions and praise.

"I didn't," said Robert, "and still don't, but it's not looking good for the flock."

"What do you mean, you still don't?" asked the sheriff. "But you said—"

"I've said a lot of things, Exalted Cyclops."

Sheriff Fuller and Deputy Halpin cringed. Billy tried not to smile.

"What's that supposed to mean?" asked the sheriff, obviously offended.

"You know what it means," said Robert. "I only zeroed in on them because they were nosing around, and it didn't fit. The more pressure I apply, the deeper it gets. I still don't have any concrete evidence, and I may never have any. Sure, this looks promising from inside these walls, but their trials won't be conducted here, and this whole house of cards will come crumbling down. Don't forget, had I put the same pressure on your little social group, I'd likely have gotten the same results. How do you think that would turn out in court?"

Dale and Ricky wanted to protest, but they knew better.

"You'd all be skipping justice as you always do, the judge being the actual Cyclops. What are you, anyway—a Terror? Or maybe a Kleagle, or some other equally disgusting or stupid thing?"

"Now, hold on there a minute. We helped you—"

"Helped get me off your backs," said Robert. "The defense is going to push this back over to your stupid little club, and voila, reasonable doubt. Some favor, bigot. Besides, don't go thinking you guys are off the hook yet. For all you know, this elaborate trap has been set for you."

The sheriff burned red with anger but kept his mouth shut. Ricky gulped. *Who knew where Stallworth's plans were really leading them? Maybe this was a trap for them, after all?*

"I'll bet that got your attention," said Robert. "But relax. I'm just fucking with you. No, it's the Antioch boys who did this. They're running scared. You can smell it in the air. It's only going to be a matter of time now. So get ready."

Ricky exhaled with relief. The last thing he wanted was Stallworth pulling him into the interrogation room. He'd seen enough to know how that would turn out. The sheriff remained offended but let it go. He'd made a deal with the Devil and had no choice but to see it through. The sooner they got rid of Stallworth, the better.

"Get ready for what?" asked the sheriff. He was afraid of the answer.

"For the dominos to fall." Billy finally entered the conversation. "Do you think they'll run or start killing each other?" he asked Robert.

"Both."

"Jesus Christ!" the sheriff exclaimed.

"The sheep will turn into wolves and devour one another," said Robert.

"What are we going to do?" asked Ricky.

"Take down the shepherd. What else?"

CHAPTER SIXTY-SIX

"*In the sweet by and by, we shall meet on that beautiful shore…*" the devout parishioners sang as Robert carefully pulled open the large wooden doors of the church. He knew his attempt to remain inconspicuous would be difficult, but Robert underestimated the level of failure he'd find.

"In the sweet by and—" The voices stopped abruptly as the organist halted the melody in mid-chorus. The crowd turned to look at the unwelcome intruder standing at the rear of the church.

Robert removed his hat, nodded to the silent gawkers, and walked to the pew in the back row. He was greeted with a scowl from the man sitting near the aisle, but the detective was unmoved. The seated man pulled his legs in to allow Robert to pass. Robert would have none of it, and he put a hand on the man's shoulder, insisting that he and his entire family move over so that he could sit on the end. Reluctantly, the man relented, although with obvious displeasure.

"I see we have a visitor," announced Brother Eustice from his pulpit. "Are you sure you're in the right place, brother?"

Robert nodded.

"This is the house of the Lord," the preacher continued. "All men are welcome. I'm afraid you've missed our service, Detective. This was our last hymn, but since you've come all this way, I can deliver an impromptu sermon for your benefit."

A few groans were heard from a row of bored looking teen-agers two rows in front of Robert. The sound from the group was quickly met by stern looks of disapproval from their parents.

"I'll try to keep it somewhat brief since it's gettin' dangerously close to the children's lunch hour." Brother Eustice laughed. He nodded to one of the deacons standing in the corner, and the man nodded in return. Robert saw that it was none other than Joe Bob Duncan, who was taking hold of a long pole. Robert didn't flinch, but instead watched with curiosity at the man's behavior.

The preacher opened his Bible and flipped to one of the many bookmarks. He began to read. "Behold, I send you out as sheep in the midst of wolves; so be wise as serpents and innocent as doves."

Brother Eustice looked up to find the detective's gaze burning into his eyes. Robert stared unblinking at the preacher. He remained aware that Joe Bob was slowly creeping down the side aisle to the right with the long, wooden pole in his hands as Buck McEwen approached on the left.

"Beware of men; for they will deliver you up to councils," the preacher continued, "and flog you in their synagogues, and you will be dragged before governors and kings for my sake, to bear testimony before them and the Gentiles."

The two men crept closer. Robert pretended he didn't notice, but he shifted slightly so that he could reach into his pocket without hesitation when the time came.

"When they deliver you up, do not be anxious how you are to speak or what you are to say; for what you are to say will be given to you in that hour; for it is not you who speak, but the Spirit of your Father speakin' through you."

The men were in position, Joe Bob at the end of the aisle, and Buck standing just out of sight over Robert's left shoulder. Joe Bob reached over and moved the wooden pole towards the detective. Robert reached into his pocket and pulled out a small stack of dollar bills with a rubber band around it, then dropped it into the straw basket at the end of the pole.

Brother Eustice smiled. Robert gave a little nod. He stood to leave, but paused to look at Buck, who glared at him with contempt. Robert turned toward the congregation.

"Brother will deliver up brother to death, and the father his child, and children will rise against parents and have them put to death," Robert finished the quote.

Gasps of horror rose from the pews. Brother Eustice continued to smile, as did the detective. But they were the only ones. Robert glanced at the row of pews on the left and saw Charles Ray Wilson watching with the rest, so he subtly nodded in recognition and made his way toward the rear door. Buck hesitated a moment, then stood aside.

Robert moved past him, opened the door, and turned around one more time, and quoted the New Testament, "Beware of false prophets, who come to you in sheep's clothing but inwardly are ravenous wolves. You will know them by their fruits."

CHAPTER SIXTY-SEVEN

An emergency meeting was called by the prophet after the Sunday service for the deacons of the church. The other members of the congregation left, including the men's wives, but the seeds of doubt clouded their minds. Everyone in the county knew about the bodies that had been found at Dead River, and everyone knew the detective had been interrogating the members of the Antioch church. Despite the arrest and release of Sheriff Fuller and the alleged involvement of the Klan, it didn't take a genius to figure out who the real suspects were.

"This is a bad idea," Cooter objected. "It makes us look guilty."

"That's 'cause we are guilty," said Joe Bob.

"Shut the hell up!" shouted Charles Ray.

"No, you shut up," replied Joe Bob. "Don't think we didn't notice the way Stallworth looked at you."

"What's that s'posed to mean?" asked Charles Ray.

"Don't act dumb, Judas," said Cooter. "Junior told us about you bein' a snitch."

"What? What the hell are you talkin' about? I didn't—"

"How come he nodded at you like that?" asked Earl. "And how come you just snuck in to the sheriff's office for a few minutes and left when it was your turn to be questioned? I heard all about it. Somethin's fishy about it."

"You're the cop," Charles Ray pointed out. "If anyone is cooperatin' with the cops, it's you."

"You dumbass," said Cooter. "If you go blabbin', we'll all go down. The only thing we can do is stick together."

"That ain't what that detective says," said Jeremiah.

"What did you tell him?" asked Buck.

"Nothin'," Jeremiah did his best to assure the big man. "I ain't told him nothin'."

"That ain't what I heard," said Earl. "The word is that Brandine's been talkin'."

"What!" shouted Cooter. "You keep that slut—"

Jeremiah lunged at Cooter. They fell to the floor, taking a small table with hymnals stacked on it with them. Joe Bob, Buck, and Earl pulled them apart. Charles Ray stood alone, feeling unwelcome.

Brother Eustice spoke at last. "That's enough, you idiots."

"Don't talk about my wife like that!" Jeremiah shouted, still in a rage.

"Brother Yates," Eustice said, raising his eyebrows.

"What I meant to say was, it would be in everyone's best interests if you were able to keep that fine woman of yours in check," Cooter spat.

"That's better," said Brother Eustice. "And that sentiment goes for all of us. I told y'all from the beginning to keep your mouths shut and stick to the story. You boys are crackin' the second that dumbass detective comes around."

"He ain't that dumb," said Buck.

"No, he ain't," Brother Eustice agreed. "All the more reason to keep your mouths shut. Now, has anybody seen Junior?"

The group looked around, but no one had.

"That's odd," said Eustice. "It ain't like him to miss a service."

"No, it ain't," said Buck.

"Somethin' on your mind, brother?" asked Eustice.

Buck didn't answer. The whole business stunk, and it was getting worse by the minute. He had a feeling that they were rats on a sinking ship.

"At least he dropped a few bucks in the collection plate," said Jeremiah.

"That was strange," said Earl.

"What did he give us?" asked Joe Bob.

"Us?" asked Brother Eustice.

"What did he put in there?" Charles Ray asked.

"Who asked you?" said Brother Eustice. "We got a few questions for you that we need answered."

"No, really," insisted Buck, "what did he put in there?"

Brother Eustice wanted to protest some more, but he could see the men weren't going to let it go. So he shrugged and pulled the wad of bills out of his coat pocket.

"I wouldn't go readin' too much into it," he said, tossing the money onto the table.

The stack of one dollar bills no longer had the rubber band around it, and it opened to reveal a piece of paper wadded up and hidden inside. Buck picked up the paper and unfolded it. His hands shook, and he turned a ghostly white as if he were going to pass out.

Earl grabbed the worn flyer from his grasp and almost soiled his underpants. "Holy shit!"

He dropped the paper on the desk, and the others looked on in horror. Staring back at them was a picture of a familiar face that they had been fighting hard to get out of their nightmares.

CHAPTER SIXTY-EIGHT

"How did it go at Antioch?" Billy asked. He had wanted to go, but Robert insisted that it would be better if he went alone. Billy knew better than to ask twice. Robert had a reason for everything.

"Better than expected," said Robert, "with one exception."

"Well?"

"Eustice Adam Winchester, Jr. wasn't there."

"That is rather odd," Billy remarked. "What do you make of it? Do you think he's hiding, ran off, or met an unfortunate accident?"

"It's too early to tell, I suppose. Give it time, and I'm sure we'll find out. I made a call on his wife, but she won't talk to me. If he's hiding, he's not hiding at home. If he ran off, he didn't take his truck because it was found over by the hardware store. He returned the car he borrowed from Mr. Drury, who hasn't seen him since. As far as we know, he's out of friends, or more accurately, people he can bully to gain access to a vehicle or a place to stay. Nobody at the bus station has seen him. If he took off, he did so without a car and without funds, so I figure he's hiding out in the woods, or—"

"That was quick," Billy noted. "I hadn't expected that. If anything, I'd guess that he'd be the one doing the cleanup."

"So, hiding it is," said Robert.

"Or," said Billy.

"Or," Robert agreed.

"I guess that leaves only Cooter and the preacher left to interrogate," Billy said.

"Forget Cooter," said Robert. "He's not going to tell us anything."

"And why is that?" asked Billy.

"Take a look at the map. His place is adjacent to the swamp. Whatever happened, happened on his property. There's no way he'll be able to bargain his way out of it and he knows it. Cooter will have no choice but to find the best lawyer in the county, and the rest will follow suit. It's best we don't poke him just yet. Being smart could be contagious."

"What about the preacher?" Billy asked.

Robert smiled. "He's in there now."

"You kidding? I expected him to resist or call a lawyer."

"He came in unannounced about twenty minutes ago."

"I see," said Billy. "I don't suppose he came to confess his sins?"

Robert laughed. "Hardly. He's the great prophet, remember? He is as pure as the driven snow. No, he came in here because he wanted to catch us off guard. He's a real control freak. He thinks he'll be able to outdo us in the cleverness department."

"You mean outdo you. So, why are you not in there?"

"I sent Ricky in."

Billy raised his eyebrows. "All out of cheap perfume?"

Robert laughed. "I'm going in right now. I sent the deputy in to blow smoke up his ass. The prophet was insulted—for about a minute. He thinks he's on to me now. He'll be full of confidence when it's my turn. He's one cocky son-of-a-bitch."

"It's all fun and games until the cuffs come out," said Billy. "Are you going to ask him about Junior?"

"Who?" Robert asked. He winked, put on his game face, and entered the interrogation room.

CHAPTER SIXTY-NINE

Brother Eustice smiled when Robert came into the room. He stood up and shook the detective's hand as if they were long-lost friends. Robert played along.

"Brother Ricky was tellin' me about how you two found the remains of the poor girl. He says you're famous for findin' dead things, I mean, the remains of lost souls," Eustice said. "It is such a tragic tale. I'll pray for your success in findin' the horrible beast that did this."

"I know you will, Brother," Robert replied. He excused Ricky, and the two sat down alone in the room.

"You were mighty generous the other day," said Eustice. "That really was unnecessary, you not being a member of the congregation. We don't usually pass the plate to visitors. I'm afraid our deacons get a little carried away sometimes, take matters into their own hands. I do my best to guide them, but I'm sorry to say, I have failed them as a shepherd."

"I'm sure you do your best, Brother. I bet you not only try to guide them, but try to protect them as much as you can."

Brother Eustice nodded. "You understand much."

"More than you know."

"One of the men took it upon himself to count the donations and said that you left this," Brother Eustice pulled a folded piece of paper out of his pocket and handed it to Robert.

Robert paused, took the paper, unfolded it, and set it face up on the table. He ceremoniously searched his pockets until he found what he was looking for. He retrieved a pair of reading glasses and looked at the flyer as if he'd never seen it before.

"Ladies and gentlemen," he read out loud, "be prepared to witness the most incredible show on Earth: The Amazing and Magnificent Villanova!"

Robert took off the phony eyeglasses, put them back in his pocket, and looked at the preacher. "I don't get it."

"You left this with your donation," said Eustice.

"I did? Why would I do that?"

"I don't know. That's why I brought it up."

Robert looked at the advertisement, then at the preacher, and shrugged.

"Are you sayin' you didn't put this in the collection plate?"

"Maybe someone picked it up off the floor or it just fell in there," offered Robert.

"Wrapped up with a rubber band?"

"I thought you said one of the deacons discovered it? How would you know it was wound up with a rubber band?"

"That's what he said."

"That's what who said?"

Brother Eustice paused. "A good shepherd protects his flock."

"Protects his flock from what?"

"Let's not play games here, Detective. We both know why you've been harassin' my congregation. Everybody knows. I came here of my own accord to set the record straight so we can put this behind us. I'm sure I can answer all of your questions and ease your mind."

"I haven't asked you any," Robert noted.

"But you want to."

Robert laughed. "So you really are a prophet."

"What do you want to know?"

"I already know," said Robert.

"Know what?"

Robert smiled.

"You think you're so damn clever, don't you?" said Eustice. "Pride goeth before the fall."

"Does it? Is that a felony or a misdemeanor?"

"I came here to clear the air, and all you're doin' is playing games and wastin' my time," Brother Eustice said, backing his chair up in preparation to leave.

"You know what is a felony?" asked Robert. "Homicide. In Alabama, that'll get you a date with Yellow Mama. You know who that is?"

"'Course I do," said Eustice. "Everybody knows. It's the 'lectric chair over at Kilby."

Robert winked.

"Are you sayin' I killed that girl?"

"Girls," Robert corrected him. "You know what's also a felony? Accessory to murder. That'll only get you life."

"What's that got to do with me?"

"A good shepherd protects his flock," said Robert.

Eustice nodded and pulled his chair back to the table. "Anythin' I learn as part of a confession is protected."

"You're not a lawyer, Brother Eustice. If indeed you know something and haven't come forward with it, you are, at the very least, an accessory after the fact. Any claim you had as to why you didn't come forward until now ended when you walked in that door. You're here now. I'm here now. It's time to spill it."

"But a confession to a clergyman is protected," insisted Eustice.

Robert shook his head. "Look at me, Brother. Go on, take a good look. I'm the only protection you've got."

"You need to give me some guarantees."

Robert laughed.

"What's so funny?"

The smile on Robert's face disappeared. He leaned forward and whispered, "Nothing. Nothing's funny. Nothing at all. You want a guarantee? I'll guarantee you that I'm going to fry every last one of you sons-of-bitches unless you come clean."

Brother Eustice remained silent, conflicted in thought. Robert waited. Moments passed before, once again, the preacher pushed his chair back as if he were going to leave.

"I'm sorry," said Eustice. "I really am. I'm responsible for the souls of my flock."

"I understand," said Robert. "I can respect that. Don't say I didn't warn you though. This was your one and only chance to cut a deal. Once you leave, you and yours are on your own."

Eustice's face flinched. Robert knew he'd struck a nerve, so he pressed further. "Is there something wrong?"

"No, I mean," the preacher stammered, "I, I'm sure there's nothin' you can do about—"

"Has anyone threatened you or your family?" Robert asked. "If so, there very much is something I can do about it."

"I'm not sure," said Eustice.

"Not sure?"

"It's just that my boy—"

"Jeremiah Thomas? I saw him the other day," Robert stated.

"No, the other one. Junior."

"Oh, yeah. We talked to him several times," said Robert. "You did?"

"Sure we did. No offense, Mr. Winchester, but he is an odd duck of sorts. He was telling us all kinds of crazy stuff. After awhile, we didn't know what to believe. Charles Ray said, I mean, it doesn't matter. I'm not at liberty to discuss it with you, but it'll all come out eventually anyway."

Eustice was speechless.

"Look, don't take it to heart," Robert said with sympathy. "I didn't get along with my old man, either. But I never went so far as to— Well, like I said, it doesn't matter."

"What are you talkin' about?"

Robert shrugged. "I've said too much already."

"You ain't said nothin'," Eustice protested. "You either seen him, or you ain't."

"Is he missing? Would you like to file a missing persons report?'"

"You said you talked to him. That's a lie. My boy ain't never talked to you. You're playin' games."

"I'm playing games!" Robert exclaimed as if offended. "You come in here saying you know something about a double homicide, but won't tell me a thing unless I give you unnamed guarantees. Only then, I find out what you're really in here for is to get help finding your good-for-nothing piece-of-shit spawn."

"How dare you! The Lord—"

"Can it with the Bible talk, Eustice. If you want my help to find your boy, you better drop the bullshit act and play ball."

"You got him, don't you?"

Robert almost laughed. The preacher was practically foaming at the mouth. What was left of his confidence had abandoned him only minutes into the interrogation. It had taken hours to wear down Jeremiah.

"You don't want me to find him," Robert said, "and you know why."

"What?" Eustice was at a loss. "Why?"

"You said it yourself. I find dead things."

"Why, you heartless bastard!" spat Eustice. "That's my boy you're talkin' about. He has a wife and children who need him."

"He's nothing to lose our heads over."

Eustice balled his hand into a fist, but caught himself and hit the table instead of the detective. He stood up to leave.

"I see you're not going to take me up on my offer," Robert said. "Just as well. I wasn't going to offer you a damn thing anyway. You see, I know it was you, Brother. Directly, indirectly, it's all you. Every last bit of it. You're going to fry, no matter what. I'm going to see to it personally."

Brother Eustice didn't want to hear any more. He walked to the door and knocked, waiting for one of the deputies to let him out.

"But I am curious about one thing," Robert added.

Eustice pretended he wasn't listening.

"How was the show? Was he really amazing and magnificent before you cut him in half?"

The door opened and Eustice left, his blood boiling with anger. The only thing that had him more worried than his missing boy was the detective. His men had been right. Stallworth was much smarter than they'd given him credit for. No mere mortal could know so much. The man was a demon. He had to be destroyed.

CHAPTER SEVENTY

"**W**here's your damn brother?"

Jeremiah jumped. He hadn't heard the old man come up, and he was shocked that he'd used that kind of language in front of Brandine.

"I ain't seen him."

"Liar!" Brother Eustice shouted. "The Lord detests lyin' lips! Tell me where he is!"

"Am I my brother's keeper?"

Brother Eustice swung his walking stick, but Jeremiah was too fast. He backed away from his irate father just in time. It was too bad the lamp and end table weren't as lucky. The table hit the floor with a thud, and the lamp shattered into a thousand pieces.

"How dare you quote the good book to me, boy! I know you went off with him in the woods."

Brandine was visibly shocked. Jeremiah had sworn to her that he'd avoid his brother, especially when it came to being in a remote location.

"I don't know what you're talkin' about," replied Jeremiah, proclaiming his innocence.

"You went off with him into the woods last Thursday. He told me he was takin' you—," Brother Eustice paused. Jeremiah pretended he hadn't noticed. "Takin' you out huntin' for squirrels," Eustice improvised. "Are you sayin' you didn't go?"

"We were goin' to, but somethin' came up," said Jeremiah.

"Somethin' came up? What came up?"

"I don't know," said Jeremiah.

Eustice swung his staff, but Jeremiah grabbed a cushion off the sofa and used it as a shield.

"Cut it out! You're bustin' up my place!"

"Quit lyin'!"

"I ain't lyin'," Jeremiah insisted. "Somethin' came up."

"What came up?"

"It was all my fault," Brandine spoke up for the first time. "I'm sorry, Papa Winchester. I was havin', uh, female troubles. I thought it might be the baby. I asked JT to take me to the doctors. I didn't want to cause no trouble."

Eustice turned to the girl. He caught his breath and put his walking stick down. "I'm sorry to hear that, little lady. Is everythin' okay with the baby?"

"Yes, sir, I was just bein' silly. It's my first child you see and—"

"No reason to apologize, sweetie. You need to take care of that little one." Brother Eustice turned back to Jeremiah, but his voice lost the tenderness he'd used with Brandine. "You go find your brother. I need to have a few words with him."

"Where am I supposed to find him?" asked Jeremiah

Brother Eustice raised his staff but stayed his hand. He glared at his youngest son. "Figure it out, and do it quick. We got a new mission to discuss."

Eustice nodded to his daughter-in-law, leaving the trailer in shambles. Once he was gone, Brandine turned to her husband.

"I thought you promised me you'd stay away from Junior."

"I tried, but he insisted. He forced me."

"What did you do?" Brandine asked, afraid of the answer she knew was coming.

"Never you mind. I did what I had to do. You heard what my paw said, don't you see?"

"What do you mean?"

"Paw sent him, Brandine. Paw sent him."

"Sent him to do what?"

"We weren't goin' to hunt squirrels. I was the squirrel. Don't you get it? Paw sent Junior to kill me."

Stallworth had warned him about his older brother. He knew what was up as soon as they set out. Squirrel hunting? As if. He played along, amazed at how well Junior covered up his true intentions. It didn't matter. He hadn't been fooled. As soon as the opportunity came, he pulled the trigger. Junior tried to beg. It was unbecoming. He pleaded and promised all kinds of things. Jeremiah didn't fall for it. Now, his father had confirmed his suspicions.

"What? That's crazy. Why would he do that?"

Brandine felt sick. She'd known the truth ever since the detective showed up, but swore to herself it wasn't true. When JT came home smelling like a whore, she ranted and raved and accused him of seeing another woman. She threw him out of the house, only to let him back in the next day. She knew in her heart that he hadn't messed around on her, but she preferred that lie to the truth.

"I didn't want to do it," Jeremiah started to cry.

"It's okay, baby. I'm so sorry." Brandine took her husband in her arms. She hated Junior, but couldn't fathom how horrible it must have been for a man to have to kill his own brother—self-defense or not. "I know how much you loved him."

"No, not Junior, not Junior!" cried Jeremiah. "I didn't want to kill that girl."

Brandine held her husband and closed her eyes. They wept together for all that was lost and all that would be lost still. There was no more pretending.

"What are we goin' to do?" Jeremiah asked. "What are we goin' to do now?"

"That detective." The words left Brandine's mouth as if spoken by someone else. "You got to get rid of him."

Jeremiah froze. He looked at the young woman he'd fallen in love with as if he'd never seen her before. "What do you mean?"

Brandine looked into Jeremiah's eyes. Tears no longer fell down her cheeks. Sadness no longer gripped her voice. It had been replaced with a tone as cold as steel as she relayed her cruel instructions. "Get rid of him."

PART FIVE:

RETRIBUTION

One crime has to be concealed by another.

Seneca the Younger

CHAPTER SEVENTY-ONE

Robert was ushered into Sheriff Fuller's office as soon as he entered the building. He suspected that something was up when he saw that the parking lot was full. His suspicions were confirmed by the electricity that hung in the air.

An elderly gentleman with graying hair and a scowl permanently attached to his face was seated in the sheriff's chair. The sheriff was standing behind the man's left shoulder, and a young fellow who appeared to be in his early thirties, wearing an impeccable custom made suit, was behind the right shoulder. Dr. Hall and Billy Watts stood in the corner behind them. Robert was left standing alone as if he were facing a firing squad.

"So this is the detective I've been hearing so much about?" the old man seated behind the desk asked.

"Detective Robert Stallworth," Sheriff Fuller said, "I'd like you to meet Judge Mason Parker."

Robert nodded, but stayed silent. He knew Parker by reputation only, and it wasn't good.

"We've been getting a lot of complaints about you," said Parker.

When the detective offered no comment, the judge continued, "It seems you've been harassing the good people of this county with little to show for it. I'm here to tell you, it's going to stop, and it's going to stop now."

Robert gave no indication that he'd heard a word of what the judge had said.

"Are you listening to me?"

"I'm can hear you," Robert replied after a momentary delay.

"But you're not listening," replied the judge. "I can make one phone call and you'll be handing out parking tickets by the end of the day."

"I doubt that."

"What! How dare you? I know the governor personally. Don't test me, young man."

"Who complained?"

"That's none of your concern."

Robert laughed.

"Is there something you find amusing? You're in deep shit, Detective. I'm warning you not to test me."

"With all due respect, your honor, you have your job to do, and I have mine."

"If you want to keep that job, you'll listen to what I'm telling you. I'm not someone you want to get on the bad side of."

"Neither am I. I'm doing my job, and I'm going to continue to do my job no matter whose toes I have to step on. We have two bodies we've fished out of the swamp, and until I lock up the people responsible, I'm not changing a thing."

"Three," the man wearing the suit said.

"Pardon?" asked Robert.

"We have three bodies now," the man replied.

"This is District Attorney Vaughan," said the sheriff. "We got an anonymous tip at the crack of dawn. Ricky responded right away and found Eustice Winchester Junior's remains. He'd been shot."

"Multiple times," Dr. Hall added. "I'll do the full assessment later, but my first impression is that whoever killed him had a score to settle."

Robert glanced at Billy, who nodded in return. It had begun.

"According to our reports, the deceased father asked for your help in finding his son," the judge said. "He said that the boy was in danger and begged you to address the situation, yet you laughed at him and refused to help. Is that true?"

"Something like that," said Robert.

"You seem to find this amusing. Care to let us in on the joke?"

"It's not amusing, but it's also not surprising."

"And it's not going to stop there," said District Attorney Vaughan.

"Not by a long shot," Robert replied.

"Well, let me let you in on a little joke you might not find so funny," Judge Parker said. "There are rumors that someone put a hit out on you."

Robert laughed again.

"You find that funny?" asked Vaughan.

"I hate to break it to you, but that's not the first time," said Robert. "Billy," he turned to Watts, "tell them what's right about it."

The men looked at the retired detective.

"It's right on schedule," said Billy.

"I don't know what kind of game you're playing, but it's not something I want conducted in my county," Judge Parker said. "I heard about the crap with the pretend Klan rally and arrests, and I have no idea how you got everyone to go along with that."

"Yes, you do," said Robert. Billy winced.

"Why, I—" the judge protested.

Robert dared to interrupt the man in mid-sentence, "Tell me, Sheriff. Ricky didn't happen to find anything else with Junior's body, did he?"

"Like what?" asked Fuller.

"Like two heads," said Robert.

Billy looked at Dr. Hall, and they both did their best to suppress a grin.

"I don't know what you're going on about, and I don't care," the judge said. "I didn't come here to nitpick. I came here because we have serious allegations of a dereliction of duty. Someone filed a complaint."

"Do you know who killed those girls?" the district attorney asked Robert.

Judge Parker stewed in anger. He was used to being in control, and this was twice he'd been interrupted. What was worse was that he'd lost the room. No one seemed to care who he was or why he was there. Somehow, that damned detective had shifted the whole conversation.

"Ask Judge Parker," said Robert.

"What?" the judge stammered. The mention of his name snapped him back to attention. "How would I know?"

Vaughan smiled. Dr. Hall and Watts smiled. Sheriff Fuller smiled. Robert looked at the judge and raised an eyebrow. Judge Mason Parker hesitated, locked in an internal battle. Moments later, he sighed and the scowl left his face. He sat back in defeat and offered up one name.

"Brother Eustice Elijah Winchester."

CHAPTER SEVENTY-TWO

"**I** only wish you'd consulted with me before."

Robert and Billy went to the courthouse in Carrollton after their run-in with Judge Parker. The district attorney had insisted on it.

"We didn't have enough evidence," said Robert.

"You don't have any from what I can see," said Vaughan. "Have you gotten anywhere with the interrogations?"

"It depends on what you mean by anywhere. We've gotten somewhere, or else Junior wouldn't have been murdered."

"That's not going to help us. What's also not going to help us is if you end up next."

"That's not my intention," said Robert.

The lawyer sat back in his leather chair and took a few breaths, deep in thought. After a moment, he continued, "You said something about the heads. Do you think you can find them?"

"I doubt it," said Robert. "I suspect that it was Junior who saved them, and he's no longer able to tell us anything."

"Why do you think he had them?"

"Just a hunch," said Robert. "They are a strange bunch of miscreants indeed."

"Why all the theatrics with the fake Klan arrests? That's only going to make it more difficult for me when we get to court."

"Maybe, maybe not. I'm not finished with that yet."

Vaughan leaned forward, intrigued. "Do tell."

"And ruin the surprise?"

The lawyer laughed. "You are a clever one, aren't you? Judge Parker was outraged. He completely underestimated you. I'm not going to make that mistake, but if I may make a suggestion?"

"Please do."

"Don't underestimate me. I'm not one of those hillbilly ambulance chasers. I went to Yale."

"I could tell by the suit," said Robert.

They laughed.

"You're alright, Stallworth."

"Call me Robert."

"I'm Garland. Now, what can you tell me? How are you going to handle the irate judge or the assassination threat, being that I'm sure it's all part of your plan?"

"Well, now that I've been officially rebuked by a high-standing member of the court, no doubt at the direction of the holy man, and I have seemingly dug a hole for myself, not to mention my questionable tactics and dubious acts of overstepping my authority, I'm persona non grata. My reputation is in ruins. I'm a bad cop. It is appropriate at this juncture that I be relieved of my command and have to take an embarrassing demotion. I'll surely be relegated to having to answer to a superior who will be brought in to take over the investigation and lead it into a, shall we say, more advantageous direction for our current suspects?"

"The good cop," said Garland, smiling.

Robert winked.

CHAPTER SEVENTY-THREE

Robert waited in the church's parking lot for the services to end. The last stanza of *Nearer My God to Thee* told him that, any minute, the throng of faithful would pour out of the large, wooden double doors.

When the hymn was finished and the crowd came out of the building, the look of apprehension on the faces of the pious told Robert that he was as welcome as a plague of locusts. He leaned against the front of his car, tipped his hat and nodded to the people as they walked past, who either gave him nasty looks or ignored him altogether. When the majority of the congregation had dispersed, Robert stood alone to face Brother Winchester and the Antioch Pentecostal Church deacons who had gathered in a semi-circle around him.

"Good day, brothers!" said Robert. "I believe it's time we had another chat."

"We're done talkin' to you, heathen," said Buck.

The others mumbled their agreement.

"You got a lot of nerve comin' over here like this, after what you done," said Charles Ray.

"After what I've done?"

"Our beloved prophet has just buried his boy, and you came here to harass us again?" said Charles Ray in disgust. He'd been working overtime trying to return into the good graces of his fellow deacons, and he used every opportunity to promote himself. When word of Junior's demise had gotten out, Charles Ray panicked. He had packed a suitcase just in case, but had few places he could run off to and none where he wouldn't easily be found. "Brother Eustice came to you for help, and you mocked him. Now Junior is dead. That's on your head, Demon!"

"And you think I killed him?" asked Robert.

"You didn't do anythin' to stop it," said Earl.

"Neither did you, Deputy."

"Don't be tryin' to turn us on each other. You've been doin' that all along, pretendin' that I'm workin' in cahoots with you," said Charles Ray. "That's not goin' to work anymore. We're on to you." Charles Ray hoped his assertion would be believed.

"Take a good look around you, gentlemen," said Robert. "My guess is that, when you do, you'll see who killed Junior. Or then again, maybe not. Where's Jeremiah Thomas, Reverend?"

"He had urgent matters to attend to," interjected Joe Bob. "And what do you mean by that?"

"You tell me, ex-Marine," said Robert.

"Silence!" shouted Brother Eustice. "Evil men and imposters will proceed from bad to worse, deceivin' and being deceived. Be gone, Demon! We know your kind. We've faced the wicked before and triumphed! I cast you out! I'd tell you to repent, but it's too late for you, Devil. The lake of fire awaits you, and there is nothin' you can do about it."

"Is that a threat?" asked Robert, unmoved by the fiery sermon.

Eustice laughed, and the others joined in.

"If you only knew."

"Oh, I know," Robert assured them. "I know. I know what happened to the magician. I know what happened to the girls. Notice I said girls. I couldn't help but observe in our little discussions that not one of you referred to the word in the plural sense. Did Brother Bullshitter actually convince you chumps that it was the same girl, resurrected by an evil spell?" Robert laughed.

The detective could see his comment hit its mark. The deacons had the tell-tale signs of guilt and confusion. Only Winchester's expression remained firm in its indignant rage.

"I know what happened to Junior, too," said Robert.

Nobody said a word. In truth, Robert was as full of bullshit as he accused the preacher of being. He didn't actually know anything. It was all a bluff, but his instincts told him he was right on the money. He'd convinced the DA and the judge that the odd man out was the culprit, so maybe it would work again.

"You don't know squat," said Buck.

"Don't I? Don't you?"

"What's that supposed to mean?" asked Joe Bob.

"Don't listen to him, brethren!" Brother Eustice exclaimed. "Through his shrewdness, he will cause deceit to succeed by his influence, and he will magnify himself in his heart. He will destroy many while they are at ease."

"Are you at ease, Brother Eustice?" asked Robert. "Are any of y'all? From where I'm standing, I'd say no. You're going down, all of you. It's only a matter of time."

"Be gone, Satan!" shouted Winchester. "I cast you out!"

"Are you going to use some magic dust, or will a bolt of lightning strike me?"

Brother Eustice smiled his toothless, evil grin. "Stand still and you'll find out."

CHAPTER SEVENTY-FOUR

"**Y**ou take that back!" Jeremiah screamed. Vernon had been teasing him about the stain on his trousers. He had been humiliated in front of all the kids in the schoolyard.

"JT needs a diaper. JT needs a diaper," the bully sang. "The little baby peed his pants."

"I did not!" Jeremiah shouted, doing his best to hold the tears that were beginning to run down his cheeks.

"Look, he's crying, too! I told you he was a baby!" Vernon laughed.

He didn't laugh long. Out of nowhere came the first blow. The sharp punch to the back of his head sent the boy crashing to the pavement. A quick succession of blows followed. In less than a minute, the bully's face was covered with blood oozing from his broken nose and several loose teeth. By the time Mr. Grady pulled his attacker off, Vernon had been beaten to a bloody pulp.

"Eustice Adam!" the man chastised the boy in his grasp, "what the Devil has gotten into you?"

Eustice said nothing, his jaw clenched in anger.

"What's the reverend going to say?" asked the vice principal. "You should try to be more like your older brother. He's as gentle as a lamb." The man pulled the enraged boy to the office, leaving the injured bully behind.

Jeremiah wiped his tears and looked around. No one made eye contact, and no one would. They'd think twice before messing with him again as long as Junior was around. He loved his brother and longed for the day he could prove himself worthy of his respect.

Cooter nudged him, and he jumped. He'd been lost in a memory, something that had been happening often lately. Jeremiah was glad to be brought out of it.

"He's outside," Cooter whispered. "You know what to do."

Jeremiah nodded and handed the collection plate to Cooter. As stealthily as he could, he made his way to the back of the church, taking care to grab the bolt action Remington .30-06 rifle on his way out.

Jeremiah took care not to be seen or heard as he disappeared into the trees at the rear. Once he was sure he'd travelled a safe distance, he crouched low and slowly moved around the perimeter until he spotted the detective leaning against the hood of his car in the church parking lot. Jeremiah moved with purpose as he got into position.

He found a good spot in the shadows of a large oak tree and rested his gun on a small boulder. Jeremiah checked his weapon and flicked off the safety. He eyed the detective through the scope until he was confident he'd be able to drop his prey without difficulty. Then he waited.

Ten minutes later, the church doors opened and the congregation exited the building. Jeremiah smiled smugly when he saw the obvious resentment the members showed to the policeman. His belief that he was doing the Lord's work was heightened by the hatred his fellow parishioners felt towards the detective. Nobody would miss him. Jeremiah was doing them a favor. He'd be a hero. It would almost make up for what he'd been forced to do to Junior.

When the crowd thinned, only his father and the deacons remained. As they'd been instructed, the men stood well out of the assassin's way. Jeremiah took a deep breath and put the rifle to his shoulder. He looked through the scope until he saw the detective's head square in the crosshairs. He placed his finger gently on the trigger.

Jeremiah let go of the trigger and sat back. His hands were shaking and his heart was beating erratically. *What the hell's the matter with you?* He couldn't understand it. He'd shot his brother without hesitation, but he seemed unable to fire on the enemy, whom he hated. *Get it together!*

Jeremiah took several deep breaths until he felt calm again. He moved back into position with resolve. There would be no more delays. It was time he took care of the whole group's problems with one fell swoop.

He positioned the rifle until, once again, he saw the detective's head square in the crosshairs of the scope. There was no wind, and he was well within range. Stallworth was as good as dead. Jeremiah calmly positioned his finger on the trigger.

The sound of the police siren almost made him fire off a round. Instead, his hand jerked away from the rifle, and he took another deep breath.

Who the hell is that? he asked himself with annoyance and no small amount of relief. He watched as the fat, bearded policeman exited his state police cruiser and limped up to the front of the church.

CHAPTER SEVENTY-FIVE

Whoop! Weeahh! The sudden chirps howled through the silent afternoon, causing the men to jump. Robert's gaze followed the preacher and the deacons as they turned and spotted the approaching police car, the red and blue bubble-gum lights flashing on the roof. They watched as the vehicle pulled up next to the detective's and a large man with a gray beard exited.

"Howdy, neighbors!" the man's friendly voice boomed. "Detective," he addressed Robert with a hint of disdain.

"Sergeant," Robert replied, his normally cocky voice full of hesitation. "What are you doing here?"

The man gave the detective a dirty look, but ignored the question and walked over to the men standing in front of the church. He introduced himself and shook each man's hand, one by one. He continued to ignore Robert, opting instead to speak to the others.

"I'm John Turner of the Alabama State Police, and I've been sent here to apologize to you men personally. Detective Stallworth's ill-advised antics and deplorable behavior have gotten the attention of those at the highest level in our state."

"Sergeant Turner, if I may have a word with you?" interrupted Robert.

"We'll have more than a few words, but you'll have to wait your turn," replied the officer. He turned back to the men and said in a considerably friendlier tone, "It seems our friend here has forgotten who he works for."

Brother Eustice and the boys laughed at the detective's humiliation.

"If you'll excuse me for a minute," whispered Turner.

The sergeant turned and walked past the detective to the rear of the police cars. Robert followed. Their distance was meant to assure that they were out of the laymen's earshot, but the level of their voices in the heated argument left little in the way of privacy.

"This is not open for discussion," said Turner. "I'm in charge now, and you'll do as you're told, or you're fired."

"You don't have the authority," Robert objected.

"The hell I don't. You can cry and whine all you want, but it's a done deal. You've stepped on enough toes with nothing to show for it. Face it, you don't have a clue what's going on."

"But these men—"

"What about these men? Don't you think you've harassed them enough already?"

"But they are—"

"Right, sure they are. First, it was the Klan. Hell, you even arrested the damn sheriff. Now you're messing with these fine Christian gentlemen."

"But—" Robert tried to explain.

"But nothing," said Turner. "It's over. We're done here. I'm not buying into your suspicions—"

"You don't understand," pleaded the detective. "I've interrogated each one of them and—"

"Interrogated? Did you detain them against their will?"

"Well, not exactly—"

"Jesus H. Christ! You really bungled this big time."

"You don't understand. Question them yourselves and you'll see."

"I intend to, if they'll agree. Frankly, I don't know why they would, except to get revenge on you. Don't you worry, Detective, I'll get to the bottom of things. It'll all be on the official record. How you ignored the preacher's pleas to help find his boy; how you threatened an officer of the law, practically accusing a county deputy of a double homicide; how you detained another for hours, then sent him home in a purposeful attempt to cause marital problems. I heard that you even disrupted Sunday services. Have you no shame, man?"

"It wasn't like that," said Robert.

"It better not be! The governor won't stand for it. Judge Parker is an ordained minister, and he won't stand for it. I'm a devout follower of Reverend Austin Sterling of the First Baptist Church of the Nazarene, and I won't stand for it. I don't know what happened to you in the army, but it wasn't good. Your father would be ashamed of you."

Robert looked like he was close to tears. He wanted to reply, but clenched his jaw shut and bit his tongue.

"I've heard enough from you, Stallworth. Like it or not, I'm in charge now, and what I say goes. Before this is over, I swear, I'm going to have you stand before every one of these men with your hat in your hand and beg for forgiveness. They'll probably give it to you, too, despite what you've accused them of because that's the kind of godly men they are. You wouldn't understand that, of course. There was a time you might've, but not anymore. If you're lucky, that'll be the only thing that happens to you."

"Don't be so certain I'm not right about them," said Robert. "You don't know—"

"No, you're the one who doesn't know," interrupted Turner. "These men are no longer suspects."

"But, how—?"

"But, but, but, that's all you keep saying."

Turner shook his head and momentarily glanced over at the group of men standing in front of the church. They were all laughing at the turn of events. Turner gave them a look as if to say, 'Can you believe this imbecile?' Then he went back to chastising Robert.

"They've found some bones behind the sheriff's office. Two skulls were uncovered so far," said Turner.

"What? But—"

"There you go with the buts again. Shut up and listen. Dr. Hall has two skulls in his possession right now. At this point, it seems way more likely that you arrested the guilty parties in the first place, only to ignore them and go after these innocent folk. Why, I'll never know. It probably has to do with some twisted, deep seated resentment you have against God, but I'll leave that to the psychiatrists and the Almighty to deal with. Unfortunately, thanks to you and your incompetent mishandling of the investigation, we'll likely never get a conviction. Hell, we'll be lucky to even get an arrest now."

"But the interrogations—" Robert couldn't let it go.

"Will prove that I'm right and you were overzealous in your pursuit." Turner put an arm around the detective's shoulders and softened his tone. "Look, I know you were trying to do your job. It's just that, sometimes, Robert, you get carried away. You're too clever for your own good. If it makes you feel better, I'll question each and every one of these men again. I'm sure they'll be more than okay with it. It'll be their chance to set the record straight without someone playing games and trying to trip them up. The truth will come out. These guys aren't like you. They're simple folk. They're not crafty and scheming. They'll jump at the chance to tell the truth."

Turner guided the detective to his car and opened the door for him, signaling the finality of the situation. All Robert could do was stare in disbelief.

"Don't be so despondent," said Turner. "It's going to be alright. You'll see. The truth will be much less interesting than your wild tale. In the end, you'll find it's also much easier to swallow. Now, we'll get the guys who did this and they'll pay, but in order to do that, we're going to need these men's help."

Robert looked at Winchester and the men who did little to hide their amusement at the detective's degradation.

"You've all but destroyed any chance of that, but I have faith," said Turner. "Something you seem to have lost. This will be a good thing for you, Robert. You're finally going to get a chance to find true meaning and joy again. You're going to find out what forgiveness and redemption really mean. As much as you've harmed these men, I know in my heart they're going to help us solve this crime. When the time comes, they'll even forgive you. I'm sure someone like you will never believe that, but I know it in my heart because I know their hearts. We are followers of the Lord."

Robert cast his eyes down and got into his car. Turner shut the door for him and leaned in to address him through the open window. "Go on, now. We'll meet up again soon over by the sheriff's office. We'll have to go through these men's statements one at a time, but remember, Fuller and his men might be the true suspects. We'll have to do this carefully. This time, I'll be doing all the talking. You'll just sit idly by with your mouth shut, and you'll begin to understand what I've been trying to tell you. What, no doubt, the good preacher here has been trying to tell you. Heed the word of the Lord, Robert, and you'll witness miracles."

"Amen!" erupted the men standing in front of the church.

Robert started his car and drove off, pretending not to see the sly wink Turner gave him. As far as the detective was concerned, John Turner deserved an Academy Award for Best Actor in a Homicide Investigation.

CHAPTER SEVENTY-SIX

"**I** can't thank you enough for talking to me," Turner explained. "After everything Stallworth put y'all through, I wouldn't have batted an eye if you told me to take a hike."

"Don't think nothin' of it," said Earl. "He was just doin' his job."

Turner looked at the deputy as if he were going to argue about the assessment, but thought better of it. He sat down at the small table in the interrogation room where Earl had been waiting for half an hour.

"I'm sorry I'm a bit late," said Turner. "I didn't want to seem too obvious about why we're really here."

"Why are we really here?"

Turner leaned in and replied in a whisper, "Fuller and his men have heard about the skulls we've dug up. Hopefully, that's all they know. Things are going to get ugly around here if we change directions and come after them. Stallworth messed things up enough as it is."

"Yeah, he's a hard man to like," said Earl.

Turner laughed. "Indeed. Look, Deputy Barber, I can understand you're in a delicate position here. I really can. On one hand, you're a member of the department, and Sheriff Fuller is your boss. On the other hand, you're a follower of Brother Winchester at the Antioch Pentecostal Church."

"They're not mutually exclusive," said Earl.

"No, they're not," agreed Turner. "But in your case, we know you're not one of the boys as it were. In other words, you're not a Klansman. Which means, if it turns out some of them were involved in the killing of those two girls or Junior Winchester, you weren't a part of it."

"And if they weren't, I am?"

"I didn't say that."

"But you implied it."

"No, Detective Stallworth implied it. I'm not buying it for a minute."

"And why is that?" asked Earl suspiciously. After all of the games the detective had played, he couldn't be too sure that this wasn't yet another elaborate scheme to trip him up.

"Why is Stallworth dead set on y'all being the guilty parties? Or why am I not?"

"Both."

"Fair enough," said Turner. He leaned back and took a deep breath and said, "As far as Stallworth is concerned, y'all remind him of a rather ugly incident from his past. I'm not privy to all of the juicy details, mind you, but I've been able to piece the events together well enough to see the big picture."

"Go on."

"During the war, Stallworth was a member of Army Intelligence. Everything he did was classified, and no one is talking, least of all, him. But I know enough people to have gotten the gist. At some point, he was assigned to find mass graves, which he evidently excels at, vis-á-vis his reputation. The way I heard it, some of the people who were selected to help him with the gruesome task got their abilities in a much more direct way."

"They were in on it?"

Turner nodded.

"Nazi scum," Earl said in disgust.

"Some."

"You mean?"

Turner nodded again.

"Wow." Earl was shocked. What little faith he had left in his fellow man was being eroded by the minute. After he'd seen what Brother Eustice and his fellow deacons had done, he wondered why he had any left at all.

"It didn't go well when he figured it out. For him or anyone else," said Turner. "Frankly, I'm surprised he didn't buy himself a bullet."

"Me, too," Earl replied before catching himself. Turner didn't seem to notice.

"So you can see why he suspected the Sheriff and the Klan, and even your friends at Antioch. He suspects everyone and trusts no one."

Earl nodded. "And what about you?"

"I looked at the evidence," said Turner. "There isn't any. Hell, he's got more on the sheriff than he does on you. Now that we have the skulls, I'm sure even he'll refocus his attention. It's not personal with him, no matter how it seems to y'all."

"I ain't so sure 'bout that."

"Be sure," said Turner. He leaned forward again. "Make no mistake. Stallworth is very good at what he does. He may be overzealous, but he can flat out tear you apart in an interrogation."

Earl nodded. He didn't need Turner to tell him that.

"As for me, I trust my instincts, and they've never let me down. I had one look at you boys from the Antioch church, and I knew y'all weren't the kind of men who would, or could, do something as horrible as this. To tell you the truth, I didn't suspect y'all, but I listened to Stallworth's side. What clinched it for me was Junior. There's no way one of y'all would've killed one of your own, which means it wasn't y'all in the first place. It also means that all of you are in danger."

Earl remained silent, lost in his thoughts. Turner was right. Whoever murdered Junior was also involved in the killing of the girls. It was one of them, alright. Whoever it was wasn't going to stop unless someone stopped him.

"Deputy, are you hearing what I'm saying? You're the only one who can help me here, or there's going to be more killings."

Earl nodded. Things were getting way out of control, but this could be his lucky break. It would be difficult, but if he was able to use his position in the police department to nab the others without implicating himself with the girls' homicide, he'd be off the hook. On the flip side, if he made one misstep, he'd end up in prison—or worse. In the end, Earl knew that a small chance was better than none at all.

"What do you want me to do?"

CHAPTER SEVENTY-SEVEN

Cooter Yates was not happy. After everything that had happened, and after all of his protests, here they were, meeting at his place near the swamp again.

"I told y'all a thousand times, I don't want y'all comin' here no more," he complained. Nobody seemed to care.

"Where else are we going to meet?" asked Charles Ray. "Besides, we ain't suspects anymore. You heard that cop."

"That sure was funny watching that dumbass detective gettin' his ass chewed out," Joe Bob said with a chuckle.

"It sure was," said Charles Ray. "What wasn't funny was how y'all were all thinkin' I was in collusion with him. Y'all know me better than that."

"What did you expect?" said Cooter. "It seemed a little fishy to me."

"What do you mean fishy?"

"What I said, fishy," Cooter replied. "Besides, I ain't convinced we're off his radar yet. Comin' here is a bad idea, I tell you."

"Tell it to Brother Eustice," said Charles Ray. "He'll be here in a minute. Ain't that right, Buck?"

Buck remained silent.

"What's got him all quiet?" Charles Ray asked. Joe Bob shrugged.

As predicted, Brother Winchester's sedan arrived, kicking up a cloud of dust into the stagnant hot air. The preacher got out and walked over to the group, clearly annoyed at being summoned.

"Whose bright idea was it to come out here?" he asked.

"I thought you—" Cooter said.

"It was mine," interrupted Earl.

The men looked at the deputy in astonishment.

"Who gave you the authority to—" Brother Eustice said before being cut off.

"Nobody gave me no authority. I took it," said Earl defiantly.

"Look who thinks he's a big shot now," said Joe Bob. "Buck, you want to put him in his place?"

The group turned to look at Buck. He glared at each of them, then turned back to the deputy and nodded.

"So it's like that, is it?" asked Brother Eustice. "Someone's gettin' too big for his britches. Smite thee down, oh—"

"Shut the hell up," said Earl.

Brother Eustice stopped in mid-sentence as if he'd been slapped across the cheek. The rest of the deacons were visibly shocked.

"We've gotten into enough trouble because of you," Earl continued. "From now on, we're doin' this my way."

"Who made you boss?" asked Charles Ray.

"See this?" Earl pointed to his badge. "I'm tired of y'all takin' advantage of me. I'll arrest every last one of y'all if I have to, so don't try me."

"No, you won't," said Joe Bob. "You're just as guilty as the rest of us."

"It's your word against mine, and I'm a cop. You ain't nothin' but an unemployed handyman. Now y'all listen, and listen well. We got one chance of gettin' rid of that detective, and I'm not goin' to sit back and watch us blow it by takin' any more advice from Brother Stupid here."

"Who the hell do you think—?"

"I said shut it." Earl pulled his gun from his holster and pointed it at Eustice.

"You ain't gonna shoot him," said Charles Ray in disbelief.

"I will if I have to," insisted Earl.

"Not on my property you ain't," said Cooter, pulling a pistol he'd had concealed in his overalls.

Earl turned his gun on Cooter and fired.

Blam!

Cooter fell over backwards, blood oozing from a hole in the center of his chest. He was dead before he hit the ground.

"What did you do!" Charles Ray screamed.

The group looked on in horror. Earl's hand shook as he took a few steps back.

"I, I didn't mean to," he stammered. "You saw it. He drew first. You all saw it."

Their expressions said it all. No one was going to have his back. He had no choice now. He pointed his gun at Charles Ray.

"Wait!" Charles Ray screamed, putting his hands up in an attempt to shield himself from any incoming projectiles. "I ain't armed—"

Blam!

Buck stood by in a trance. Joe Bob turned to run.

Earl paid them no mind. He raised the gun once more and pointed it squarely at Brother Eustice Winchester's face.

Blam!

CHAPTER SEVENTY-EIGHT

Following the incident at Cooter's place, the entire county went on lockdown. Roadblocks were set up throughout the vicinity; dozens of policemen from neighboring counties and close to thirty state troopers were utilized.

"Any word on his condition?" asked Captain Warner.

"Critical, but stable," replied Turner. "He's getting the best of care. It's a miracle he even survived, considering the blood loss."

"It's a good thing you and the sheriff went out there," said the Captain. "Why did you do that, anyway?"

"It was Robert's suggestion," said Turner. "You know him—always thinking ahead."

"Thinking ahead? We have a major clusterfuck on our hands, and you call that thinking ahead?"

"That was my fault, Captain. I—"

"Stallworth is in charge of the investigation," said Warner. "Everything that happens is his fault. I'm wondering if I promoted him too quickly."

"No, sir. I wouldn't agree with you at all," a gruff voice interrupted them.

Warner and Turner turned to see who had entered the office.

"Judge Parker. I'm surprised to see you," said Warner. "We don't get too many celebrities down here."

"That detective of yours is a real peach," said Parker. "I was all set to ask for his resignation myself."

"I heard."

"Got some heat from that one?" The judge coughed. It was the closest thing to a laugh that he had in his repertoire. "Maybe I still have some pull over at the governor's office, after all."

"I'm sorry," Warner said. "It's his first big case. We usually give them an unsolvable mess to learn from the first time out, but it looks like it backfired. I'll have him reassigned as soon as—"

"You'll do nothing of the kind," interrupted the judge.

"I'm sorry, I thought—"

"Yeah, yeah, I know," said Parker. "It's a real mess. We have a cop hanging on to dear life. Shot by a sniper, they say. We have two suspects shot by that same deputy, and four fugitives on the run or hiding out somewhere. What we also have is the answer to our puzzle. Obviously, these are the men guilty of the murder of those two girls, the magician in Tennessee, and at least one of their own. We'd still be standing around with our dicks in our hands if it weren't for that asshole detective. No offense intended."

"I agree," said Warner. "But what changed your mind? You were dead set on getting rid of him."

"Well, he pushed my buttons! But I also owe him one. That son-of-a-bitch preacher used my faith in the Good Lord against me. He almost had me doing his bidding for him. The low down good for nothing bastard! Stallworth set me straight. I'll admit it pissed me off at the time. But he was the only one with the balls to stand up to me. He ain't going to win any popularity contests. That's for sure. But he's damn good at getting to the truth. No, you aren't going to reassign him, if you're smart. And I know you're smart. You keep that one around."

"Sure," said Warner. He couldn't remember a time when a man of Judge Parker's stature had come to his office on behalf of one of his men.

"Mr. Turner," said the judge, "it's good to see you get away from that desk finally. How's the leg?"

"It hurts, but it's still attached, and I can walk on it." He laughed. "I'm not so sure it was a good thing, me leaving my desk, though. It appears I made a mess of things."

"I'm sure it's all part of the plan," said Parker.

The judge excused himself and left. Warner and Turner stayed silent for awhile, still dumbfounded by the unexpected visit.

"What plan is he talking about?" asked the captain.

"Robert's," Turner replied. "But I'm sure this wasn't part of it."

"How?"

"How what?" asked Turner.

"How can you be so sure? Judging by everything else I've seen, I'd say anything is possible."

"Well, when you put it that way—" said Turner. Warner was right. No one could possibly guess how deep the devious schemes of Stallworth would go.

Warner sat down and rifled through the various reports strewn across his desk. "Fake Klan rallies, phony arrests of police officials, cheap perfume." He smiled at that one. "And what's this I hear about those skulls that were found?"

Turner laughed.

"What's so funny?"

CHAPTER SEVENTY-NINE

Eyeing the machines with trepidation, Turner listened intently to the rhythmic chirping hoping no unexpected pauses would develop. The hospital made him nervous. He was afraid that, if he touched anything, it might result in the sudden death of the man lying in the bed. The trooper was relieved when the man opened his eyes.

"I see you took matters into your own hands," said Turner.

Earl laughed, but winced as a sharp pain shot up his flank. "I didn't mean to—"

"It's going to be okay, Deputy. We know you didn't. Still, there are men dead. Others are on the run. We'll have to sort this out."

"Cooter?" asked Earl, hoping it had all been a bad dream.

Turner nodded. "And Charles Ray. Shot with your gun."

"Cooter tried to shoot me."

"We know. His gun was found at the scene."

Earl remained silent about Charles Ray. He wasn't sure how he ended up shooting him. It had all gone to hell in a hurry. He just wanted to take charge to keep them all safe. Instead, he'd messed things up beyond repair.

"Do you know who shot you?" asked Turner.

"JT" said Earl. "He was the only one missin'. Besides, he was the one that was goin' to—" The deputy stopped himself. The medications were making him loopy. He had to be careful what he said.

"Going to what?"

"Nothin'," said Earl. "He was the only one who wasn't there. I think it was JT who killed Junior, too."

"What makes you say that?"

"Just a hunch. What about Brother Eustice? Is he still alive?"

"As far as we know," said Turner. "We're searching for the lot of them as we speak. What happened out there?"

"I, I don't know," Earl spoke the truth. "It happened so fast. We were talkin' about everything that had gone down, and an argument started. Cooter pulled out a gun, and I drew. The next thing I knew, he was layin' on the ground. That's when Charles Ray lunged for my revolver, and it went off. I don't remember what happened after that. I must've been shot."

"You were," said Turner, "by a hunting rifle. It doesn't make a lot of sense."

Earl didn't comment. It all made sense alright, but only when the truth came out. There would be no way to spin it otherwise now.

"This is bad, Earl," said Turner. "It's going to be even worse when you-know-who gets back."

"It's all his damn fault. If he hadn't made everybody so paranoid about the murders—"

"Easy now. I know where you're going with this, but you know as well as I do, it's not going to be that easy to explain this away. As much as it pains me to say it, it's not looking good for you boys. You were shot by a sniper. He was laying in wait for you. Now, why would JT do that? You said yourself that he was the one who likely killed his brother. Why would he do that? You were about to say that he was going to kill someone else. Who was he going to kill?"

"I, I don't know."

"Yes, you do." Turner sighed. He pulled his chair up closer to the bed and put a hand on the deputy's arm. "This has gone on long enough. It's time we put an end to it. They're cleaning house, and nobody is safe. If they can't get to you, they'll find a way to get to your wife or your kids."

Earl wanted to cry. He knew Turner was right. The preacher had damned them all to hell, and Judgment Day was nigh.

"Who was Jeremiah going to kill?" Turner asked again.

"Stallworth."

Turner gulped. His mind raced. "When was he going to do that?"

"At the church. Right before you showed up."

Turner sat back. He wondered how long the crosshairs had been fixed on Stallworth. Still, a small amount of satisfaction crept into his heart. Robert had saved his life once. Maybe he'd finally been able to repay the debt.

"We're going to find the others, dead or alive. The ones we take in are going to spin their stories, but it won't hold up. It'll be every man for himself. I'll only be able to hold Stallworth back for a little while, then he'll pounce. What do you think he's going to do when he gets wind of this?"

"I know," said Earl through his tears. "I'm sorry. I'm so sorry. It wasn't supposed to be like this."

"I know it wasn't," said Turner. "But it is like this. It's time you picked which side you're on."

"What am I goin' to do?" Earl bawled. "What am I goin' to do?"

"Shhh, be strong, Deputy Earl Barber. You are an officer of the law. Get those tears out of your system and be a man. Whatever mess you've gotten yourself into is only going to be fixed one way, and you know the way. I'm not one to quote the good book, especially after what Winchester did to y'all, but it's as good a time as any."

Earl closed his eyes and let his resistance fade away. He waited to hear the words that he knew were coming—his new command from on high.

Turner stood up and took Earl's hand in his, then spoke from the scriptures.

"And ye shall know the truth, and the truth shall set you free."

CHAPTER EIGHTY

"**M**r. McEwen, we've got the place surrounded," Sheriff Fuller announced through the megaphone. "Come out with your hands in the air."

The Fairview Inn on the outskirts of Palmetto was the last place Buck would've been found normally, which, in his mind, made it the perfect place to hide out. He had parked his truck in the woods and walked through the forest in the waning light of the evening. He checked in under an alias, but the desk clerk paid him no heed. It wasn't the sort of place where questions were asked. All the same, he woke to find the authorities waiting for him in the parking lot.

Ring! Ring! Ring!

The phone made him jump. He ignored it. He knew it was the cops. They were everywhere.

"Buck," the megaphone chirped again. "We know you're in there. Please come out now before someone else gets hurt."

Buck fingered the shotgun. He knew he'd never be able to shoot his way out of the motel alive. It was futile. The end was near.

Ring! Ring! Ring!

"Think of your family," the sheriff implored.

Poor Gracie, he thought. She'd ignored the horrible things people had told her about his past. She saw the good in him. He loved her. He had repaid her love and kindness with his acts of depravity. She'd been wrong about him. He was a bad man.

"Buck, please. We don't want to hurt you. We know you didn't shoot Earl, or Cooter, or Charles Ray. We just want to talk to you. Please, surrender now, and it'll all be okay."

It wasn't going to be okay. They knew about the girls; about what they'd done. How could he face anyone?

Ring! Ring! Ring!

Buck looked at the gun in his hands. He knew there was only one way out.

CHAPTER EIGHTY-ONE

Understanding his dire position, Joe Bob surrendered without a fight. After the shootings, he had run off to hide in one of his cousin's hunting cabins outside of Pleasant Grove, but it didn't take long for them to track him down. He'd stopped off at a small store for a few staples on the way, and his car was parked right outside the cabin. He was unarmed. It was as if he'd wanted to get caught.

The cops brought him back to the sheriff's office in Carrolton, and he waited in the interrogation room. They'd offered him a chance to make a phone call, but he turned it down. He had no one to call. He was too ashamed.

"Mr. Duncan," Turner announced as he came into the room and sat across the table from Joe Bob. "I see you've managed to survive."

"For now," said Joe Bob.

"Right," Turner agreed. "For now. It seems you boys from the church have been busy. I just don't get it. I thought y'all were men of God."

"So did we."

"But here you are."

"What can I say?"

"What do you want to say?"

Joe Bob laughed. He didn't want to say anything, but at the same time, he wanted to say everything. "Don't I get a lawyer?"

"Do you want a lawyer?" asked Turner.

"I s'pose not."

The answer stunned Turner. His face showed his surprise, and Joe Bob laughed again.

"What's so funny?"

"Nothin'. There's nothin' funny," said Joe Bob. "Well, almost nothin'. What was funny was how you chewed out that stubborn detective. I bet he don't look so stupid now, does he?"

"Did he ever?"

Joe Bob shook his head and chuckled. "I see. That was just another one of his games to try to get us to talk, wasn't it?"

"I doubt if the good detective knew the deputy was going to start shooting everybody."

"No, that was your doin'."

"Mine?" Turner asked indignantly. "Do you blame everyone else for anything that y'all do?"

Joe Bob stopped laughing. "You don't know the half of it."

"Suppose you tell me."

"This ain't about Earl, or Cooter, or Charles Ray. This is about those girls they found in the swamp."

"Well then, tell me about that."

"No, I don't believe I will. Why should I? You're like a used car salesman."

"I am? How so?"

"You're just here to reel me in. Pretty soon, you'll make some excuse, telling me you have to check with your manager. Let's cut the crap right now. Go get your manager. I have plenty to tell him."

"My manager?" asked Turner.

Joe Bob smiled again. "Listen up. I don't want a lawyer, and I don't want to talk to any flunkies. Go get me Stallworth. He already knows most of it anyway. I don't know how, but he had us pegged from day one. Go get him, and I'll fill in all the dirty details for him. Isn't that what you want?"

"Sure, sure," said Turner. "I'll get him. I'm curious as to why the about-face, though. First, none of you want to say a damn thing, especially to Stallworth. Now, you ask for him specifically. Tell me why."

"I told you. He already knows. He fuckin' knows. He understands. He'll make sure that bastard gets what's coming to him."

"What bastard?"

"The prophet, that damned prophet."

CHAPTER EIGHTY-TWO

Ring! Ring! Ring!

The phone kept ringing, only adding to the panic in the small, worn down motel room. Buck was frantic. He glanced out of the window from behind the corner of the thick, green curtain. The cops were all over the place, hunkered down behind their squad cars, their firearms at the ready.

Ring! Ring! Ring!

"Shut up!" Buck yelled at the phone. Why couldn't they just leave him alone? He didn't want to hurt anyone. He had only done what he was told was right.

Ring! Ring! Ring!

Buck put the end of the barrel in his mouth and reached down, his long arms barely making it to where the trigger waited for him.

"Buck!" the sheriff implored over his megaphone. "Don't make us come in there. Put your gun down and walk out slowly with your hands up!"

Ring! Ring! Ring!

The pressure was too much. He set the shotgun aside and picked up the receiver.

"What do you want?" he cried into the telephone.

"Buck, it's me. Robert," the calm voice answered.

"Robert?" For a brief moment, Buck had forgotten the detective's first name.

"Robert Stallworth. We need to talk."

"I'm done talkin' to you! It's all your fault!"

"You know better than that, Buck. This isn't like you. None of this is like you."

"What do you know about it? You said I was a pervert."

"Come on, Buck. You know the game we were playing. Look at where you are. There's no more time for games. It's time we put that aside and hashed this out, man to man."

"It's too late for that. It's all over."

"No, it's not. I know what you're thinking, Buck. I've been there myself. Don't do it. It's not what you want."

"How do you know what I want? You don't know anything."

"I know you were the only one I talked to who was bothered by what the preacher did; what he made you do. That has to count for something."

"I didn't want to—"

"I know you didn't."

"I'm not a pervert."

"I know you're not. You're the only one of them who has a conscience. Don't let them do this to you. It's what Winchester is counting on."

"What, what do you mean?"

"You were set up, Buck. He's waiting for you to kill yourself so they can blame it all on you. Think about it. You're the big man. You have the past. It's why you were there in the first place."

"But, but, I, I—"

"Yes, I know. Don't fall for it, man. You're better than that."

"But how can that be?"

"I've seen enough to know, Buck. I told you the last time we talked that you were a patsy. Now you see what I mean."

"I didn't want it to be like this."

"Of course, you didn't. You wanted to be a good man. You wanted to trust someone. You still do. This time, trust the right person. I'm here to help you, Buck. There's still time to be a good man."

"It's too late. The things I did—"

"It's not too late. Look, I'm not going to lie to you. This isn't going to be easy. This is going to be the hardest thing you've ever had to do. But it's the right thing. You know it in your heart. If you don't do it, he's going to get away with it. You'll take the blame for all of it. You know that's not what happened. You know it wasn't your fault. You were trying to be a good person. You were trying to do what was right. Only, in your heart, when you were doing those things, you knew there was something wrong about it. I'm not asking you to do that again. I'm not asking you to trust me without reaching into your own heart. Do what your heart tells you is the right thing to do. Not the easy thing, Buck, the right thing."

"I don't know, I don't know."

"Yes, you do. You're scared. It's okay. You should be scared. But listen closely, Buck. I'm offering you something you'll only get one shot at. I'm offering you the most valuable thing you've ever been offered."

"What? What are you offerin' me? I'll go to jail. I'll be executed. I'll be humiliated. What can you offer me that'll help me now?"

"The one thing you've always needed, Buck. The one thing you've longed for your entire life. It's not for me to give it to you. It's for you to take. All I can do is offer you the chance. You'll be doing the heavy lifting. You do it, you'll earn my respect. But what's more, you'll earn what you need, what all of us need."

"What do I need?"

"Redemption."

The word hit Buck like a bolt of lightning. He felt its sting, then its warmth as it touched his soul. Stallworth was right. He'd been right from the beginning.

Buck put the phone back in its cradle without another word and looked at the shotgun in his hand. He sighed, took a deep breath, and gently set it on the bed. He slowly opened the door and stepped out into the sunlight, his hands in the air. Whatever was to come, he was going to face it like a man. The time for lies and evil deeds was over. Redemption had been offered, and it was his for the taking. Buck McEwen was going to take it.

CHAPTER EIGHTY-THREE

"We have a visitor," Deputy Smith announced, opening the door to the sheriff's office.

"Are you going to tell us or keep us in suspense?" asked Dale as Robert, John Turner, and Billy looked on.

"A Brother Eustice Elijah Winchester and his attorney, Mr. Douglas Lee, Esquire, have waltzed in through the front door."

Everyone in the room stood up.

"Did you arrest him?" asked Fuller.

"Ricky is taking care of it."

"This I gotta see," said the sheriff, walking to the door. The other three men sat back down. Fuller glanced at them in surprise. "Y'all coming?"

"We'll be along in a bit," said Robert. "Book him and let him stew for awhile. He wants special treatment, but he needs to learn he came to the wrong place for that."

The sheriff laughed and headed out of the room, pausing as Robert gave him another suggestion.

"His lawyer is going to start fishing. Let him know, we ain't biting."

Fuller made his way to the front as Ricky and Brian were leading their new prisoner to one of the holding cells in the back. He was instantly accosted by Winchester's irate lawyer.

"What is the meaning of this? My client came here of his own accord."

"He's under arrest, Doug. You know the drill."

"On what charge? He's committed no crimes."

"That'll be up to a jury to decide. In the meantime, he'll be just fine in the back."

"What are the charges? When will bail be set?"

"Accessory to the attempted murder of a police officer, homicide, homicide, homicide, etcetera. There will be more in time. It'll be up to the judge to set bail, but you know as well as I do, there ain't going to be none."

"Homicide? I do believe you've made a mistake."

"What's the matter, Doug? Didn't you get the proper retainer? Your boy is in deep shit. You should be happy. You're going to have plenty to bill for."

"What homicides? We only came here over concern about the boy."

"The boy?" asked the sheriff.

"Jeremiah Thomas," answered the attorney. "We believe he's in danger."

"Do you, now? Well then, come right in, and we'll sort it out."

"We believe that some of your men are the ones putting him in danger. Don't be coy with me, Dale. I've heard about your department's little escapades. There are rumors about a couple of skulls being found under your nose. Perhaps I should leave you my card in case you need it."

"Perhaps," said Dale. He waved off the attorney and headed back to his office. Winchester's lawyer was going to be awfully disappointed when he found out the truth about the skulls.

"Well?" asked Billy when the sheriff returned.

"Winchester's stewing in the back. When do you want to talk with him?"

"Let him wait," said Robert. "He has his lawyer with him anyway. He's not going to tell us a damn thing. I think I'd better have a word with the one who doesn't want to exercise his right to an attorney first."

Robert stood up and stretched. He winked at Billy and Turner, and he headed to the interrogation room to talk to the ex-Marine.

CHAPTER EIGHTY-FOUR

"It seems we meet again, Mr. Duncan," said Robert. "I hope we can dispense with the bullshit now."

"Are you still offerin' up a deal?" asked Joe Bob.

"Deal? What kind of deal?"

"I'll tell you everything. You said before that the first one gets the deal."

"I hate to break it to you, but you ain't the first one."

Joe Bob figured as much, but he had no choice but to bargain for whatever crumbs might be left on the table. "You know, I'd wager that it didn't happen the way Earl is sayin' it happened out there. He shot Cooter and Charles Ray in cold blood. He was about to shoot Brother Eustice, too, but JT got him first."

"Cooter was armed. Earl is a deputy."

"Charles Ray wasn't," stated Joe Bob.

"He lunged for the weapon."

"Shit he did." Joe Bob laughed. "Earl is just tryin' to save his own neck."

"So are you."

Joe Bob knew the detective had him there. "Hey, I'm offerin' what Earl ain't. I'm here talkin' to you without a lawyer. You, Detective Stallworth. I asked for you personally because I know you're the smart one. You told me way back when to come clean, and I'm takin' you up on it. Surely, what I got to tell you is worth something."

"That depends."

"On what?"

"On what you want and what you have to tell me," said Robert. "You know how this works. If you would've been honest and forthright in the beginning, we wouldn't be in this mess right now. But you weren't. So, here we are. I really don't see what you can tell me now that I don't already know. Besides, I have a better offer on the table."

"I already told you, Earl is lyin'."

"I'm not talking about Earl."

"Then who? Buck ain't goin' to tell you nothin', even if you find him."

"We found him yesterday. He's itching to tell me everything. Hell, he's begging to tell me."

"I bet he don't tell you he stayed behind to watch while Brother Eustice raped and strangled the girl the first time. I bet he don't tell you it was him who shot that girl the second time. I bet he don't say jack about that magician. It was him who sawed that poor bastard in half. Shit, if you made a deal with that psycho, you made a deal with the Devil. He's a pervert, anyhow. How's that gonna look on the stand? You'd do better to talk to me. I'm a bonafide war hero, a decorated Marine."

"So now you're a Marine," said Robert. As he'd predicted, the deacons were turning on each other. It was long overdue.

"I've always been a Marine. I just needed a little remindin'."

"You don't honestly think you're going to walk after all the things you've done, do you?"

"No, I ain't askin' for that," said Joe Bob. "I know I'm goin' to jail. I deserve it. We all deserve it. I'll accept my fate and take it like a man, as long as you promise me that damned preacher goes down the hardest. It was him that put us up to everything. He needs to hang."

"And how are you going to help me do that?"

"I'll tell you everything, from beginning to end. I'll tell you the hundred percent truth, which Buck or Earl ain't gonna do. I'll do it so no one can say otherwise, or catch me in lies, or so forth. I won't downplay my role in the whole mess. I killed before. You already know that. Hell, I was a Marine. I got paid to kill. I'll look them lawyers and that judge straight in the eye and tell them the way it was. I'll tell them folks on the jury what they need to hear. You'll get your conviction, and then you can do whatever you want with me. I won't plead. I won't beg. I'll take it like a man, like a Marine."

Robert sat back. He looked at the man in front of him. Joe Bob sat upright, as if he were at a military tribunal. The man made a persuasive argument. He'd look great on the stand, with his G.I. Joe demeanor and matter-of-fact delivery. A little remorse, but full acceptance of guilt thrown in, and the jury would be ready to pin a medal on his chest. Robert had a fleeting idea of having Mr. Duncan show up in court dressed in full military regalia but dismissed it. Nevertheless, Joe Bob was prosecution gold. If he did well enough, he might even be able to avoid execution, in lieu of life behind bars. If—

"I tell you what I'm going to do," said Robert. "I'm going to bring the district attorney in here, and we're going to go over everything from beginning to end, over and over again. If I catch you lying even once, your ass is mine. If not, and you do as you say you'll do, we'll do everything in our power to keep you off of death row. But bear in mind, that's not a promise. You'll be sentenced however you're sentenced, and I don't want to hear a peep about it. No lawyers. No recanting. No bullshit. Do we have a deal?"

Joe Bob offered his shackled right hand. Robert buried his disgust and shook it.

"We have a deal, Detective."

"We have a deal, Marine."

CHAPTER EIGHTY-FIVE

Eustice sat next to his attorney in the interrogation room, looking like he didn't have a care in the world. He casually puffed on his filter-less cigarette, waiting for the detective. When Robert entered the room with a sharply dressed man beside him, Eustice did his best to hide the swarm of butterflies that made a sudden appearance in the middle of his gut.

"Who you got with you, Detective?" asked the preacher. His attorney shot him a dirty look to remind him that he was to say nothing and to let his representative do the talking. Eustice paid him no mind. He was in charge. The sooner everyone learned their place, the sooner he'd be going home.

"You brought your lawyer, so I brought mine," Robert said with a smile.

The district attorney introduced himself, reaching out to give Douglas Lee a firm handshake. Brother Eustice barely nodded in the man's direction.

"I only come in here to discuss my boy," said Eustice. "He was actin' in self defense when that rogue deputy attacked us. You need to call off your men before someone else gets hurt."

"What my client is trying to say is that there are several witnesses who can attest to the fact that Deputy Earl Barber acted in an unofficial capacity and murdered two men in cold blood with the intent to kill my client here, along with every other man present that day. Jeremiah Thomas was acting within his rights when he, unfortunately, was forced to protect his life and that of his immediate family, along with the lives of Buck McEwen and Joe Bob Duncan. Even then, he only meant to disarm the murderous scoundrel, not to kill him."

"My boy is an excellent shot," added Eustice, staring coldly into the eyes of the detective. "If he wanted someone dead, they'd be dead."

"I'm sure he is," said Robert, who met the man's gaze without a hint of concern. "His brother could attest to that."

"Why you son-of-a—" Brother Eustice exclaimed before being cut off by his attorney.

"My client came in here of his own accord to set things straight. There have been a lot of accusations thrown around. Accusations that, I must say, are not only unwarranted, but insulting as well. Mr. Vaughan," he said, addressing the district attorney, "I hope you have evidence to back up these claims, or mark my words, I'll make sure that justice is swift when it comes to reparations. My client's reputation has been irrecoverably besmirched."

"We'll let the detective handle things at this point, Mr. Lee," Vaughan responded. "When the time comes, I'll be more than happy to do my part to make sure justice is served."

"We want guarantees," said Douglas Lee. "My client—"

"Fuck your client," said Robert, his eyes never leaving Brother Eustice's angry glare.

"Pardon me?" said Lee.

"You heard me," said Robert. "I said, fuck your client, and his son. Your power is gone, Prophet. Poof! There's no one left who's buying your bullshit. In fact, they're all clamoring to be the one to drive the last nail in your coffin. Too bad for them, I'm keeping that privilege for myself."

"You are a fool to wait for a day that will never come, brother. Your days are numbered," replied Eustice.

"Did your client just threaten an officer of the law?" asked Vaughan.

"No, he did not," said Lee. "What he meant to say was—"

"They are numbered unto the Lord, who will smite thee with vengeance for your baseless attacks upon his servants," finished Eustice.

"Ooooh!" replied Robert with a phony shiver. "Scary."

"You won't be laughin' for long," said Eustice.

"What my client is—" Lee tried to interrupt again.

"What your client is doing is trying to gather his courage for the upcoming storm. He believes his false bravado will sway things. He knows Jeremiah's fate is already sealed." Robert leaned in and whispered to the preacher, "All that live by the sword shall perish by it."

Brother Eustice laughed. "So be it, Detective. It's too late to stop now. Save those prayers for yourself."

"What your client trying to say—" Vaughan said, much to Lee's dismay.

Robert leaned back and smiled. "It's time I prophesized a bit, Winchester. Any minute now, my boss is going to come in here and chew me out. He's going to offer you an apology, but then explain, with as much regret as he can muster, how he's unable to release you just yet, until we get a few things clarified. He'll tell you how it's for your own protection, etcetera. It doesn't matter how you respond because, either way, you'll be sitting in lockup until the arraignment. Then he's going to demand that I go speak to your son's wife, Brandine. She'll have something urgent to tell me that requires my immediate attention. I'll do as I'm ordered to do and run straight over there, where I'll be assassinated by JT. Except, that's where the prophesy takes an unexpected turn. Care to tell us, oh holy one, what's really going to happen out at your son's place?"

"You bastard!" Eustice lunged at the detective, only to be stopped by the handcuffs and chains that pulled against the bolted-down table.

"If he wanted me dead, I'd already be dead and all that, right?" said Robert. "What about what I want?"

"You leave my boy alone!" Eustice cried, his anger turning to alarm.

"I heard about his mission out in the parking lot in front of the church that day," said Robert. "It seems he missed his chance. It's my turn, now."

"He was only doin' what—" Eustice stated before stopping himself.

Robert raised his eyebrows. "Go on."

Brother Eustice fought a battle with what little was left of his soul. Even the life of the only son he had left wasn't enough to change his priorities.

"He was only doin' what the Lord instructed," finished Eustice.

Douglas Lee, Esquire, breathed a sigh of relief. The district attorney shook his head. He had known from the beginning that it wasn't going to be that easy.

Robert nodded. "So am I."

A knock on the door signaled the end of the interrogation. John Turner entered the room. He chastised the detective for the heavy handed way he'd treated the esteemed preacher, and then he apologized to Winchester and Lee. Nobody in the room said a word as Turner continued his tirade. When it was over, he turned to Stallworth and instructed him to make haste to Jeremiah Winchester's trailer because his wife, Brandine, had a pressing message to impart to him.

Tears welled up in Eustice's eyes. Robert looked at him, this time with pity and sadness on his face. The die had been cast. Eustice was no Jesus; he was closer to Judas. He was no longer the prophet. That distinction now belonged to Stallworth.

CHAPTER EIGHTY-SIX

Jeremiah watched through the trees as the unmarked police cruiser pulled up to the trailer. He was grateful; he'd waited a long time for this.

Rain had been falling since the previous afternoon, and Jeremiah was wet and tired. Although the precipitation had diminished to a light drizzle, he was already soaked. The cool November air cut through his wet clothing, and it was all he could do to keep from shivering.

Jeremiah got into position. He held his rifle in place, looked through the scope, and waited for the detective to exit the vehicle. He waited. He waited some more.

Something was wrong. No one got out of the car. Jeremiah set the gun down and pulled out his binoculars. He scanned the area in front of his home, but nothing stirred. Why didn't Stallworth get out?

The sound of a twig snapping made him jump. He turned his head to his right, but nothing was there. Jeremiah took a deep breath. He was getting paranoid. He listened intently to the sounds of the forest. The light rain and creaking of the trees made it impossible to hone in on the source of every noise. After a few moments, he laughed and whispered to himself, "You're gettin' jumpy. Get a hold of yourself. What would Junior say?"

The last revelation made his insides burn with shame and regret. He hadn't wanted to kill his brother. He had to. Junior was going to murder him. Jeremiah couldn't let that happen. He had a baby on the way.

Thinking about Brandine and his future child deepened his depression. Who was he kidding? He wasn't going to be around to raise any child. He was going to prison, thanks to that stupid detective. Jeremiah felt his depression morph into rage. Stallworth was going to pay for what he'd done. If Jeremiah was going to jail for murder, he had nothing left to lose.

A noise in front of the trailer caught his attention, so he grabbed his binoculars and scanned the area again. Three more police cars pulled up, flanking the detective's car.

"Damn!" he spat. He'd hoped he'd get a clean shot at Stallworth and at least get a day or two before they drove him out of the woods. He knew the area better than anyone, and he had a multitude of places he could hide. He'd stashed supplies here and there to facilitate his escape. No matter now, he thought. He was going to take care of business whether the whole world looked on or not. Stallworth was as good as dead.

Jeremiah set the binoculars down and picked up his rifle once again. He got into position and intently watched the driver's side door of the detective's cruiser. As soon as the man emerged—*blam!*

Another twig snapped, and he swiveled to his right. His heart sunk. Stallworth was standing less than ten yards away, his service revolver pointed straight at Jeremiah's head.

"Looking for me?"

CHAPTER EIGHTY-SEVEN

Garland Vaughan stared out of the window in his office and contemplated his next move. The arraignment was imminent, and he was ill-prepared.

The detective had done an amazing job, without a shred of evidence to back him up. He'd also opened up can upon can of worms that would undoubtedly be seized upon by Douglas Lee and milked for every ounce of reasonable doubt that he could squeeze out of it. In the end, it would be the lack of evidence that would hamper them, unless Vaughan played his cards right.

"You wanted to see me?" the voice behind him asked.

Vaughan waved a hand, instructing the man to take a seat. Without turning his chair around, he asked, "What are we going to find out about Stallworth that we don't already know?"

"We've dug up what we can, but it wasn't that easy," the man explained. "The files are classified."

Vaughan already knew that. It's why he called in favors. He needed more. If there was dirt, Douglas Lee was going to find it. It was imperative that Vaughan get it first.

"But," the man continued, "we weren't without resources. It's not much, but there has to be more."

"I know there's more. That's why I hired you," Vaughan said. He continued to sit with his back to the man. It was better that way.

"Lee's been poking around, too. He has his friends, and we have ours."

"Again, that's why I hired you. What are they going to find out?"

"Nothing they'll use."

"And how do we know this?" Vaughan hated this part of his job. The detective was on the good side and deserved respect, but when the shit hit the fan, Vaughan knew that Winchester's attorney would stop at nothing to get an acquittal. Their entire case came down to Stallworth. If they could discredit him, it would go a long way to serving their purpose.

"Because no one is talking."

"What do you mean? Someone is always talking."

"What little we've got is all we're going to get. Look, Vaughan, if you don't want to pay me, that's okay. I'd prefer it if we just skipped this assignment and moved on."

That got Vaughan's attention, and he swung his chair around. His only response was one raised eyebrow.

"Between you and me, there's a huge cover-up over there. I stopped asking as soon as I started. Someone's—"

"Someone's what?"

"Someone's going to get killed if we keep asking."

"Someone?" asked Vaughan. *What the hell did Stallworth get himself involved in during the war?*

"I'm not going to follow up on it. That's as plain as I can say it."

"If our boy is the one in danger, this could be bad for him. Lee will pursue it."

"I don't think it's Stallworth who needs to worry."

"Then who?"

"Whoever keeps asking," explained the man. "They would've taken care of the detective a long time ago unless he took measures to prevent it. He's too clever not to."

Vaughan nodded. He hadn't known Robert long, but he had no doubt that the man plotted his actions ahead of time. Yet there was a restless streak in him, almost to the point of carelessness. One never knew when the man was bluffing. He kept everybody off balance.

"Whatever happened during the war, it wasn't Stallworth who caused it. He discovered it. Some kind of deal was made. Officially, they used what he'd given them for Nuremburg, and they buried the rest. I'm not sure that's all they buried, but whatever happened, it isn't ever going to see the light of day. The detective stays alive, and the secrets stay hidden."

"Can you guarantee that?" asked Vaughan.

The man nodded. "It's bigger than Alabama."

That's all Vaughan needed to hear. He dismissed the man with a wave and turned to stare back out of the window. Somehow, the revelation made him feel better. If Robert could keep the competing interests of the various international factions of the Military Industrial Complex at bay, the legal maneuverings of a Pickens County defense attorney should be of little concern.

Yet something nagged at the district attorney. He knew that, like it or not, he'd have to breech the subject with the detective. It would be awkward for him. His military deferment to attend an Ivy League college generally made him uncomfortable when questioning people about their service in the war. It made him feel ashamed, as if he'd shirked his responsibility for personal gain at the expense of others.

It made him feel ashamed because he knew that he had.

CHAPTER EIGHTY-EIGHT

"Are you sure it's okay for you to be seen with me in public like this?"

Robert joked.

They'd agreed to meet up at *Samson's Bar and Grill*. Located a half-block away from the courthouse, the watering hole was a favorite of the county establishment. When Vaughan invited him there with the excuse of having a few drinks, Robert knew there was much more to the meeting than a friendly get together.

"From now on, we're a couple," said Vaughan. "At least, until the trials are over."

Robert nodded and took a sip of his beer.

"Winchester's lawyer—" Vaughan began.

"Douglas Lee," said Robert.

"Right. Douglas Lee."

"Esquire," Robert added.

They both laughed.

"He's been trying to dig up dirt on you," said Vaughan. He watched Robert's face, but the detective showed no sign of concern. If anything, thought Vaughan, he looked amused.

"I'd advise against that, but who'd listen to me?"

"Why is that?" asked Vaughan. "Why would you advise against it?"

"I'm sure your man told you," said Robert. He looked at Vaughan and lifted his glass.

"He didn't tell me shit. It's what he didn't tell me that concerns me."

"He didn't quit on you yet? Ask for a different assignment?"

"That concerns me as well."

Robert nodded and took another sip of his beer. He set it down on the table and replied, "Don't be concerned, Councilor. It's a dead end. I work for the state police. If they can't get the files, your man's not going to. Neither is Lee. I'm sure whomever he sends will soon find out that it's a fool's errand, and they'll switch tactics."

"I'm not completely convinced" said Vaughan. "We have to be prepared for everything."

"You can't be prepared for everything. I guess that's something they don't teach you at Yale. Germany taught me otherwise."

"It always comes to that, doesn't it?"

"Not really," said Robert. "Look, you don't have to have this conversation with me. I don't give a rat's ass what you did or didn't do in the war. I only want the Antioch members to pay for what they've done. If you'll make that happen, then you're my new best friend. If you want to know what kind of dirt they're going to present in court about my time in the service, I can assure you, there will be none. Not that there's no dirt, mind you. War is a dirty business."

"And why are you so sure they're not going to suggest some improprieties? I'm not saying they'll have something concrete to present. Of course, they won't do that. All they need is something they can allude to in front of the jury. It won't matter if it's stricken from the record. What'll matter is that the jury thinks you're tainted in some way. All that top secret crap will only make you look shadier."

"They're not going to even bring it up," Robert said.

"How can you be so sure?"

"Because there's a line that even Douglas Lee won't cross."

"That's where you're wrong. He's going to do anything he can to save his client. Winchester is looking at the death penalty."

Robert laughed. "He's not going to bring it up. If he does, Winchester will be looking for a new lawyer."

Robert winked. Vaughan swallowed hard at the implication.

"Just what did you get yourself involved in over there?"

"Our concerns are in Alabama," said Robert. "Oh, and lest we forget, Tennessee."

"Our ace in the hole."

The men raised their glasses in a toast.

"The Amazing and Magnificent Villanova," said Robert. "The poor bastard."

"Yeah," Vaughan agreed. "I've been in touch with the Memphis DA. Gibson has already been released. In the meantime, we're keeping a separate file on the Antioch boys in regards to that crime. We'll push for extradition if all else fails."

"If we don't hang him here, he's likely to walk there," said Robert.

"We don't really have shit. Any chance we'll find those skulls?"

"It's not going to help us much now. I suspect that was Junior's doing, and they'll pass along any blame they can his way. He's not alive to defend himself," said Robert, "but I haven't given up yet. I've had other things to attend to lately, not to mention, I can't let on that we're still looking for them. We've already found them, remember?"

They laughed.

"Where do you come up with this crap?" asked Vaughan.

"It's a gift," Robert said. "Has Lee brought up the excavation behind the sheriff's office yet?"

"Nope," said Vaughan with a smile.

"The arraignment or the trial?" asked Robert.

"The trial, I'm sure. He knows Winchester isn't going to get off at the arraignment. He's just going to use that to see what we have."

"Then why not bring up the skulls?"

"Because Douglas Lee wants an audience he can wow with the big reveal."

"Sucker," said Robert.

"Esquire," corrected Vaughan.

They laughed.

"What concerns me is all that phony Klan crap you pulled during the investigation," said Vaughan. "It's going to cause a lot of reasonable doubt they can use."

"No, it won't."

"Again with the certainty," Vaughan said. "Why do you say that?"

"Take a look around you," Robert waved toward the people in the crowded bar room.

"Yeah? So?"

"Who do you think is wearing those robes? Unless we get an all black jury, I'm sure at least half of them will be absolutely certain that the Klan had nothing to do with the crimes in question."

"That's pretty harsh," said Vaughan.

"I calls it like I sees it," said Robert. "The boys at the Antioch church were the only ones who would fall for that because none of them were involved in the Klan. It's the one good thing I can say about them. Of course, that didn't prevent them from doing what they did."

"No, I suppose not." Vaughan took a sip of his beer and voiced his concern. "We don't have the strongest of cases. All we have is circumstantial evidence and their confessions."

"Which they'll retract once we get going," said Robert.

"Right."

"Yet the jury will hear it, whether they're told to disregard it or not," said Robert. "And we'll have Lee's stumbling and bumbling when he takes our bait. That's not going to help his client."

"Yes, but he'll recover," said Vaughan. "Don't underestimate him. He may not be a Yale man, but he knows what he's doing. What's more, he knows his county. I'll be standing there in my Italian suits, and you'll be there, the most unpopular guy in the state. Lee and Winchester will be the locals. Lee will play it like it's the Civil War all over again, and we're the Yankee carpetbaggers come to burn Richmond to the ground."

"You forgot the Lord," said Robert. "Winchester will have them convinced we were sent by the Devil."

"He'll never take the stand," said Vaughan. "Lee won't let him."

"Oh, he'll take the stand alright," argued Robert. "He'll insist. Brother Stupid won't be able to resist the lure of a captive audience."

"Then we'll have him." Getting a chance to cross examine a nut like Winchester is a prosecutor's dream, thought Vaughan.

"Will we?" Robert knew better.

CHAPTER EIGHTY-NINE

Robert laughed, almost spewing out his beer. The others looked at him and waited.

"What's so funny?" asked Dr. Hall.

"A lawyer, a doctor, and two detectives walk into a bar…" Robert joked.

They'd agreed to meet up at *Samson's Bar and Grill* as soon as the arraignment was over. None of them expected to be drinking at such an early hour.

The arraignment was over in less than a thirty minutes. An initial request to dismiss all charges by the defense was quickly rejected, followed by a plea of not guilty and a request for a speedy trial.

"I didn't see that coming," said Watts, speaking about the events at the courthouse.

"Short and sweet, eh Billy?" Robert winked.

"What do you make of it?" asked Watts.

"They're putting the bum's rush on us," Vaughan replied. "It's a sound strategy."

"No change of venue?" asked Dr. Hall.

"Why would they do that? The county is full of bumpkins who think Winchester is a prophet, with the rest being kinfolk. We're the bad guys in their eyes," said Robert.

"Well, you are anyway." Vaughan laughed.

"So sayeth the Yale man," replied Robert.

"Will we be ready?" asked Watts.

"It's doubtful we're going to find any more evidence to go along with our big pile of non-existent evidence we already have, so I'd have to say yes," Vaughan said. "We're as ready as we're going to be."

"Then let's get this show on the road," said Robert, raising his glass.

The others met his mug with theirs, and the men took a swig in unison.

"When are the other arraignments?" asked Dr. Hall.

"Tomorrow," said Vaughan. "None of them have any money, and subsequently, no representation. They won't enter a plea; they'll ask for a public defender, and then a preliminary hearing will be scheduled. Nobody is in any hurry. Winchester's trial will set the tone, which can be good or bad. Once we get them on the stand, one or more will likely recant, throwing a monkey wrench into our plans. If Winchester walks, they'll likely walk with him, confessions or no confessions."

"There's always Tennessee," said Watts.

The men nodded unenthusiastically. They recognized that whatever transpired at Winchester's impending trial was likely to carry over for the lot of them in Memphis. There would only be justice for the murder of the magician if justice was found for his daughters.

"What should I do with your modern art masterpiece on the tarp in my office?" asked Dr. Hall.

"We should photograph, tag, and bag them until the trials are over," said Vaughan. "Then we'll give them a proper burial."

"Why wait?" asked Hall. "They're creepy as hell. And that's coming from a forensic pathologist."

"I'm not done with them yet," said Robert.

"I know what you're thinking, but if you find the skulls now, it would only complicate things," said Vaughan. "From what Duncan and McEwen said, it was likely Junior's doing. We'll already be wrestling with his ghost, if it comes to that. It might be better to let that go."

Billy laughed. "You don't know Robert," he said. "If there's a body part to be found, he's a bloodhound on the hunt."

Robert took a swig of beer, but kept quiet.

"Are you hearing me, Detective?" Vaughan asked.

Robert heard him, but paid the man no heed. He didn't work for the district attorney. In the end, he was going to do what was right, no matter the cost. He'd compromised in the past and had lived to regret it. Recognizing it was the only reason he was still living didn't ease the guilt. He wasn't going to do that again.

Robert set his empty mug on the table and stood up to leave. Before he turned to go, he made a single promise that no one dared to question.

"When the time comes, Lacey and Laura Henderson will be buried whole."

CHAPTER NINETY

Jeremiah Thomas sat in the interrogation room, waiting for Detective Stallworth to arrive. Initially, he'd had a mind to request an attorney, but he didn't know any. He had little in the way of funds, so he'd need a public defender, although he had no idea how to ask for one. His father had hired the best defense attorney in the state. But then again, his father had more money than anyone suspected. He'd been raiding the collection plate for years. It was the Lord's will.

The door opened and, much to Jeremiah's relief, the fat detective with the long, white beard entered instead of Stallworth.

"Good afternoon, Mr. Winchester," Turner said as he sat down. "I'm sorry I've kept you waiting so long. I got tied up with a lot of nonsense on the way over here."

"It's okay. It's not like I'm goin' anywhere," Jeremiah replied, motioning to the shackles that kept him in place.

"Yeah, I'm sorry about those, too. Are they too tight? Do they need to be loosened a bit?"

"No. They're okay, I s'pose, but thanks anyway," said Jeremiah.

"I'm sorry, I didn't introduce myself. I'm John Turner." The detective reached over and shook Jeremiah's hand. "You can call me John if you like. Should I call you Mr. Winchester or Jeremiah?"

"JT"

"Then JT it is. Those are my initials as well." Turner smiled.

Jeremiah liked the man. The way he looked at him with kind, but sad eyes; the way he talked in his soft, southern drawl. He was everything Stallworth wasn't.

"I'm not going to lie to you, JT. You're in a lot of trouble," said Turner as he opened a manila folder and shifted through a few forms. "I wish it weren't so. I heard that your wife is expecting. Ah, what a joy a child can bring to a young couple. Is this your first?"

Jeremiah nodded.

"It's scary. Being responsible for the welfare of such a fragile thing, but it makes you a man. Everyone pats you on the back and gives you a cigar, but nothing compares to seeing your wife holding your baby for the first time. You'll be filled with pride and love. You'll swear that you'll do everything you can to protect them both, come hell or high water. Of course, some take that oath more serious than others."

Turner set down the papers and folded his hands, placing them over the file on the table. He frowned and looked at the man across from him.

"You were once a baby, and your daddy swore that same oath. He counted his blessings and promised to raise you right, promised he'd be there for you when times got tough. Times are tough, JT, and right now, your paw is throwing you to the wolves."

"He wouldn't—" A lump trapped the words in Jeremiah's throat.

"He already did, son."

Jeremiah held back the tears that welled up in his eyes. He remained silent, not only because he didn't want to start crying in front of the policeman, but because he didn't know what to say.

"What is also happening right now is that Detective Stallworth is talking to Brandine. He's telling her that you are in here throwing her to the wolves."

"That lyin' son-of-a-bitch! I would never—"

"But you are. Imagine how scared she is, expecting her first child and all. Her husband soon to be executed as a child killer. Her family name and reputation in shambles, and to top it off, she's likely to go down as an accessory. Ten years, maybe? I don't know, but long enough to predict what'll happen to your child. Foster homes can be so cruel, especially when the sins of the parents follow the child around. Who knows? Maybe it'll be for the best. Maybe a decent family will adopt the poor thing."

Turner looked at the pages in front of him. From what Jeremiah could see, they were some kind of official documents with an unrecognizable State Seal embossed along the top.

"Did you know the girls you raped and murdered were adopted?" asked Turner, motioning to the birth certificates on the table. "From that orphanage in Tennessee that was all in the news a couple of years ago. You know, the one where they were stealing kids from their parents and selling them on the black market. I hear none of them were ever returned."

Turner shook his head. "It must be a hard burden to bear, losing a child like that and knowing they're out there somewhere. Not knowing if they are hurting, if they need you, and not being able to do anything about it. Never knowing what happened to them." He looked up at Jeremiah. "I guess you'll learn about that soon enough. Brandine, too."

"She ain't done nothin'!" Jeremiah pleaded, no longer able to keep the tears from running down his face.

"I'm so sorry, JT. I truly am." Turner sighed.

"Mr. Turner, you can't let this happen to her. She ain't done nothin'. I swear!"

"Call me John."

"John, please! Don't let them do this!"

"It's not up to me. It's up to you."

"Me? What can I do? I'm in here, chained to this table."

"You can start by telling me the truth. All of it. You can tell it to the jury at your father's trial."

"I can't do that. He's my daddy."

"And he's done so much for you."

"You don't understand!" Jeremiah cried. "He's not like other men. He's a prophet from God."

"Is he? Did God tell him to saw that magician in half?"

"The Lord hates those who practice the Dark Arts. We was only doin' what he commanded. Besides, it was Buck who did that."

"Did you help to hold him down?"

"No, me and Junior took the girl to the truck."

"Did you rape her?"

Jeremiah sat upright as if Turner had slapped him across the face.

"I ain't no pervert. I didn't touch her. We was savin' her from the Devil's grasp."

"Is that why you took her? To save her? Is that what you tell yourself?"

"It's the truth."

"Your father raped her. Did the Lord command that as well?"

"It wasn't rape. She was to be his bride!"

"She was twelve, maybe thirteen."

"She was older than that," Jeremiah proclaimed, even though he knew the policeman was probably right.

"You keep saying she. There were two of them."

"She came back after we—"

"Chopped her into little bits."

Jeremiah closed his eyes and shook his head. He wanted it all to go away. His chin fell down on his chest, and he wept. Moments passed without a word being spoken until his sobbing faded.

The quiet of the room was interrupted by the sound of the door opening. Jeremiah looked up to see his nemesis standing before him.

"He's ready," said Turner, standing and motioning towards the now empty chair he'd been sitting in.

"Ready for what?" asked Jeremiah.

"For me," said Robert, taking the seat across from him.

Turner smiled and started to leave.

"But I thought you—" said Jeremiah, his voice cracking with emotion.

"Thought I was what?" asked Turner. "On your side?" Turner shook his head in disgust. "Robert, show him."

Jeremiah looked at Stallworth. Robert pulled out a photograph from under the birth certificates in the file on the desk and presented it to the distraught man.

"I call it *The Bone Puzzle*."

CHAPTER NINETY-ONE

Jeremiah averted his gaze. He didn't want to look at the photograph.

"What's the matter?" Robert asked. "Not your cup of tea? Everyone's a critic."

"You're one sick bastard," said Jeremiah.

"Hey, I just put it together. Y'all did the work. What was that like, cutting up a beautiful little girl? You must've enjoyed it. You did it twice."

"She came back. I don't know how, but she did. It was the Devil's work."

"It sure was. Tell me, how did Pops talk y'all into it? It was a tad extreme."

"You don't understand. We didn't know it was goin' to turn out that way."

"How did you think it was going to turn out?"

Jeremiah shrugged his shoulders. He had no answer.

"You're not going to be able to distance yourself from this, son. Three innocent human beings were murdered in cold blood and dismembered. You killed your own brother. You shot a police officer. You tried to shoot another."

Jeremiah hung his head. Everything the detective said was true.

"I take particular offense to that last one," said Robert. Jeremiah showed no indication that he'd heard him. "At least you could look me in the eye when I'm talking to you."

Jeremiah looked up. "What do you want me to say? It's all your fault I'm sittin' here. If it weren't for you, my brother would still be alive; Cooter and Charles Ray, too."

"Is that why you wanted me dead—for revenge?"

"No," said Jeremiah. "I mean, yes, but… I don't know. She—"

"She? Are you telling me it was Brandine's idea?"

"No, she had nothin' to do with it," Jeremiah insisted.

"Sure she did," said Robert. "She called and personally asked me to come out there. She set me up. And now, from what you're telling me, it was all her idea in the first place."

"That ain't what I'm sayin'. You're puttin' words in my mouth."

"We've already arrested her, Jeremiah. She's ready to sing like a canary. Hell, she was one of the first to cave under pressure. Watts and I went out there when we were talking to you the first time. You remember; when I went out to get you something to eat. Instead, we took a drive out to your place and had a long chat with your wife. I'm sure she told you all about it."

Jeremiah was noticeably shaken. Brandine hadn't gone into specifics about the conversation she'd had with the policemen. By the time Jeremiah had gotten home at that late hour, smelling like cheap perfume, thanks to the asshole detective, she'd given him hell. He'd tried to plead his case, but she'd looked at him in disbelief. She made him feel as if she'd never be able to trust him again. Now he finds out that she'd been keeping even bigger secrets from him. He was livid and more than a little scared. What the hell had she told the detective about him? What was she telling him now? What was she going to tell him in the future?

"Your father was sitting right where you are sitting when I got the message that Brandine needed to see me. He had that smug look on his face. You know, the one that makes you want to punch him in the nose."

Jeremiah snorted despite himself. He knew that look all too well.

"He must've known what the plan was, which makes it premeditated. You'll find out soon enough the significance of that in the legal sense, but I digress. When I told him that I already suspected that it was a trap, and that if anyone was going to end up on the wrong side of a gun, it was going to be you, do you know what he did?"

Jeremiah said nothing, but by his expression, Robert could see he was all ears.

"Nothing, he did nothing. I told him that we already knew that whatever trouble you'd gotten yourself into was all his doing, and that it was fruitless to pile more misery onto the only son he had left. I told him that there was a very real chance that you'd be killed in the process. Then I asked, no, I pleaded with him to come clean, if for no other reason than to spare your life. He was unmoved. He sat there with his fancy lawyer, none the worse for wear and tear over your awful fate. Truth be told, he just doesn't care about you. Brother Eustice only cares about Brother Eustice."

Jeremiah wasn't surprised in the least. His father was a selfish prick and would remain so until the end.

"Then there's poor little Brandine," Robert continued. "In all fairness, she had nothing to do with your foray into homicidal madness. I'm sure she would have disapproved, if you'd bothered to confide in her before you followed the mob to Memphis. But you didn't. Initially, she'd offered up pertinent information about your whereabouts in an effort to save you. She wanted so much to believe in you. She wanted you around to help raise that child. She wanted a normal life with a good marriage to a good man. Unfortunately, she didn't marry one. She married you."

Jeremiah remained silent. The words stung but were sadly accurate.

"In a strange turn of events, it was the conversation with Brandine that told us we were on the right track and eventually led to this. Don't be hard on her though, she was only trying to help. Of course, once she realized what you'd done, she wised up. Well, as wise as she's capable of, anyway."

The sarcastic insult didn't set well with Jeremiah, but he kept his mouth shut. *I told that dumb bitch to keep her mouth shut!*

"A woman will usually do whatever she feels is in her best interest to do. And a mother will almost always do whatever she can to protect her child. In a last ditch effort to hold it together, she did what she could for you. Unfortunately, it didn't work. I'm still breathing, and now she's in as much trouble as you are. There's only one card left for her to play. Do you want to guess what that is?"

"She wouldn't turn on me," Jeremiah said.

"No?"

"She loves me."

"No doubt. Nevertheless—"

Tears welled up in Jeremiah's eyes. His sins were coming down on both of them. What had he done?

"The sad thing is that, despite what she thinks, there's little she can offer us. We have no reason to offer her a deal. On the other hand, I have every reason to prosecute her to the fullest extent of the law."

"Don't. I'm beggin' you."

"The two of you tried to murder me, son."

"Please, I'll do anything."

"Such as?"

"I'll confess. Whatever you want me to say, I'll say it."

"That's not going to be good enough."

Jeremiah knew what the detective wanted. "I'll testify in court."

Robert nodded. He pulled out the photograph one more time and held it up for Jeremiah's inspection. Jeremiah clamped his eyelids shut.

"Open your eyes, boy. I insist."

Jeremiah looked at the collection of bones on the tarp. The grotesque image made his stomach retch.

"I'm going to need something more than a full confession and your testimony in court if you want me to drop the charges on Brandine," Robert said as Jeremiah stared at the grisly photo. "Actually, I'm going to need two things."

PART SIX:

REDEMPTION

Bad men are full of repentance.

Aristotle

CHAPTER NINETY-TWO

The selection of the jury drew the expected complications. Vaughan would have preferred a secular panel of jurists. Lee wanted only the most stringent of the faithful. Lee did his best to weed out members of secret societies of racial purity; Vaughan brushed past any indication such things existed. As it turned out, in Pickens County, Alabama, a non-religious jury of non-racists was wishful thinking. Vaughan agreed with Robert's summarization. Klan members and cult members were as close to a jury of peers Winchester could ask for.

Soon after the jury was selected, the court was adjourned for the Christmas holidays. The fireworks on New Year's Eve would pale by comparison to a very different kind of pyrotechnics slated to begin on January third.

The courthouse was packed on the first day of the trial. From his vantage point in the third row behind the prosecution, the detective could see that the majority of the people were there to support the accused. Robert was disgusted by the display. The good Christian folks of Pickens County had already decided that the preacher was innocent. He was being persecuted for his godly beliefs by agitators from Birmingham.

Robert ignored the ugly stares from the gallery. They didn't matter. He only hoped that the madness didn't spread to the jury.

At the request of the district attorney, Dr. Hall wasn't present. He'd be summoned at a later date to testify, and it was Vaughan's opinion that his reputation would be sullied by sitting next to the detective. Robert understood. He was a pariah and proud of it.

"Take off your hat!" the bailiff said in an unnecessarily rude voice to one of the yokels who made his way to the back row. The man shot the bailiff a dirty look, but did as he was told.

"That was harsh," Watts noted.

"Contempt of court," said Robert.

Watts chuckled. The heavy handed way the court officials treated the good citizens of the county explained a lot about the animosity the locals had toward everything government. The insular world in which the courthouse thrived ensured that this fact was lost on those within.

"Tuck in your shirt!" the bailiff shouted at another man who had entered the room. Once again, his outburst was returned with an icy glare.

"I'd hate to see what he does when someone mixes stripes with solids," said Robert.

Watts bit his tongue to keep from laughing out loud.

The members of the gallery were plainly insulted by the lack of respect the bailiff showed them. Grumblings arose. The bailiff used the opportunity to display his dominance by addressing the room as a whole. "Men need to tuck in their shirts and remove their hats. Women need to keep their chattering down. I will forcibly remove anyone who fails to comply."

Complaints could be heard rumbling throughout the audience. The bailiff took exception to the outburst. "I said shut up!"

"What an asshole," Robert said, in no way attempting to whisper.

Watts laughed.

"Who said that?" The bailiff was livid. He stuck out his chest, flexed his muscles, and pushed through the bar that separated the public from the trial participants. With a menacing gait, he walked to where Robert and Billy were sitting.

Robert met his glare with amusement. The smirk on his face only added to the bailiff's bad disposition. It was all Watts could do not to lose it. He knew Robert kept a poker face better than most. The smirk was planted there on purpose.

"I said no disruptions! You and your friend will have to leave," the bailiff insisted.

Robert ignored the man. The bailiff reached for his baton. As if on cue, the two detectives moved their suit jackets to the side in unison, revealing the badges attached to their belts. The bailiff froze, his baton half way out of its sheath.

"Y'all are supposed to be on the other side of the bar, in the place designated for law enforcement," the bailiff said.

Robert noted a subtle cracking in the man's voice. His day was getting better already.

The two detectives let their jackets fall back into place and remained where they were, daring the bailiff to pursue the matter. Giggles erupted from a few rows behind them, which put the bailiff back on track, chastising those who he could intimidate.

"Shut up or I'll clear the courtroom!"

The room fell silent, and the bailiff strutted to the front, pretending that the detectives hadn't made a fool of him.

"You know he could've made us leave," Watts whispered.

"Until he went for his nightstick," said Robert.

"What was he going to do with that?" Watts chuckled. "Beat us senseless?"

"I'd of shot him right between the eyes," joked Robert.

"All rise!" the bailiff commanded as a gray haired wiry man with black robes entered. Everyone stood. "Oye! Oye! Oye! The Circuit Court of Pickens County, Alabama, is now in session, the Honorable Judge Samuel Foley presiding!"

The judge took his seat on the bench and casually tapped his gavel, obviously bored by the over-the-top performance of the bailiff.

"Thank you, Porter. How are the wife and kids?"

"Good, Your Honor," the bailiff replied, noticeably proud by the personal attention paid upon him and his family by the esteemed judge. "My oldest will be going into the Navy soon. I tried to talk him into joining the Marines, but you know how kids are."

"They never listen." Judge Foley laughed. "Semper fi!"

The district attorney stole a glance at Robert and winked. It had taken no small amount of finagling by Vaughan to assure Foley was assigned to the case. It would pay off when Joe Bob Duncan took the stand.

"Helen," Foley addressed the court reporter, "I trust you had a Merry Christmas and a Happy New Year."

"Why yes, Your Honor," she replied. "I went to my sister's. She's been a might under the weather lately. It's the arthritis again."

The judge shook his head with concern before continuing, "District Attorney Vaughan, Mr. Lee, are we ready to proceed?"

"Yes, Your Honor," Vaughan replied.

"We most certainly are, Your Honor," Douglas Lee responded with a flair, leaning extra hard on his Southern drawl. Robert fought the urge to roll his eyes. It was bad enough the ham was wearing a seersucker suit with a red bow tie. The detective was sure, if he'd had suspenders on, he would've hooked both thumbs under them and arched his back, in a piss poor parody of a W.C. Fields backwoods hick politician.

"Bailiff, please commence," said Foley.

"As bailiff of the Circuit Court of Pickens County, I, Porter Tyndale, present the case before us today: the state versus Eustice Elijah Winchester, for the charges of trespassing on state property in the commission of a felony, grand theft auto, carnal knowledge of a juvenile, obstruction of justice, transportation of a juvenile across state lines with carnal intent, kidnapping, conspiracy to commit murder, forcible rape of a juvenile, mutilation of the corpse of Lacey Henderson, mutilation of the corpse of Laura Henderson, capital murder of Lacey Henderson, and capital murder of Laura Henderson."

An audible buzz echoed through the room as the charges were read one by one. It lent weight to the seriousness of the crimes and diminished some of the resolve the gallery had in regard to the holiness of Brother Winchester. Bailiff Tyndale let the sound fade away without admonishing the crowd. Robert thought the bailiff was as shocked as the rest of the assembly when he realized what the trial was about.

"Will the accused please stand," the judge announced. It was not a question.

Brother Winchester and Douglas Lee stood, their body language equal parts humility and indignation.

"How do you plead?"

"I stand before you an innocent man, Your Honor," Brother Eustice declared. "I am but a most humble servant of our most Holy Lord."

"Amen!" the crowd shouted.

"Order! Order in the court!" Judge Foley said, incensed over the inappropriate outburst. "Bailiff, I order you to remove anyone who further disrupts these proceedings!"

"Yes, Your Honor," Bailiff Tyndale said with more than a hint of sadistic glee at the prospect of pushing his weight around.

"Mr. Lee, please counsel your client to only answer the questions asked of him. A simple plea of not guilty is all that is required. We'll not have any more proselytizing. Is that clear?"

"Yes, Your Honor," Douglas Lee replied, "and we offer our apologies to the court. My client is unfamiliar with the law. I'm afraid he's more comfortable in the house of the Lord than in a courthouse. I do believe this is the first time he's ever set foot in one."

"Your Honor, please," Vaughan interrupted. "Do I need to object before we've even begun?"

"Your complaint is duly noted, Mr. Vaughan. I'm not going to warn you again, Mr. Lee. You are dangerously close to a contempt of court charge."

"Yes, Your Honor," Lee replied. "My humble apologies."

"Is there any reason we can't proceed?" Judge Foley asked.

"No, Your Honor," said Vaughan.

"May I approach the bench?" asked Lee.

"Here we go," whispered Watts.

The prosecutor and the defense attorney stood before the judge's bench and a spirited whispered discussion went on for several minutes. Judge Foley waved the pair off and sat back, shaking his head.

"I'll ask again, is there any valid reason we can't proceed?"

"No, Your Honor," Vaughan answered once again.

"No," Lee said, his pregnant pause drawing a look of disapproval from the robed man on the bench. The attorney pretended he hadn't noticed before eventually adding, "Your Honor."

"Is Lee trying to piss off the judge?" Watts whispered.

"Mistrial, maybe," Robert said and shrugged. He was unconcerned about Lee's theatrics. Once the gruesome facts of the crime were presented, the petty shenanigans of the lawyer would soon be forgotten. As talented as Lee was in causing distractions, there was nothing in the world that could compete with the photographs that Dr. Hall would introduce into evidence. They'd be passed, one by one, to the jury. Every member was going to get an eyeful. There would be no unseeing what Brother Eustice and his merry band of killers had done.

CHAPTER NINETY-THREE

District Attorney Garland Vaughan kept his opening remarks brief. He wanted what little evidence he had to have the greatest impact when presented. The majority of his case was circumstantial and hearsay. It was imperative that he make the most of what he had, so he gave his usual civic duty speech to the members of the jury. He thanked the jurors for their sacrifice, while reinforcing the need for them to see that justice prevailed.

When it came time for the lawyer for the defense to make his opening statement, the courthouse got a full measure of the considerable theatrics of Douglas Lee, Esquire. He pranced around the room; at times, barely speaking above a whisper, at other times, shouting to the rafters. He flailed his arms wildly when speaking of the horrible deeds of the dubious detective in persecuting a man of God. He folded his hands in prayer when softly describing how the humble preacher withstood those unfounded attacks on him and his flock.

Weeping could be heard from the gallery when Lee talked about the death of Junior Winchester, inferring that he'd been cut down in the prime of his life by the detective himself. Robert noted that more than one member of the jury had wiped tears away during the absurd accusation.

Billy nudged Robert. "We might be in trouble."

"Wait till they see the pictures," said Robert.

Lee went on for more than an hour, pouring everything he had into his presentation. He knew, once he was finished, it would be the state's turn to present their case, and the holy man image he needed to maintain for his client would be chipped away, bit by bit. The bigger the monument he built now, the better the chances that something would remain later.

Judge Foley looked on with amusement. Normally, the cases he presided over were little more than he said, she said domestic disputes or petty crimes. Not this time. The big guns had been brought out—Douglas Lee was involved.

The judge knew he'd have to keep his gavel handy. Lee had a reputation for dramatics. Secretly, Judge Foley was a fan of the man's performances. He looked forward to having a front row seat for what was surely going to be an exciting event. Being the judge, he'd have to make sure he gave the impression that he was non-biased. That meant putting a damper on Lee's act whenever he pushed it too far. But he reasoned, it didn't mean he couldn't enjoy his job for a change.

During Lee's opening statement, Vaughan sat quietly at his desk, shuffling through his papers, looking bored. Thirty minutes into Lee's presentation, he placed the files in a neat pile and poured himself a glass of water. Ten minutes later, he glanced at his watch. Ten minutes after that, he yawned a few times and began to visibly nod off. The third time his head fell to his chest and popped up, he drank another glass of water. He propped up his head on his hand and yawned again.

Robert laughed when Billy yawned in response. Billy nudged Robert, who looked over at the jury in time to see three members yawning.

Robert felt better. As good as Lee was, Vaughan wasn't going down easily. This was going to be a fight.

Lee ignored Vaughan's subtle antics, but the restlessness of the jury told him it was time to wrap things up. He'd sowed the seeds. He'd water them sporadically throughout the defense's case whenever possible. When it was his turn, he'd nurture the saplings with everything at his disposal.

In the end, despite his insistence to the contrary and against his best advice, he knew Winchester was adamant about taking the stand. There was little doubt he would use it as a pulpit. It would all come down to the preacher whether he was convicted or not. It's just as well, thought Lee. It's Winchester's life that's at stake.

Douglas Lee had nothing to lose. He'd been paid up front. He'd get a lot of publicity. He was going to present a monster of a case, which would only add to his reputation and his future success at attracting lucrative cases. If he won, he'd be hailed as the best defense attorney in the state, maybe the country. If he lost, it would be his client's doing.

It didn't matter to Lee if Winchester was executed. No matter what cock-and-bull story Eustice had spun for him, he knew damn well that the old pervert was guilty as sin. He had no idea how the detective had figured it out, but he had. Now, however, the prosecutor had to prove it.

When Lee finished and took his seat, Judge Foley motioned for Vaughan to present the prosecution's case. The district attorney stood up, cleared his throat, and began.

"Judge Foley, ladies and gentlemen of the jury, citizens of Pickens County, the state calls Buck McEwen as its first witness. Mr. McEwen, please take the stand."

CHAPTER NINETY-FOUR

Buck McEwen, escorted by a burly prison guard, entered the courtroom through a door at the judge's right. He was wearing an orange jumpsuit and was shackled at the wrists and ankles. The guard paused and unlocked the chains in full view of the jury. Vaughan was furious. He had little doubt that Lee had arranged the display, probably with an unofficial contribution to the guard's retirement fund. Vaughan made a mental note to remind Lee of the rule of reciprocation when the opportunity arose.

Buck took the witness stand, and the bailiff approached him. Buck raised his right hand and placed his left on the Bible that the bailiff held out to him.

"Do you hereby swear to tell the truth, the whole truth, and nothing but the truth, so help you God?" asked Bailiff Tyndale.

"I do," said Buck.

Shouts of 'Praise be!' and 'Amen!' erupted from the gallery. Winchester clenched his eyes shut and bowed his head as if whispering a prayer to the Almighty. Judge Foley reached for his gavel, but thought better of it and allowed the crowd to settle down on their own.

"That didn't take long," noted Billy.

"Before you know it, he'll be leading us in prayer," Robert said with disgust.

Vaughan approached the witness and began his preliminary questions. He asked Buck his full name, where he lived, and how he knew the defendant. Buck answered in a monotone voice, as if hypnotized. Something about the way he was talking troubled the prosecutor, but he continued his questioning, hoping for the best.

"Mr. McEwen, we're just going to get this out into the open so there'll be no reason to dance around it later. Have you ever been charged with a crime before?"

"Yes."

"When was that?"

"Over twenty years ago."

"Twenty-three to be exact," Vaughan added. "Can you tell us what those charges were?"

"Statutory rape and carnal knowledge of a juvenile," said Buck, his voice devoid of emotion.

Audible astonishment emanated from the crowd. Judge Foley ignored the interruption.

"Were you convicted?"

"No, sir."

"No? Those are serious charges, Mr. McEwen."

"Yes, sir. The charges were dropped."

"I see. So you've never actually been convicted of a crime?"

"No, sir."

Vaughan paused. He could sense Buck was itching to say more, and anything at this point could only help.

"It was a long time ago," Buck explained. "It's not what you think."

"Objection!" shouted Lee.

"Overruled," said Foley. He wanted to hear the rest.

"Mary Jo was my girlfriend. We were in love. It was her folks who didn't like me. They put her up to it. But it don't matter. I ain't done nothin' like that since. You'd think people would forgive and forget, but they never do."

"Did you find forgiveness at the Antioch Pentecostal Church?"

"Yes, sir. Brother Eustice brought me in. He accepted me. He gave me a new life."

"And what did he ask for in return?" asked Vaughan.

"Nothin'," said Buck. "Well, at first—"

"Go on."

"I soon became his favorite. I was his right-hand man. If anyone questioned his authority, it was my job to keep them in line, remind them of who the prophet was."

"So you were his goon?" asked Vaughan.

"Objection!" shouted Lee.

"Sustained," Judge Foley answered. "Mr. Vaughan—"

"Yes, Your Honor, I withdraw the question," said Vaughan. He turned back to Buck and asked, "How did the others feel about your new position?"

"Objection!" shouted Lee. "Hearsay."

"Sustained."

"Allow me to rephrase, Your Honor," said Vaughan. "Mr. McEwen, did you notice a change in the way the other members of the congregation treated you when you were given a higher position in the church?"

"Sometimes," said Buck, "but it was better than the way they treated me before. I was accepted. I ain't never been accepted before that. Brother Eustice brought me in and showed me respect."

"In your opinion, is Eustice Winchester a man of the Lord?"

"Yes, sir."

"Is he a prophet?"

"Yes, sir. Well, I used to think so."

"Used to? You don't think so anymore?"

"I ain't so sure."

"Heathen!" "Backslider!" Shouts erupted throughout the gallery. Judge Foley did not approve. He slammed his gavel down to restore order.

"But you were sure back in April, weren't you?" asked Vaughan.

"Yes, sir."

"Is it fair to say you were a devout follower of Eustice Winchester at that time?"

"Yes, sir."

"And you'd do anything he asked you to do?"

"Objection!" shouted Lee, "Leading the witness."

"Sustained," Foley agreed.

"Did you go on a religious retreat with the deacons of the Antioch Pentecostal Church and Eustice Winchester back in April?"

"Yes, sir."

"Where did you go?"

Buck hesitated. Vaughan waited.

"Mr. McEwen," Judge Foley interrupted, "please answer the question."

"We went to Memphis," Buck said.

"What did you go to Memphis for?"

Buck hesitated again.

"Mr. McEwen," the judge intervened once more, "you need to answer the question."

"What if I don't want to?" asked Buck.

"You are here to testify. Is there a reason you don't want to do that?"

"I'll withdraw the question, if it pleases the court," said Vaughan. This was about to go south quickly, and he needed something from the witness to help his case before it did. "Mr. McEwen," Vaughan continued before the judge could interrupt again, "when you came back from Tennessee, did you bring anyone with you?"

"Yes, sir," said Buck, happy to move on from the incident in Memphis. "We brought Brother Eustice's bride."

"His bride?" asked Vaughan. "Did Mr. Winchester get married in Tennessee?"

"No, sir, but she was his bride-to-be. He's a holy man, so, in the eyes of the Lord, they may have already been married. I don't know."

"Is that why he told y'all you were going to Memphis? To fetch his fiancé?"

"No, sir, not exactly," Buck explained. "We needed to rescue her from bein' a pawn in the Devil's workshop. We did that and came back with her. It was then that Brother Eustice told us about their nuptials."

"How old is Brother Eustice?"

"I'm not sure," said Buck. "You'd have to ask him."

"Sixty-seven," stated Vaughan. "How old was his bride to be?"

Buck paused for a brief moment before answering, his voice barely above a whisper. "I ain't sure. Young."

"Thirteen," said Vaughan. "What was the girl's name?"

"Natalia," said Buck. "She was a gypsy."

"A gypsy?" asked Vaughan.

"That's what we all thought. She was a gypsy woman."

"But you know now that she wasn't a gypsy, don't you?"

"Yes, sir."

"And that she was only a girl? And not a woman?"

"Yes, sir."

"And her name wasn't Natalia?"

"Yes, sir."

"Not that it would make a difference from a legal standpoint, but did the girl come of her own accord?"

"No, sir."

"Who brought her?"

"Junior and Jeremiah."

"Winchester's sons?"

"Yes, sir."

"Did Winchester tell them to?"

"Yes, sir."

"That's called kidnapping, Mr. McEwen. Are you aware of that?"

"Yes, sir."

"But you did it anyway."

"We had no choice. I don't know. It weren't like that. We was doin' the Lord's work. You don't question the Lord."

"Who told you it was the Lord's work?"

"Brother Eustice."

"Did anyone touch the girl?" asked Vaughan.

Buck remained silent.

"Mr. McEwen, perhaps you didn't hear me," Vaughan repeated. "Did anyone touch the girl?"

Buck nodded.

"Please state your answer out loud for the record," Judge Foley said.

"Yes, sir."

"Who?"

"Brother Eustice."

"Did he rape her?"

"No," said Buck. "They was man and wife."

"Where were you when this happened?"

"They was in the back of the truck. I was outside, keepin' watch."

"You were watching?" Vaughan asked with disgust.

"No, they had the door closed."

"Then how do you know what they were doing?"

"I could hear it. She was fightin' him off and—"

"Fighting him off? So it was rape."

"I, I don't know."

"Where were the others?"

"Brother Eustice had everyone spread out to make sure nobody was watching us."

"Except for you."

"I was nearby just in case."

"As a lookout?"

"Yes, sir."

"What did the girl say when Winchester was finished?"

"Nothin'," said Buck. "She was dead."

"Dead? Why was she dead?"

"Brother Eustice said the Lord took her away, but it looked to me like she'd been strangled."

"Objection!" shouted Lee. "The witness is not a qualified pathologist."

"Overruled."

"What did you do then?"

"Brother Eustice told us we had to get rid of her, or the Devil would come for us all. So we—"

"You what?"

"We put her in the swamp."

"You buried her body in the swamp?"

"Not exactly."

"What exactly did you do?"

"He said we had to cut her into pieces first so the Devil wouldn't be able to find and resurrect her."

"So you chopped her body up and threw the pieces into the swamp? Like she was garbage?"

"Yes, sir."

"What about the other girl?"

"We didn't know there was another girl."

"No? When did you find her?"

"Earl brought her in his police car the next mornin'," said Buck.

"The police brought her?"

"Earl's a deputy. He found her on the road and brought her with him. She tried to run, but we found her."

"Did y'all rape her, too?"

"No. Junior wanted—. No. No one touched her like that."

"What happened then?"

"Brother Eustice said she'd been resurrected by Lucifer. We had to do the same to her as before. So we cut her up and put her in the swamp."

"You cut her up while she was alive?"

Moans and gasps rippled through the gallery. Judge Foley and Bailiff Tyndale were too engrossed in the story to pay any mind.

"No, sir."

"How did she die?" asked Vaughan.

Buck didn't answer.

"Mr. McEwen, who killed the girl?"

Buck remained silent.

"Mr. McEwen," Judge Foley said, "you are instructed to answer the question."

"I, I don't want to," said Buck.

"Why don't you want to?" asked the judge.

"I, I can't."

"I think what he's trying to say is that he wants to plead his Fifth Amendment rights," said Vaughan. "Is that correct, Mr. McEwen?"

Buck was confused. He wasn't sure what the lawyer was talking about, but if it kept him from answering, he was all for it. He nodded his head.

Garland Vaughan walked back toward his desk but stopped before taking his seat. He turned to Buck to take a parting shot.

"Mr. McEwen, you never once asked the names of the girls, did you?"

"No, sir."

"Laura and Lacey Henderson. I just thought you'd like to know." Vaughan glanced at the judge. "No further questions, Your Honor."

The prosecutor took his seat. It was Lee's turn to cross examine the witness. Vaughan had given him enough ammunition. How he used it could very well determine the way the rest of the trial proceeded and whether or not justice would be served.

CHAPTER NINETY-FIVE

Douglas Lee casually stood up and approached the witness stand.

"Mr. McEwen," he asked, "can I call you Buck?"

"Yes, sir."

"Sir? Now, we don't have to be so formal. Call me Douglas."

"Yes, sir, I mean, yes, Douglas."

"Now Buck, as I sat over there listening to your testimony, I was shocked by what I heard. Frankly, I was appalled. You've made serious allegations regarding my client, and not only my client. You've made serious allegations regarding the deacons at the Antioch Pentecostal Church. Then it hit me. You've made serious allegations about yourself. Of course, you tried to backtrack a bit by saying you didn't want to testify and so forth. But only about your own involvement. You didn't seem to have a whit of trouble accusing everybody else."

"Objection," said Vaughan.

"Sustained," the judge responded. "Is there a question hiding somewhere in there, Counselor?"

"My apologies, Your Honor." Lee bowed gracefully. "Buck, are you sure you've been completely honest about everything you've told us so far?"

"Yes, sir."

"Call me Douglas. May I remind you, you're under oath."

"Yes, Douglas," replied Buck.

"You stated earlier that your youthful indiscretions were all a misunderstanding. You were only a child at the time, dating a young girl, and her parents didn't cotton to your involvement. That wasn't exactly the truth, was it?"

"It, it was a long time ago."

"But that ain't what I asked you. You stated that the young girl in question was your girlfriend."

"She was."

"Did she consider herself to be your girlfriend, or was that solely your interpretation?"

"She was bein' pressured by her parents."

"Is that why you beat her?"

"I didn't. It wasn't like that," pleaded Buck.

"She checked herself into the hospital with a broken nose and multiple bruises. Her clothes were all torn—"

"You don't understand."

"You're right, I don't," said Lee. "You say that a lot, don't you, Buck? People don't understand."

"Objection," said Vaughan.

"Sustained."

"But you claim you put all that behind you. You said you were reborn. Is that so?"

"Yes, sir. I ain't like that no more."

"Of course not," Lee agreed. "How did you make this great change, turn over that new leaf?"

"It was the Lord."

"Right, Jesus will do that." Lee nodded to Winchester's supporters in the gallery, who responded with a round of 'Praise be' and 'Amen'. "Did you find the straight and narrow path to redemption all by yourself?"

"No, sir. It was Brother Eustice who saved me."

"The same Brother Eustice who you accuse of these horrendous deeds?"

"Well, I, he weren't like that."

"Wasn't or isn't?"

"I, I don't know."

"Clearly," said Lee. "Let's face it, Buck. Your testimony doesn't make a lick of sense. I pondered that while sitting over there listening to you cast aspersions at others—until I saw the light. You've been a bad boy, haven't you, Buck?"

"Well, I, I—"

Lee offered him no opportunity to back out. Instead, he stood there with a sad look on his face, waiting for the big man to finish.

"I have," said Buck at last.

"Did you kill that girl, Buck?"

"I ain't gotta answer that."

"Did you kill that feller in Memphis?"

"I ain't gotta answer that."

"You just did."

"Objection!" shouted Vaughan. Not that it mattered. Buck was useless to him now.

"Sustained."

"Still looking for redemption for your sins?" asked Lee.

Buck nodded his head in shame.

"You ain't gonna find it blaming others for your own misdeeds."

"Objection!"

"Sustained."

"Is it possible that the good Brother Eustice was doing his best to keep his flock from straying into the deep end of temptation, but was outnumbered by the wicked and outmaneuvered by Satan?"

"I, I don't understand."

"I'm sure you don't. At any time, did Brother Eustice try to counsel you on the wages of sin and sermonize the Lord in order to keep you on the path of the righteous?"

"Sort of."

"In the midst of these heinous acts of lust and violence, was it not Brother Eustice who offered prayers and instructions in a vain effort to turn you and your fellow deacons to the Lord?"

"He prayed."

"Did he quote the good book while doing so?"

"Objection!"

"Overruled."

"Yes, he did," Buck conceded.

"But you testified that it was his instructions that led you to the murder and dismemberment of the girls. Is that so?"

"Yes."

"How can that be? Are you claiming the righteous preacher quoted the Word of the Lord while simultaneously telling you to do the work of the Devil?"

"Yes, I mean, no. I, I, I don't know," stammered Buck.

"Did he or did he not quote the Bible during these prayers?"

"Objection!" shouted Vaughan.

"Overruled," said Judge Foley.

"He did," Buck replied.

"Well then, I'm confused," said Lee. "You first stated that you were but an innocent youth, caught in an unfortunate love affair, only to admit later that you beat and raped a young girl."

"Objection!"

"Sustained."

"Only to blame it on the girl's parents. Then you claim it was Brother Winchester who took you in and gave you a place of respect in his church. And now, you're trying to blame him for similar crimes."

"Objection! Your Honor, please!" Vaughan shouted.

"Sustained," said the judge. "Mr. Lee, if you'll be kind enough—"

"Yes, yes." Lee waved him off. "Of course. I profusely apologize. Buck, can you see what I'm getting at here? Do you really expect us to believe you when you contradict yourself at every turn."

"I'm only trying to tell you the truth," Buck explained.

"Yes, yes, the truth. Was it the truth you told Detective Stallworth the first time he questioned you?"

"Well, no."

"So you lied to the police in a homicide investigation? That's a felony."

"I told him later—"

"What he wanted to hear. Ain't that right?"

"Objection!"

"Overruled."

"Yes. He said he'd help me if I testified," admitted Buck.

"And, by then, he'd slipped you just enough information to make it seem like the details came from you, didn't he?"

"Objection!"

"I withdraw the question," said Lee. He walked back and leaned against his desk. Lee glanced at the jury with a sad, knowing look. He folded his arms, sighed, and continued, "I don't know what to make of you, Buck, but I wasn't born yesterday. I'm betting neither was the jury. How about if I give you a break, give you time to reflect on things. I reserve the right to call you back to the stand if it's required. But in the meantime, I think it's best if you had a few days to prioritize. Your Honor, no further questions."

Lee sat down and flipped open a manila file folder, pretending to scan the pages in front of him. Judge Foley motioned to Vaughan. "Redirect?"

"No further questions at this time," Vaughan said. If and when Lee called McEwen back to the stand, he'd have a chance to ask him anything that might help. Not that it was likely to matter. The prosecutor was certain Buck would recant his entire testimony.

"The witness may step down," the judge instructed.

The burly prison guard approached the bench, reattached the shackles to Buck's wrists and ankles, and led him away through the same door he'd entered the courtroom.

Vaughan glanced over to where Robert and Billy were sitting. He had a bad feeling about his next witness, but he was determined to see his plan through.

"Your Honor," Vaughan announced, "the state calls Joe Bob Duncan to the stand."

CHAPTER NINETY-SIX

Once again, a prisoner was ushered out through the door on the judge's right. As the man before, he was wearing a standard prison jumpsuit and shackles.

When the prisoner was unshackled, he took his place on the stand and swore the oath. Vaughan approached the witness.

"Mr. Duncan, are you a deacon at the Antioch Pentecostal Church?"

"Yes, sir, I am," Joe Bob said without hesitation.

"Did you attend a retreat with your fellow deacons in April?"

"Yes, sir. We were all there."

"Was Brother Eustice Winchester in attendance?"

"Yes, sir. He'd have to be, seein' that he's the pastor."

"Did you and your fellow deacons travel to Memphis, Tennessee during that time?"

"Yes, sir, but we only stayed one night and came back the next mornin'."

"What was the purpose of this trip?"

"It was under the direction of Brother Eustice. We don't question the prophet in spiritual matters."

"Did you attend a performance of the magician who called himself The Amazing and Magnificent Villanova?"

"No, sir."

"No? Did any of your fellow travelers go to the show?"

"You'd have to ask them. All I know is that I didn't."

"Did you go to the theater where the show had been held the following morning before you left?"

"Yes, sir, we did."

"What was the purpose of this stop?"

"We accompanied Brother Eustice so he could have his boys fetch a truck."

"A truck?"

"Yes, sir. The Winchester boys picked up a truck, and we all drove back to Alabama."

"What was in this truck?"

"I don't know. I didn't look inside."

Vaughan hesitated. Joe Bob was changing his story.

"What happened to the truck?"

"I don't know. Wasn't any of my business," said Joe Bob.

"Was there a girl inside?"

"Not that I recall."

"That's not what you told Detective Stallworth during the interrogation," Vaughan noted.

"I just repeated what he told me to say," said Joe Bob with all the innocence he could muster.

Lee was all smiles. He knew that Joe Bob would come around. All he needed was a little push.

Lee had made sure he got that push in the holding cell he shared with Justin Bailey. Justin was a two-time loser who was doing a stint for a parole violation. Lee could have made a small fortune off the career criminal over the years, but it was a fortune that Justin couldn't pay. He knew the dire predicament that he was in when he violated his parole, and he begged Lee to take him on as a client one more time. Lee agreed, wiping out the debt owed for past services and taking on this new case pro bono. There was only one catch. He had to put a word in Joe Bob's ear.

"Are you saying you falsified a police statement in a homicide investigation? Because that's what it sounds like," said Vaughan.

The district attorney's words got Joe Bob's attention. It was clear that he hadn't thought everything through when he changed his testimony. Vaughan looked the witness straight in the eye and leveled with him. "I hope that you are aware that you've now admitted, under oath, to committing a number of felonies, including obstruction of justice in a capital case. So, I'm going to ask you again, and I want you to think real hard before you answer."

"Objection!" shouted Lee. "Badgering the witness."

"Sustained."

Joe Bob's insides were tangled up in a knot. He had no idea what the legal jargon of the trial meant, but he played it cool. The detective had thought he was so clever, coercing the confession out of him at the police station, with all that talk about the electric chair.

It was a good thing Joe Bob came to his senses before he blabbed everything in front of the jury. His cellmate was right. There was no real evidence to prove the case against him. As long as he watched what he said from now on, he was convinced he would skate on the charges.

"Mr. Duncan," Vaughan said, "the court has already obtained several signed statements from your accomplices testifying to the fact that Laura and Lacey Henderson were in the back of the magician's truck when it was stolen and brought to Alabama by your church group. Are you claiming that every one of those statements is false?"

"I ain't claimin' nothin'," said Joe Bob innocently. "I'm only tellin' you what I saw. I can't speak for the others."

"What did you see?"

"Nothin'."

Laughter erupted from the back of the room. Judge Foley banged his gavel until the snickers abated.

"Do you find this amusing, Mr. Duncan?"

"No, sir, I don't. Three of my friends are dead; the rest are in jail. The prophet is on trial for his life. There ain't nothin' funny about it."

"You forgot to mention the more abhorrent part. A man was cut in half and his two daughters raped, murdered, dismembered, and thrown into the swamp."

"I don't know nothin' about all that," Joe Bob insisted.

"That's not what your friends say," said Vaughan.

"Objection!" shouted Lee.

"Sustained."

"No further questions, Your Honor."

Vaughan walked back to his table and sat down, clearly disgusted by the unexpected turn of events. It was Douglas Lee's turn, and it wasn't going to be pretty.

CHAPTER NINETY-SEVEN

"Mr. Duncan," Lee said, "the prosecutor raises some very interesting questions. I've read through the reports from the police interrogations, and I have to say, I'm a little confused. Perhaps you can clarify some of my concerns?"

Joe Bob sat calmly in his chair. His plan was to say as little as possible and deny everything.

Lee stood up and approached the stand. "As Mr. Vaughan previously asserted, it appears that you originally stated that you knew nothing of the events leading to the deaths of the two girls, with your knowledge limited to the initial discovery of the bones. Why is that?"

"I answered the detective's questions the only way I could. It was all I knew at the time."

"But that would change, wouldn't it?"

"Yes."

"By the time Detective Stallworth took your last statement following your arrest, you had more to say—a lot more. All of a sudden, you knew all sorts of gruesome details pertaining to the crimes, including the supposed involvement of a number of your constituents, one of whom is my client. Now you have no recollection whatsoever of even the most basics of the facts surrounding the tragic events that led us here. I find this curious. Can you explain?"

Joe Bob paused a moment to formulate his words with care. He took a deep breath, sighed, and spun his newest yarn. "I tried tellin' the truth to the detective, but he wouldn't listen. He kept at us, all of us. He even came to one of our services, interruptin' the worship, to harass and embarrass us in front of our families and friends. He cast suspicion in our direction in a most vile way. Do you know what it's like to have everyone around you think you're a child killer? They give you sideways glances and whisper behind your back. Even my kids stopped gettin' invited to play with other kids. It ain't right, I tell you. But no matter what you do, no matter what you say, it don't matter. No one believes you, 'specially not that cop. He's relentless. He never stops. He's clever, too. He tells you things you didn't know, and two hours later he slyly asks you some seemingly unrelated trivial thing, and when you answer, you say somethin' he told you as if it came from you. It's all a trap."

Lee nodded in pity as if he understood. He turned towards the jury with a sympathetic expression and waited for the prosecution's star witness to continue.

"They must've taught him that in police school," said Joe Bob. "I bet that detective graduated at the top of his class. His bosses must love him. He probably solves every case he works on, gettin' some poor schmuck to confess to whatever happened.""This is his first big case," Lee interjected.

"Objection!" shouted Vaughan. "That is irrelevant and completely inappropriate."

"Sustained," Judge Foley stated. "Let me remind the defense that the detective is not the one on trial here."

"Oh, I agree wholeheartedly," said Lee. "Brother Winchester is on trial. For his life, I might add. I disagree with the prosecution about the relevancy of this testimony, but that'll be up to the jury to decide. Would you care to continue, Mr. Duncan?"

"His first big case?" Joe Bob exclaimed. "That figures. He's determined to pin it on someone. I'll admit, he played me for a fool, and as it turns out, I was one. He had me repeatin' his lies like I was confessin' my sins before my maker, and that wasn't too far from the truth. All the time he had *Yellow Mama* waitin' in the wings."

"*Yellow Mama?*" asked Lee as if he hadn't heard the moniker before.

"The 'lectric chair over at Kilby. That damn detective hung that over our heads as if he were the angel of death himself. Look at him over there, all smug and self-righteous. He ain't from 'round here. He don't know what God-fearing good Christian folks are like. That heathen probably don't even believe in the Lord."

A round of boos and hisses erupted from the crowd. People looked at the detective with hate in their eyes. Robert ignored them.

"Brother Eustice warned us about him. Said he was a trickster. He told us he was sent by the Devil to persecute the righteous. We didn't listen 'cause we didn't understand. Well, I understand now. The preacher was right all along. He must've come from the Devil's workshop. How else could he make all of us turn like we did? Who but the Devil could've taught him to do that?"

"He learned that in the Army," offered Lee. "At least, that's what we think. They ain't saying over at the Pentagon, because we asked. They won't tell us anything about his record, except that he worked with the Russians and was involved in those death camps in some manner or another."

"Objection!" shouted Vaughan.

"Sustained," said Foley. "I warned you once already, Mr. Lee. We won't tolerate you showing disrespect to our Armed Services or our war vets. I'll not stand for it."

"I meant no disrespect, Your Honor," said Lee.

"I don't know nothin' 'bout all that," Joe Bob continued. "I'm a Marine myself. I fought at Guadalcanal. It ain't like I ain't never been under pressure before. But there's more to it than I can explain."

"Is that so?" asked Lee. "I'm not sure what you mean."

"He set us up from the beginnin'. First, he worked some kind of deal with Deputy Barber. You know how cops like to stick together. Still, I didn't think Earl would turn on us like that. But then again, he never was that bright. Then he come out to Cooter's place to meet us all. Just showed up out of the blue and started spinnin' his bullshi—, I mean, story. He even told us he'd bring us in, and he swore he could get us to confess to anythin' he wanted us to. Can you believe it? What a cocky bastard. Still, he was right about that one."

"Go on."

"He did like he said. He brought us in, one by one, to question us. He pretended it was all a trick, and he wanted us to go along."

"A trick? What kind of trick?"

"He said he suspected the Klan of killin' those girls. He said Sheriff Fuller and his men were all members, with the exception of Earl, of course. He even arrested them, only to let them go the next day. Hell, he was probably right and found out he'd get nowhere with that one. If it were the Klan, and I'm not sayin' it was, mind you, but if it were and Sheriff Fuller was involved, they'd never get it through the court system and get a conviction. Once he realized how that'd end up, he turned on us 'cuz we was the only ones left to pin it on. He knew we was just simple God-fearin' men, uneducated about the ways of the law."

"But why choose you?"

"Because we helped in searchin' for the girls," Joe Bob explained. "He ain't from 'round here. He don't know no one. All he had was the old man who found the first bones, the sheriff, and us. The old man is a nigger, but he's too old. Besides, everybody knows Lucius ain't that sort. Then he went after the sheriff and his men. When the judge threw that out the window, he come at us. And he kept comin'. It kept gettin' worse and worse. Junior turned up dead. Earl freaked out and tried to kill us all, puttin' poor ol' Cooter and Charles Ray in their graves. They trapped Buck in a seedy hotel and hauled him in. If someone didn't do somethin', there ain't no tellin' where it would've stopped. So I did what I had to do."

"You did what you had to do?"

"I turned myself in. Some other detective started questionin' me, but I could see the writin' on the wall. I asked for Stallworth, and I told him everythin' he wanted to hear. He ate it up with a spoon, too, 'specially the sick parts. That's what he really wanted anyway. I think it turns him on."

"Objection!" Vaughan shouted. "Your Honor, please, this is outrageous."

"Overruled," Judge Foley announced.

Robert and Billy looked at each other. Trouble was brewing on the horizon.

"That's quite an accusation, Mr. Duncan," said Lee. "Why would you say something like that?"

"Because of that picture he keeps showin' everyone," said Joe Bob.

"Picture? What picture?"

"Not long after he showed up, we kept hearin' rumors 'bout him. They said that he kept the body parts they fished out of the swamp in a special room over at the coroner's. But not covered up, or put in containers, or anything. No, the stories said that he had them displayed, lyin' on a tarp on the floor, in the middle of the room."

Muffled groans drifted from the crowd.

"Well, let me tell you, them rumors were true. He took pictures. He loved to show them to us, too. He liked to see our reaction when he shoved his favorite one in our faces. He even has a name for it."

"A name? That is disturbing," Lee said with disgust. "Why would he do that?"

"I told you. There's somethin' wrong with him."

"So you say. What does he call it?"

"The Bone Puzzle."

The room erupted in an audible display of revulsion. A large woman in the back row fainted and was quickly attended to by those around her. An elderly man in overalls escorted his wife outside before she could empty her stomach on the tile floor. Judge Foley half-heartedly tapped his gavel for show, exhibiting no genuine effort to silence the courtroom. Robert ignored the whispered insults that drifted his way and stared nonchalantly at the front of the room, fighting the urge to wink at Bailiff Tyndale, who glared at him.

The crowd settled down after a few minutes, and the judge ordered a fifteen minute recess before letting the cross-examination continue. That was fine with Lee. The longer the jury had to process Joe Bob's testimony, the better it was for his client. Vaughan saw no reason to protest. The audience wasn't going to like it any better when it was his turn to redirect the lying SOB, so there was little cause to hurry.

Robert and Billy kept their seats as the room emptied. Neither had any wish to mingle with the local hillbillies, who were known to lynch undesirables on occasion.

"I see you made quite an impression in the short time you've been here," said Billy.

"It's a gift," Robert answered.

"Were you as popular in Germany as you are in Alabama?"

"Almost, but I don't live in Germany."

"So, what do you think?" asked Billy.

"I think I need to change that title."

CHAPTER NINETY-EIGHT

Stepping out of the side room wearing his shackles, Joe Bob was escorted by the guard back to the stand after a short recess. Douglas Lee had no more questions, preferring to quit while ahead. Garland Vaughan had no choice but to redirect the witness, even though he knew it would do little to help his case. Unless—

"Mr. Duncan," Vaughan said, "to summarize your testimony to this point, you originally told the police you knew nothing pertaining to the investigation. Then you not only told them that you were involved, but you went into great detail about the horrendous events, and you specifically named those in your group and spelled out the actions each took. Now you're claiming, once again, that you have no idea what this trial is even about. Is this an accurate account?"

"I, I don't know how to answer that," stammered Joe Bob.

"It either is or it isn't," said Vaughan. "Yes or no?"

"Which part?"

"Right. That's my point. Which part is correct, and which part is a lie? You're under oath in a capital murder case involving the rape, murder, and dismemberment of children. So, to simplify my question, are you a liar?"

"Objection!" shouted Lee.

"Overruled," Judge Foley stated.

"I, I ain't lyin'," Joe Bob explained.

"You have to be," said Vaughan. "You've given nothing but conflicting statements from the beginning. They are diametrically opposed."

"I don't know what that means."

"It means you are a liar."

"Objection!"

"Overruled."

"I ain't a liar. I was just scared is all. That detective—"

"You're scared of the detective? I thought you were a Marine."

"I was."

"Oh, so you were a Marine. I didn't know that was possible. I was told that once a Marine, always a Marine. But I may be wrong. How does the Marine Corps feel about lying, Mr. Duncan?"

"Objection!" shouted Lee.

"Overruled," Judge Foley spat. Lee winced at the tone of the judge's voice. He clearly didn't appreciate one of his fellow servicemen obviously perjuring himself.

Joe Bob stuck to his newest story. "I was just sayin' what he wanted to hear."

"He wanted to hear the truth. Isn't that what he told you?"

"Yes. I mean, he said that, but—"

"So you told him the truth. Isn't that right?"

"Yes. I mean, no. I, I don't know."

"What do you mean yes, no, I don't know? Did you or did you not tell him the truth?"

"Sometimes."

"Sometimes?" Vaughan asked incredulously. "So, if you were only telling the police the truth sometimes, what were you doing the rest of the time?"

Vaughan waited. Joe Bob didn't answer. He glanced about the room, hoping Winchester's lawyer would object, or that the judge would bang his gavel on the bench and rescue him. But no relief came. The room grew silent. The audience was on the edge of their seats, waiting for the shameful words to come out his mouth.

"Lyin'," Joe Bob replied, his voice a whisper.

The crowd erupted with sneers and groans.

Judge Foley tapped his gavel several times. "Order! Order in the court!"

"What do we call someone who lies, Mr. Duncan?"

"A liar."

"Are you a liar, Mr. Duncan?"

Joe Bob nodded his head, keeping his eyes down.

"We can't hear you."

"Will the witness please answer so that the court reporter can hear," instructed the judge.

"Yes," said Joe Bob forcefully. "I'm a liar. Is that loud enough for you?"

"I'm warning you, Mr. Duncan," Judge Foley said angrily. "I'll hold you in contempt of court if you speak to me in such a manner again."

"Are you lying to us right now?" asked Vaughan.

Joe Bob found himself back where he'd started. His cellmate had convinced him that, if he'd just stick to his story, everything would work out. For awhile there, he'd almost believed that it had. He'd snookered the district attorney the first time around, and Winchester's lawyer paved the rest of the way. But then they took a break, and when they came back, everything had gone to hell. Either the district attorney suddenly got his shit together or that damn detective put a word in his ear. No matter now, he was screwed.

Luckily, his cellmate told him of a Plan B, just in case. It was the only card he had left, and he played it.

"I refuse to answer on the grounds it might incriminate me."

"No further questions, Your Honor," said Vaughan. He strutted back to his desk, giving Lee a sly smile on the way. Before he sat down, Vaughan glanced at where the detective had been sitting, but Stallworth was gone. He wondered what could've dragged Robert away from such a pivotal moment in the trial. There was an infinite number of possible scenarios, though only two outcomes. Either it was going to be very good, or very bad.

CHAPTER NINETY-NINE

The trial was set to resume at nine o'clock the following morning. Vaughan knew he'd be up most of the night in his office preparing, but he made the time to grab a quick bite and head over to Dr. Hall's office. Stallworth was up to something, and Vaughan was determined to find out what it was.

"It's good to see you again, Garland." The medical examiner greeted him and escorted him toward the back office. "I hear it was a rough one today."

"I've had worse, but just barely," Vaughan replied.

"Tomorrow you'll have another shot at it," quipped the doctor.

They walked past the big coolers and down a long hallway until they got to the detective's unofficial space. Dr. Hall unlocked the metal door and waved the prosecutor in. Vaughan took a deep breath and steadied himself before entering.

Billy looked up and smiled when the men entered. Robert's expression never wavered, his only acknowledgement that the visitor had arrived was a subtle nod. His attention was riveted on the grisly display lying on the tarp in the middle of the floor.

"Good God!" exclaimed Vaughan. "Is this necessary? Don't you think it's time we put these girls to rest?"

"It is now," said Robert.

Vaughan looked at the pile of bones and saw that they were now complete. The skulls had been placed at the apex of the skeletal remains. "How? Where did you find them?"

"We've released Brandine without charges," Robert stated. "For the time being. I thought you'd want to know. You'll have to amend your witness list. She's not going to testify."

"Excuse me?" Vaughan was outraged. "You have no authority to do such a thing."

"Judge Parker signed the order," said Robert. "She's gone."

"What? Why would you do that?"

"Lacey and Laura are going to be buried whole, just like I said they would."

"Even if that means the killers walk free?"

"If you do your job, that won't happen."

Vaughan was furious. "If I do my job? What about yours? Where's my evidence? You bring me this case full of holes and beg me to take it on, then hamstring me at every turn. That isn't the way it works, Detective."

"You need to take a deep breath, counselor," Robert replied in a steady tone, "before you forget yourself. We're only one day into the trial. Things are just getting interesting."

"Interesting? Is that what you call it? I don't know if you've noticed, but our case is falling apart. The only thing we've established with our first two witnesses is that nobody can believe a word they say. Oh, that and that you're the reincarnation of Satan. Did you have a look at the people seated around you, by any chance? They're ready to acquit Winchester already. Hell, half of them are probably joining his church. How the crowd goes is often how the jury goes. What do we have left? A disgraced deputy? These country people aren't going to understand a word Dr. Hall says, and they'll dismiss it outright. Your testimony is only going to make Winchester look like a martyr. Lee has already set up his defense against your pile of bones here to make you look like the sicko. What do we have left? Jeremiah Winchester? He's not going to testify against his daddy, even if you let his wife go."

"What do you think you were going to get out of Brandine?" asked Robert. "She's not going to testify against her husband, and we can't make her. Lee will play up the fact that she's expecting, and we'll look like bigger assholes for locking her up. We had to let her go. At least, for now."

"Damn it, Robert, the woman set you up to have you murdered."

"She wasn't the first, and she won't be the last."

"Is that all you have to say? That's rather flippant, considering the circumstances."

"You're going to be just fine, Garland. I have faith in your abilities."

"Gentlemen," Billy interrupted, "please. This is getting us nowhere. We're all on the same side."

"I thought we were," said Vaughan.

Robert ignored the comment.

"Where were the skulls found?" asked Vaughan.

"On Junior's property," said Robert.

"How did you find them?"

"Jeremiah."

"Fuck. When Lee finds out, he's going to use it to cast suspicion on Winchester's kids; first, the dead one, and if that doesn't do it, then, the youngest one. By that time, JT will have sworn that his father's innocent in regards to the two girls. He'll cave when it comes to the shooting of his brother and the deputy, or take the Fifth. Either way, he'll be a killer in the eyes of the jury. Eustice will be sitting pretty. We already know he's more than willing to let the rest of the men burn to save his own skin—kin or no kin. You released Brandine for naught. Jeremiah is going to be a better witness for the defense than he will be for us."

"Will he?" asked Robert. "I think you've misjudged the boy. Call him to the stand, but leave questions about the skulls out of it, for the moment. Let Lee bring those up when he's ready. The later, the better."

"We have to let him know," said Vaughan. "It's evidence."

"You submitted the evidence. My now famous photograph. We didn't hide anything. It was everything we had at the time, and we submitted it. Has Lee asked for an updated list?"

"No."

"And he's not going to. Because a new one doesn't have that name attached."

Vaughan smiled. *"The Bone Puzzle."*

"Unless Jeremiah mentions it, which is a very real possibility, Lee is waiting to use the skulls we found behind the sheriff's office," said Robert. "So we save Jeremiah's testimony for last."

"But if he defends his old man and takes the heat himself, we'll be closing on a bad witness."

"What's our choice? Me?" said Robert.

The men laughed.

"Jeremiah will make his choice, and we'll have to make due," said Robert. "And what's Lee going to do?"

"He'll ask for a dismissal for lack of evidence."

"And Judge Foley?"

"Denied."

"And Lee has his turn," said Robert. "He'll bring up the skulls. Ouch! He can't bring back any of our witnesses. They're all liars. Remember?"

"Except for you," noted Vaughan.

"Oh, he'll be done with me after the first pass. I wouldn't worry too much about that."

"I wouldn't be so confident if I were you," said Vaughan. "He's a shark in the courtroom. He's practically drooling on himself to have a go at you. I doubt once will be enough."

"That's what Waldemar Hoven thought," Robert said.

"Who?" asked Dr. Hall.

"Never mind. It's not important," said Robert. "Don't worry about me. I'll be just fine. So what's that leave him?"

"Jeremiah," said Billy. "That doesn't instill me with confidence."

"You're forgetting the other Winchester," said Robert.

"If Lee lets him testify," said Vaughan.

"I can't see how he can stop him," said Robert.

"If they're on the edge of acquittal, he'd be stupid to take the stand," said Vaughan.

"Unless—" said Dr. Hall.

"Unless what?" Vaughan asked.

The group turned towards the medical examiner. What did he know that the rest of them didn't?

"Did you see the commotion on the picnic grounds across from the courthouse, by any chance?" Dr. Hall asked.

"Yeah, I was going to ask you about that," said Billy. "What's that all about?"

"They're putting up one of those giant circus tents."

"Circus tents?" asked Vaughan. "You have to be kidding me. The circus is coming to town right next to the courthouse during the trial?"

"No, not the circus," Dr. Hall explained. "It's even better than that. There's going to be an old fashioned Christian revival."

"Good Lord," said Billy.

"Something like that," said Dr. Hall.

"That'll do it," said Robert. "The old windbag won't be able to resist his captive audience. He'll testify, alright."

"I'm not sure that'll be a good thing," said Vaughan. "The jury might be compromised by the revival. It might work against us."

Robert indicated the tarp at their feet. "They'll have to ignore this."

Garland Vaughan wasn't at all convinced that wouldn't happen.

CHAPTER ONE HUNDRED

Earl had been fantasizing about his dramatic entrance into the Pickens County courthouse for weeks. When the time came, he could barely contain his enthusiasm. He'd hear the bailiff call his name, then he'd slowly enter through the double doors at the back of the room. Wearing his dress blues, with his newly won Medal of Valor pinned on his chest, Earl would limp up to the podium as the crowd looked on with awe. He was a hero, wounded in the line of duty, here to secure justice for the victims.

Things could not have been more different when the day came. Porter, the bailiff who Earl had known for a number of years, although neither had ever quite gotten along, called his name with a hint of sarcasm. Or at least that's how it sounded to Earl. The deputy ignored the insult and hastened to make his entrance, pulling open both doors simultaneously and stepping into the crowded room in all his uniformed glory. *Wham!* The doors slammed into his back with a thud. Mocking laughter, which echoed through the room, was only mildly rebuked by Judge Foley's halfhearted tap of his gavel. Earl thought he detected a smirk on the judge's face, which, as a decorated and recently injured officer of the law, he felt he didn't deserve.

The deputy straightened his back and walked to the front of the courtroom with a noticeable limp. Earl hadn't fully recovered from the gunshot wound and generally played up his disability for sympathy and respect. Unfortunately, his limp appeared to those watching to be the result of the doors smacking him on the ass and proved to be yet another stimulus for humiliating laughter at his expense.

The oath he took from the stone-faced bailiff felt like a brutal slap to the face and elevated his perpetual dislike of the bailiff to one of deep seated hatred. Earl took his seat in the witness box as the prosecutor approached.

"Deputy Earl Barber," Vaughan asked, "is it true that you are a follower of Brother Eustice Winchester and a deacon in the Antioch Pentecostal Church?"

"No, sir, I am not," stated Earl.

"You aren't?"

"To clarify, I was, but I'm no longer affiliated with that den of vipers."

Boos and hisses erupted from the gallery. Judge Foley glared at the assembly, but made no move to silence their disapproval with his gavel.

"I see," said Vaughan, "and when did you sever ties with the organization?"

"When they shot me."

"Objection!" shouted Lee.

"Overruled," the judge replied.

"Are you saying I wasn't shot?" Earl asked Lee defiantly.

"Please, only address me at this time, Mr. Barber," said Vaughan. "But at one time, you were a member? Is that correct?"

"Yes, sir, it is."

"Were you a member in April of last year?"

"I was."

"Did you attend the retreat with the pastor and the rest of the deacons at that time?"

"I did."

"Where did y'all go?"

"We went to Tennessee. Memphis. We came back to Alabama the next day."

"What did y'all do in Memphis?"

"We stayed at a hotel while Brother Winchester and Buck McEwen went to a show. The next mornin', we went by the theater, and Eustice's boys hopped into a truck. Then we came back to Alabama."

"Is that all that happened in Memphis?"

"It's all I can recall."

"What was in this truck that y'all picked up?"

"Some stage props from a magic show."

"Is that all?"

"That's all I saw. But it ain't like I was lookin' inside. The truck was Winchester's business. He didn't explain himself, and I didn't ask."

"Where did y'all bring this truck when ya'll came back to Alabama?" asked Vaughan.

"To Cooter Yates' property, outside of Vienna."

"Did anyone else go with y'all or meet you there?"

"No, sir. Although a couple of the deputies from work came by in the afternoon and brought me to the office. I was on duty for the night shift."

"I see. And when did you return to the Yates' property?"

"Early the next mornin'. When I left the sheriff's office."

"Did you return alone?"

Earl shifted in his seat. He was determined to avoid any questions about the magician. He wasn't on trial for that, and, so far, there had been little focus on the events in Tennessee. Earl knew that eventually there would be, and everything he said now would come back to haunt him. He had stuck to the truth in regard to being picked up by his fellow lawmen and not being around when the first girl met her demise. If only he hadn't returned the following morning, he might've been able to get out of the entire episode. But he had returned.

"At first," said Earl.

"At first?" asked Vaughan.

"As I was drivin' back to Cooter's place, I spotted a girl in the road."

Murmurs drifted up from the gallery. Judge Foley tapped his gavel for silence.

"A girl?"

"Yes, sir."

"Who was this girl?"

"I don't know," explained Earl. "I tried to get her to talk, but she wouldn't tell me nothin'. Not even who she was or how she got there. So I put her in the back of the car. I planned to bring her in once I was done at Cooter's place. I figured her to be a runaway or somethin' who got lost out in the woods overnight. We hadn't gotten a call about it, so chances were that it hadn't been noticed that she was gone yet. She probably knew she'd be in trouble when her folks found out, which would explain why she wasn't talkin'. It happens more than you know."

"I see. That is troubling."

"You don't know the half of it."

"What happened when you got to Cooter's place?"

"I could tell somethin' horrible had happened there, but no one was sayin' nothin'. While I was talkin' to the boys, the girl must've climbed out of the car and ran into the woods. Everybody went to look for her. They all seemed real anxious 'bout it, but I didn't put two and two together at the time, much to my disgrace. I wasn't the lawman I thought I was, or we wouldn't be here now."

"What happened?"

"They found her. Before I knew it, they had her tied and gagged. They was all talkin' like she had been there before. They kept sayin' they had to do what they'd done the night before."

"Which was?"

"I don't know. I weren't there, but I gathered that they thought she was a reincarnation of another girl; a girl they killed and threw into the swamp. I, I didn't know what to say or what to do."

"You're a lawman. What do you mean you didn't know what to do?"

"I know, I know, but you don't understand," Earl pleaded, tears welling up in his eyes. "These were my friends.

Men I loved and trusted. And the preacher—, the preacher—, my God! He had me believin' he was a prophet; he had us all believin' that. 'Sides, I weren't the only one carryin' a gun. What do you think they'd a done to me if I whipped out my revolver and started waving my badge 'round?"

"So what happened next?"'

"They was talkin' 'bout things I didn't understand. Junior was arguin' that he wanted a go at her."

"A go at her?" asked Vaughan.

"You know, a go," Earl explained.

"And what did you do?"

"I was goin' to pull out my revolver and put a stop to the madness. I swear I was. I couldn't just stand there while he raped the girl."

"Did you?"

"I didn't have to. Buck shot her in the face."

Gasps reverberated through the courtroom. Even Judge Foley looked shocked by the revelation. He reached for his gavel but fumbled it.

Bailiff Tyndale came to the rescue. "Order! Order in the court!" he barked, his voice cutting through the cacophony like a drill sergeant on an artillery range.

When the room grew quiet once again, Vaughan continued, "What did you do then, Deputy?" The revulsion in the prosecutor's voice when he uttered the word *deputy* was not missed by Earl or anyone else within earshot.

"They talked 'bout how they needed to saw the body up and dump her in the swamp— like last time. I didn't know what they was talkin' 'bout. Last time? It's not like they was gung ho 'bout explainin' it to me, neither. Anyway, Brother Eustice wanted Buck to do it, but he refused. Joe Bob insisted that Eustice take a turn, bein' that he had weaseled out before. Eustice said he would, but he started cryin' like a little bitch."

"Objection!" shouted Lee.

"Sustained," Judge Foley replied. "You'll watch your language in my courtroom, Deputy Barber."

"Yes, sir, I mean, Your Honor," said Earl. "Anyway, Eustice babbled quotes out of the Bible and speakin' in tongues like he always does, so it was left to the rest of us. I didn't want no part of it, but I was outnumbered. I had no choice."

"You helped cut up the body?" Vaughan asked.

"I had no choice."

"What did y'all do with the body parts?"

"We wrapped them in pieces of tarp and threw them into the swamp."

"Who told you to do these things?"

"Brother Eustice," said Earl, raising his right hand and pointed a finger at the accused seated next to his attorney.

"Did you tell anyone about what happened?"

"No, sir."

"Well, why not? You're an officer of the law."

"Because I was implicated at that point," Earl exclaimed. "I was scared. What could I do? I had blood on my hands. I just wanted it all to go away."

"But it didn't, did it?"

"No, sir. Old man Lucius fished out that foot. We got called in. It looked, for a moment, like nobody would find anythin' else, but Jarvis brought out the bloodhounds. Once they found the other foot, I knew things would get bad. Still, after a few weeks, nothing happened, and we started to breathe again. That's when that fucking detective showed up."

Judge Foley slammed his gavel on the bench. "I told you about that language. I'm not going to tell you again!"

"Yes, Your Honor, I apologize. Slip of the tongue."

"You mean Detective Stallworth?" asked Vaughan.

Earl nodded.

"What difference did he make?"

"He kept findin' more parts. I don't know how, but he did. No one in the department liked him. He made us all nervous. Even Sheriff Fuller wanted to get rid of him, but he wouldn't go away. He kept diggin' and diggin', askin' and askin' questions, again and again. He tricked us. He even arrested the sheriff."

"The sheriff?"

"Yeah. Said it was a Klan thing. He said he knew we wasn't part of that, and he needed our help. It was all bullsh—, I mean, it was bull. He set us up. He asked endless questions and kept tellin' us things he couldn't possibly know. Things I didn't even know. Pretty soon, he had us suspectin' each other of talkin'. The next thing we knew, Junior was dead. There was a rumor that we was all goin' to get it sooner or later. Someone was cleanin' house. Finally, that other guy showed up."

"Other guy?"

"John Turner. He's from the state police, too, but he ain't like that Stallworth fella. He's a good guy. Once I talked to him, I knew I had to start actin' like a lawman again. So I arranged a meetin' out at Cooter's place. I wanted to talk some sense into the boys."

"That didn't turn out like you wanted it to, did it?"

"No, sir. Cooter pulled a gun. I had to shoot him. I didn't want to. He was my friend. Then Charles Ray went for me, and the next thing I knew, I'd shot him, too. It was horrible. I don't know what happened next. I woke up in the hospital. I'd been shot. The docs said I was lucky to be alive, but I don't feel so lucky. Cooter is dead. Charles Ray is dead. Junior is dead. Those girls are dead. If only I'd acted like a deputy sooner, who knows? But I didn't because I was a coward. I didn't because I believed in the prophet. But he ain't no prophet, and he ain't never been one. He's a false prophet."

Another round of boos and hisses echoed from the gallery. The judge tapped his gavel, and the room grew silent once again.

"You said before that you wouldn't be here if it weren't for the detective. Is that how you still feel?"

"No, sir. He was just doin' his job. I'm here because I wasn't doin' mine. I'm here because Eustice Winchester is a murderin' scumbag."

"Objection!" shouted Lee.

"Sustained," the judge answered.

"No further questions, Your Honor."

Garland Vaughan took his seat. Things were marginally looking up; marginally, because it was Douglas Lee's turn with the witness.

CHAPTER ONE HUNDRED ONE

Resisting the urge to address the witness by his first name, Lee asked his question without a hint of sarcasm, "Deputy Barber. That is right, isn't it? You are still a deputy?"

"Yes, sir. Why wouldn't I be?"

"Why not, indeed? It seems up to the standards of the department."

"Objection!" shouted Vaughan.

"Sustained."

"Apologies all around, Your Honor," said Lee. "I guess I'm just reacting to the report about Sheriff Fuller's arrest and all these allegations of belonging to nefarious social clubs with dubious reputations. I withdraw the comment. Deputy Barber, you stated earlier that you never saw anyone except the members of your church group when y'all returned to Alabama after your foray into the wilds of Tennessee, is that correct?"

"Yes, sir."

"That is, until you returned the following morning, on your own, in a vehicle supplied to you by the department. Is that correct?"

"It is."

"When you passed a wayward child hiding in the woods, is that what you said happened?"

"Yes, sir."

"Were you on the late Mr. Yates' property at that time?"

"No, sir. I believe it was state land."

"So, you have no idea who the girl was or how she got there?"

"Not at the time, no."

"But you picked her up anyway."

"I'm a police officer. It's my job to tend to such things."

"Were you on duty at the time?"

"No, sir, not at the time, but—"

"But you were still in uniform?"

"Yes, but—"

"And you were driving a marked police vehicle at the time?"

"Yes. I didn't have time to go home first."

"No? Why is that?"

"I had to get back."

"Why?"

"I, I don't know exactly. We had unfinished business, I guess," stammered Earl.

"Unfinished business?" asked Lee. "What kind of unfinished business?"

"I, I, well—"

"Y'all were digging a well?" Lee turned to the crowd and made a goofy face. The audience responded with laughter.

"Order! Order in the court!" Judge Foley silenced the room with his gavel.

"Was the girl part of your unfinished business?" asked Lee.

"Well, no."

"No? But you just claimed that several members of your group said she had been there the previous day and y'all needed to repeat whatever it was that was done to her, or something like that. I can have Miss Godsey read the transcript if it helps," offered Lee. "Helen, please go to—"

"That won't be necessary," interrupted Earl. "Yes, that's what they said."

"Who said?"

"Some of the guys."

"Be more specific, if you can."

"Cooter, maybe. Charles Ray. I don't know."

"You don't know?"

"I can't remember exactly who said what," said Earl.

"I see," said Lee. "But you remember that it was Junior who stated that he wanted to take advantage of the poor thing."

"Yes, sir."

"Are you sure?"

"Yes, sir."

"Because I'll understand if you're not. Your memory does seem to come and go."

"Objection!" Vaughan shouted.

"Sustained," said the judge.

"And you said it was Buck McEwen who killed the girl?" asked Lee.

"Yes, sir."

"And you're sure about that as well?"

"I'm sure."

"Not Brother Eustice?"

"No, sir, but he wanted it done," said Earl.

"How do you know that? Did he specifically order Buck to shoot the girl?"

"Well, no."

"Did Brother Eustice have a gun pointed at Buck?"

"No."

"Did Brother Eustice have a gun pointed at you?"

"No."

"Did Brother Eustice have a gun pointed at any of the members of your group?"

"No."

"Did Brother Eustice have a gun pointed at the girl?"

"No."

"At any time during the incident?"

"No."

"Did Brother Eustice have a gun at all?"

"Not that I know of," Earl conceded.

"Did anyone else have a weapon?"

"Sure. We all did. Or, at least, most of us."

"Yet you claim that everything happened according to Brother Eustice's commands?"

"Yes, sir. He's the prophet," said Earl.

"I thought you said he wasn't a prophet. Helen, please—" Lee turned towards the court reporter again.

"I say that now, but at the time, we all thought he was," Earl interjected.

"Right, right. You say that now, but then you thought different. Are you to have us believe that, even though most, if not all, of y'all were armed, Brother Eustice made y'all rape, murder, dismember, and dispose of two children in Dead River Swamp, just by telling you to do it?"

"Well, when you say it like that, I know it sounds dumb." Earl tried to explain.

"Agreed," said Lee. He turned towards the audience and rolled his eyes. Another round of laughter greeted him.

"What other dumb statements are you prepared to make today, Deputy?"

"Objection!"

"Overruled."

Vaughan kept his composure but noted the judge's reaction. Foley was enjoying Lee's performance as much as the crowd. The district attorney could only wonder how entertained the jury was by this point.

"Earlier you stated that after Buck killed the girl you brought there in your official police vehicle while wearing your official policeman's uniform, Buck insisted that Brother Eustice dismember the girl because he hadn't taken part in the grisly task the day before. Is that correct?"

"That's what he said."

"And you also said that Brother Eustice refused yet again to participate in this heinous act, to the point of throwing himself prostrate on the ground and wailing. Is that also correct?"

"Well, yes."

"Then, as the other members actually did those horrible deeds, Brother Eustice spent his time quoting the Bible, talking in tongues, and praying to the most Holy Jesus?"

"That's not exactly what I said."

"Helen, please read—"

"Okay, okay. It's what I said," Earl interrupted. "Yeah, he prayed, but it was only to get out of doin' his fair share."

"His fair share?" gasped Lee.

"We all had to do it," Earl explained, "but not him. He couldn't get his hands dirty like the rest of us because he's a holy man. What a crock."

"Whoa, calm down there, fella!" Lee said. "Take a deep breath." Lee paced around the courtroom as Earl fumed silently on the stand. The lawyer made eye contact with the members of the jury as well as the audience in the gallery as he summarized his cross examination. "We believe you, Deputy. Buck McEwen murdered the girl you brought there, then the rest of the men, most of whom were carrying weapons, you included, took turns sawing up the corpse to dispose of the pieces in the swamp while the only guy not armed refused to be a part of it and prayed to the Lord, in vain, while the atrocities were carried out. Does that about sum it up?"

"You're twistin' my words," Earl argued.

"You keep saying that," said Lee. "I've had about enough of it. Miss Helen, please read the first two sentences of the last statement that Deputy Barber made. Verbatim, as he made them."

The court reporter skimmed through the paper tape in front of her until she found her place. When she was ready, she looked to the judge for approval. Judge Foley nodded, and she commenced reading from the tape.

"We all had to do it, but not him. He couldn't get his hands dirty like the rest of us because he's a holy man," read Miss Godsey.

A round of 'Amen' and 'praise the Lord' arose from the gallery. Lee looked over at the jury for effect. Their pious expressions told him it was time to wrap this up.

"Deputy, I think we can all understand what happened out there now. Thank you for your testimony. No further questions, Your Honor."

Lee took his seat next to Winchester, whose head was bowed and his hands folded in prayer. He had a lot to be grateful for. He had faith in the Lord, and the Lord was going to set him free.

CHAPTER ONE HUNDRED TWO

Not to be suckered into fortifying the defense's case, Vaughan waved off any further questions of the witness, and the trial broke for lunch. He waited for the room to clear before grabbing his briefcase and heading for the door. Robert and Billy lingered by the exit so that they could share a few words on the way to *Samson's*. Before they made it outside, a commotion on the courtroom steps got their attention.

"What the hell is going on out there?" asked Billy. He poked his head outside before retreating quickly back into the lobby.

"Well?" asked Vaughan.

"Protestors," Billy explained. "Probably from that tent revival set up across the street. It looks like they pelted Earl with eggs."

Vaughan winced and remarked, "Poor deputy."

"Fuck him," said Robert. Billy and Garland looked at him. "That asshole drove up to Memphis with the lot of them and sawed Villanova in half. He already admitted to cutting up the girl and throwing her in the swamp. I'd say eggs are the least of his worries."

"Yeah, but he had on his dress uniform with the shiny Medal of Valor attached," said Vaughan mockingly.

They laughed.

"Well, when you put it that way," said Robert, "I withdraw my statement."

"What about us?" asked Billy. "My wife bought me this tie. Egg yolk wouldn't go well with this shirt."

"Follow me," offered Vaughan. "We'll go out the back way."

Garland led the group down a hallway and around a corner until they came to a service entrance. The trio exited the building and crossed over an empty field behind the courthouse. Once they were a safe distance away, they paused to watch the mob.

"Who's the guy with the megaphone?" asked Robert.

"That's Reverend Beecher," explained Garland. "He's a distant relative of Winchester from Clay County. He has his own congregation of miscreants outside of Ashland. He's called in the troops from every nook and cranny in the region. They've only just begun to arrive."

"So there's more hillbillies on the way?" asked Billy. "Wonderful."

The men walked to the bar and grill to grab a quick bite to eat and strategize before it was time for the trial to resume. Once seated at their usual table, they ate quickly while discussing Vaughan's next move.

"Why didn't you redirect the deputy?" asked Billy.

"What was the point?" said Garland. "He was only likely to say something else to clear Winchester. I was afraid of having him up there, but if I hadn't called him, Lee would've. It's better that we got that out of the way as early as possible. At least, Lee won't have any cause to call him back up. We're done with Barber for now. We'll charge him later, once we're done with Winchester."

"Agreed," said Robert. "So who's next? Me or Hall?"

"Hall," said Vaughan. "If I had my way, I'd call JT, but you feel pretty adamant about saving him for last, against my better judgment. Please, convince me again, if for no other reason than to put my mind at ease."

"I've been working on the boy," said Robert. "Unlike Duncan, he's being kept by himself over in Fairview. The only person who's been allowed to see him is Turner. Oh, and I arranged for a short visit from Brandine."

Billy laughed. "You clever boy."

"Sheriff Clanton owes me a favor," Robert continued. "Anyway, give John a couple of more days. He assured me that the Winchester boy is starting to look up to him as a father figure. The Good Lord knows he needs one who ain't a huge pile of donkey dung. He'll talk some sense into the boy."

"How can you be so sure?" asked Garland. "Besides, I might be able to stretch it past tomorrow and over the weekend, but come Monday morning, ready or not, we'll be calling him up."

"That's all we'll need," said Robert.

"Again, how can you be so sure?"

"Good cop, bad cop. Brandine will bring him a picnic basket Saturday and tell him everything we told her to tell him—how his daddy is turning on everyone and rolling over on him and Junior. Turner is going to bring in his pastor for a good round of sermons and confessions come Sunday morning. Sunday night, I show up with my newest work of art."

Robert reached into his pocket and pulled out an envelope. He wiped the cheeseburger grease from his fingers on a napkin and carefully removed a five-by-seven glossy photograph, which he held up for his companions to see. Billy almost choked on a French fry in a fit of laughter, while Garland just shook his head.

"You are too much, Detective," said Garland. "Do you have a colorful name for this picture as well?"

"After all the bad reviews, I kept it simple this time," said Robert. "It's called *Yellow Mama.*"

CHAPTER ONE HUNDRED
THREE

Up on the stand, Dr. Hall sat patiently and waited while Garland and the defense attorney argued in whispers with the judge. Once their argument was settled with a dismissive wave by Judge Foley, Vaughan approached the witness stand. The prosecutor threw in a few questions about the pathologist's credentials to establish his expertise, which went uncontested by Lee. Vaughan quickly moved to the details of the evidence.

One by one, photographs of the assorted body parts were introduced and passed to the jury. Each had numbers and letters attached. Most of the photos were taken at the point of recovery in the Dead River Swamp. The dozens of photos made their way along the two rows of jurists. Vaughan glanced towards the defendant's table and noted that Winchester looked to be asleep while Lee absently shuffled through a stack of papers in front of him. He knew it was all a show. Vaughan was certain Lee's attention would perk up when he got to the last picture.

"Tell me where this particular photograph was taken?" asked Vaughan.

"At the medical examiner's office," answered Hall.

"It is rather grisly, isn't it?"

"I work in the morgue, sir. They're all grisly."

"Yes, yes, of course. Can you tell me when the photograph was taken and describe its contents?"

"This photograph was taken a couple of months ago. As discussed earlier, the various bones were retrieved from the swamp sporadically throughout the summer. We knew almost instantly that they were the remains of at least two separate individuals of identical size. It was quite unusual, and we improvised to gain a clearer picture of what we were dealing with. Once identified, we placed the bones in their appropriate places on the tarp. By the time this picture was taken, two distinct skeletons lay side by side. Their genetic makeup and similarities were striking, which helped us determine the approximate age and gender of the victims. We also hypothesized that they were most likely twins with a strong chance of the sisters being identical."

"I see," said Vaughan. "That was highly resourceful of you."

"Thank you."

"Could you tell the cause of death?"

"Good question, Mr. Vaughan," said Hall. "We could not initially be certain of the exact cause of death, due to the fact that we had incomplete cadavers in an advanced state of decay."

"Yet you stated on the coroner's report that the cause of death was homicide."

"That was never in question. Both victims were dismembered using a saw, as determined by the blade marks on the bones. Each part was disposed of separately in a wide area in the swamp. It was clear that whoever the perpetrator, or perpetrators, were, the remains were meant to be hidden."

"Yet you found them," said Vaughan.

"I didn't," responded Hall. "The investigators found them. And with great effort, I'm sure. I doubt it was a pleasant task."

"I doubt that it was," Vaughan agreed. "Can you verify that this photograph is authentic, and that it contains the same anatomical parts recovered in the Dead River Swamp and only those?"

"I can."

"Is it your conclusion that there was more than one killer involved?"

"It is. It is our conclusion that the two victims were killed, dismembered, and disposed of within a short time span. No more than one or two days apart. A great amount of effort would have been required to accomplish this. It is unlikely, if not impossible, for one person to do all of this in the time allotted. Nor is it practical. No, at least two if not more people were involved in this crime."

"In your opinion, did the murders take place at the point of recovery of the body parts?"

"No. They were cut up and individually wrapped in pieces of tarp, then brought to the area of disposal by someone familiar with it."

"Why do you say familiar with the area?"

"It's very remote, and it would be easy to get lost or be spotted by an unexpected hunter or fisherman. It's our conclusion that the persons involved are from this area."

Exclamations erupted from the back of the courtroom. The very idea that one of their own would do such a thing struck at the core of the local inhabitant's sense of security and serenity.

"No further questions, Your Honor."

CHAPTER ONE HUNDRED FOUR

"**M**r. Hall—" said Lee.

"Doctor," the witness corrected him.

"Right. Doctor." Lee glanced at the audience in full view of the jury, his expression a mixture of innocence and derision. "Have you performed any successful operations lately?"

"Objection!" shouted Vaughan.

"Sustained," said the judge.

"Sorry, Your Honor. I forgot all the doctor's patients are already dead."

Laughter echoed across the chamber from the back of the courtroom. Judge Foley tapped his gavel in disapproval, but the smirk on his face revealed his amusement at the disparaging comment.

"I'm a forensic pathologist," stated Dr. Hall. "I don't have patients. If you'd like, I'd be happy to give you a tour of the morgue. That is, if you think you have the stomach for it."

More laughter erupted from the audience. Even a few of the jurists showed their appreciation of the joke. Judge Foley reached for his gavel. This time, he gave it a more resounding slam on the bench. Gone was his expression of pleasure.

"Touché, Doctor, touché." Lee laughed. "Speaking of strong stomachs, the last photograph entered into evidence has had its share of controversy. Is it true that a title of a most inappropriate nature has been appointed to it?"

"It has been referred to by a title, yes. I'm not sure it's inappropriate though."

"You're not? Tell us again what it's called."

"*The Bone Puzzle*," said Hall.

Groans of disapproval drifted up from the gallery. The judge ignored the interruption, allowing the noise to dissipate on its own.

"And you find this distasteful moniker appropriate?"

"It's accurate. That's what it is—a bone puzzle. We used it to help us solve the case."

"We?"

"The investigative team."

"Who is in charge of this investigative team?"

"Detective Robert Stallworth."

"And is he the one who came up with the name for the photograph?"

"He is."

Negative rumblings could be heard in the courtroom. Once again, these were ignored by the judge.

"Was the detective highly involved in the investigation?"

"Of course," said Dr. Hall. "He's in charge."

"How much input did he have in your assessments of the evidence?"

"We discussed the case in an open forum, but my official conclusions were my own, based upon sound logic and science and the evidence we had."

"Logic, you say?" asked Lee. "Based upon the evidence? What evidence might that be?"

"I'm not sure I understand the question. We've provided—"

"A bunch of gory pictures and a slew of unsubstantiated assumptions," interrupted Lee.

"Objection!" shouted Vaughan. "If he's going to ask the witness a question, he should allow the good doctor to answer."

"Overruled," said Judge Foley. "I'll allow you a little leeway this time, Counselor, but I advise you to keep in mind that the prosecutor has a valid point. The next time you ask a question, wait for the answer, even if it's one you don't want. You always have the option of not asking it."

Vaughan was outraged, briefly considering a sidebar or a recess to the judge's chambers. He quickly changed his mind. It was clear to him that Foley was leaning towards the defense, and antagonizing the man further would do little to help his prosecutorial efforts.

"I appreciate that, Your Honor. I'll withdraw the question and comment, if it so pleases the court. We'll move on." Lee glanced at the jury, prompting them to pay extra attention to his next line of questioning. "Where were we? Oh yes, assumptions and conclusions. Would you say that that's a possible pitfall in your profession, Doctor?"

"Yes, sir, it is."

"Incorrect assumptions could lead to erroneous conclusions which, in turn, could lead to faulty arrests and unjust convictions. In a capital case with multiple suspects, such as this one, innocent men could be executed. This must be a heavy burden for you to bear."

"It can be."

"Yet you felt unhindered by doubt and uninhibited in your employment of uncorroborated evidence. Or, if I can put it more bluntly, no evidence at all, in this case, in which your conclusions, made from flimsy assumptions, impugn my client and risk his life."

"I examined the evidence and made my conclusions. The only assumption I made was that the guilty party's lawyer would refuse to accept my conclusions as the only logical one that could be made. On that assumption, I was proven right by this line of ridiculous questioning," said Dr. Hall.

"Dr. Hall, I'll ignore your unmerited taunt. Let's cut to the chase, sir. You seem to draw a lot of conclusions about things that are not at all certain. Case in point: you assume that there was more than one criminal, that they were from the area, that the victims were murdered, that they were murdered in another location, that they were identical twins, and that they were murdered, sawed up into little bits, and discarded in the Dead River Swamp within days, if not hours, of each other. All of this without a single definitive shred of evidence to prove it. That is quite impressive, I must say."

"Objection!" shouted Vaughan. "Is it the defense's intention to give their closing statement, or is there a question in there somewhere?"

"Sustained," said Judge Foley.

"Of course, of course. Apologies all around," said Lee. "Let me state my questions plainly then. Dr. Hall, do you have any direct, irrefutable, physical evidence to prove, without a shadow of a doubt, that someone from our area committed these crimes?"

"No."

"Or that there was more than one killer?"

"No."

"Can you state exactly where the girls were killed?"

"No."

"All assumptions, as I stated," said Lee. "Dr. Hall, do you have, in your possession, any irrefutable evidence that directly links my client to the murder, dismemberment, and disposal of the two victims?"

"No."

"No further questions at this time, Your Honor, though I do reserve the right to call upon the witness, if necessary, at a future time."

"Agreed. Prosecutor?" the judge looked at Vaughan.

"No further questions at this time, Your Honor," replied Garland.

"Agreed," said Judge Foley. "You may step down, Doctor."

Vaughan noted the disdain in the judge's tone when he said the word doctor. Things weren't going well and his next witness was the one person in the state of Alabama with a talent for making enemies.

"The court will recess until nine o'clock sharp tomorrow morning," the judge announced. "Will the state's next witness be ready to take the stand?"

"Yes, Your Honor," stated Vaughan.

"And who will that be?" asked Foley.

"Detective Robert Stallworth of the Alabama State Police," said Vaughan.

Boos and hisses once more rose from the gallery, which the judge ignored. Bailiff Tyndale called for everyone in the room to rise, and Foley left the courtroom as the protests continued. Vaughan looked at Lee, who grinned at the prosecutor before turning toward his client. Winchester rose and accepted the shackles from the guard. The accused and his uniformed escort walked side by side, like old friends, towards the exit, to the accompaniment of whispered encouragement from his faithful followers.

Vaughan kept his head down, preferring to ignore the nasty looks that came his way. He knew that he was nothing more than a harbinger of Satan in the eyes of the gallery. He sighed and mentally prepared himself for the following day when none other than Beelzebub in all his demonic glory was slated to take the stand. God help them all.

CHAPTER ONE HUNDRED FIVE

Friday morning came much too soon for Garland Vaughan. He knew that his case would be won or lost by how well the detective fared on the stand. Vaughan warned the trooper on multiple occasions to be wary of the defense attorney, but he got the impression that Stallworth was unfazed by the man's reputation or his antics so far. But Vaughan knew it could be costly to underestimate the courtroom skills of Douglas Lee.

The walk to the courthouse was a bad omen of things to come. Reverend Beecher's tent revival had gained momentum. Even at the early hour, hymns were being sung with gusto as the preacher shouted fire and brimstone sermons into a megaphone. His followers had multiplied in number and seemed to be growing every day.

Vaughan was concerned about the effect the protests would have on the jury. Even through the closed windows and solid walls of the stone courthouse, the boisterous dissonance of the faithful would no doubt be heard. The insanity of the devoted was often contagious, as evidenced by the crimes that brought them to this point.

Once the judge and jury were seated, the trial resumed. Bailiff Tyndale called for the state's next witness with a fanfare typically reserved for monarchs. Everyone in the room turned to see the man himself. In a disappointing display of understatement, Robert casually stood up from his place in the third row behind the prosecutor's table and walked up to the witness stand like he was on a Sunday stroll. Vaughan was frustrated, if not surprised, that the detective chose to wear his usual nondescript cheap suit instead of his state police dress uniform. They'd argued about it the night before, but Robert had shrugged off the lawyer's suggestion.

Robert was sworn in and took his seat, ignoring the whispers of disapproval that rippled through the gallery. Vaughan approached his witness.

"Detective Stallworth," he asked, "could you briefly describe your qualifications for the court."

"I'm a homicide detective for the Alabama State Police," said Robert without further elaboration.

"Yes, we know that. But what kind of experience do you have?"

"I graduated from the Alabama State Police Academy after the war and entered the Major Crimes Division. I've been involved in many investigations since then, the vast majority involving charges of kidnapping, rape, and/or murder. I was also a member of several task forces involving conspiracies of a similar nature as well as those where explosives were detonated in an attempt to kill, maim, or terrorize individuals or groups of people. Eventually, I settled into investigating homicides as my primary duty."

"Have you been effective in your occupation?"

"Very."

"Would you say that you have solved some, most, or all of the cases you've been actively involved in?"

"Most. Although convictions are never certain."

"Don't I know it." Vaughan chuckled.

Some brief laughter followed Vaughan's lighthearted remark.

"Would you say your job is difficult?"

"Usually," said Robert.

"Would you care to elaborate?"

"Even when the perpetrator is obvious, we still have to prove it. That isn't always easy since it requires that a jury agree with us. Many times, the crimes are committed in small communities, and the people involved are known to those who'll decide their fate. It's often hard to see someone you've known your entire life as being capable of doing some of the horrible things we present to them. On the flip side, occasionally it's hard to see them not doing those kinds of things. Even when uncontested, we have to deal with the gritty details of what one human being is capable of doing to another. We have to inform the family members of their loss. It's never easy."

"I can only imagine," said Vaughan. "I guess that last part is the hardest—telling people their loved ones met an untimely end."

"No," said Robert.

Vaughan paused, surprised by the detective's unexpected answer. "No?"

"It's worse when there is no one to tell," said Robert.

"Sad."

"It's a crime in itself."

"What do you do then?"

"What we always do," said Robert. "We find the bastards. Someone is dead. They aren't coming back. It doesn't matter whether a thousand people pick up torches and pitchforks and march in the streets, or if no one cares. I care. I am their advocate. I am their family. Somebody kills, they're likely to do it again unless someone stops them. I'm that someone, and I don't rest until I do."

"I don't suppose you make a lot of friends, do you?"

"No, I don't. Believe it or not, occasionally people are grateful when I find the person or persons who killed their loved one and bring them to justice. Everybody should be grateful that there's one less killer on the loose. You and I both know that the dead can no longer speak for themselves. The guilty, on the other hand, rarely shut up. They always have plenty of friends to attest to how they're really nice people, and it's all a misunderstanding. The courtroom is always full of people wringing their hands over the fate of some murderous scumbag. That doesn't sway me in the least. I'm the one who sees firsthand what they did. I know who the victims were before their lives were cut short for some trivial reason by a maniac on a rampage. I see the pain and loss in the family's eyes. I'm there when the bodies are laid to rest. I weep at their loss. And then I get angry. It's my job to clean up the mess, and clean it up is what I do. So no, Counselor, I don't make a lot of friends. So be it. You don't call your friend when you find your wife, or your husband, or your mother or father, or, God forbid, your children beaten and bloody on the floor. You call me, and you expect results. You expect justice. Rest assured, you will get it because I'm going to get it for you."

A few boos and hisses drifted up from the gallery, but not as many as before the detective had taken the stand. Their resolve about the detective's nefarious motives had been mildly diminished. Douglas Lee kept his head down until the muffled sound of sacred hymns seeped in through the walls. The preacher he hired was doing his part. But if the detective kept doing as well as he had so far, Winchester was going to need all the help he could get.

"Tell us how you became involved in this investigation," said Vaughan.

"I was assigned."

"So, you had no previous knowledge of the victims, suspects, or location prior to this investigation?"

"I did not. Prior to my arrival here last summer, I haven't been to Pickens County. As far as the victims or suspects, prior knowledge was impossible."

"And why is that?"

"Because we had no idea who any of them were."

"Yes, yes, of course," said Vaughan. "But that all changed."

"It did."

"Dr. Hall explained in his testimony how you and the other officers found the various bones and how you pieced them together to come to the conclusion that the victims were prepubescent identical twin girls. Kudos on that, but the way. Excellent work."

"Thank you."

"Please tell us how you eventually found out who the girls were. Were there reports of missing identical twins?"

"No, there were not."

"Isn't the disappearance of identical twins unusual?"

"It is."

"Yet you found the answers."

"The fact that it was so unlikely was a clue in itself. Because of that, we broadened our search area. If the victims had been local girls, we'd have known about their being missing. We knew the girls came from somewhere; someone would know they were gone. If they weren't reported missing, it meant that their parent or guardian was either involved or incapacitated. Due to the condition of the girls, we leaned towards the parent, or parents, having met a similar fate, although we didn't rule out other possibilities. In the end, our suspicions were confirmed. Their father had been murdered. Sawed in half, to be exact."

Cries of horror rose up from the gallery. Judge Foley grabbed his gavel to restore order.

"Objection!" said Lee. "My client isn't on trial for any other offenses, much less ones that occurred in separate jurisdictions."

"Who said anything about your client being guilty of other offenses? Does the defense wish to add a statement from the accused, perhaps a confession?" said Vaughan.

"Overruled," said Judge Foley. "And I'm warning you, Mr. Vaughan, another outburst like that and I'll hold you in contempt."

"Sorry, Your Honor. I withdraw my last statement."

Lee sat back down, clearly perturbed by the exchange. Vaughan couldn't have been more pleased.

"How did you track down the girls's origin?" asked Vaughan.

"It wasn't easy. I can't take the credit; it was a team effort. Once we had it narrowed down to the most likely possibilities, we still found ourselves without a clue to which way to go. There was, however, one piece of evidence that didn't fit. So we let that lead us to the Promised Land."

Vaughan nodded and looked at the Bailiff. Tyndale picked up a paper bag and presented it to the court. Inside was a red jewel. Vaughan showed it to Robert.

"Is this what I think it is?" asked Vaughan.

"It's fake," said Robert. "Costume jewelry, though very unusual."

"I don't imagine you see things like this every day?"

"I've never seen one like it."

"Neither have I. Where did you find it?"

"In the ditch on the side of the road, about a quarter mile from Cooter Yates's place."

Soft chatter rose from the courtroom. Winchester was slowly losing the support of the crowd.

"What was it doing there?"

"That's what I wondered," said Robert. "It didn't fall out of the sky. It was quite the mystery until one of my colleagues brought us the poster."

"Right. The poster," said Vaughan as he nodded to the Bailiff again.

Tyndale retrieved the billing from the theater in Memphis.

"The Amazing and Magnificent Villanova," said Vaughan, reading the large type on the advertisement. "He does present a mesmerizing image. I see what you mean about the jewel. It looks like the same one that's on the magician's turban. Who's this? Natalia the Gypsy? What can you tell us about this Villanova fellow and the gypsy girl?"

"Villanova's real name was Richard Henderson. Villanova was his stage name. He adopted identical twin girls from the Tennessee Children's Home Society, the one that was in the news a couple of years ago for human trafficking. He used them in his act, only showing one at a time so they could disappear and reappear as if by magic. The possibilities were endless for someone who makes their living by presenting illusions for entertainment purposes. A fact, I can only imagine, that was not lost on the magician. Natalia was the stage name of the girl, who he billed as a gypsy. Lacey and Laura Henderson were the real names of the two girls he adopted. It was quite resourceful of the magician. That is, until his illusion proved to be too real for the members of the Antioch Pentecostal Church to handle. The table saw was an unfortunate part of his act. Winchester and the boys have a difficult time telling the difference between what's real and what's an illusion, which led to the saw being employed in the very real demise of the famed magician. The boys from the Antioch church aren't the brightest bulbs in the box."

"Was this the same magic show that Eustice Winchester and Buck McEwen attended the night before they allegedly abducted the girls?"

"Yes, sir, it was. It was Villanova's truck that the suspects admitted to stealing. The girls were inside."

"But they thought they only had one girl?"

"From all accounts, that is the general consensus, at least until Deputy Barber showed up with the other one. In their ignorance, they thought the Devil was playing a trick on them and had resurrected the first girl, whom they had murdered, dismembered, and disposed of in the swamp the previous evening. So they killed her again and repeated the gruesome procedure."

"That's quite a story. How do you know all this?"

"They told me," said Robert. "All of them. Separately, with little variation."

"They just came in and told you?"

Robert laughed. "It wasn't that easy. They required a little prompting, but we got there eventually."

"I'm going to ask you a difficult question, and I don't want you to take it the wrong way. Detective, did you present the details of your allegations to them, and when they repeated them back, you used that as a confession, as the defense has suggested?"

"Of course not," said Robert.

"But the distinguished Mr. Lee has raised the concern?"

"What else is he going to say? Defense attorneys always say that." Robert turned towards the jury and continued, "When the news is bad, shoot the messenger, eh?"

Several members of the jury smiled and nodded. Judge Foley said nothing. Lee was furious but pretended it was of no consequence. Winchester turned pale.

"So, are you saying that it's possible that the suspect's recollection of the incident is tainted?"

"Suspects lie all the time. It takes awhile to get at the truth. When they start telling you things that only the killer or killers could know, some of which you don't even know, and it matches the physical evidence, you start to put the pieces together. Most people tend to minimize their own involvement, but when it comes to their buddies, they'll throw them to the wolves if it means saving their own skin. Some have a conscience and spill the beans regardless of the consequences; others will do whatever they can to avoid punishment. No price is too high."

"In your opinion, which category does the defendant fall into?"

"No price is too high. He's had opportunity after opportunity to come clean. He's refused every step of the way, even when it came to his own offspring. He's a sociopath."

"Objection!" Lee shouted.

"Sustained," said Judge Foley.

"In my opinion, he's a sociopath," said Robert to the jury. "He doesn't believe he's done anything wrong, and, consequently, he takes no responsibility for his actions. It's all about him. It's always all about him. The holy man act is just that—an act. He's not a prophet; he's a murderer. Oh, sorry, I mean, in my opinion, he's not a prophet."

"He's an alleged murderer," added Vaughan.

"No, not alleged. He's a murderer."

"Objection!"

"Sustained."

Robert shrugged. He wasn't taking back his statement. The jury was instructed to disregard it, but Robert knew better. Winchester was guilty, and there weren't enough legal procedures or fancy maneuvers by Douglas Lee that was going to change that.

Stallworth looked over the audience that had been whispering behind his back all week. Many still cursed him under their breath but not one of them returned his gaze. He turned his eyes to the jury, and, one by one, he looked at them. Each man, in turn, met his stare, and there was an unspoken understanding between them. Detective Stallworth had done his part. The rest was up to them.

CHAPTER ONE HUNDRED SIX

"**M**ister Stallworth," said Lee.

"Detective," Robert corrected him.

"Right, Detective," Lee said mockingly as he had when addressing the medical examiner. As before, he made a face to the audience in full view of the jury. Only, this time, nobody seemed to be in on the joke. Trying to show no outward sign that he was aware of the disconcerting change in the room, Lee continued his inquiries. "You stated earlier that, after the war, you attended the Alabama State Police Academy. Before—"

"Correct," interrupted Robert. "Graduated at the top of my class."

"I didn't ask you that, but I'm happy to see you hold yourself in such high regard."

"I'm not the one who calls himself Esquire," joked Robert.

The room erupted with laughter. Even Judge Foley found it hard to hide his amusement. Lee was furious, but brushed it off. If the detective wanted to pick a fight, he'd give him a fight.

"Before that, you stated that you served in the war."

Before Lee could get the next sentence out, Robert interrupted him again. "Yes, sir. I served my country in its time of need. Did you?"

Lee ignored the taunt. He wasn't about to admit that he hadn't. "What did you do during the war?"

"I was assigned to Army Intelligence in the European theatre. Where did you serve?"

"I'll be the one to ask the questions here," said Lee.

"So you didn't."

"Your Honor, I implore you to—"

"I'm a Marine, Counselor. You implore me to what?"

"I request that this man be considered a hostile witness," said Lee.

"As you wish," said Judge Foley. "That is, unless the state has any objections."

"None whatsoever," Vaughan replied. "I'm not surprised that the accused considers the police to be hostile to his cause."

Lee fumed but hid his anger and resumed. "What did you do specifically in Army Intelligence?"

"Specifically, that's classified information," said Robert.

"Objection," said Vaughan. "This is completely irrelevant to the case."

"Your Honor, the state's case is built upon the detective's testimony. I must be allowed to question the qualifications of such a witness to properly provide my client with the best defense as is required by law under the Constitution."

"I'll allow it for the moment," said Judge Foley, "but this better lead somewhere relevant. Make your point, and let's get on with it."

"Thank you, Your Honor," said Lee. "Now, as I asked earlier, what specifically did you do during your time in Army Intelligence?"

"As I stated earlier, specifically, it is classified information. I'm not allowed to divulge, and you're not allowed to ask under the articles of treason. You'd understand that if you had served. Since you didn't, I hope that clarifies it for you."

"Classified? How dramatic," said Lee. "I suppose you took down the Third Reich all by yourself? Again, with the delusions of grandeur."

"Did I say that? Miss Godsey, can you read my testimony?"

"Do not address the court reporter," Lee said in a huff. "You answer only to me. Is that understood?"

Robert shivered in a mock pretense of fright. "Careful, Esquire, you're starting to intimidate me."

Laughter rang out. Judge Foley tapped his gavel for order.

"Is this a joke to you, sir? A man is on trial for his life."

Robert's face turned serious. He stared into the attorney's eyes, unblinking. "Do you think you have to remind me of the horrors of this investigation? I was the one who pulled the rotting body parts out of the swamp, one by one, and pieced them together. You made quite a show of disrespect about Dr. Hall's involvement. It was quite entertaining. I assure you, it wasn't amusing when he was picking the flesh off of the bones of two young girls. What's funny is that I don't remember seeing you there during any of this. By funny, I mean, pathetic. Show some damn respect, sir. If not for me, then for Lacey and Laura."

Lee turned towards Judge Foley for a smidgen of support. There was none to be found. The defense attorney knew better than to look at the jury. Not at this moment. So he went back to the witness and doubled down on his attack.

"Classified or not, Detective, I've been able to uncover a small amount of information on your time overseas. You were involved in those horrid accounts of mass burials and labor camps equipped with ovens to dispose of the dead. Isn't that true?"

"I can only speak about what is public knowledge. Yes, I was involved. If, by involved, you mean recovering the bodies of the deceased and gathering evidence to use in the tribunals at Nuremburg. I readily admit that my actions led to the deaths of several human beings, if you consider the scum of the SS to be human beings. Personally, I beg to differ. Once again, I was there; you were not."

"*Personally.* That's an interesting choice of words. Did you personally watch any of the accused hang as result of your enthusiastic investigating?"

"No."

"No?" exclaimed Lee with exhilaration. He'd caught the detective in his first lie, and he felt like a lion, ready to pounce on an unsuspecting antelope in the wilds of Africa. "Are you sure about that?"

"I'm sure," said Robert. "The men I saw hanged were executed because of their own sins, not because I found out about them."

"But you said you weren't at liberty to discuss it. Despite that, here you are discussing it."

"Only what's been unclassified. Do you want to continue this dog and pony show, or are we going to get on with this trial? Ask what you want to ask and stop beating around the bush. I've got nothing to hide."

"It seems to me you have a lot to hide," said Lee. "All that top secret stuff you allude to."

"You mean, you allude to," said Robert. "Let me spell it out for you, Esquire. War is a dirty business. You get dirty doing the business of war. I did what I was sent there to do, and I'd do it again. For every man hanged, there were a thousand— no, many, many times more than that—who died because of what those men did."

"How many got away?"

"Too many. Then again, one is too many. You referred to me as being overzealous in the performance of my duty. Is that possible? Can one be overzealous when confronted with evil?"

"Perhaps one can," said Lee, "if one pushes so hard they make the innocent pay for the sins of the guilty."

"They were all guilty."

"Were they?"

"Yes, as is your client."

"You don't know that."

"Yes, I do. So do you. So does everyone in this room."

"Your Honor, please—"

"I warned you before, Mr. Lee. Those are your questions. Don't ask them if you don't want them answered."

"Did your time in the service affect your mental stability?" Lee asked, turning back to Stallworth.

"Define mental stability."

Laughter erupted once again. Things were not going well for Douglas Lee or his client, but the audience was enjoying it.

"Have you had trouble dealing with the things you saw?"

"Of course. But I found a way to handle it. I had to; I still see those things. How different do you think it is digging up buried corpses from one continent or another?"

"The difference between murder and war," said Lee.

"They are one and the same."

"That's not a very patriotic thing for you to say."

"Says the guy who wasn't there."

"This is getting us nowhere," said Lee.

Judge Foley's gavel came down hard on the bench. He openly glared at the defense attorney, then he announced a pause in the proceedings. "The court will take a short recess. I want to see both attorneys in my chambers immediately."

CHAPTER ONE HUNDRED SEVEN

"**A**re you out of your mind?" Foley asked the attorney for the defense. "I allowed you to question the detective in matters that are known to the public, but you are taking things too far. If classified information gets disclosed on the stand, it will be a felony, as you well know. Not to mention, it is highly inappropriate and irrelevant to your case. You could be disbarred, the detective arrested, and I could be thrown off the bench. I'm not ready to retire so you'd better get your act together."

"I'm sorry, Your Honor," Lee said, his voice notably shaken. "Things didn't go as I planned."

"I sure as hell hope not," said the judge, "or you might as well tell your client to confess and opt for a plea. He's going to death row for sure if you keep this up, and you'll be looking at a stint in prison as well."

"I have no choice but to question the detective," said Lee. "Drilling holes in his case is the only chance my client has. He's entitled to the best defense. What else can I do?"

"You can stick to the parameters of the incident that led us here. Further attacks on Detective Stallworth's character will not be tolerated. In particular, any pertaining to his military service. Am I making myself clear, Counselor?"

"Yes, Your Honor."

"Douglas," the judge continued, his voice noticeably softer, "I understand your position. I really do. I was once a defense attorney myself. But think of it this way, I'm doing you a favor. The detective is making you look like a fool."

Lee nodded but kept his mouth shut. He was going to have to up his game and do it quick.

"Mr. Vaughan." The judge acknowledged the prosecutor. "Is there anything you care to add?"

"No, Your Honor," said Vaughan with a straight face. "I agree. Mr. Lee is making a fool of himself."

Judge Foley frowned at the slight but let it go. Up until this moment in the trial, Vaughan had borne the brunt of Lee's attacks. His witnesses had fallen apart, one by one, on the stand. He needed a victory, however temporary, and he deserved a moment of satisfaction after the detective so brilliantly destroyed the competition. The trial wasn't over yet. The tables would undoubtedly turn again.

"Let's get back out there before the jury forgets why we're here," said Foley. "If you like, we can dismiss the witness and pick up again on Monday morning. An extended weekend might do us all good."

"I'd prefer to be allowed to continue for the time being," said Lee.

"With the detective? Are you sure?"

"Yes. I insist."

Judge Foley understood. The last thing Lee wanted to do was break for the weekend on such a low note. The jury would have too much time to think about the day's testimony.

The three men returned to the courtroom, and the trial resumed. Lee was granted another chance at the detective, and he knew he was going to have to give it everything he had.

CHAPTER ONE HUNDRED EIGHT

"**M**r. Stallworth," said Lee.

"Detective," Robert reminded him.

"Detective, is it alright if I ask you more questions?"

"I'm not stopping you."

"Wow, you really are a hostile witness," noted Lee.

"I have a low tolerance for stupidity."

"Ouch. Well, I admit that's a bit deserved. I apologize for this morning's exchange. It wasn't my intention to impugn your time in the service."

Robert remained silent, making no acknowledgment of Lee's phony gesture.

"Detective, a photograph has been entered into evidence and exhibited earlier, showing a collection of bones on a tarp. By all accounts, it was you who created the display and gave it a name. That being, *The Bone Puzzle*. Is this correct?"

"It is."

"Do you find it appropriate to find such levity with things of this nature?"

"It's descriptive of the item."

"Yes, that is what the good doctor said as well. However, it does seem a bit harsh."

"Not as harsh as how the girls ended up in the picture."

"Indeed," said Lee. "For once, we agree. When discussing your résumé earlier, you stated that you were a part of a task force investigating groups of conspirators involved in nefarious acts of violence. Would you care to elaborate on that?"

"What is your question?"

"Who were these clandestine groups?"

"You mean, who are?"

"Oh, so they are still around? I was under the impression that you were so effective an investigator that you stopped at nothing to bring the guilty to justice. Between your earlier admission that some of the guilty walked free, despite your best efforts, during the war and now your admission that you've been unable to stop the current band of miscreants plaguing our state, I'd say you've overstated your success."

"What's your question?"

"Are these unnamed groups still around?"

"They aren't unnamed. We know who they are. If not every member, certainly the primary agitators."

"Is that so? Who knows?"

"The state police, the FBI, multistate task forces, you name it. It's no secret."

"But you implied that these organizations are secretive."

"They try to be. But when you wear goofy white robes and burn crosses on people's lawns, you tend to stick out."

Several members of the audience giggled.

"I would think you do. Is this common in our area?"

"Are you feeling alright, Counselor, or are we pretending here? You know damn well what I'm talking about." Robert leaned forward and stared straight into Lee's eyes, causing the attorney's knees to buckle a little. "Spare us the phony bullshit, sir, and cut to the chase. None of us are getting any younger here."

Lee glanced at the judge, hoping he was going to rebuke the detective for his use of foul language in the courtroom, but it appeared Stallworth would be given leeway in his testimony from here on out. Since the judge chose to ignore it, Lee did likewise.

"You have investigated the Klan?"

"We continue to investigate the Klan," said Robert. "And, as you know, I'm not at liberty to discuss the details of an ongoing investigation."

"First, it was classified, and now, it's an ongoing investigation. It's always something with you, isn't it? Whatever you don't want to talk about, you make some excuse why you can't talk about it."

"It's not me who doesn't want to talk about it. I'm not allowed to. Consider it a favor, Esquire. As before, it's not something you really want to hear."

"Let me be the judge of that."

"I thought Samuel Foley was the judge here. You're just an attorney."

"And you're just a detective."

"Not just a detective. I'm the detective who's going to send your client to the electric chair for what he did to those girls."

"What he allegedly did."

"What he did."

"So you say."

"I do. Is there anything else you wish to ask me, Mr. Lee, or are we going to spar like this all day?"

"Mr. Winchester and his friends weren't your first suspects in this case, isn't that true?"

"It is."

"Who were your first suspects?"

Robert opened his arms in an arc. "Everyone."

"Cute, but you know what I mean. Isn't it true you made other arrests before my clients were even questioned?"

"Sort of."

"Sort of? So you admit you thought others did the crime before you zeroed in on my client?"

"No. They were suspects from the beginning, but like I said, so was everyone. I eventually whittled it down to them being persons of interest. No one else made the cut."

"Yet you arrested the sheriff himself and some of his men during a Klan rally. If they weren't suspects, why would you do that?"

"I didn't."

"Excuse me? Did you say, you didn't?"

"That's what I said."

"But we have records to prove—"

"No charges were ever filed."

"But arrests were made.'"

"Not officially. You might want to re-check your records, Esquire."

"Now you're splitting hairs."

"Am I? The Klan rally wasn't a Klan rally. The arrests weren't really arrests. It was all a show, an illusion, much like the late magician was known for—only with better results."

"Is that normal operating procedure for a homicide investigation?"

"It's ironically appropriate, given the circumstances of the magician's death. The accused seemed to have a problem from the beginning differentiating illusion from reality, so we gave them yet another illusion to ponder."

"So you tricked them?"

"You bet your sweet ass we did."

Laughter once again erupted throughout the room. Instead of being morally outraged by the detective's lack of decorum, Judge Foley was as amused as the rest of the crowd. Even the pious court reporter giggled at Robert's colorful language.

"Why didn't you suspect the sheriff and his men? Aren't they members of the Klan?"

Lee's question ended the merriment in the courthouse. The unpleasant secrets of Pickens County were not to be discussed in a public setting, much less in court. Lee's faux pas wasn't gaining him any additional support from the audience or the jury.

"The Henderson sisters weren't killed by the Klan."

"And you know this how?"

"They were murdered by Winchester and his followers."

"Again with the certainty. How can you eliminate the sheriff and his men so easily? Is there any evidence presented that might lead us to believe they could've been involved in this crime?"

"None."

"Really? Are you as certain of that as you are of my client's guilt?"

"I am."

"Is there any evidence you've not presented that might say otherwise?"

Lee had him, and he knew it. Robert paused and shifted in his seat, his gaze drifting down and away. *Bingo!*

"None."

Lee did his best to conceal his excitement. Vaughan had failed to mention the two skulls dug up from behind Sheriff Fuller's office. Lee was sure that they didn't think he'd found out about them. The medical examiner never mentioned them. Now, the detective lied on the stand to protect that evidence from disclosure. It was perfect.

Lee resisted the urge to ask for an updated list of evidence prior to the start of the trial, precisely for this reason. He would spring it on the jury, in due course, when he presented his case, and what a surprise it was going to be.

"No further questions at this time," said Lee before adding, "Your Honor. I request the opportunity to question this witness further if deemed necessary."

"Granted," said the judge, amazed at such a stupid request.

After all the expectations he'd had regarding the famous Douglas Lee's courtroom reputation, Judge Foley was disappointed with the day's proceedings. As a former defense attorney, it took Foley all of two minutes to recognize that Stallworth was the last person you wanted on the witness stand. He was a prosecutor's wet dream. Now, Lee was requesting another go at him in the future, as if the beat down he'd already received wasn't sufficient. His ego was getting the better of him. Whatever it was, Foley thought that Lee better have a trick up his sleeve, or his client was toast.

Lee did have a trick—two of them. He couldn't be more pleased with himself. Neither could Vaughan.

CHAPTER ONE HUNDRED NINE

Robert left town for the weekend. He hadn't been home in ages, and he knew he'd get little rest with Reverend Beecher's old fashioned fire and brimstone Christian revival going on in Carrollton. Although, after his testimony, he was seen as less of a pariah than he had been the previous day, Robert knew it would be short-lived. By the time Beecher spent the weekend sermonizing the apocalypse, on Monday morning the detective expected to be right back on top of the list of demonic influences that brought the most pious Brother Eustice to his wretched state of martyrdom.

He drove straight to Birmingham that Friday evening, took a long hot shower, and fell asleep within seconds. It was well past ten a.m. when he woke to the sound of Mrs. Anderson's polite knocking on his screen door. Robert begrudgingly rolled out of bed, slipped on his robe, and ran his fingers through his hair before answering the relentless tapping that had interrupted his well-deserved slumber.

"Good morning, Mrs. Anderson. It's always a pleasure to see you," said Robert, flicking the small metal prong out of its eyehole and pushing open the screen door.

"I saw your car in the driveway and came over to give you your mail," the elderly woman said without a hint of geniality in her voice.

Robert nodded and reached down with both hands to pick up the large, brown paper grocery bag at the woman's feet. He took a step back and motioned for his neighbor to enter his small but well kept house.

"You know, in my day, a woman wouldn't dare be caught dead entering a man's house unescorted, particularly when that man was a bachelor and dressed only in his skivvies. It's not proper."

"I'm wearing a robe," said Robert.

"And a fine robe it is, I must say. Nevertheless, I wouldn't want any of the neighbors to see me and besmirch my reputation. My late husband, as you know, was an honorable man whose memory I shall never blemish, even by misunderstanding."

"I wouldn't hear of it," said Robert in his best Southern drawl. "Please, allow me a moment to put on some proper attire, and I'll gladly meet you on the front porch with a freshly brewed cup of coffee."

"And take off that wonderful robe? I'll hear none of it. Besides, your coffee brewing skills are much to be desired. I'll forgo my usual sense of decency and make us both a cup of suitable brew. If you'll kindly lead me to the kitchen, sir, I'll commence the arduous task at hand."

"But what will the neighbors say?" protested Robert. "I wouldn't want to be the cause of such scandalous gossip regarding your chastity, my fair maiden."

"I have given birth to six children. The horrid Japanese took the only good one of the bunch; the rest, nothing but a pack of ungrateful vagabonds and ne'er do wells. If you promise to check your carnal instincts, I'll enter your humble abode."

"And if I don't?"

"I'll come in even quicker!"

They laughed. Mrs. Anderson brushed past Robert and headed for the kitchen. Robert closed the door with his elbow and followed her, carrying the grocery bag filled to the top with letters and advertisements.

Robert plopped the bag on the table and sat. He removed the mail from the bag one handful at a time and sorted through it, tossing the majority of the contents in the garbage can in the corner. More often than not, his shoddy marksmanship sent the errant correspondence to the floor, much to Mrs. Anderson's disapproval.

"It's no wonder you're still single," she said, her back to him as she prepared the percolator. "Your aim is poor."

Robert laughed. The elderly widow had lived next door to him since he bought the house. Her husband had passed away not long after, and Robert did what he could to help look after her. Lord knows, her sons never bothered to. In truth, she did more for him than he ever did for her. Gathering his mail while he was away was the least of it.

"It's the sleeves on this robe," complained Robert. "They impede my athletic prowess."

"Don't you go blaming your fine apparel. If anything, it gives you an air of sophistication. Like Rhett Butler."

"Frankly, my dear, I don't give a—"

"Mr. Stallworth!" Mrs. Anderson turned around and wagged her finger.

They stared at each other in silence for a brief moment before starting to giggle.

"Well, it is a rather nice robe," agreed Robert.

"Wherever did you get such an exceptional one?"

"This rather attractive woman, who shall remain nameless, gave it to me a few years ago for Christmas. It is my most treasured possession."

The percolator whistled, and Mrs. Anderson poured two cups of the hot elixir. She handed one of the cups to Robert and sat down, holding the other cup carefully with both hands so as not to spill its steaming contents onto the tablecloth.

"She must be an extraordinary woman, with such fine taste. You should marry her at once."

"It never leaves my thoughts, but alas, our age difference is too great."

"Why, I never!"

"I meant that I'm much too old for her. I'm afraid I'd be unable keep up with the sprightly vamp."

"Of course, that's what you meant."

They laughed again. All jokes aside, Robert did treasure the bathrobe his kindly neighbor had given him. It was high on a short list of his belongings that he'd grab on the way out of his house if it ever caught on fire, God forbid. Mrs. Anderson was like a mother to him. More, in fact, than his real mother ever had been. Robert was a son to her. Despite a slew of relatives on both sides, they were the only true family each had.

Robert mindlessly shuffled through his mail as they drank their coffee. When he saw the nondescript letter with the odd lettering and no return address, he stopped. Robert held the envelope in his hands without opening it.

"Is something wrong, dear?" Mrs. Anderson asked.

"No, not really," said Robert.

"What's that one?"

"There's only one way to find out," Robert answered and ripped open the top. He retrieved the letter, unfolded it, and gently placed it on the table.

"My goodness!" Mrs. Anderson exclaimed. "Is that blood?"

"More likely red paint," said Robert. "Blood doesn't work as well as you think it does when you're trying to use it like ink."

"And you know this how?"

Robert looked up.

"Oh, right," said the elderly woman. "What a nice job you have, Robert."

"Why, thank you, Coralee."

"What does it say?"

"Nothing," he joked. "You have to read it."

"Wise guy."

They chuckled again.

"Some nonsensical Bible verses telling me I'm going to burn in hell. I guess it's supposed to scare me."

"Does it?"

"What do you think?"

"I doubt it. You're already going to hell, heathen."

Robert's head popped up, a look of shock on his face.

"That's what my pastor has been telling us all week," she said.

"Is that so?"

"Oh yes, and much more. He said you're the Devil for persecuting that poor preacher over in Pickens County."

"And what did you say?"

"Nothing."

"Nothing?"

"Nothing. But I found a new church."

"Why, Mrs. Anderson, you've been going to that church for over forty years."

"Forty years too long."

"I don't know what to say." Robert was stunned. He knew word was sure to get around about the Winchester trial. But he hadn't considered that the madness insisting that Brother Eustice was a prophet and that he, Robert Stallworth, was, in fact, the bad guy had spread as far as Birmingham. It was a bad omen.

"You don't have to say anything. I've heard rumors about what happened over there. I don't ask you about your work, and I'm not about to start now. But I know you. If you're convinced he's the one that did those terrible things, that's good enough for me."

"Why, thank you. That means a lot."

"You don't have to thank me, either." Coralee Anderson reached across the table and took one of Robert's hands in hers. "I know you're getting threats, and there's mobs of people who say the worst about you, but never forget, for every one of them, there are many more like me. I think about those poor girls and pray for their souls every night. Believe me, a lot of us do. We're counting on you, Robert.

You may not see us, but we're in your corner, cheering for you all the way. There's only one thing we ask for in return."

"What's that?"

"Send that bastard to hell."

CHAPTER ONE HUNDRED TEN

When Robert received the phone call on Sunday, he was furious. Not only had Joe Bob recanted on the stand, Vaughan now informed the detective that Buck had secured himself legal counsel. Under the advice of his lawyer, he filed a complaint with the Justice Department, claiming that his prior testimony was illegally acquired under duress and was, therefore, inadmissible in court.

According to District Attorney Vaughan, rumors had it that Douglas Lee persuaded a colleague to take on Buck's case pro bono. Additional rumors had it that a similar arrangement would be forthcoming within days regarding Deputy Barber. Jeremiah Thomas Winchester was the last of the dominos left to fall, and, if not for Stallworth's foresight in having JT moved, he'd undoubtedly already be compromised.

On Sunday afternoon, Robert headed over to Fairview on his way back to Carrollton. He hoped that between Brandine's visit the previous day and John Turner's constant intervention, Jeremiah would be ready to go the following morning. Stallworth pulled into the parking lot of Sheriff Clanton's office and headed inside. He reached into his pocket on the way in to assure himself that the photograph of Alabama's two thousand volt means of execution was ready, and he made his way to the holding cells in the back.

"Robert," Turner greeted him by the first gate that gave access to the prisoners. "I didn't expect you so early."

"Hey, John. Things have turned south on us. The rest of the deacons are lawyering up."

"Yeah, I figured as much. Some smooth talker came around here yesterday, nosing around."

"Damn!"

"Don't worry. He's probably wandering around Talladega looking for our boy."

"Thank God!"

"The only way JT sees a lawyer is if he asks for one. So far, he's not mentioned it. I doubt he's going to."

"I wish I could be as certain as you," said Robert. "So is he primed and ready to see me?"

"I wanted to talk to you about that. I don't think you should."

Robert didn't like the sound of that. Without Jeremiah, all they had was county officials and circumstantial evidence. His testimony was vital to their success.

"I don't think I heard you right," said Robert. "Why wouldn't I?"

"Look, I know this is going to be hard to understand, but there's something more at stake here; something bigger than Eustice's conviction."

Robert couldn't believe what his friend was saying. "What could be bigger than that?"

"Redemption," said Turner.

Stallworth said nothing. Turner waved his friend into a small office in the corner and closed the door. The men each took a seat at a small metal table. Robert waited.

"I know this is going to sound crazy, but I've spent a lot of time with the boy," Turner said. "At heart, he's not really a bad kid. Just a little confused."

"A little?"

"Well, maybe more than just a little. What do you expect? With a father like Eustice and a brother like Junior—"

"Who he murdered."

"Who he had to murder," continued Turner. "He got into something he couldn't get out of."

"He's not going to get out of it—ever."

"So be it. He knows that. He's not asking to be excused. He's not expecting to be set free."

"What's he asking for?"

"To be forgiven," said Turner.

"That's not up to me."

"Maybe not for the girls, or Villanova, or even Junior, or Barber. But he wants your forgiveness for what he's done to you, and what he tried to do."

"What makes you say that?"

"He told me."

Robert shook his head. "John, you've been around long enough to know—"

"True repentance, when I see it. I know there's a lot at stake here. I know how naïve I'm sounding, but you have to trust me."

"It's not you I don't trust."

"I know that, but I'm telling you. I'll put my reputation on the line if I have to."

"That's exactly what you're doing. What's more, you're putting mine. The man pointed a gun at me with his finger on the trigger."

"And I stopped him."

"Yes, you did," said Robert. He paused and let out a sigh. "I never thanked you for that, by the way."

"You didn't have to. You did the same for me once. Do you think I've ever forgotten that?"

"John, I can understand your feelings on this, I really can. Do you think I've never had a time when I didn't stop seeing the criminal I was sending to the gallows as a criminal and more as a man? Do you think I've never questioned my resolve, or questioned the morality of putting a man to death, or had a moment of regret about my part in it? I'm not made of stone."

"I know. That's why I'm begging you."

"He's a killer."

"He never said he wasn't. That's why I'm going to bat for him here. He's not denying a damn thing. He's ready to go out there and put his deepest, darkest sins on display for the world to see. He's ready to stand up and take responsibility for his actions. No, actually, he's begging to. If you go in there playing the bad cop—"

"What? I'll make him shit his pants? Good."

"No, not good."

"Fuck him. He should be scared. He should be scared of me," said Robert.

"He is. Believe me, he is. He's terrified of you."

"More than his father?"

"More than his father," said Turner.

"Then what's the problem?"

"He's going to go on that stand tomorrow and spill his guts. Unlike everybody else involved in these unspeakable crimes, Jeremiah isn't going to minimize a thing he did, or tried to do. He's also not going to try to save the others. He's going to do what he knows in his heart needs to be done, and he's not going to expect less of anyone else. Quite the opposite. It's the actions of the others, trying to run from the truth, that exposed the hypocrisy of his own. He's done with that."

"I'll make damn sure he is."

"No. He needs to do this by himself, without your manipulation."

"Why? As long as he does it, I'm satisfied," said Robert.

"If he does it because he's scared, he's not confessing his sins with a pure heart. He needs to do it when he doesn't have to. It's important."

"To who?"

"To him. To me. The fate of his soul is on the line."

"And if he chickens out? If he changes his mind, then what? The lot of them will walk."

"Memphis still has a crack at them for Villanova. The Feds have a shot at them for kidnapping. They'll get theirs, sooner or later."

"I prefer sooner. For this. I made a promise."

"To who? Yourself?"

"To Lacey and Laura. They're laying on a tarp in my office. Do you know how many hours I've spent with them? Just the three of us? Alone? You know I respect you, John. You know I'll do anything for you, but you can't ask me to do this. The girls need me."

"They're already dead, Robert."

"So is Jeremiah. He just doesn't know it yet. You'd better get used to it."

"I know. He knows. That's why it's so important. We've prayed together. I tell you, I know his heart."

"No man can know what's in another's heart. You've prayed with him? That's what got him in this mess in the first place."

"And it's what's going to get him out."

"I don't know…"

"Give him a chance. No one else ever has."

Robert sat in silence. Turner sighed. He did his best, but he understood where Stallworth was coming from. He'd seen too much to ever have that level of faith in another human being, much less a confessed killer like Jeremiah Winchester. Robert had already gone above and beyond, allowing the boy's wife to walk without charges. That gesture alone surprised him, but John knew that it was part of one of the detective's manipulative schemes.

John had known Robert for years. He owed the man his life. He watched as Stallworth rose through the ranks of the state police, stopping at nothing to get justice for the victims of some of the worst crimes one could imagine. He'd heard the rumors about what had gone on overseas during the war. Stallworth was famous for his nose, his ability to find hidden dead things. He was famous for his interrogations. John respected those talents in a fellow lawman, more than most.

It was the other things Stallworth was famous for that left him unsettled. All those schemes. Turner was convinced that, if Robert Stallworth wasn't a detective, he'd be the most dangerous criminal a cop could ever run across.

Robert stood up, reached into his pocket, and pulled out an envelope. He put it unopened on the desk and turned to leave.

"Thank you, Robert. I owe you one."

"No, you don't."

"Then Jeremiah owes you one."

"He knows what he needs to do."

Turner escorted Robert to the iron gated door that separated the prisoners from the rest of the world. He unlocked the door, opened it, and re-locked it once the detective went through. As Robert turned to go, he called out, just loud enough for his friend to hear, "No matter what happens tomorrow, tell Jeremiah I forgive him."

THE BONE PUZZLE

PART SEVEN:

RESURRECTION

Cancel my subscription to the Resurrection,
Send my credentials to the House of
Detention,
I got some friends inside.

The Doors

CHAPTER ONE HUNDRED ELEVEN

Garland Vaughan absorbed the news about Jeremiah's redemption with skepticism. He'd heard the same thing in regard to Joe Bob, only to watch him recant everything on the stand. Since then, Buck McEwen and Earl Barber had gotten lawyers and were now renouncing their testimonies. Vaughan knew it had all been secretly arranged courtesy of Douglas Lee, but there was no evidence that he'd be able to present to the bar association that would warrant a reprimand, and none that would sway the Honorable Judge Samuel Foley.

What troubled Vaughan the most was the lack of physical evidence he had. His case hinged on the testimony of a pack of self-proclaimed liars whose reputations were as depraved as that of the accused. Although Dr. Hall had held his own when questioned by Lee, Vaughan wasn't convinced that the jury would understand the implications. Detective Stallworth, on the other hand, had eviscerated the defense when testifying, but Vaughan understood that when it came time for deliberation the state would need more than an over-eager policeman to send the preacher to death row.

As Jeremiah Winchester was escorted to the stand, Vaughan took a deep breath. He had to play his cards just right, or all would be lost. Brother Eustice's conviction could be jeopardized by a single question phrased incorrectly as well as any he failed to ask. When the guard removed Jeremiah's shackles and Bailiff Tyndale swore the witness in, Vaughan exhaled and counted to ten, then approached the witness stand.

"Mr. Winchester, how are you related to the defendant?" he asked.

"He's my paw," Jeremiah answered.

"Is he more than that?"

"I ain't sure what you mean. How can he be more than that?"

"Indeed," said Vaughan. "What I mean is, does the defendant hold any other position of authority in your life in addition to being your father?"

"Not any more. He was once my pastor, my spiritual guide, but all that changed."

"When did that change?"

"After the girls. After Junior. After everythin'," said Jeremiah. "It weren't all at once. I wanted to hold on, to believe, but—"

"But?"

"I just can't no more. He was everything to me. I believed in him. I loved him, but he don't believe in me. He don't love me. He don't care 'bout nobody but himself."

"What makes you say that?"

"It's the truth. We was all there, doin' what he wanted, doin' what he told us to do. He had us all convinced that the Lord talked through him, that he was a prophet. It was a lie."

"Heathen!" someone shouted from the back row. "Devil!" yelled another. Judge Foley banged his gavel for order. Bailiff Tyndale puffed out his chest as his eyes scanned the audience, pretending that his intimidating stance would be enough to dissuade further outbursts from the locals.

"Jeremiah, did you travel with Eustice and your fellow deacons to Memphis last April?"

"Yes, sir."

"And what was the purpose of that trip?"

"Officially, we were not to question the motives of the prophet, but we was to tell our wives and such that we were goin' on a spiritual retreat. We weren't supposed to tell them that we were leavin' the area, or anythin' specific. We was told it was the Lord's will."

"And unofficially?"

"When we headed to Tennessee, there was some complainin', so Paw pulled out a poster. It had an evil lookin' foreigner on it. Hell, it looked like Satan. The poster was 'bout some magician. As soon as I saw that, I had a feelin' what we was goin' up there for."

"And why was that?" asked Vaughan.

"'Cuz I remembered when CW came 'round a few months before that, tellin' us about the time he'd seen the show in Nashville. He had Paw all up in arms 'bout the devilish things goin' on. Once he got to tellin' of the poor fate of the gypsy girl, I knew the old man wouldn't let it go."

"CW?"

"I don't know his name," explained Jeremiah. "He's some distant kin or somethin'. We call him CW 'cause he thinks he's a singer. He plays the steel guitar and is always braggin' 'bout the Grand Ole Opry, as if he were a star. CW stands for Country and Western, or so he says."

"And you say his story got Eustice all wound up?"

"Oh yeah," said Jeremiah. "Paw was convinced the magic guy had hypnotized some unfortunate gypsy refugee and forced her to do all kinds of unspeakable things, like worship the Devil and who-knows-what-all. He said it was our moral duty to rescue the poor girl and bring her into the fold. He wanted to personally see to it that she was instructed in the ways of the Lord so she could follow the righteous path. All that kind of crap."

"Sinner! Repent!" a few enraged shouts came from the gallery, but they dissipated before Foley could reach for his gavel.

"Crap?" asked Vaughan.

"I didn't mean it like that," said Jeremiah. "I meant 'cause that weren't what Paw was really after."

"No? What was he after?"

"He just wanted the girl."

"How do you know that?"

"After we got back, he told us she was to be his wife. It weren't right. She was just a child."

"How did she end up in Alabama?"

"We took her," said Jeremiah.

"We?"

"Me and Junior. We was in the magician's dressin' room when she come in. Paw told Junior and me to grab her and put her in the truck. The rest of 'em come out in a bit, and we high-tailed it back to Alabama. I drove, and Junior rode in the back with the girl, which I weren't real keen on. We already had her tied up, but if you knew Junior, you'd know better than to argue with him. I drove kinda reckless so he'd get knocked 'round a bit. Teach him a lesson, and maybe he'd keep his hands to himself."

"You thought he was going to rape her?"

"I wouldn't have put it past him, but I don't think he went that far. She was to be Daddy's, and he knew better than touch one of Daddy's girls."

"One of?"

"Figure of speech, but it were well known that Paw would counsel a young sweet member of the congregation when he saw the opportunity. They'd be rumors every once in awhile, but Buck would put an end to that, and you'd never hear them again."

"Objection!" shouted Lee. "Hearsay!"

"Sustained," said the judge. "The witness will refrain from repeating unsubstantiated rumors not pertinent to these proceedings."

Jeremiah didn't understand a word the judge had said, but he nodded his head anyway. All he knew was the truth.

"What happened when you got back to Alabama?" asked Vaughan.

"We went to Cooter's place, out in the sticks. When we opened up the back of the truck, the girl was in there with Junior. Paw wasn't happy about her state, and he whacked Junior with his cane. But he did that all the time anyway."

"Her state?"

"Her skirt was hiked up a bit. I'm sure Junior took some liberties, but I don't think he debased her, thanks to my reckless drivin'."

"What happened then?"

"Paw sent us off to keep a look out. Buck hung back with his gun, which we took as more of a threat to us. But that's what he always did. Paw got into the truck with the girl and shut the door."

"Liar!" "Judas!" came shouts from the back of the room.

"Order!" yelled Foley, banging his gavel.

"All you men just stood by and let him do that?" asked Vaughan.

"I told you, Buck had a gun."

"So did most of you."

"It weren't up to us. The prophet had spoken. We didn't argue with commands that came from God."

"He's not God."

"He might as well have been to us. Now, don't get me wrong. Some of the men were grumblin'. They weren't happy about the way things were going. I think they were shell-shocked after what had happened with the magician."

"What happened with the magician?"

"Paw forced them to kill him because he refused to confess his sins and give his soul over to Jesus. It was over before they knew it, and it was just settlin' in. Then we get back and find out Paw just wanted the girl for himself. We was pissed, but what could we do? We was all involved by that point."

"You could've rescued the girl, like you should have done in the first place."

"She was dead by the time we got back."

"Dead? Who killed her?"

"Paw said it were the Devil. Buck said when Paw came out of the truck, she was dead. She was alive when he went in there with her and shut the door. You tell me."

"Why did he kill her?"

"She resisted, I suppose."

"Objection! Hearsay!"

"Sustained."

"I'll re-word the question," said Vaughan. "How did she die?"

"She looked like she'd been strangled. Her clothes were all messed up, and we could see she'd tried to fight him off."

"What happened then?"

"He told us we'd have to get rid of her or the Devil would come for us all. So he told us to cut her body up into small pieces. After that, we scattered them in the Dead River Swamp."

"You did that, too?"

"We all did. The prophet commanded us."

"What happened after that?"

"It was dark, and we went to sleep. The next morning, Earl came by. He had the same girl with him, only she weren't dead. We were scared. She run off into the woods, but we found her and dragged her back. Junior wanted a turn with her. He said Paw already had his, and she was his now because he was the prophet's heir. Buck wasn't goin' to let that happen, so he shot her dead."

"Buck killed her?"

"He was doin' her a favor," said Jeremiah. "She was dead anyway. After that, we cut her up again and dumped her into the swamp like we had the night before."

"Why?"

"The prophet commanded us to."

"I have to say, Jeremiah, that's a lot to ask of people. You'd think that, at a certain point, some of you would've resisted."

"We was starting to, but we was already in too deep. Besides, we had cut up the dead girl the night before, and there she was again. Whatever doubts we had 'bout the Devil playin' tricks on us were long forgotten. Only the Devil could do such a thing. The prophet had warned us, and we couldn't explain it any other way. You had to be there to understand."

"I'm glad I wasn't," said Vaughan.

"I wish I hadn't been," said Jeremiah, "but I was."

"Do you still believe the girl had been resurrected by the Devil?"

"No, that was all a lie, too. They were twins. The other one must've been hidin' in the truck. It was loaded with the magician's props and whatnots. She must've sneaked out and got lost in the woods. The lawmen found two sets of bones, so there had to be two of them."

"What happened after that?"

"Some ol' coon found a foot. When we found out 'bout it, we all got together to help in the search, hopin' to keep them from findin' the other bones. But Jasper brought them damn dogs, and they found some more. We thought we was doomed, but nothin' ever came of it. That is, until that detective came 'round. He started diggin' them bones up like he put them there himself. He took one look at us and had us pegged from the beginnin'. He knew we weren't goin' to tell him nothin', so he tricked us."

"Tricked you?"

"He staged some Klan rally and arrested the sheriff and a few of his men. Then he came to us, beggin' for help. We thought he was dumber than a stump, and we took the bait. It took us about two minutes to figure we was in some kind of trap, but he weren't done. He sprayed perfume on me, kept me out all night, and turned my wife against me."

Laughter erupted from the gallery. Even Judge Foley chuckled as he tapped the bench for order.

"It weren't funny at the time," said Jeremiah. "Like I said, he's a real assh—. I mean, he's full of tricks. Pretty soon, he had us turnin' on each other."

"How did he do that?"

"I don't know, but he did. Junior took it upon himself to be the avengin' angel. He was itchin' to show Paw he was worthy, so he started investigatin' on his own. He was convinced someone was sellin' us out. That's when he showed up out of the blue and took me out to his special hidin' spot in the woods in back of his place. I knew what he was goin' to do, so I had no choice."

"What did you do?"

Jeremiah paused to compose himself. A tear rolled down his cheek, and he reached up and brushed it off. Vaughan saw Lee lean forward, ready to pounce, waiting for yet another witness to invoke the Fifth.

"I shot him," said Jeremiah.

Seemingly shocked by the incriminating statement, Vaughan turned back to the witness. "You killed him?"

"Yes, sir."

"You do know that you don't have to make statements like that. You have the right not to admit criminal guilt."

"Maybe I do legally, but not morally. What I did was wrong. What we all did was wrong. Junior was goin' to kill me. I had to protect myself. But we all know the truth is that, if we ain't done what we'd done, it never would've come to that. I'm tired of makin' excuses and blamin' others. I ain't gonna do that no more."

Vaughan glanced over at Robert. The detective looked surprised. Next to Stallworth sat John Turner, the expression on his face that said everything was turning out just as he'd expected.

"What happened after that?"

"The detective kept at it. Paw told me it was up to me to put a stop to him. So I waited for a chance. Stallworth showed up at the church one day, so I did what I was told to do and took the rifle. Before I could get a shot off, John showed up."

"John?"

"John Turner," said Jeremiah. "He's another detective. He showed up, and I had to wait for another chance. But like

I said earlier, the detective is a clever one. In the meantime, the deacons were starting to waver, so the prophet had me take precautions. When Earl showed up and started shootin', I had to take him out. After that, we was all screwed. The only chance I had was to finish the job on Stallworth, so I lured him over to my place and waited in the brush with my rifle."

"You were going to shoot the detective?"

"I was goin' to, but he got the jump on me. I should of known better, but I was desperate. We'd have gotten away with everythin' if he hadn't shown up. At least that's what I told myself at the time."

"And now?"

"We was guilty. He didn't make us do those things. We did them. He just figured it out. I don't know how, but he did. I can hate him all I want for that, but it's not really his fault. He was just doin' what he gets paid to do, which is more than I can say for a lot of folks 'round here."

"Boo!" "Hiss!" "Traitor!" The shouts of disapproval rose once again from the gallery. As usual, the judge tapped his gavel for order, and the bailiff pretended that he wasn't going to put up with the interruptions, without actually doing anything about it.

"Did, at any time, Detective Stallworth or any other police officer give you any of the details of this case and make you recall them as a confession, or in any other way compromise your testimony in this case?"

"No, sir."

"Did anyone offer you special treatment or cut a deal for a reduced sentence to secure your testimony?"

"No, sir."

"Is everything you are saying today the truth?"

"It is."

"I only have one more question for you, son. Why have you come here and so plainly admitted your part in these horrendous crimes?"

"Because it's the right thing to do," said Jeremiah. No longer able to keep his emotions in check, he sobbed uncontrollably. "All my life, I've been preached to and told to do what's right, only to be coerced and intimidated into doin' wrong. All my life! I convinced myself that, as long as I did what I was told, it were the right thing to do, even when I knew, in my heart, it was wrong. It's easier than you think to be led astray. I ain't doin' that no more. I know what we did was wrong, and ain't no preacher, or so called prophet, or anyone else goin' to convince me otherwise. I don't need no lawyer, or jury, or judge to tell me nothin' I don't already know. What we did was wrong, and we deserve to be punished for it. What I did was wrong. I'm going to be punished for it, and I know it. I'd be lyin' if I said I weren't scared 'bout it, but enough is enough. I'm here telling you all the truth, whether you want to hear it or not. I'm doin' it 'cause, just once in my whole life, I want to do the right thing because it's the right thing to do. The fact that no one expects that says everythin' I need to know 'bout this wretched world we live in. Maybe that'll be the only comfort I have when I reach the gallows."

"No further questions, Your Honor."

CHAPTER ONE HUNDRED TWELVE

"**M**y goodness," said Lee, "I got a lump in my throat listening to your story; especially the part about how you weren't going to blame others for your own sins. Just a word of advice in the future, son; the next time you give such a noble speech, you might not want to pepper it with baseless accusations, blaming other people for your own despicable acts."

"I ain't blamin' no one," Jeremiah protested. "I admitted what I done."

"No. What you did was justify what you did and minimize it," said Lee. "Let's go over it, shall we? You said that you killed your brother in self defense."

"He was gonna kill me!"

"Are you a prophet?"

"What? No—"

"Then how do you know he was going to kill you? Did he say he was going to kill you?"

"No, of course not. But he had a gun."

"So did you."

"Yeah, but—"

"But what? Did you go out there with him with the intent to murder him?"

"No, I wouldn't—"

"Then why were you carrying a gun?"

"Because, I, I had a feelin'."

"You had a feeling? You must be a prophet, then. You stated earlier that you knew why your father was allegedly taking you to Memphis. Oh right, you also stated that you didn't know. It's all so confusing. Hold on now. Didn't you say that it was you and your brother who kidnapped the girl? Isn't that correct?"

"Paw told us to."

"Did he? So you say. But you're the one who actually did it."

"Yes, but—"

"You said that you were also the one who shot Deputy Barber. Is that correct?"

"Yes, but—"

"And you tried to murder the detective—twice?"

"Yes, but—"

"I'm hearing a lot of buts in there for someone who wants to stop blaming others. You also stated that it was Buck, and not Eustice Winchester, who murdered the girl."

"One of the girls. But not the first one."

"The one that you said you didn't see killed and really have no way of knowing for sure who killed her. Is that correct, or did your miraculous talent for prophecy bestow upon you such knowledge?"

"No. It was Paw who killed her."

"And you saw that happen?"

"Well, no."

"So you don't really know for sure?"

"I guess not."

"Did you take part in the dismemberment and dispersion of the deceased?"

"Yes, sir, but I didn't want to."

"So you say. But you did it anyway?"

"Yes, sir."

"As did the others?"

"Yes, sir."

"Did your father?"

"No. He wouldn't do it."

Jeremiah's answer sent a wave of approval through the crowd. Whispers of "Praise be!" and "Amen!" resonated in the packed courthouse.

"What was he doing?" asked Lee.

"Prayin' mostly."

"No doubt for your souls," said Lee. He gave the jury a look of consternation before returning his gaze to the witness. "Is there anything you're leaving out of your testimony?

Vaughan felt his gut tighten, but he pretended the question was of no concern. It wasn't time to reveal the truth about the skulls, and he didn't want Jeremiah to inadvertently spill the beans.

"No, I mean, I don't think so," said Jeremiah.

"You admit to being a cold-blooded murderer and you accuse your own father of heinous crimes, and now you sit there and lie straight to my face. And not only to my face, you lie to the honorable judge, the fine citizens of Pickens County, and, worst of all, to our esteemed members of the jury who have taken time out of their busy lives to see that justice is done. Why are you lying?"

"I'm not lyin'."

"You said earlier that all of the deacons were in on the murder and dismemberment of the first victim. You said you all went out into the swamp and disposed of the body parts."

"They did."

"They?"

"We."

"All of them?"

"Yes, all of them."

"Don't you mean us?"

"All of us."

"Then, how the hell did Earl Barber show up the next day with the other girl and not know anything about what happened the night before?"

"Well, that's because he left before—"

"You just said that you were all there."

"Except for Earl, I meant."

"Except? There is no except. You've perjured yourself under oath. You sit up there and give a fine speech about doing the right thing and taking responsibility, then you lie and accuse others and make excuses for your own actions. The only thing you said that I find believable is when you confessed to first degree murder."

Douglas Lee turned away with a dramatic show of disgust and looked at the jury, pretending to mutter to himself, "I've been doing this too long to be surprised when a killer turns out to be a liar."

"But you're twistin' my words. I—"

"No further questions, Your Honor," Lee interrupted. "Unfortunately, I may be forced to recall this witness, with your approval."

"Granted," said Judge Foley. "Mr. Vaughan, have you any more questions for the witness?"

"No, Your Honor," said Vaughan, feigning defeat, then adding, "The state rests."

Brother Eustice leaned closer to Douglas Lee, and the two exchanged a few whispers. Lee stood up and addressed the courtroom.

"I move for a dismissal, Your Honor. The state has shown no evidence to support their scandalous and unwarranted allegations. Furthermore, I demand an apology from not only the prosecutor, but also from the state police for their vicious attack upon my client's reputation. I—"

"Hold it right there, Counselor," interrupted the judge. "Let's not get ahead of ourselves here. You are in no position to demand anything at this point. Your client has been accused of murder, Mr. Lee. I haven't agreed to your request for dismissal, nor shall I. We will convene here tomorrow morning at nine o'clock, and you can present your defense."

Lee nodded and assured his client that it was now only a matter of time before he'd be exonerated. Vaughan kept his head down and exited through a side door. In truth, he wasn't at all convinced that Winchester wouldn't walk. A guilty verdict was far from certain, and Vaughan would be surprised if Lee didn't have a trick or two up his sleeve yet to play.

The circus tent revival had infected half the county, and all it would take was one member of the jury to cause a mistrial. The surviving members of the Antioch church were scrambling to save their own hides, and their testimony was tainted. As the only man left standing with a conscience, Jeremiah was positioned to take the fall for the lot of them, and the rest would be happy to see him do it, even his own father. On the other hand, they had the skulls, they had the detective, but most of all, they had the scumbag who had created the entire mess, who was dying to run his mouth. Vaughan knew all he had to do was to let him do it.

CHAPTER ONE HUNDRED THIRTEEN

Douglas Lee started his defense by calling up character witnesses. One by one, they raved about what a fine man Eustice Winchester was. Example after example of godly devotion and charitable works by the esteemed preacher were presented in great detail by the assorted members of the community without as much as a rebuttal from the prosecutor. When the fourth witness was going to be called up to the stand, Vaughan asked for a sidebar.

"Your Honor," said Garland, "Mr. Lee has eight more of these witnesses slated to testify. I'm not planning on asking a single question of any of them. Can we please wrap this up so we can get on with it?"

"Your Honor," Lee countered, "the jury has heard terrible accusations about my client. It is imperative that I'm able to present a more accurate portrayal of his character for balance."

"Mr. Lee," said Judge Foley, "you've done that. The prosecutor is right. There's no point in beating a dead horse. Unless the witnesses have something pertinent to the crimes of which your client is accused, the court isn't interested in hearing their testimony."

"Very well, Your Honor," said Lee.

Vaughan walked to his table and sat down. Lee wasted no time in calling his next witness.

"The Defense re-calls Deputy Earl Barber to the stand."

The back doors of the courtroom opened and Earl entered. Bailiff Tyndale swore him in, and he took his place on the stand.

"Deputy Barber," Lee asked, "when you testified earlier in the trial, you made quite a few conflicting statements. Why is that?"

"It's hard to remember all of the details," said Earl.

"Is it? I don't know, but if I was involved in such horrific crimes such as these, I think I would remember them."

"That's the problem."

"I don't understand," said Lee.

"I was told to say so many things, I can't always get them straight," explained Earl.

"Told to say? By whom?"

"By that detective."

"Objection!" shouted Vaughan.

"Overruled," said the judge.

Vaughan turned and glanced at Robert and Billy. They shrugged. It had begun.

"Which detective?" asked Lee.

"Detective Stallworth," said Earl.

"Are you saying that Detective Stallworth told you to lie on the stand?"

"Not in those words, but in effect, he did."

"In effect?"

"He's too smart to come right out and say it as such. Instead, he tries to trick you. It worked, too, except it's hard to keep track of everythin' sometimes, so I get mixed up."

"I'm sure you do," said Lee. "So then, let's keep it simple. Just tell us what you know for sure, and leave out all of the things you were supposed to say. Did Eustice Winchester order you to kill anyone?"

"No, sir."

"Did you see Eustice Winchester kill anyone?"

"No, sir."

"Did Eustice Winchester order you to do any of the other crimes of which he's accused, such as theft of a truck, or rape, or dismemberment of a corpse?"

"No, sir."

"Well, that is quite a change in your testimony, I must say. How did you and your fellow church members become involved in this mess in the first place?"

"We were asked to help look for the missin' body after the foot was found in the swamp. We volunteered because it seemed like the right thing to do."

"And that's it? You unwittingly became suspects in these unspeakable crimes solely because you offered to help?"

"Yes, sir. We didn't know what we was gettin' into. It just happened that we was away on retreat when these things occurred, so we had no alibis 'cept each other. I suppose that's why we was all brought in on it. That way, none of us could vouch for each other. Instead, we turned on each other out of fear."

"But why would you implicate each other in crimes you didn't commit?"

"We was scared. The detective confused us. He kept at it with his story until we could no longer tell what had actually happened and what he had told us." Earl turned to the jury and added, "I know it sounds crazy, but that's what happened. He has this way about him that makes you paint yourself into a corner. I can't explain the rest."

"You don't have to," said Lee. "I got a taste of that myself."

Lee chuckled and glanced around the room before turning back to the witness. "So, you are saying now that you had nothing to do with any of this?"

"I'm not saying anythin' about it no more," said Earl. "Under advice of counsel, I refuse to answer the question on grounds that I might incriminate myself."

"I see. So now you are recanting everything?"

"On advice of counsel, I refuse to answer the question on grounds I might incriminate myself."

"Is that how you are going to answer everything I ask you?"

"When it applies to me."

"And when it applies to Eustice Winchester?"

"What do you want to know?"

"Is he guilty of these crimes?" asked Lee.

"No."

The gallery exploded in cheers. Judge Foley allowed a few seconds to go by before banging his gavel on the bench and calling for order.

"You once believed that Eustice Winchester was a man of God, but you stated that you no longer believe that. What do you say now?"

"Objection!" shouted Vaughan. "This is completely irrelevant to this trial."

"Overruled," said the judge. He turned to the witness and stated, "You may answer the question, Deputy."

"Even Peter denied knowin' the Christ three times," said Earl. "It is to my great shame that I am a weak and sinful man. I pray that my sins will be forgiven."

"You didn't answer the question," prompted Lee.

"There's much I don't know, but I know one thing for sure. Brother Eustice Winchester is a prophet of the Lord."

"No further questions, Your Honor," said Lee. His announcement drowned out by the cries of 'Amen!' and 'Hallelujah!' from the audience.

Vaughan declined a redirect of the deputy. Barber would just refuse to answer any questions that might hurt Winchester while reinforcing the defense's case whenever he could. At this point, Earl was nothing more than a character witness for the preacher.

Lee called up Buck again. As Earl had done, he recanted everything and blamed Stallworth for any previous damaging testimony. As an extra measure, Buck broke down in tears at the end, openly begging Eustice for forgiveness while proclaiming the preacher to be a prophet sent from on high.

Once again, Vaughan waved off asking the witness a single question.

Lee skipped over a return visit with Joe Bob Duncan. The last thing he'd said on the witness stand was to declare himself to be a liar, so regardless of what he'd have to say now, it wouldn't help.

Gospel music from the church revival outside drifted in through the windows. Every witness Lee had called so far had proclaimed Winchester to be a holy man. Not one shred of physical evidence directly linked his client to the crimes of which he was accused. Lee could smell victory, but he was wise enough to know that it was in those moments that it all could fall apart.

"Your Honor," Lee addressed the judge, "if it please the court, may we resume presenting our case tomorrow? It's getting a bit late in the afternoon, and I think it would be better for everyone if we started fresh."

"No objections, Your Honor," said Vaughan.

"In that case, we will adjourn until nine a.m.," said Foley.

Lee was relieved. Nobody had asked who his next witness was going to be. It was perfect. The next morning, he'd blow the case wide open. He'd exact revenge on the man who had humiliated him. Most importantly, he'd all but guarantee that Eustice Winchester would once again be a free man.

CHAPTER ONE HUNDRED FOURTEEN

Onward, Christian soldiers, marching as to war. The melody drifted into the courtroom from the revival tent outside. Judge Foley made his entrance, and everyone present took their seats on what would hopefully be the last day of the trial.

The local merchants would be sorry to see it end. The influx of visitors had filled their coffers substantially. Reverend Beecher's flock numbered in the thousands, all awaiting acquittal of the most holy Brother Winchester. For the local police, the trial presented a great deal of anxiety. If Winchester was found guilty and sent to the gallows, it was almost certain that a riot would break out. No matter how many reserves they brought it, they'd be outnumbered if the going got rough. The pressure was on to set Brother Eustice free, and that pressure was felt outside the courtroom as well as inside.

With the cross of Jesus going on before! sang the choir from the tent next door.

"Is the defense ready to proceed?" Judge Foley asked.

"We are, Your Honor," said Douglas Lee. "The defense re-calls Detective Robert Stallworth."

A round of boos and hisses greeted the detective as he made his way to the stand. Random shouts of 'Heathen!' and

'Devil!' accompanied his taking of the oath. Robert ignored them and took his place in the witness box.

"Mister Stallworth," Lee began.

"Detective," Robert corrected him.

"Right, Detective, you testified earlier that there was no additional evidence that might lead us to believe that someone other than my client was involved in this case. Is that true?"

"It is."

"And you're sure about that?"

"I am."

"I find that rather hard to believe."

"I'm sure you do," said Robert.

"You previously testified that, at one time, everyone was a suspect, up to and including Sheriff Fuller and members of the police department. Isn't that so?"

"Yes, at one time, everyone was a suspect until they could be eliminated."

"And you eliminated them all?"

"No."

"No? I'm not sure I understand you," said Lee.

"Deputy Earl Barber was never eliminated as a suspect."

"But the rest of them have been."

"Yes."

"I find that rather odd, considering what you found buried behind the police station."

Robert remained silent.

"You're being awfully quiet about that, aren't you, Detective?"

"You didn't ask me a question."

"You think you're so clever, don't you? Well, I'll bet you don't think you're so smart now."

"Which question should I answer? If I think I'm clever or if I don't think I'm smart?" asked Robert. Laughter came from the jury box.

"The defense would like to, once again, present to the jury Exhibit R, the photograph taken by the detective, otherwise known as *The Bone Puzzle*."

Bailiff Tyndale retrieved the item and handed it to Robert.

"Do you recognize this as being the same photograph as before?" asked Lee.

"Yes."

"It shows two almost complete skeletons, does is not?"

"Yes."

"Tell me, Detective, what are the most obvious parts of the skeletons that are missing?"

"The skulls."

"Correct, the skulls. Why aren't the skulls in the photograph?"

"We didn't have them at the time," said Robert.

"But you have them now, don't you?"

"We do."

"Then why wasn't another photograph taken with them?"

"It was."

"Really? I don't have it."

"You didn't ask for it."

"I asked for all evidence to be handed over when I took this case," said Lee.

"We didn't have it at that time. When we found them, we catalogued them, and another photograph was taken and put in the respective file. It's up to you to ask for it, but you were so enamored by the title I gave this one, you weren't interested in looking at it."

Lee felt his face flush with anger. The detective was right. He had overlooked it for that very reason, never expecting to be called out in court over it. It was time to put the detective in his place.

"I asked you earlier about what was found buried behind the sheriff's office."

"No, you said something about it, but you didn't ask me anything," said Robert.

"Well, I'm asking you now. Isn't it true that two skulls were dug up from behind Sheriff Fuller's station?"

"Yes."

The crowd erupted with cries of astonishment. Judge Foley banged his gavel to restore order in the room.

"Yet you refused to reconsider the sheriff's department as suspects?"

"Yes."

The gallery grew agitated. That level of corruption in the police department could never be tolerated.

"How could they not be?" asked Lee.

"I didn't consider it relative to the investigation," said Robert.

The audience went berserk. This time, all the gavel banging the judge could do would not restore order. Bailiff Tyndale strutted out to the gallery, grabbed the arm of a local disruptive hayseed standing in the aisle, and forcibly escorted him out. By the time he came back to remove another, the crowd had calmed down and taken their seats.

"No further questions, Your Honor," said Lee. "However, I will request that a thorough investigation be conducted immediately and that the detective be removed from the state police and charges brought against him as soon as possible."

"I'm leaning toward doing just that," said Judge Foley. "What a disgrace."

Robert showed no concern and sat back. He winked at Billy, who bit hard into the side of his mouth to keep from laughing.

CHAPTER ONE HUNDRED FIFTEEN

"**D**etective Stallworth," Vaughan asked when it was his turn to question the detective, "there seems to be a lot of explaining for you to do. I, I'm not sure where to begin."

"Begin wherever you like," said Robert.

"Is it true that two skulls were found buried behind the police station?"

"It is."

"Yet it never occurred to you that this might implicate members of Sheriff Fuller's department in this crime?"

"No, it didn't."

"How can this be?"

"Oh, it can be," said Robert.

"I'm not understanding this at all."

"That's because, like Douglas Lee, Esquire, here, you're not asking the right questions."

"You could be right. I guess someone who asks a lot of questions for a living like you do becomes an expert at that."

"That's in your job description as well, Counselor."

"That it is," agreed Vaughan. "Okay then, let's stop with the shenanigans. Why weren't the skulls found behind the police station considered pertinent to the investigation?"

"Because they weren't related to our case."

"And how do you know this?"

"Because they were canine skulls."

The audience buzzed with puzzlement.

"Come again?"

"Canine skulls," said Robert. "They came from a pair of dogs. Gunner and Apache, to be exact. They were police dogs that were buried out back after their retirement and demise. We got a tip that some bones were buried there, and we did our due diligence, just in case. We didn't want to leave any avenue of investigation open without the proper attention paid to it."

"I see," said Vaughan. "But you also said that the two skulls that belonged to the murdered girls were later found. I know this to be a fact because I looked at all the evidence and saw them for myself."

"Yes, we found those as well."

"Where did you find them?" asked Vaughan.

"On Eustice Winchester's property," said Robert.

The crowd exploded with cries of condemnation. Judge Foley banged his gavel repeatedly.

"No further questions, Your Honor."

CHAPTER ONE HUNDRED SIXTEEN

"**H**ello? Mr. Lee," Judge Foley said for the third time, "we're waiting on you."

"Uh, sorry, Your Honor," Lee replied. "If you'll allow me one minute to confer with my client."

"We've given you ample time."

Lee and Eustice were in the midst of a heated argument, their whispers beginning to morph into shouts when the judge interrupted them again.

"Mr. Lee!" Foley banged on the bench with his gavel.

"If it pleases the court, I'd like to ask for a brief recess," pleaded Lee.

"Denied! Counselor, this trial has gone on long enough."

"But, Your Honor—"

"In my chambers!" Judge Foley slammed his gavel on the bench and headed to his office. Douglas Lee pulled away from a noticeably perturbed Winchester and followed the judge, his head down. Garland Vaughan picked up a file and casually strolled into the back office behind them, smirking at the detective on the way out.

Once seated behind his desk, Foley waited for Lee's explanation.

"Your Honor, I was completely caught off guard by this. All I'm asking for is—"

"—for the rest of us to wait while you get your shit together," the judge finished the sentence for him. "This is unacceptable, Douglas. I expected a lot more out of a man with your reputation. What the hell is the matter with you?"

"But the detective—"

"The one I had to rescue you from the first time around. I warned you to stay away from him, which, by the way, could be seen by some as overstepping my boundaries as judge. If it were not for the professionalism and discretion that Mr. Vaughan here has shown, we could be looking at a mistrial. Thank you again, Garland, for your patience in this matter."

"Don't mention it, Your Honor" said Vaughan.

"As for you, I told you not to ask questions unless you wanted those questions answered. I shouldn't have to tell you that. You're not a first year law student."

"They were hiding evidence," countered Lee.

"I object to that allegation," said Vaughan.

"You don't have to," said Foley. "Douglas, unless you have concrete proof to support your assertions, you'd better have an apology ready."

"But, I—"

"Counselor!"

"Okay, I apologize. I, I made a mistake."

"Accepted," said Vaughan, "provided you don't do it again. Who you really need to apologize to is the detective."

"Oh, come on!" exclaimed Lee.

"Oh, come on what?" said the judge. "But don't worry. I won't make you do that, if only for the sake of your client. He's the one you should apologize to. Now, we are going to go out there and wrap this up. No more delays. I'm not telling you what to do, but you'd better have a plan. If you'll take my advice, and, if it's okay with Garland here, I'd advise you to move on from Stallworth. He's eating your lunch."

Lee nodded and composed himself before they resumed their places in the packed courtroom. *Rock of Ages* wafted in through the open window to greet them.

"Is there anything else you'd like to ask the witness?" implored the judge.

"No, Your Honor," said Lee.

"Mr. Vaughan, do you have any questions for this witness?" asked the judge.

"No, Your Honor," replied Vaughan, barely containing the smile threatening to appear on his lips.

"The witness is dismissed," said Judge Foley.

Robert nodded and walked back to his spot next to Watts. Billy grinned. "Eustice Winchester's property?"

"Eustice Adam Winchester," said Robert.

"Junior," countered Billy.

"To be exact," said Robert.

"Clever boy."

CHAPTER ONE HUNDRED SEVENTEEN

Another stanza from the choir next door drifted in from the window behind the jury. *Not the labors of my hands can fulfill thy law's demands.*

"Mr. Lee?" asked Judge Foley.

Lee and Eustice stopped their whispered disagreement in mid-sentence. Lee glanced at the judge, then back at his client one more time, pleading his argument with his eyes to no avail. Eustice nodded vehemently, and Lee bowed his head momentarily before standing.

"Your Honor, the Defense wishes to call Brother Eustice Elijah Winchester to the stand."

...thou must save, and thou alone.

"Praise be!" a rotund woman with a ruddy complexion shouted from the second row.

"Glory, glory, glory!" answered a wiry fellow wearing overalls.

Nothing in my hand I bring...

Winchester stopped before Bailiff Tyndale and put his hand on the Bible. He gazed into the bailiff's eyes with a fiery glare and whispered, "Go on, Porter, bless us with your pious duty."

The bailiff gulped and asked for the oath, his voice cracking under the strain. "Do you swear to tell the truth, the whole truth, and nothing but the truth, so help you God?"

"Sanctify them in the truth; your word is truth. I do."

"You may be seated," said the bailiff as he retreated.

Wash me, Savior, or I die.

"Mister Winchester," said Lee.

"You may call me Brother, as we are all children of the Lord," interrupted Eustice.

"Amen!" came from the gallery.

While I draw this fleeting breath...

"Okay then, Brother Winchester, many a vile thing has been said about you during this trial. What do you say about all of that?"

"Blessed are they which are persecuted for righteousness' sake; for theirs is the kingdom of heaven. It hurts when those you love speak ill of you, but you bear it all the same, for who am I to deny forgiveness when it is I who needs to be forgiven most of all?"

"Forgiven? If you are innocent, like you say, what is it that you need forgiveness for?"

"Let he amongst you who has not sinned, cast the first stone. We are all sinners, Brother Douglas. Are we not?"

See thee on thy judgment throne...

"You know the crimes of which you have been accused."

"I am aware. I must confess, such wickedness I was oblivious could exist in this world, much less in Alabama. But, alas, here we are."

"Are you saying that you or your followers took no part in these offenses?"

"I am not here to speak for my neighbors, but to answer for my own transgressions."

...let me hide myself in thee.

"What are you saying?"

"What are you askin'?"

"Are you guilty?"

"I am," said the preacher. He paused to allow the whispers to circulate the courtroom before continuing, "but, of what?"

"Forgive me if I must ask these repulsive things, but I must. Did you kidnap the girls?"

"No, I did not kidnap any girl. I stand accused of this, yet, even when lyin', not one of my flock has ever said that I did such a thing."

"I'm not sure what you mean."

"Accordin' to the testimony, which is questionable at best, I didn't drive the alleged stolen truck. In fact, I don't believe anyone has been able to produce this ghost truck. I'm no policeman or lawyer, but I think if someone is accused of stealin' somethin', that somethin' should be proven to exist."

"I never thought about it that way," said Lee. "You make a good point. So you are saying you didn't steal a truck or kidnap anyone?"

"Of course not," said Brother Eustice. "Why would I do that? I already own a Buick, but I can barely drive that thing myself. What am I going to do with a truck?"

"I don't know. When you put it that way, it doesn't make much sense."

"There ain't no other way to put it, but what do I know?"

"Some of your fellow church members have claimed that you instructed them to do these things."

"I heard what they said," said Eustice. "Why would that matter?"

"It matters because, if you told them to do it, then you are as guilty as they are."

"I've told them many a thing over the years: how to be righteous men, how to treat others as they wish to be treated, how not to lie, or lust upon loose women. It seems that they've not listened to those instructions. Why would they listen to others?"

"But if they did."

"If they did right by my word, is it I who should get the credit? If they do ill, should I be to blame?"

"If they felt coerced into action, some might consider you an accomplice."

"Perhaps," said Eustice, "and if I did my best to prevent such happenings? What then?"

"It all depends. Did you?"

Eustice sighed. "I've always tried to be there for my flock; to give comfort when I can; to give sound advice when asked; to give spiritual counsel to those in need. Sometimes, I come up short. I am but a man. I live with that shame every day."

"Did you murder the girls?"

"I did not murder the girl."

"Do you know who did?"

"I will not speak upon my brothers."

"You can be made to testify."

"By whom? Satan? He has sent his best to trick us, but I was not fooled, unlike my brothers. I tried to warn them, but they heeded my warnings as much as they heeded the rest of my instructions."

"Did you have any part in these crimes whatsoever?"

"Yes."

"What part did you play?"

"Spiritual guidance, but as I said before, I was unsuccessful, or we wouldn't be here."

"I think I'm beginning to understand now," said Lee. "You accompanied the men to prevent them from committing such atrocious deeds, yet despite your best efforts, they did these horrible crimes anyway. After that, you tried to protect them, even from themselves, but still were unable to do so. Is this correct?"

"It is as you say. I have failed my brethren."

"No further questions, Your Honor."

Lee sat down, relieved that Winchester didn't say anything stupid. The angelic voices of Reverend Beecher's Gospel Revival sang another hymn, one that would have an unexpected effect upon the prophet of the Lord.

CHAPTER ONE HUNDRED EIGHTEEN

"**M**r. Winchester," Vaughan asked when it was his turn to question the preacher.

"Call me Brother," interrupted Eustice.

"As I said, Mister Winchester, you stated that Satan sent someone to trick and deceive you. Would you care to elaborate on that?"

"Evil men and imposters will proceed from bad to worse, deceivin' and bein' deceived. One such demon sits amongst us now, cloakin' the truth with his wicked lies."

"Are you talking about yourself?" asked Vaughan.

"Objection!" shouted Lee.

"Sustained."

"Who is it that you speak of?" asked Vaughan.

"We all know who I speak of," said Winchester. "Through his shrewdness, he causes deceit to succeed by his influence. He will destroy many while they are at ease." Eustice turned to the jury and asked, "Can't you smell the sulfur in the air, brothers, or has the evil one ensnared you, too, with his trickery?"

"Will the witness please address me and me alone?" said Vaughan.

"Sure, that's what you want, isn't it? You want to keep that cloak of deceit over the eyes of the righteous men of the jury, my peers. You want to keep them in the Devil's grasp so that they will unwittingly do the deeds of the Evil One, thus, castin' their own souls into the fire." Eustice turned to the jury again. "Heed my warning, brothers, for the Lord has spoken, that no advantage would be taken of us by Satan if we are not ignorant of his schemes."

"Judge Foley, I implore you to instruct the witness—" said Vaughan.

"When the preacher quotes the Good Book, he speaks from a place higher than my bench," said the judge. "I will not chastise him for that."

Choruses of "Amen!" and "Praise the Lord!" rose from the gallery.

"What just happened?" whispered Billy.

"I don't know, but it's not good," said Robert.

"Speak plainly then, Brother," said Vaughan, trying a different tactic. "Who is it among us that you say has been sent by the Devil?"

"Stallworth. Curse his name," said Winchester. "It's obvious. Only he knew where the bones were buried. Only he knew where the gypsy girl came from and what happened to the conjuror that held her captive. The deacons of my flock were weak, I admit that, but none of them told of their righteous actions. No, the detective knew it all, but how? How could he know? There is only one answer: sorcery."

The gallery erupted with shouts of rage directed at Robert. Cries of "Devil!" and "Satan!" echoed throughout the room. A middle-aged woman seated behind him made her way to the aisle and flung herself on the hard tile floor while babbling in tongues.

"Order!" shouted Judge Foley. "Order in the court!" He banged his gavel repeatedly on the bench. "Bailiff, remove that woman from the courtroom!"

Bailiff Tyndale helped two of the men in the audience drag the woman out the back door. He then walked up the aisle with his chest puffed out, one hand on his baton, daring anyone in the room to continue their outbursts. By the time he took his place next to the bench, the room had grown silent, with the exception of the choir outside, whose beautiful rendition of the religious classic drifted in through the open window behind the jury box.

Shall we gather at the river...

"So you admit that you and your group kidnapped the girls from Tennessee?"

...where bright angel feet have trod?

"I admit nothin'. As a shepherd seeketh out his flock that are scattered, so will I seek out my sheep, and I will deliver them out of all places where they have been scattered in the cloudy and dark day." Eustice turned towards the jury. "You've seen the poster with the vile fiend emblazoned so boldly upon it. Only a pitchfork and horns were missin'. The poor gypsy girl's eternal life was at stake. Could I, a prophet of the most high, ignore her plight? Would not each of you have done the same for such a damsel in distress?"

Yes, we'll gather at the river...

"You keep saying girl. There were two girls," said Vaughan.

...the beautiful, the beautiful river.

"There was but one. The rest is more trickery of the Devil."

Gather with the saints at the river...

"But I fear, lest by any means," Eustice continued, "as the serpent beguiled Eve through his subtlety, so your minds should be corrupted from the simplicity that is in Christ."

...that flows by the throne of God.

"Two skeletons were found," said Vaughan.

"Lies!" Eustice shouted.

On the margin of the river, washing up its silver spray...

The preacher stared at the detective and pointed a finger at him. "You are of your father, the Devil, and you want to do the desires of your father. He was a murderer from the beginnin' and does not stand in the truth because there is no truth in him. Whenever he speaks a lie, he speaks from his own nature. For he is a liar, and the father of lies."

...we will walk and worship ever, all the happy golden day.

Eustice turned again and faced the jury. "Resist the Devil, and he will flee from you."

"Amen, Brother," one of the men of the jury responded. Robert noted that three others nodded their heads in agreement.

"This can't be happening," said Billy. "He's admitting guilt."

"It's not going to matter," said Robert. He looked at Billy with disgust in his eyes. "He's going to walk."

The beautiful, the beautiful river…

"Lacey and Laura Henderson," said Vaughan. "You killed them both and had them dismembered and thrown into the swamp. Didn't you?"

…that flows by the throne of God.

"One girl!" insisted Eustice. "Bewitched by the Devil, she was! The wicked sorcerer, Villanova, had cast his spell on her. I was unable to exorcise the demon that possessed her. I tried, oh Lord, with all my heavenly might, but it was not meant to be. Beelzebub would not release her soul and snatched her away from my grasp. It was then that I saw the trap that had been set, so I did what I could to protect my flock from the world that could never understand. We were doin' the Lord's work! For we wrestle not against flesh and blood, but against principalities, against powers, against the rulers of the darkness of this world, against spiritual wickedness in high places!"

Grace our spirits will deliver…

"Two girls," insisted Vaughan. "Twins. And you murdered them in cold blood."

…and provide a robe and crown.

Eustice addressed the jury. "Put on the whole armor of God, that ye may be able to stand against the wiles of the Devil."

"Yes, Brother," four of the jurists replied.

"Oh my God!" said Billy. "They're buying this crap."

"Fucking Alabama," said Robert.

Vaughan looked over at Robert and Billy, clearly distressed. The writing was on the wall. No matter what came out of Eustice Winchester's mouth now, he was going to be a free man. There would be no consequences for his actions.

"You had their corpses sawed into pieces and thrown into the swamp," said Vaughan.

Shall we gather at the river...

"Satan had set his trap well. We hid what was left of the gypsy girl to confuse the Evil One, but alas, the Father of Lies is a clever one. The next mornin' he resurrected her and had one of our own bring her back to cause confusion and tempt my flock into turnin' from the narrow path. Not on my watch."

"Praise be!" someone shouted from the gallery. Murmurs of approval accompanied the outburst. The bailiff and judge ignored it, complicit in its implication.

"My brothers," Eustice addressed the jury, "remember the word of the Lord. And they may come to their senses and escape from the snare of the Devil, havin' been held captive by him to do his will. You are all righteous, Christian men. You know what to do."

The courtroom erupted with a chorus of 'Amen' and 'Glory be.' Vaughan watched in horror when Judge Foley himself closed his eyes and lowered his head in prayer. He glanced at the jury to see the men holding hands and whispering prayers as if caught up in the Holy Spirit. Vaughan looked frantically at Robert and Billy. Watts appeared to be sick; Stallworth's face was flushed with anger.

Eustice sat back and smiled.

CHAPTER ONE HUNDRED NINETEEN

Appalled at the maddening effect that the preacher's words had on the jury, Vaughan pushed the only button he could think of. "Two girls."

"One," Eustice replied, the twisted grin of victory on his face. "Resurrected by Satan, but sent back forever to the fiery pit of hell by the prophet of the Lord. Members of the jury, fear not. The Devil has done his best and been conquered by yours truly. Believe in me, and this mess will be put behind us forever. Let the dead rest in peace, and we'll all find peace in return."

Shall we gather at the river... the angelic sounds of the chorus drifted in through the open window. Members of the audience began to sing along.

...the beautiful, the beautiful river...

Vaughan had nothing left. His shoulders fell in defeat as he turned and walked back to his table. Even Douglas Lee looked defeated, not comfortable with the win he'd acquired for his now undisputed guilty client.

Gather with the saints at the river... By now the whole room, save for the two detectives and both attorneys, had joined in. Even the judge and bailiff sang along.

...that flows by the throne of...

Everyone stopped in midsentence as their eyes were drawn to the back of the room and the two people who now stood in the doorway. Vaughan looked up, his face a mixture of shock and jubilation. Robert and Billy turned around.

"Claire!" said Billy.

Robert smiled.

At the rear of the packed courtroom stood two figures, hand in hand. One, an attractive woman with auburn hair and a pirate's smile; the other, a girl dressed like a gypsy, identical in every way to the girl on the poster, and identical to the two girls whose bones lay upon the tarp in Dr. Hall's back room.

"This cannot be!" shouted Eustice. "You are dead! We killed you!"

Douglas Lee sprung out of his chair. "Objection! Your Honor!"

"Be gone, Satan!" Eustice continued to rant, foam spitting out of his mouth. "This cannot be! I saw you cut up with my own eyes! We buried you in the swamp! Go back to the depths of hell where we sent you!" He went into convulsions, his speech deteriorating into incoherent mumbling.

"Order!" shouted Judge Foley to no avail. He looked towards the bailiff who seemed frozen into place, unable to move or take his eyes off of the reincarnated Gypsy girl standing at the rear of the room.

"Your Honor," pleaded Lee. He glanced towards the prosecutor and let his objection die in his throat. Vaughan was smiling. Lee looked over at Stallworth, who gave him a wink.

Bailiff Tyndale was joined by one of the guards, and they forcibly removed Eustice Winchester from the room. The preacher was sobbing uncontrollably and shouting obscenities at invisible demons that only he could see. The rest of the courtroom was surprisingly silent, unable to process what had occurred just moments before.

Soon our happy hearts will quiver, with the melody of peace.

CHAPTER ONE HUNDRED TWENTY

The group waited in Vaughan's office while the jury deliberated. They didn't have to wait long.

"How the hell did you find her?" asked Billy.

"As Robert would say, I dazzled them with diligence, Mr. Watts," said Claire.

"I'm in awe of you, Miss Montgomery," said Vaughan.

"Why, thank you, darlin'." Claire laughed as she took a bow.

Robert said nothing, letting the big smile plastered across his face do his talking for him.

"Cat got your tongue, darlin'?"

"I would have never guessed in a million years," Robert muttered.

"That's because you said they were twins. Whatever gave you that idea?" Claire responded.

"Triplets?" said Dr. Hall. "Identical triplets? What are the odds?"

"I'm sure they're up there," said Billy. "But how did you figure it out?"

"There were three cribs at the Tennessee Children's Home Society, but only two girls. Something about it didn't set well with me. That monster who ran things over there was peddling human babies. She had no conscience. My heart ached for all the parents who had been separated from their children. As hard as I tried, I was unable to do anything about it, but that didn't stop me from trying."

"I'm sure it didn't," said Robert.

"I eventually tracked the missing girl to Maryland. I must've looked like I'd seen a ghost when I first set eyes on her. Lucky for the sweet thing she'd found a good home."

"What's her name?" Robert asked.

"Lilah," said Claire, "Lilah Dunlap. She didn't even know she had sisters. Unfortunately, she'll never get to meet them now."

"The gypsy costume was a nice touch," said Billy.

They laughed.

A knock on the door interrupted their meeting. Vaughan's secretary poked her head inside and announced, "The jury has reached a verdict."

The group made its way back to the courtroom. The gallery was still packed, but the crowd was subdued. An occasional banging drifted in from the open window, the sound of Reverend Beecher's revival tent being dismantled. Gone were the fervent supporters of Brother Winchester. No one wanted a part in his evil doings anymore, lest the Devil come for them next.

"All rise!" Bailiff Tyndale called out as Judge Foley took the bench.

"Has the jury reached a verdict?" he asked.

"We have, Your Honor," said the foreman of the jury.

He handed a piece of paper to Tyndale, who, in turn, handed it to the judge. Foley opened it and silently read the words before handing it back. The bailiff gave it to the foreman.

"Would the jury please read the verdict," said Foley.

"We, the jury, find the defendant, Eustice Elijah Winchester, guilty on all charges."

Vaughan expected cries of dismay from the crowd, but none came. As far as the people of Pickens County were concerned, the sooner Winchester and his bunch were put away, the better.

"What does the jury recommend for sentencing?" asked Foley.

"The members of the jury are unanimous, Your Honor. We recommend the death sentence."

Judge Foley wasted no time in sentencing the preacher, eager to wash his hands of the whole mess. "I hearby reprimand the convicted to the Alabama Correctional Facility at Kilby State Prison, where he will be held until such time as his execution can take place. Mr. Winchester, do you have any last words you wish to say?"

Brother Eustice looked pale and sickly. His knees buckled as he fought to stand and find the right words. He sobbed. "I, I, I was only doing the Lords work!" Tears fell down his cheeks as he threw himself on the floor in front of Judge Foley's bench. "Mercy! Have mercy on me, I beg you! It wasn't me. It was the others! Buck did it!"

Bailiff Tyndale nodded to the guards who stood nearby. They made their way to retrieve the broken man, each grabbing one arm to pick him up from the floor.

"It was Jeremiah and Junior!" Winchester pleaded with the jury. "I was only takin' up for them because they're my kids. You understand, don't you? You can't do this! You'll pay for this! I'm a prophet of the Lord!"

"Mr. Winchester, get a hold of yourself," said the judge with disgust. "You're becoming a spectacle. Have a modicum of dignity, for Christ's sake."

"Blasphemy!" Winchester screamed. "You'll all rot in hell!"

"I sentence you to death by electrocution," said Foley, clearly disgusted by the pathetic display. "May God have mercy on your soul."

"Sinner! You're all goin' to burn in hell!" Winchester yelled as he was dragged from the courtroom. He gave one more look over his shoulder and spotted Robert. "Satan! Father of Lies! You did this!"

Robert looked at the distraught man and winked.

"Classy," whispered Billy.

"He had it coming," said Robert.
"I couldn't agree more," said Claire.

CHAPTER ONE HUNDRED TWENTY-ONE

Eager to be finished with the sorrowful conclusion of the preacher's trial, the crowd thinned out with the exception of the prosecution's team. There was a lot of catching up to do, and it gave them time to decompress after the ordeal of the last six months.

A solid hour passed before Stallworth and the group made their way out of the courthouse. Claire spotted a handsome young couple waiting under the shade of an oak tree next to the parking lot and guided Robert in their direction. Claire introduced Robert to Lilah and her parents. It was all the detective could do to keep from crying as he looked into the innocent face of the little girl. The only thing he knew about her sisters were the bones on the tarp in the back room of the medical examiner's office. All three had been identical. Now he knew what they looked like before the boys from the Antioch Pentecostal Church had gotten hold of them. They were beautiful.

Robert knelt down and addressed the child. "Your sisters were named Lacey and Laura, and they looked exactly like you. They were the bravest girls who have ever lived. I'm sorry that I couldn't have been there for them when they needed me, but they left you something to remember them by." He reached into his pocket and retrieved the plastic ruby that had once decorated the great magician's turban. "I call it

The Holy Relic. Without it, I never would've caught the monsters who did this. Your sisters were heroes."

Robert stood up and patted Lilah's head before brushing away a tear from his eye. He thanked the girl's parents and walked over to where Vaughan and the others waited, giving Claire time to say her goodbyes.

"Did you just hand over state's evidence to that girl?" asked Vaughan.

"I don't know what you're talking about," Robert replied.

Vaughan shook his head, but his smile gave away his approval.

Claire walked her guests to their car, then made her way to the others as they gathered on the courthouse steps.

She retrieved a small box and card from her purse.

"What's that?" asked Dr. Hall.

"It's a gift for a special someone."

"Well, if you insist—" joked Billy.

"Not you, darlin'. We all know who it's for."

"Detective Stallworth, the Devil incarnate," said Vaughan.

Robert bowed. He took the box from Claire and began to open the card.

"No, not yet," she teased.

Robert raised an eyebrow.

"It's to celebrate your big win, but you have to save it until all this is over."

"It is over. Winchester is going down," Robert protested.

"Not Winchester," said Claire. She waved her arm in the direction of the courthouse. "All of this."

"Oh," said Robert, dejected.

Billy smiled and cleared his throat. Only then did the hidden meaning become clear to Robert.

"Oh!" he said again, this time with exhilaration at the promise of a life together with his true love once his quest to catch evil men was a thing of the past.

The group walked to *Samson's Bar and Grill* and ordered a round of drinks to celebrate. The district attorney briefly excused himself to take a call, returning to the table with news of the latest developments.

"Earl Barber has been arrested," Vaughan announced.

"It's about time," said Billy. "What's going to happen to the rest of the boys?"

"I'm expecting to hear from their lawyers anytime now," said Vaughan. "They'll be looking to cut some deals, but I'm not feeling overly generous at the moment."

"I figured as much," said Billy. "With Eustice's conviction, theirs is all but assured."

"What about Jeremiah?" asked Robert.

"He hasn't asked for a deal, but I believe, if he plays his cards right, we might be willing to cut him some slack," said Vaughan. "He's the only one of the bunch who showed remorse."

"There might be hope for the boy yet," said Billy.

A lone reporter approached the group, holding a large camera. "May we get a picture of the team that put the murderer away for the *Alabama Star*?"

"Sure, but leave me out of it," said Vaughan.

"Are you sure? You're the district attorney who defeated the great Douglas Lee. This might help you come election time," said the reporter.

"I'm not so sure about that. As much as I would like to, I can't take any of the credit. Smile for the camera, Robert. It's all yours."

"I'm out, too," said Billy.

"Me as well," echoed Dr. Hall.

"Come on now, I didn't do any of this alone," Robert protested.

The men didn't want to hear it. They shrugged and moved away.

"Well, only if the delightful Miss Claire Montgomery stands with me," said Robert.

"Oh, I couldn't, darlin'," said Claire.

"Nonsense," said Robert. "That scumbag was laughing at us until you showed up. He was going to walk for sure."

"He's right," said Vaughan. The others nodded in agreement.

"Besides, with a mug like mine, I'll end up buried in the back pages. With you, on the other hand—"

"He's right about that one, ma'am," said the reporter.

"Hey!" Robert said. "Don't go agreeing too quickly with that."

They laughed as Robert held Claire close to his side, and the flash went off.

"Thanks a bunch," said the reporter. "It's a hell of a thing what that preacher did. Too bad they'll never get justice in Tennessee for that Villanova thing. Sawed the bastard in half, ouch!"

"They'll get justice," said Vaughan. "He'll be extradited and stand trial for that one, too."

"I, I thought you heard," said the reporter.

"Heard what?" asked Dr. Hall.

"Brother Eustice hanged himself in his cell," the reported informed them.

"What!" Vaughan yelled.

"Yep. I guess his conscience wouldn't let him go on."

"He had no conscience," said Billy. "He's a sociopath."

"Was a sociopath, darlin'," Claire agreed. "Was a sociopath."

"And a coward," added Robert. "May he burn in hell."

Everyone present had the same reply. "Amen."

EPILOGUE

Purvis Johnson sat in his rocking chair, reading the newspaper in the dying light of the Alabama sun. He enjoyed sitting on the front porch of his newly built home, especially when the weather was mild, as it was on that January evening.

His house was nothing more than a shack, hastily thrown together with clapboard siding in a haphazard fashion by day workers hired piecemeal. He had employed an excavating crew in the beginning, only to stiff them on the bill and run them off his property. Then there was Willie, buried under the septic tank nearby. Purvis couldn't decide which memory gave him more pleasure.

The old man rifled through the paper until he'd read enough. He placed the sections back in place, folded the paper, and set it on his lap. He glanced again at the photograph on the front page. Some nondescript policeman was mugging it up next to a gorgeous dame.

"I'd smile, too, if I had that piece of eye candy on my arm," Purvis said out loud.

The story attached had been a doozey. Even by Purvis's standards, it ranked up there. Some magician had been sawed in half and his twin daughters kidnapped, raped, dismembered, and thrown into Dead River Swamp. Although Purvis wasn't particularly fond of the raping part—after all, he wasn't a pervert—he did appreciate the aesthetic quality of sawing a magician in half. It was almost worthy of him. The name of the swamp was an extra bonus: Dead River Swamp. It was perfect.

The old man pulled out a Camel cigarette and lit it with one of the matches he'd collected from the Winecoff Hotel. He liked to save them for special occasions, and this one felt just right. Purvis took a deep drag of tobacco laden smoke and exhaled into the cool, evening air. He glanced at the picture again, making sure to catalogue the people it portrayed and the related story attached in his photographic memory.

Purvis remembered everything. He always had. Most people thought he was little more than an imbecile, and he played the part so as not to disappoint them. It made things so much easier for him. He'd hidden his gift of intellect his whole life, as he hid the other things. One begat the other, he reckoned. It's why he'd been so successful at carnage and remained free to wreak havoc in an unsuspecting world. Every creature had its purpose, and he'd been exceptionally adept at his.

Thinking about the wonderful story he'd read in the newspaper, Purvis took another long drag off his cigarette and leaned his head back, exhaling the grey plume towards the spider strategically perched in its giant web overhead.

"Now, ain't that sumthin', Edgar?"

THE END

ABOUT THE AUTHOR

CLAYTON E. SPRIGGS is the author of the critically acclaimed Johnson Road mystery/thrillers. His novels include Johnson Road, Billy, and Peterson County Murders. He lives in southeast Louisiana with his lovely wife, wonderful children, and his beloved beagle, Bo. He can be contacted at:

cespriggs@pennmillpub.com

THANK YOU

Dear Reader,

You may not be aware of how difficult it is for a self-published author, like myself, to get reviews. I don't have a publicist to promote my books or a staff of marketing personnel to hustle reviews. I depend on my readers for support. I would greatly appreciate it if you would please take a few minutes to post a review where you purchased this book. What did you like about *The Bone Puzzle* and would you recommend it to your friends (star rating)?

Thank You.

Clayton E. Spriggs

ACKNOWLEDGMENTS

The author wishes to thank everyone who has contributed to the successful completion of this novel. Although there are too many to name them all, special appreciation goes to Jennifer, Jesse, and Louaine for all that they've done and continue to do for me. I love you all. I also would like to thank Gerard and Dina for the great covers and Kit for the outstanding editing. Most of all I wish to thank my readers without whom I would never be motivated to get past the first paragraph.

JOHNSON ROAD

Book One of the Johnson Road Saga

When Purvis Johnson fell on hard times, he agreed to sell most of his land to a real estate developer. Before long, the dirt road that once served as his makeshift driveway became a paved street. Newly constructed houses sprung up on both sides. Families moved in and the quiet neighborhood was on its journey to becoming the suburban utopia promised by the American Dream.

A girl goes missing. Detective Robert Stallworth, an Alabama State Trooper known for his ability to find missing things, is assigned the case. As Detective Stallworth and the local sheriff work together to solve the case, mysterious events continue to take place on Johnson Road.

One by one, tragedy will strike them all. By the time the dreamers realize they are trapped inside a nightmare, it's too late. Something has gone terribly wrong inside the dream -- something evil -- something on Johnson Road.

Buy *Johnson Road* today to discover the truth about who is behind the horrifying events.

PETERSON COUNTY MURDERS

Book Two of the Johnson Road Saga

They cornered a killer... and unleashed his full potential...

Detective Robert Stallworth can't shake the horrors he witnessed that fateful day on Johnson Road. As the unexpected deaths and disappearances grow, the detective's desire to catch the killer has morphed into a personal vendetta...

When the FBI and US Marshals take the case, the Peterson County police expect a quick arrest, but Robert isn't so sure. Recognizing the killer's calling cards won't stop the murders unless the detective can find him first. As they uncover the terrifying truth about their prime suspect, Robert races against time to thwart the psychopath before he demonstrates what he's truly capable of...

Peterson County Murders is the second book in the Johnson Road Saga, a series of thrilling mystery novels. If you like gut-wrenching twists, psychological suspense, and masterful storytelling, then you'll love Clayton E. Spriggs' twisted tale.

Buy *Peterson County Murders* today to see if one man can stop a killer from becoming a legend...

BILLY

A Tale of Terror

Hidden away in the cypress swamps of the Atchafalaya Basin, a cabin sits on pilings driven into the murky waters of Bayou Noir, home to the Cajun family known as the St. Pierres. One dark night, a newborn arrives — unwelcomed and unwanted. Over time, he grows into something to be feared, chained, and hidden away in the attic. When the rising water from Hurricane Katrina reaches Bayou Noir, the St. Pierres are forced to confront the terror that awaits them in the attic.

In the aftermath of Hurricane Katrina, when a group of college kids looking for survivors in Bayou Noir disappears, Detective Nicholas Vizier and a band of local gator hunters are hired to search for the missing students. What they find is more than they bargained for. They find Billy.

From the cabin in the swamp, to the confines of St. Elizabeth's Institute for the Insane, to the haunted ruins of Lost Bayou Plantation, *Billy* will send you on a terrifying adventure. So prepare yourself for the horror that you'll encounter with every turn of the page.

Buy *Billy* today and discover the terror that awaits whomever is brave enough to venture into Bayou Noir.

www.ingramcontent.com/pod-product-compliance
Lightning Source LLC
Chambersburg PA
CBHW032257020726
47495CB00001B/148